SPOTLIGHT

SPOTLIGHT
ON THE RUNWAY

BESTSELLING AUTHOR
Melody Carlson

BOOK FOUR

ZONDERVAN®

ZONDERVAN

Spotlight
Copyright © 2010 by Melody Carlson

This title is also available as a Zondervan ebook.
Visit www.zondervan.com/ebooks.

Requests for information should be addressed to:
Zondervan, 3900 *Sparks Dr. SE, Grand Rapids, Michigan* 49546

This edition: ISBN 978-0-310-74821-2

Library of Congress Cataloging-in-Publication Data

Carlson, Melody.
    Spotlight / Melody Carlson.
        p.   cm. — (On the runway ; bk. 4)
    Summary: Paige and Erin Forrester head to London, England, where
    Paige will appear on one of Britain's top television shows, as the global
    attention surrounding their fashion-focused reality television show reveals
    the benefits and perils of stardom.
    ISBN 978-0-310-71789-8 (softcover)
    [1. Reality television programs — Fiction. 2. Television — Production
and direction — Fiction. 3. Fame — Fiction. 4. Fashion — Fiction. 5.
Sisters — Fiction. 6. London (England) — Fiction. 7. England — Fiction. 8.
Christian life — Fiction.] I. Title.
PZ7.C216637Sop 2010
[Fic] — dc22   2010018737

Cover design: *Jeff Gifford*
Cover photo: *Dan Davis Photography*
Interior design: *Patrice Sheridan, Carlos Eluterio Estrada, Tina Henderson*

Printed in the United States of America

14 15 16 17 18 19 20 /DCI/ 19 18 17 16 15 14 13 12 11 10 9 8 7 6 5 4 3 2 1

SPOTLIGHT

Chapter

1

I never wanted to be famous. I know there are people, like my best friend Mollie, who probably don't believe me. Of course, that's because Mollie would absolutely love to be famous. Unfortunately, Mollie's acting career is on hold because her baby is due in about three months.

Since I *never* wanted to be a celebrity, I'm experiencing some real culture shock over what's happened since our show *On the Runway* became a real hit. According to our producer, Helen Hudson, we're one of the hottest reality TV shows running right now and sponsors are lining up. This is totally great news — and I am happy for my sister, Paige, because this is her dream. But I'm still not comfortable with all that comes with it.

My general dislike of the limelight is not because I'm some highly evolved Christian who is too holy and humble to want to hog all this attention. Paige's theory that my fame-phobia is a result of my poor self-image isn't exactly right either. In fact, I think my self-image is fairly normal. I mean, how many young women — or old women — look in the mirror and absolutely adore what they see? Well, besides Paige.

But honestly, I'm pretty much okay with my looks. And most of the time, despite having a drop-dead-gorgeous sibling, I'm thankful that God made me the way he did.

My discomfort with celebrity is basically selfish—I happen to like my normal life and I enjoy my privacy, and I'd rather fly beneath the radar of the paparazzi than be running from them.

I think being in Paris last month gave me a false sense of obscurity-security, because Paige and I were able to film our episodes and go about our daily lives with very little intrusion from the media. Of course, Paige was a little troubled by this.

"It's like no one even knows who we are," she said as we walked through the Charles de Gaulle International Airport unobserved.

"Or they just don't care," I teased. And, really, Paris is kind of like that—subdued and slightly aloof. I think Parisians, totally unlike Americans, aren't too interested in celebrity spotting.

But Paige seemed bummed. Her way to protest was to sport her newest pair of Gucci sunglasses, hold her chin high, and strut through the terminal like she was a real star. And I'll admit I noticed heads turn. I'm not sure they knew who she was, or cared, though: she is simply an eye-catcher.

Fortunately, for Paige, we were spotted and even photographed when we arrived at LAX the next day. By then I had on sunglasses too, but mine were to hide the dark circles beneath my eyes after a mostly sleepless night during the eleven-hour flight.

"Is it true that you and Benjamin Kross were vacationing together in France?" a reporter from one of the gossip shows asked Paige as we waited to spot our luggage in baggage claim.

Paige smiled and tossed her head. "We were with a number of interesting people in France," she said brightly. "Benjamin was there for a few days as well."

"What did you think about Benjamin's settlement with Mia Renwick's family?" the reporter persisted.

"I think it's really none of my business." Paige smiled.

"What about rumors that you and Dylan Marceau are engaged?" the other reporter asked next.

Paige laughed. "They are just that—rumors."

"But are you involved with Dylan Mar—"

"I think Dylan is a brilliant designer and he's a good friend."

Just then I spotted some of our luggage on the carousel, and I abandoned my sister to her adoring paparazzi in order to help our director, Fran, drag the bags off. Sure, we might be "famous," but we still carry our own bags. At least most of the time, anyway. Blake has reminded me more than once that his offer to carry my bags, do shoulder rubs and pedicures, run errands, take out the trash—or whatever—is still good if the show wants to take him along with us. So far I don't think the show is too interested in Blake.

Unfortunately, Blake's interest in the show doesn't seem to be going away. And way too often, despite me asking him not to, he wants to talk about it. So why am I surprised when he starts in after our fellowship group? Several of us, including Lionel, Sonya, and Mollie, decided to extend the evening by meeting at Starbucks for coffee, and I've just taken a sip of my mocha when Blake brings it up.

"Did you guys hear that Erin is going to London next month?" he announces.

"Yeah, and she's not even excited about it." Mollie rolls her eyes at me.

"It's not that I'm *not* excited," I protest. "It's just that we haven't been back from Paris for that long. And we're trying to plan my mom's wedding and—"

"Excuses, excuses . . ." Mollie waves her hand. "You are off living the life and all you do is complain, complain."

I frown at her. "Really? Do I complain that much?"

She gives me a sheepish smile. "Well, I might exaggerate a bit. It's only because I'm jealous. I would so love to go to London."

"Me too," Blake chimes in.

Mollie makes a face at Blake. "But you already got to go with Erin to Paris, so if anyone gets to go to London with her, it should be me."

"FYI," I remind her, "Blake went to France with *Benjamin Kross*, not me." And, okay, I know I'm doing this as much for Lionel's sake as for Mollie's, since he already questioned why Blake made that trip. I'm not sure if he was jealous or merely curious, but it's a topic I try to avoid.

Things have been a little awkward with both guys since I returned from the trip and put the brakes on both relationships. As soon as I got home from Paris, I called both Blake and Lionel and told them the same thing: that Paige and I had made a pact not to date for a while and to focus on the show.

"Yeah, Erin didn't actually invite me." Blake turns to Lionel, almost like he's trying to get a reaction. "And when I got to Bordeaux, she already had a French boyfriend."

"You know that Gabin was *not* a boyfriend." I shake my finger at Blake. "He's just a good friend." We'd been over this several times already.

"Yeah, but he gave you that great bag." Mollie points to

my black Birkin bag, which has kind of become my signature piece of late. Not because it's such a fashion statement as much as it's really great for carrying my camera and junk.

"So what are you going to be covering in London?" Lionel asks me.

"Isn't it Fashion Week there?" Mollie suggests.

"Actually Fashion Week London isn't until September," I explain. "And the show will probably send us back to London then. This trip is to coincide with a new British TV show. It's kind of like *America's Next Top Model*. Paige is going to be a judge and we'll use that for an episode, then we'll do some episodes on the Brit fashion scene. And we'll stay at the May Fair and —"

"The May Fair is like the swankiest hotel in the coolest fashion district in London," Mollie explains. "I looked it up on the Internet and I was pea green with envy."

"And you're not excited about that?" Sonya asks me. She's been the quiet person in the group tonight. As usual, I wonder if she's still feeling a little out of sorts because of her breakup with Blake. And because she might secretly blame me for losing him, although I'd beg to differ. Sometimes I catch these glances from her and, despite Blake's assurance, I suspect Sonya isn't totally over him.

"It's not that I'm *not* excited," I say for the second time. Like is anyone listening. "It's just that —"

"Oh, admit it," Mollie pushes in. "You're like the heel-dragging, reluctant little starlet. Your TV show is handed to you on a silver platter and you turn your nose up and —"

"It was *not* handed to me," I protest. "It's Paige's show. I'm just a secondary character, if that. I'm the lowly camera girl and —"

"Not true," Blake interrupts. "That makeover episode in Paris sent your popularity soaring."

I frown at him. "And how do you know that?"

He grins. "Because I pay attention to these things."

"So do I," Mollie tells me. "And, whether you like it or not, that episode turned you into a star. So get over it."

Okay, now I don't have a response.

"I think they're right," Lionel confirms. "I saw that episode too, and I'm guessing that your role in the show is going to change."

"*Is* changing," Mollie interjects.

"And you're not happy about that?" Sonya looks like she'd love to slap me.

"It's just not what I wanted," I try to explain. "It's Paige's gig, not mine."

"Did you even listen to Eric's message tonight?" Blake demands with a twinkle in his eye.

I consider this. Eric is an assistant pastor at our church and he led the fellowship group tonight. But at the moment I'm blank. "I listened," I tell him. "But I'm having a hard time remembering ..."

"Eric said that God sometimes puts us in bad situations for good reasons." Mollie grins at me like she thinks I'll give her a gold star.

"Oh, yeah." I nod. "Thanks, Mollie."

"Like Joseph," Lionel reiterates. "Sold as a slave by his brothers, then falsely accused and put in prison—talk about some hard situations."

"But God had a plan," Blake adds. "He worked it together for good."

I nod, knowing where this is going. "You guys are right. I do have the wrong attitude about the show."

"You need to see your TV show as an opportunity," Blake tells me. "You can be a light in a dark place, Erin. Remember that night in Bordeaux?"

"What night in Bordeaux?" Lionel asks with a creased brow.

I tell everyone about Blake's bonfire idea. "It's like everyone was starting to get into a big fight," I explain. "Our hostess was having some issues. Paige was caught in the middle. Yet somehow Blake managed to get everyone gathered around a campfire and we sang and stuff and then, before the evening ended, Blake actually gave his testimony and it was pretty cool."

Lionel actually gives Blake a fist bump. "That *is* very cool. Way to go, Blake."

Blake smiles and I can tell he appreciates this coming from Lionel. I must admit it's a relief to see a couple of Christian guys acting more like brothers than competitors.

"So maybe you need to remember Joseph next time you feel like complaining," Mollie tells me. "He didn't exactly like being sold as a slave or doing time, but he did his best and God used him in some big ways."

"And the bigger your role on your show becomes, the more visible you'll be," Lionel says. "And the more influence you'll have ..."

"To be a light in a dark place," Blake finishes.

And so that's my new attitude—or it's what I'm trying to adopt as my new attitude. I obviously need God's help to carry it off. But my goal now is to do my best job, and even if I don't particularly love being on the show, I'll give it my all and just see what happens. I thought that would make everyone happy—especially everyone working on the show.

Unfortunately, I quickly discover that might not be the case. The following week, after previewing a couple of the Paris episodes, Paige and I are in a planning meeting with Helen and Fran and the rest of the crew when Helen suggests that my role in the show has changed.

"I know that you like filming the show," she tells me. "But I see the show going a different direction now. We no longer need a camera girl."

"What do you mean?" Paige demands. "You can't take Erin off the show. I need her!"

Helen laughs. "No, of course we're not taking her off the show. *On the Runway* needs her too, Paige."

Paige has a relieved smile. "Oh, you scared me."

"Sorry." Helen pats her hand. "What I'm saying is that Erin needs to become more of a partner now."

Paige's forehead creases ever so slightly. "A partner?"

"Yes. No more remaining behind the scenes. The fans are connecting with Erin in a big way now. She needs to come out of the background and become a featured costar."

"A featured costar?" Paige looks unconvinced.

"Of course, you'll still be the host," Helen assures her. "But Erin will play a more significant and visible role alongside you."

"How, exactly?" Paige glances at me then back to Helen.

"Mostly by being herself." Helen smiles at me like I should get this. But frankly, I don't.

"We want Erin to bring her opinions about fashion onto the screen," Fran injects. "You two girls are so different. Sometimes it's hard to believe you're really sisters." She laughs. "But it's apparent that our fans are diverse as well. And we've gotten some great viewer responses in regard to topics like green design and economical fashion."

"So we've decided we need to include more segments along these lines," Helen finishes for her. "And Erin is the perfect one to take us there."

Everything in me wants to stand up and protest—to remind everyone in this room of our original agreement, that I am merely "Camera Girl" and that it's acceptable for me to remain a wallflower. But at the same time I remember the conversation at Starbucks on Saturday night. I remember how my friends challenged me to change my attitude and let God use me however he wants in regard to the show. So how do I back down now?

Paige lets out a little laugh then shakes her head. "Okay, I'll admit that *sounds* like a sensible plan and, naturally, we want to expand our audience. But there's one itty-bitty problem."

"What's that?" Helen adjusts her glasses and peers at Paige.

Paige makes what feels like a patronizing smile at me. "We all know how stubborn my little sister can be. Of course, Erin would never agree to this, *would you, Erin?*"

Now all eyes are on me, and with a furrowed brow Helen points her silver pen in my direction. "Is that right, Erin? Are you still going to play the spoiler?"

I clear my throat, which suddenly feels like sandpaper.

"Speak up," Helen urges.

"Actually . . ." I glance at Paige then back at Helen. "I am actually . . . sort of . . . open."

Paige's jaw drops ever so slightly. "Open? Open to what?"

"Open to . . . you know . . . whatever. I mean, if the show needs me to step up, well, I'm willing."

Helen clasps her hands together. "I just knew you'd be game, Erin. I felt it in my bones. When I saw the initial footage from Paris I said to myself, our little Erin is finally growing up!"

Suddenly they're all talking and making plans, and it's obvious that they've already given this some serious thought, but when I glance over at Paige, who is sitting silently, I can tell she's not really on board. And the way she's looking is reminiscent of something . . . something I'd nearly forgotten . . . something that happened a long time ago.

When we were little—I was in kindergarten and Paige was in first grade—my sister begged my parents for gymnastic classes. Her friend Kelsey was bragging about how she was going to become an Olympic gymnast (which never happened), so Paige insisted she needed lessons too. My parents eventually agreed, but Dad decided both Paige and I should be enrolled in the academy so that I wouldn't feel left out. Naturally, I was happy to be included since I already loved jumping, climbing, and rolling around like a monkey. But after a couple of months at the academy, which I thoroughly enjoyed, Paige's interest started waning until she refused to go at all.

Years later, I learned by accident that Paige's reason for quitting gymnastics was simply because I'd been outshining her and she did not like to be second best at anything. Although I continued going for a while, it wasn't long before my sister convinced me that gymnastics was silly and the outfits we had to wear were even worse, and that it would be much more fun to take dance classes instead. Naturally, she turned out to be far more gifted and graceful at ballet than me. And, once again, she was back in her comfort zone—where she reigned.

Spotlight

Although my sister has grown up some since then—she's matured a lot these past few months, and our relationship is stronger than ever—I still suspect that some of her old habits die hard. Forcing Paige to share the limelight with me could come with its own set of challenges. Which brings to mind Joseph ... and how his own brothers sold him to strangers. Okay, I'm pretty sure my sister wouldn't sink quite that low. But it does give me pause to wonder.

Chapter 2

"*I know you'd hoped to find your bridesmaid* gowns in Paris," Mom says to Paige as we carry an assortment of dresses into the changing area of a new Rodeo Drive boutique that Paige insisted we had to try, "but it's so much more fun doing this together."

"I agree," I tell Mom as I head into a fitting room. "After all, it's your wedding. You should have a say in what we wear."

"And worst-case scenario," Paige calls from her room, "is that we have to get our dresses specially made. But I know a certain designer who might be willing to help us out . . ."

I laugh as I pull the rose-colored satin dress over my head. "Yeah, I'm pretty sure Dylan Marceau would drop everything to make Paige a gown."

"Especially if I promised to wear it on our show," Paige says. "Are you ready yet, Erin?"

I strain to zip the fitted dress, then emerge from the dressing room, holding my hands out. "Ta-dah."

Paige presses her lips together then shakes her head. "Too boring."

I go over to the three-way mirror to see for myself. "I don't know. I think it's got potential."

"This one is much better." Paige strikes a pose in the lacy pale pink dress. Admittedly she looks pretty. But what else is new?

"It seems too frilly to me," I tell her.

"*Too frilly?*" She looks at me like I have dirt on my face.

I glance over at Mom, comfortably seated on the velvet-covered divan, and I can tell she's unsure. "I think you both look lovely."

"But which dress do you like better?" Paige asks as she struts back and forth like she's on a runway. "See how this skirt moves. And this delicate pink shade would look gorgeous in a garden wedding."

"But it doesn't really go with Mom's dress," I tell my sister. While Paige and I were in Paris, Mom found a two-piece dress at Neiman Marcus. It's an elegant ivory satin. Mom tried it on and fell in love with it and, despite her promise to let Paige help her with this, she impulsively purchased it. Paige acted like that was okay, but I could tell she wasn't too pleased. I suspect she's not overly fond of the dress or that Mom made the decision without consulting her. But I keep thinking, *this is Mom's wedding* — why shouldn't she get what she wants?

"Of course it goes with Mom's dress," Paige argues. "Almost anything would go with Mom's dress ... anything stylish that is." She frowns at my choice.

"This is stylish," I say. "It's a classic style and Mom's dress is a classic." I point at Paige. "That dress looks pretty on you, but it's too fairy-princess-like to look good with Mom's sophisticated dress."

Mom nods. "You know, Paige, I think Erin might be right."

Paige's expression looks like Mom just slapped her. "*What?*"

Mom points to my gown. "I'm not saying that dress is the exact right dress, but it would go well with my dress. They do have a similar style."

"As in boring."

Mom sighs. "Maybe some of us prefer boring, Paige."

"I'm sorry, Mom." Paige holds up her hands. "I think your dress is lovely. But I don't see why Erin and I need to mimic you. We can express a little more creativity than that."

"But it's Mom's wedding," I finally say. "Maybe she wants something more classic. Something timeless like pearls and roses," I suggest.

"Yes." Mom stands and comes over to where Paige and I are standing in front of the three-way mirror and nods. "I do like the idea of pearls and roses, Erin."

Paige is scowling now. "So suddenly Erin's the fashion expert. Is that what you're saying?"

"I'm not trying to step on your toes or diminish your gift of fashion sense." Mom shakes her head. "We all know that this is your territory. But perhaps Erin's style is more like mine."

"But Erin doesn't really *have* style," Paige says quietly. And, okay, maybe that's true. Or maybe it used to be true. Lately I've been trying harder; even Helen and Fran think I've come a long way. So why is my sister trying to pigeonhole me again?

I look at our reflections, the three of us, in the mirror. There's Paige, the tall, willowy, beautiful blonde — often compared to our handsome dad when he was alive, and more recently to a young Grace Kelly. And then there's Mom and me ... average-looking brunettes of average height with green eyes and even features. Can't Paige see the difference?

Mom, who's standing between us, slips her arms around

our waists and smiles. "Two beautiful daughters. I don't care what you girls wear to the wedding—I know it will be perfectly lovely."

And so, not wishing to cause any further ado, I go back to the fitting room and remove the rose-colored dress and try on the next. But it's horrible compared to the first one, and the third one is all wrong.

"I don't think this shop has what we're looking for," I tell Paige quietly. The saleswoman is hovering nearby nervously and I suspect she knows who we are, which is just one more good reason we decided to do a reconnaissance mission before allowing the show to film us shopping for bridesmaid dresses. We wanted to avoid pressure.

"Thank you for your help," Paige tells the woman politely. "We'll keep these dresses in mind." Then we gather our things and leave.

"So I think I understand what you want," Paige tells Mom as we walk down Rodeo Drive. "Do you have any objections to checking out Chanel?"

"Well ..." Mom sighs. "I would prefer to stay within our budget."

"But if we do the wedding episode, Chanel might be within your budget." Paige pauses in front of the Coco Chanel boutique. "We can at least look."

"You're right." Mom nods as she reaches for the door. "We can look."

"And if we like what we see here, we can ask Fran to speak to them and perhaps we can use their boutique in our show."

As we walk through the boutique, I realize that I'm not nearly as irritated as I used to be when Paige would drag me to shops like this. It's not that I enjoy it exactly, but after being in Paris and experiencing the language barrier combined with some of the Parisian attitude, I don't find Rodeo Drive nearly as intimidating as I used to. Naturally, the salespeople recognize Paige, and as soon as she lets our intentions out of the bag, we become the center of attention—the manager even offers us wine and chocolate.

"We only want to look today," Paige explains. Then she tells the manager that our mom already purchased her dress and we now need to find something compatible. "Something classic and timeless," she says, using my exact words, "that would go well with pearls and roses."

And, okay, I'm trying not to gloat here, but maybe I'm not as fashion-challenged as my sister would like to have me think. As it turns out, Chanel has some good, albeit expensive, options. The manager even offers to have a few more things sent to the store that we might like to consider when we return.

Paige gives her a business card and promises that someone will call to see about setting up a show. "Of course, we wouldn't want to do it during normal business hours," she tells her. "We don't want to disrupt your regular customers."

"I'm sure we can accommodate your needs," the woman assures her.

"Well, I think we're on the right track," Mom says as we walk down Rodeo Drive. "And, really, hasn't this been fun?"

I'm thinking "fun" might be overstating it a bit. But I try to maintain my party face as we walk over to the restaurant where Mom had made late-lunch reservations. Fortunately, Paige seems to have forgotten our earlier disagreement, and she tells Mom another amusing story about something that happened in Paris.

"It's hard not to be jealous," Mom says when our salads arrive. "But Jon has promised me that we'll go to Paris sometime."

"Why not for your honeymoon?" Paige suggests.

"I'd rather go in the fall or spring," Mom tells her. "Besides, Jon is looking into an Alaskan cruise."

Paige makes a face. "Really? That is what you'd want to do?"

Mom smiles. "I think it sounds rather nice . . . and relaxing."

"Not to mention beautiful. I'd love to do something like that just for the photo opportunities alone."

"Not me . . ." Paige gets a dreamy look. "If I were going on a honeymoon, I'd choose a location like Paris. Or maybe somewhere in Italy . . . like Tuscany . . . or maybe even the Riviera."

"Maybe Eliza will let you use her place," I tease.

Paige gives me her exasperated look. "Yeah . . . right."

"And if you were taking a honeymoon somewhere on the Riviera," Mom persists in this line of craziness, "who might you be taking it with?"

Paige laughs. "Oh, that's undetermined."

"So you don't see either Benjamin or Dylan in that picture?" Mom's tone is hopeful.

I watch Paige's reaction. She and I talked about this very thing on our last night in Paris. Maybe it was because I'd surprised her with the Birkin bag, but Paige turned very sisterly that evening. And during a heart-to-heart about our recent relationships, we both decided we weren't in a good place to be seriously involved with guys right now. As I recall we agreed to put the show ahead of romance. We both felt there's enough drama without adding more of our own in the area of romance. At least that's how I remember it.

But now Paige almost looks like she's in another world — as if she's imagining herself honeymooning with someone, like Dylan or even Benjamin, on the Riviera. "Oh, you never know," she says mysteriously to Mom.

Mom sort of laughs, but I can tell she's uneasy with this response. I simply stab my fork into my salad and realize that when it comes to Paige and matters of the heart, I probably should not trust my sister too much.

Paige excuses herself from lunch early. She doesn't say why or where she's going, but since we came in separate cars, it's not really a big deal.

"Do you think she's seeing Benjamin?" Mom asks me as we share a piece of lemon cream pie and coffee.

"I don't know," I admit. "The truth is, I've been wondering."

"Paige didn't tell me too much about his unexpected visit to France ..."

I give Mom the nutshell version of how Eliza subversively invited Ben, and how he surprised everyone by showing up with Blake in tow. "I know Eliza's reason for inviting Ben was to distract Paige from Dylan. But it seemed like Paige kept both guys at a distance. And when Dylan returned to New York, I got the impression that he wasn't too happy about it."

"Meaning he wanted to be more involved with Paige?" Mom scoops some of the meringue off the top of the pie with her spoon.

"That's what I suspected. And Paige seemed to confirm it by telling me that she didn't want to be seriously involved with anyone." I frown down at my coffee. "In fact, we kind of made a pact."

"A pact?" Mom looks surprised.

"To keep our romantic lives on hold ... you know, so we could focus on the show better."

Mom smiles. "Perhaps that's easier said than done."

24

I nod. "And when Benjamin showed up in Paris a couple days later ... it was the night before he was going home and Paige went to dinner with him ... and now I'm starting to wonder."

"If they're getting back together?"

I shrug. "I don't know."

"What about you and Blake?" Mom persists. "Did you go to dinner with him in Paris too?"

"No ... Blake had to go home a couple of days before Ben. He had classes and stuff."

"Smart boy."

"I guess. He's been smart not to pressure me too much about our relationship. I kind of told him that I was taking a break for now."

"Because of your pact with Paige?"

I consider this. "Maybe. Or maybe I think I need a break."

Mom chuckles. "Smart girl."

"Why?" I study her.

"Oh, it just sounded like you were getting in a little over your head."

Okay, now I sort of regret confiding in Mom after I got home from Paris. I told her a little about Gabin and Blake and Lionel and how weird it was to have three guys semi-interested in me at once.

"You're only eighteen," Mom continues.

"Almost nineteen," I remind her.

She smiles. "Yes. And a mature *almost nineteen*. But I still think you're wise not to get too involved right now. Take your time."

I nod as if I agree. And, actually, I *do* agree. Yet there's something about my mom telling me to *take my time* that makes me want to do just the opposite. Unreasonable, yes. But it's true.

Mom glances at her watch. "Well, as delightful as this has been, I've got to get back to the station."

"And I have an appointment with Helen at four thirty," I tell her.

"That's kind of late in the day for an appointment."

"It was last minute. She called this morning."

"So you're meeting Paige there?" she asks as she signs the check.

"Paige isn't going."

"You mean just you and Helen are meeting?"

I suddenly realize that I never really told Mom about Helen's new plan to make me Paige's costar. The truth is I've been avoiding this sticky subject, especially when Paige is around. But I realize that Mom will hear about it sooner or later. So as I drive her back to the station, I give her a quick rundown.

"Oh, that's wonderful, Erin," Mom exclaims. "I can understand Helen's thinking — that's a great plan."

"I guess." I let out a frustrated sigh.

"But you're still reluctant?"

"The funny thing is that I'm actually willing."

"So what's the problem?"

I glance at her and wonder why she doesn't know the answer to her own question. But then, when it comes to Paige, my mom can be a little dense sometimes. It's like Paige is her blind spot. Once again, I miss my dad. I have a feeling that if he were alive he would totally get this. "The problem is" — I try to think of a good way to say this — "Paige."

Mom nods. "Oh . . . is Paige reluctant to share the stage?"

"What do you think?"

Mom laughs. "I think you have your work cut out for you."

I'm pulling into her station's parking lot now, maneuvering my Jeep toward the entrance to drop her off.

"But if anyone can make this work, you can, Erin."

I frown at her. "How's that?"

She taps the side of her head with a knowing smile. "You'll figure it out."

"I hope so."

"Thanks for the lift," she tells me as she gets out.

"And thanks for lunch."

"By the way, I really did like the bridesmaid dress you picked out." She winks at me. "And Paige is coming around too."

I nod and wave, watching as my mom hurries into the building. Not for the first time, I consider the dynamics among the three of us—Mom, Paige, and me. I realize that I'll never completely figure out what it is about Paige that makes Mom treat her the way she does. It's kind of like she's protecting Paige. I guess, to be fair, I've learned to do pretty much the same thing. But sometimes ... I wonder, *is it a good thing?* Or are Mom and I simply allowing Paige to get away with being a brat—she throws a tantrum and we turn our heads and look away, almost like a form of enablement? And yet, Paige is Paige ... even when she's acting spoiled, most people seem to still love her. And, according to Helen Hudson, Paige's fan base just keeps growing, so why would Helen want to change anything about her? Of course, Helen doesn't have to live with my sister. Even if she did, she might eventually discover, like Mom and I have, that it's a lot easier to let Paige have her way.

Someone behind me honks, and I realize I'm still parked in the loading zone by the news station. As I pull out into traffic, I decide that I'll probably never fully understand my sister.

Chapter

3

As I drive through town, my phone rings and, seeing it's Mollie, I pull into a handy parking lot to answer it. "What's up?" I ask, knowing that with Mollie it could be anything. Her hormones combined with her broken heart are playing havoc with her emotions lately.

"Where are you?" she asks in a slightly desperate tone.

"Uh ... Seven-Eleven."

"Why?"

"Because I just pulled in here to answer the phone."

"Where are you going?"

So I tell her about wedding shopping with Paige and Mom and how I'm on my way to meet with Helen Hudson.

"Meaning you don't have time to talk?"

I glance at the clock on my dash. "Actually, I do have time. What's going on?"

"I don't think I can do this, Erin."

"Do what?"

"Have this baby."

"But … you're like six months pregnant, Mollie. You need to have the baby —"

"I don't mean the giving birth part. I mean I don't think I can keep it and raise it." She starts to sob and I don't know what to say. What in life prepares someone to counsel her best friend about being a single mom?

"So what brought this up today?" I ask a bit helplessly.

"I saw this real estate commercial on TV," she sobs. "This family — a dad and a mom and two little kids and a dog. I just fell apart."

I'm trying to wrap my head around this. "A TV ad upset you?"

"Yes — they were a *family*, Erin," she cries. "*They were buying a house!* Don't you get it? I will never be able to do that. My child and I will be destined for — for poverty."

"Oh …" I try to think of something comforting. "A lot of single moms make it, Mollie."

"I'm not strong enough to parent this child alone."

"Then maybe you need to rethink this, Moll … I mean, maybe the baby needs a different kind of home."

"You're telling me to give my baby up?"

"I don't know." Okay, now I know I've stepped over the line. I also have an overwhelming sense of déjà vu; this is what happened the last time Mollie and I talked about the baby.

"You're just like my parents, Erin. And everyone else for that matter. Why is it that *no one* encourages me to keep my own baby? *Why*?"

Talk about being caught between a rock and a hard place. Didn't *she* just say she can't do this — can't be a single parent? Really, what am I supposed to tell her?

"Sorry I bothered you," she says finally. "I just thought my best friend would have something more encouraging to say."

"Fine. I do have something to say."

"What?"

I take in a deep breath. "Okay ... you need to take this one day at a time, Mollie. You need to kind of step back and take care of yourself, and your baby, and you need to trust that God will show you what to do next. Remember he promises to give us what we need for today. *Just today.*"

"Okay ..." She sounds a little calmer now.

"Okay."

"So why didn't you just say that in the beginning?"

I control the urge to yell that I'm not a trained therapist and that I'm doing the best I can here. "And, one more thing."

"What?"

"You need to stop watching commercials like that."

She actually kind of laughs, which is a relief, like she's crawled in off the ledge now.

"Seriously," I add. "Some ads are psychologically designed to trigger an emotional response. You should see my mom when this particular coffee ad comes on. She's like a basket case."

"Okay. I'll just say no to commercials."

"That's right." I look at the clock again. "And I need to go talk to Helen now."

"So what's up? Something new with the show?"

I realize I haven't told Mollie my latest news, and so I promise to give her a full update later. She begs me to stop by her house on my way home.

"Okay," I tell her. "It'll probably be close to six by then."

"That's okay," she says quickly. "It's not like I have a life anyway."

As I drive to the studio, I consider how much of a life I have—or don't have. Besides work, it seems that most of my spare time has been spent with Mollie. I realize she's in a very needy place right now, and spending time with her has been good overall. I know that I promised to be a better friend to her, but sometimes I feel selfish—like I should be able to do what I want to do.

The truth is I actually miss Blake. I miss his phone calls and going out with him. And, to be honest, I miss Lionel too. I'm starting to wonder if this so-called pact with my sister wasn't just a figment of my imagination. Or perhaps it's one more way for Paige to keep me under her thumb while she goes out and does whatever she feels like, even if it's a huge mistake—so that I'll be available to pick up her pieces. And what would happen if I blew my life to smithereens and she was the one who had to clean it up?

"Sorry to call this meeting at the last minute," Helen tells me after her assistant, Sabrina, tells me I can go into her office.

"That's okay." I sit down in one of the leather chairs and wait.

"Did you tell Paige we were meeting without her?"

"It's not like I purposely *didn't* tell her," I admit. "But it just never came up."

"How did the bridesmaid dress shopping go?"

I roll my eyes then laugh. "It'll probably make a good show. Paige wants to film it at the Chanel boutique and the manager seemed to be game."

"Of course she's game. It's free advertising."

"Right." I wait, wondering exactly why Helen didn't want Paige here this afternoon.

"You've probably guessed why I wanted to keep this meeting private today?"

"I suspect it has to do with Paige's attitude about having me as her new costar on the show."

Helen nods with a coy smile. "Yes … you and Paige are both smart girls. But you have a different kind of smarts. Paige is sharp and savvy when it comes to fashion, and has wit and charm. In fact, the girl is amazingly gifted."

"I know."

"But you seem to have a gift of empathy and a sense of reality that our viewers love too, Erin. And that's no small thing."

I kind of shrug. "Thanks."

"The question is how to get both of you girls on the screen without shutting Paige down. That's why I've invited you here today."

"Okay …" I nod. "I get that."

"For starters, I want to say that your opinions matter to the show, Erin."

"Right." I realize she's perfectly serious, but I almost want to laugh since my opinions have never been much of a consideration before.

"I've observed you in the past, at our planning meetings," she continues. "I've seen that glazed-over expression you get, as if you couldn't care less what we do or don't do. I know that fashion is not your thing."

I hold up my hands helplessly. "Hey, Paige is my sister. She's the expert. That doesn't leave much room for me in that arena."

She adjusts her glasses, narrowing her eyes at me. "And yet I think you understand it a lot more than you usually let on. It's as if you are so used to taking the backseat when it comes to Paige that you don't even try."

"I'm sure that's partially true. But it's also true that I'm not that into fashion. There are two main reasons I've stayed interested in the show." I hold up one finger. "First of all, because I do care about my sister, and both Mom and you felt she needed Jiminy Cricket by her side. But to be fair, I think she's grown up a lot and that part of my role could be lessening." I hold up my second finger. "Secondly, my motivating reason is that working in film and TV was always my goal. So getting to be part of the camera crew has been a real education."

"Yes. But it's my opinion that to learn the most about TV and film, people should immerse themselves completely. That means experiencing all aspects of the industry. I believe the best directors are multitalented—behind the cameras, in front of the cameras, writing, editing, promoting . . . you name it and they can do it. Take Woody Allen, for instance. He's done it all and, in my opinion, he's brilliant."

I consider this. Woody Allen's not my favorite Hollywood example. "How about Charlie Chaplin?"

She nods eagerly. "Exactly my point. He acted, wrote, directed, produced—the works. The man was pure genius." She picks up a pen and shakes it. "And that brings us back to you, Erin. I want you to appreciate that you will learn more about this business if you'll take your role costarring with Paige seriously."

"I plan to."

She looks a bit surprised. "Really?"

"Seriously, I do plan to. I think it's a great opportunity. I already have a show I'd like to discuss with you."

"Really?"

"Remember how I wanted to do a show that focuses on models and body image and eating disorders and how all of this impacts the average American woman?"

She nods slowly. "Yes. I realize we ran out of time in Paris. But that's the kind of episode that can be filmed anywhere. Perhaps it's less offensive to the international markets if we handle it right here in Los Angeles anyway."

"That makes sense."

"So …" Helen presses her lips together. "I'm making an executive decision. I want you to take the lead in that show. Talk to Fran and do your research and we'll see how it plays out."

"Okay."

"But I also want you to help Paige with this transition, Erin. The last thing we want is for her to shut down. We need her to make the show work. No Paige … no show. And I have a feeling, since you've known her a lot longer than we have, that you probably have some basic understanding of how the girl works."

"Or at least some coping skills," I offer.

Helen laughs. "Yes, I'm sure none of us can completely comprehend how that pretty head of her's works. But, don't be fooled, it does work."

"Don't worry, I know that."

"And somehow you've got to do your best to make sure that you two work together." She gets a serious look. "I know that's a lot to ask, Erin. But I have a feeling you can deliver."

This sends a shiver of insecurity down my spine, but I put on a brave face. "I hope so."

"Good." She claps her hands now, her signal that we're done here. "So consider yourself officially promoted." She stands.

"So does my promotion mean I get a raise?" I ask hopefully.

Helen laughs. "Why don't you ask your agent to make an appointment with me? We can discuss renegotiating your contract."

I nod. "Okay. I will."

So on my way out to the parking lot, I decide to give Marty Stuart a call. Paige and I both signed on with Marty several months ago. Jon produces and co-hosts the *Rise 'n' Shine, LA* show and Marty is his agent too, and, although Marty hasn't done much more than negotiate our original contracts, he's a good guy.

"Hey, Erin," he says to me as if we're old friends. "What's up?"

I quickly fill him in on my meeting with Helen and how she suggested he contact her. "Do you think I was out of line to ask for a raise like that?" I finally ask.

He laughs. "Not at all. But it's my job to negotiate it with her."

"Oh, good."

"I've been thinking it's about time to renegotiate for both you girls. With the show's new level of popularity, the stakes are rising." He promises to get back to me and hangs up.

Feeling very much like an adult, I get into my Jeep and drive home. As I drive, I consider how I can make the episode about fashion and body image work for the show. For starters, I think I need to come up with a strong title—something that will grab viewers' attention and make them want to watch. I play with a number of ideas and finally decide on: "Killer Style: What Happens When Fashion Turns Lethal?"

Okay, it might be a little too extreme for our demographics, but it's a start. And, really, according to some of my research, a few models have actually died from complications of eating disorders. Plus, I know that millions of young women are affected daily by the images of super-thin models. The truth is I've struggled with my own body image as a result of the constant exposure to the beauty myth that *thin is so in.* Spending time in Paris and around some stick-thin models didn't help much either, although I try not to give in to that kind of warped thinking.

I recently read a statistic that most fashion models weigh about a fourth less than the average American woman. One-fourth less! I find that both astonishing and disgusting.

As I stop for a red light, I notice a billboard with yet another overly thin and scantily clad model holding a very expensive bottle of designer cologne and gazing at it as if she's in love with it, when in reality she's probably just wishing it were a milkshake. I have to wonder—why do we as a culture put up with this crud? And am I, by being part of a TV show about fashion, aiding and abetting in the degeneration of the mental health and well-being of the American woman? Okay, that's probably overstating it. But I have to wonder.

As the light turns green, I remind myself that Paige, while naturally thin, isn't of the anorexic variety. She does seem to respect health issues. Also, I tell myself, I will do what I can to reeducate our viewers. If that's even possible. I sigh as I envision the image of the little Dutch boy sticking his finger in the wall of the dike in order to hold back the floodwaters threatening the entire town. This won't be easy.

Chapter
4

"What's so interesting?" *Mollie asks as she* returns to the family room with a pizza box in hand. We started watching an indie movie that Lionel recently recommended to me, but it's turned out to be kind of a bomb. So I've switched gears and am now plugged into my laptop.

"Research," I tell her.

Mollie drops the cardboard box onto the coffee table, something she would not do if her neat-freak mom were home, but since her parents are on a Mexican cruise right now, celebrating their twenty-fifth anniversary—a trip they booked almost a year ago and Mollie insisted they take—Mollie has let the house get pretty messy. "What are you researching?"

"In my new role as costar Helen is letting me put together a show about how fashion impacts the body image of the average American woman."

Mollie laughs sarcastically as she rubs her bulging, round stomach. "Probably not as much as pregnancy does." Thanks to her lime green warm-ups, combined with her red curly hair and short stature, Mollie reminds me of a chubby leprechaun today. Not that I would ever, in a million years, say this to her.

"Right …" I look back down at my screen. "It says here that in a recent survey, twenty-seven percent of teen girls felt media pressure to have a perfect body."

"Only twenty-seven percent?" She frowns as she takes out a slice of pizza. "That seems pretty low to me."

I nod as I reach for a piece. "I know. But maybe not all the girls surveyed were honest. Think about it—no one likes to admit to feeling media pressure. But it's a well-known fact that most American women don't like their bodies. Where do you think those ideas come from?"

"From being bombarded with images of beautiful women … probably starting with our first Barbie doll." She flops down on the sectional and turns off the TV.

"Exactly." I nod as I take a bite. "I never did like Barbies."

She laughs. "Not me. I *loved* my Barbies."

"Why?" I ask. "Why would you love something that made you feel like you didn't measure up?"

"Barbie was so perfect." With her pizza suspended halfway to her mouth, Mollie gets a dreamy look. "Those long slender legs and cute little feet … those perky boobs—and now that I think about it, she never even needed a bra. And she looked fabulous in every outfit. Man, that girl could even make army boots look good." She sighs and takes another bite.

I control myself from throwing a pillow at her. "But how did that make you feel back then? More importantly, how does it make you feel now?"

"Fat." Mollie looks at her rounded belly with a slightly astonished expression, as if she can't quite believe it herself.

I try not to laugh.

"And short. And plain. And ugly." She sighs.

That makes me feel more like crying. "But that's all wrong," I tell her. "You are adorable, Mollie. Sure, you've gained weight because you're pregnant, but that's a temporary thing. Otherwise, you are petite and pretty, and your hair and coloring is stunning. You're a doll. And I don't mean a plastic one either."

She smiles at me. "Thanks."

I decide to google something. I've heard that Barbie's dimensions would be pretty strange if she were a real woman. "Listen to this," I say suddenly. "It says here that if Barbie were human she would be nearly six feet tall and weigh about one hundred pounds, which means she would be so grossly underweight that she'd have stopped menstruating and could never have children. Plus her nineteen-inch waist would have difficulty supporting her nearly forty-inch bust, which would probably result in serious back problems. And her feet are so small she probably wouldn't be able to walk."

Mollie shakes her head. "Poor Barbie."

"*Poor Barbie?* What about the poor American woman who will never be happy with her body because she's so stuck on the idea that she should look like Barbie? And yet the madness continues as these same women buy their little girls more Barbies. *What is wrong with this country?*"

Mollie laughs. "Lighten up, Erin. It sounds like you're suggesting we start a Barbie-burning campaign."

I ignore her as I continue to read more alarming statistics.

"Even if there were no more Barbies, there'd still be fashion models," Mollie persists. "I'll bet their height and weight ratios are almost as extreme as a human Barbie. I've heard of six-foot models weighing around a hundred and ten pounds. Walking skeletons."

"That's true." I nod and point to my computer screen. "But listen to this. Did you know that the average American woman weighs about one hundred forty-five pounds, wears a size eleven to fourteen, and is about five foot four?" I consider this. "Hey, that means I'm taller than average. Who knew?"

"And I'm almost average." Mollie sounds hopeful. "All this time I've been thinking I was short."

"According to this article, we've all been brainwashed by the media." I shake my head. "No wonder we obsess over our appearance so much. It's like we've been trained to measure our self-worth based on our physical looks."

"Pathetic." She wraps a string of cheese around her pizza and takes another bite.

I nod. "It really is. And, think about this, Mollie. You and I are okay looking. I mean, we don't have any serious defects or —"

"You mean besides my oversized stomach."

"You know what I mean. It's like we're relatively attractive. But what about other girls — ones who have serious challenges like obesity or physical defects or terrible acne — how do you think they feel?"

"Maybe they don't care."

I frown at her. "You think they don't care?"

"You know … maybe they just give up on the whole stupid beauty thing and get on with their lives, become doctors or lawyers or missionaries."

"In that case, they'd be the lucky ones. I could be jaded, but I seriously doubt that too many women in this country *don't care* about their looks. Or if they do, they're the exception." I continue skimming websites, gathering facts, and I realize that "Killer Style" is a show that *On the Runway* has a moral responsibility to do. "And get this," I tell Mollie. "The diet industry alone generates nearly fifty billion dollars a year. How is that even possible?"

"Because everyone wants to be thin." Mollie sighs. "Okay, you're depressing me now, Erin. The truth is I want to be thin too."

"Give it a few months."

But I'm actually depressing myself too. It's hard to believe how American women have been victimized by the beauty myth—that we're only worthwhile if we turn heads. It's like this faulty thinking has seriously handicapped us and impaired our reasoning. And in my opinion Los Angeles is particularly messed up. When I read about things like extreme dieting, bulimia, anorexia, plastic surgery, hair removal, implants, teeth caps, liposuction, and everything else … I feel like it's hopeless.

I close my computer and think, once again, about the little Dutch boy with his finger in the dike. I can't remember how that story ended. Did he remove his finger and drown in the flood or what? Also, he only had a small hole to plug. The hole I'm seeing is more like Niagara Falls or Lake Meade. How do you stop something like that?

For the next several days I obsess over my research until it's almost all I think or talk about. By Sunday afternoon, Mollie is fed up. "Enough already," she tells me as we're finishing up lunch at the mall. We stopped here after church to shop for some maternity clothes, since Mollie has outgrown just about everything in her closet. "Did you even listen to this morning's sermon?"

I nod. "Yeah ... we can't change other people, we can only change ourselves. I get it."

"But"—she points her index finger in the air—"when we change ourselves, it can change the way we see others."

"Give the girl a prize," I tease.

"It was a good sermon."

"So what did it mean to you personally?" I ask.

She gets a thoughtful look. "I think it means that I need to quit focusing on Tony so much. I need to accept that he does not want to be a dad ... doesn't want to marry me. I need to let it go. Then I won't keep seeing him as ... well, as the devil."

I frown. "You see Tony as the devil?"

"Not literally. But sort of ..."

"Wow." I shake my head. "I didn't know that."

"I'm not exactly proud of it. But sometimes it feels like he got me into this mess ..." She holds up two tightly balled fists. "And then he runs off like a great big chicken ... and I get so angry that I'd like to seriously injure him."

"You should let that go, Mollie."

Her fists go back down. "I know. For the sake of the baby, I'm trying to forgive him, but it's not really a one-time-and-it's-done-with kind of thing."

"I can understand that."

"Well, hopefully by the time the baby comes, I'll have completed the process."

I smile at her. "I admire how grown up you're being, Moll. I'm sure I wouldn't do half as well if I were in your shoes."

"Speaking of shoes, I need to find some more comfortable ones since my feet seem to be getting bigger too. Mom told me that her feet grew two sizes when she was pregnant with me. Can you believe that?"

I just shake my head. And, no, I can't believe it. I wasn't exaggerating when I told her that I wouldn't handle it too well if I were in her shoes. I honestly don't know how she does it ... and more than that, how she will manage to do it when the baby does come. I cannot wrap my head around it.

So I'm determined to be the best friend I can to her. If that means picking out maternity clothes and sensible shoes, I can do that. But when Mollie begs me to go to the baby department to look at the cribs and things, I start to inwardly balk. I want to tell her to get real—I mean, she doesn't even know if she's keeping the baby! Why make things worse by looking at this stuff? And yet I manage to keep my opinions to myself.

"Isn't this adorable?" she says as she shows me her favorite nursery arrangement—turquoise blue baby furniture and magenta and lime green bedding.

"It seems kind of bright to me," I admit. "Do babies really like these kinds of colors?"

"I read that bright colors stimulate brain development." She runs her hand over the rail on the crib. "It's supposed to increase the baby's IQ."

"Oh ..." I wander over to a more traditional nursery setup with white painted furnishings and pale blue and yellow bedding. "I think I'd go more for this," I tell her. I pick up a teddy bear and pretend to rock it like a baby. "More soothing." Just then I feel someone watching me and I look up in time to see a teen girl pointing her phone at me with a triumphant grin.

"You're Erin from *On the Runway*, aren't you?" she calls from where she's standing with a woman I'm guessing is her mom.

I know I now have a choice—I can become indignant

and snarl at her ... or I can smile and act nonchalant. Fortunately I have the good sense to go with the second option. She takes her shot and then I turn my attention back to Mollie as she comes over to look at the more subdued nursery set.

"Yeah ... this is actually pretty nice. Much calmer." I hand her the teddy bear and she sighs. "I can't believe it's only three months away."

I press my lips together. No way am I going to stick my foot in my mouth right now. Especially with that teen girl close enough to overhear us.

"Mom told me I can move my bedroom down to the basement if I want." She gently sets the bear against the pillow in the crib. "I can make it into an apartment for the baby and me."

"Are you going to do that?"

"I don't know." She pats the bear's tummy. "I'm thinking about it."

It's so hard to respond. Although I want to be encouraging to Mollie, I don't want to encourage her to keep her baby, because I honestly don't see how she can manage to parent a child and finish school and have much of a life. But if I tell her how I really feel, I know I risk upsetting her. Best to keep my mouth shut.

So I keep my opinions to myself as we continue to shop. I chat about other things as I drive Mollie home from the mall, telling her about the plans for our next show. "Paige got Chanel to agree to let us film there while we pick out bridesmaid dresses." Then I tell Mollie about how Paige and I disagreed on what style would be best.

"No way." Mollie laughs. "You stood up to your sister's sense of style? Are you nuts?"

"But the dress Paige wanted would look weird with what Mom plans to wear. And it *is* Mom's wedding."

"But Paige *is* the fashion expert."

I consider this. "Yes. Paige is an expert when it comes to fashion. But maybe she's not the only one."

"So you're an expert now too?"

"Helen seems to believe in me." I hold my head higher. "And, sure, Paige and I have totally different taste. But maybe I've let her overshadow me too much. I mean, I know what I like. And I kind of know what looks good on me. Or at least I'm starting to figure it out. Admittedly, Paige has helped me with that some. But I also know what I don't like."

"Such as?"

"Such as expensive designer clothes. I honestly don't see why style has to be expensive."

"And you helped me find some good deals in maternity clothes," Mollie points out. "You actually found some pretty stylish pieces too."

"Thanks."

"So maybe you're right. Maybe you do need to step outside of the Paige shadow and let your own style shine."

"Yeah. That's what I'm thinking." I nod eagerly. "In fact, that gives me an idea."

"What?"

"I think I'll ask Helen if I can do my own kind of shopping spree for a show sometime. With cameras following me, I could gather up my own wardrobe of environmentally friendly and economically affordable threads — and do it with style."

"That sounds like fun."

"And I have some other ideas too. Maybe it's time to push

the envelope a little. How much *haute couture* can our viewers stand anyway?"

Mollie laughs. "Well, if they're anything like your sister, they will never tire of it."

"But what if their wallets are more like yours?"

Mollie nods. "Good point. You should go for it, Erin. I think you have some great ideas. By now you must know enough about how the show works to make some good pitches."

After I drop Mollie off, I go directly home and start putting together a plan for shows I'd like to pitch. The first episode is "Killer Style," and although I have gathered a lot of statistics and ammunition, I'm not totally sure how we would shoot it. I do know I would like to interview some models, hopefully ones who've been through some body-image struggles but who aren't still suffering from eating disorders. Like Paige Geller—I'll bet she'd do an interview. That could give it a more positive spin. The next show I'm calling "Cheap Chic." It would be about economizing the closet—how big style doesn't need to cost big bucks. And the third show I'm calling "Haute Green"—about how high fashion doesn't have to harm the planet.

I think these are all good, viable ideas for *On the Runway* episodes, but at the same time I know Paige is not going to like any of them. Well, except maybe the body image one since she's already agreed to it. But I'm hoping that Helen and Fran will like them and agree to produce them. More than that, I'm hoping that we can get a least one of them in the can before it's time to go to London. I'm also hoping that I can actually carry this off. I realize that means I need to get comfortable in front of the camera. I need to exude more confidence. And to do that, I think I need to practice.

Ideally, I would approach Paige and ask her to coach me. But I doubt that either one of us is ready for that. I consider asking Blake for help—I'm sure he'd be willing and probably even be good at it—but it kind of goes against my keep-the-guys-at-a-distance policy. Not that I plan to maintain this "pact" indefinitely. But I guess I want to do it just long enough to prove to my sister that it is actually doable.

Finally, I decide to ask Mollie for some assistance. After all, she seemed interested, and the distraction might be nice for her. Plus, she's taken a number of acting classes and knows how to run a camera. I simply hope it doesn't set her up to think she's part of the show or cause her to feel jealous. I don't want that. But, to my relief, she seems genuinely pleased when I call and explain my idea—and she's still enthused after I clarify that she won't be an actual part of the show. "It's more about getting me ready to take on a bigger role," I say. "Like an acting coach."

"Sounds like fun. I'd love to help," she eagerly tells me. "When do we start?"

"As soon as you want."

"I've got an idea. How about if you come over here and help me move my bedroom stuff down to the basement? Then we can use that as our studio since it has more room."

I gladly agree and we decide to go ahead and get started tomorrow afternoon. Mollie promises to study some of the previous *On the Runway* episodes in order to determine what it is I really need to work on. And I'll bring my camera equipment so we can critique my performances.

Whether this will work or not still remains to be seen. But at least it won't be as embarrassing or painful as it would be if I were doing it with Paige on an actual set. The worst-case scenario is that the practice doesn't help, and I tell Helen Hudson that she needs to rethink the whole costar plan. But the truth is, I actually hope it does work, because I think the episodes I want to do are both interesting and necessary.

Chapter
5

"*I wonder if you should be moving heavy* things," I say to Mollie. We've just started to dismantle her bedroom and I'm beginning to have second thoughts.

"Oh, it's probably okay." She sets a drawer full of folded T-shirts on her already-crowded bed, then stoops down to pull out another drawer.

I watch her hunched over as she tugs on the bottom drawer, which seems to be stuck, and wonder what I'd do if she suddenly went into premature labor or, even worse, tumbled down the steep basement stairs while carrying down a piece of furniture. "What would your mom say?"

She shrugs. "Mom's not here, remember?"

I glance around her jam-packed bedroom, the same room she's had her whole life, and it's showing its age. Last year, her design goal in this room was to create "shabby chic," but I think she struggled with the chic part. "You know, Mollie, I think we need to make some kind of a plan."

"A plan?" She frowns up at me.

I bend down and help her dislodge the stubborn bottom

drawer, which is stuffed with old jeans, and I set it on the bed. "Yeah. A plan. For starters, let's check out the basement and decide where things are going to go down there so we only have to move them once. Okay?"

She nods. "Yeah, that makes sense."

But once we're down there, I realize we need more than just a plan. We need some Merry Maids. "This place is kind of a mess," I say to Mollie as I pluck a string of cobweb from her hair. "I can't believe your mom wants you to live down here."

"Well, since they moved the laundry room upstairs, she never comes down here anymore. I guess she doesn't clean down here too much either."

I nod. That seems fairly obvious.

"It's kind of depressing, isn't it?"

I nod again. "That wall color doesn't help much." It's sort of grayish beige. Maybe it's greige.

"I remember when Dad threw a bunch of leftover paints together and mixed them up to get this."

I look down at the carpet, which is also beige and in need of a good cleaning. Then, against the wall, there's a beige couch and matching beige chair. "This place is like a sea of beige," I tell Mollie.

"Pretty dreary, huh?"

"You're sure you want to do this?" I peer at her curiously, thinking that her overly crowded bedroom is starting to look a whole lot better.

"My parents kind of want me to move down here," she says quietly. "I think it's so they can pretend this isn't happening."

"You mean the baby?"

She nods with sad eyes. "Dad's kind of in denial. I think

he's hoping that my pregnancy will be like a bad case of the flu … it'll eventually just go away."

My heart hurts for Mollie, but I don't know what to say.

"And my mom is planning to turn my room into her office," she continues. "She thinks she's going to start writing a book."

I look around the dreary space, trying to imagine some way to make it more habitable. "What if we painted the walls a more cheerful color?" I suggest.

Mollie brightens for a moment and then shakes her head. "That'd be nice, but according to my pregnancy book, I'm not supposed to breathe paint fumes. It's bad for the baby."

"Yeah, that makes sense." I look around the room more carefully now and I suddenly begin to imagine it differently— like after a makeover.

"It's hopeless, isn't it?" Mollie goes over and sinks down onto the couch, and I can see the dust fibers floating through the dim light that's coming through the high, dingy window.

"No." I shake my head. "It's not hopeless at all. In fact, I'm starting to get a vision."

"A vision?" Her brow creases. "Huh?"

"Do you trust me?"

"Trust you to do what?"

"Makeover this room."

She laughs. "I don't think you could make it any worse than it already is, Erin. Sure, I trust you. What's your vision?"

"Well … I'm still working on it. But you could start running a vacuum down here while I go check into some things. Okay?"

"Okay." She stands up with a slightly hopeful expression. "You really trust me?"

She smiles. "Actually, I do. Your room is pretty cool and you've always had a better sense about stuff like this than me."

"Are you still into shabby chic?"

She shrugs then makes a sheepish smile. "When it's done right."

"Okay ... I'm going to go pick up paint and a few other things while you do some cleaning down here."

"Do you need some money?"

"We'll figure that out later." Then I head out and, hoping that I'm not biting off more than I can chew, drive over to the closest home improvement store, where I find a color called sea glass green. The guy tells me he can mix it in the low VOC kind, which makes it safer for Mollie's baby. So, remembering that Mollie has always liked green, I decide to go with this peaceful shade of pale blue-green. While the guy's mixing it, I look around thinking *shabby chic ... shabby chic ...* And yet nothing in this store really seems to fit.

But then I see a pile of rugs on sale, and one of them reminds me of a rug in my grandmother's house—a braided rug her mother had made out of old fabric. This rug, though not handmade, is still interesting. Its soft shades of blue, rose, and green would brighten up that blah beige carpet. Then, after it's rolled and loaded onto an oversized cart, I head back to pick up the paint. But on my way, I pass by the outdoor furnishings and spot a set of white wicker chairs and a table marked fifty percent off. However, I realize there's no way those will fit in the back of my Jeep Wrangler.

That's when I call Blake, who has just finished his last class of the day. I explain my dilemma, the dreary basement, and how I want to help Mollie. The next thing I know, he's offering to borrow his dad's pickup and help me out. Blake arrives as I finish paying for this stuff, which is relatively cheap.

"Do you need some help with the painting?" he asks as we load things into the back of his dad's truck.

"Sure," I say eagerly. "That'd be awesome."

"I could call some guys from church," he suggests. "We'd finish it really quick."

"Great." I glance at my watch. "I have to make a couple more stops, but maybe you can head over to Mollie's now—I'll meet up with you in an hour or so."

"Will do."

"And don't let Mollie down there while you're painting," I say as he's getting into the cab. "Paint fumes are bad for the baby."

He nods. "Gotcha."

Next, I go to the discount fabric store across the street. I honestly don't know what I'm looking for, but I do have the pale green paint sample with me. Again, I'm thinking *shabby chic ... shabby chic.* I'm also thinking I need to hurry. That's when I notice a table of decorator fabrics that are marked down to twelve dollars a bolt. A woman explains that they're the ends of discontinued bolts but promises they have at least six yards of fabric on each. So I grab a fairly heavy bolt of pale green and white stripes, a bolt of pastel plaid, and a bolt of multicolored pastel polka-dots. As I purchase these bolts, I have no idea how I'll put them to use. Mostly I want something to transform the ugly beige sofa and chair as well as to create cushions for the wicker chairs.

Finally, I stop at my favorite import store. I'm not even sure what I'm looking for exactly, but I'm hoping for a few items that will cheer up the basement. I stick to my pastel color scheme and emerge from the store with some lamps, a large watercolor print that I think Mollie's going to love, a soft pink throw, and some candles and other accents. As I drive toward Mollie's house, I'm becoming more and more excited at how cool that basement could end up being. At least that's what I'm hoping for.

I carry some things down to the basement to discover that Blake's paint crew consists of Blake and Lionel. As surprised as I am to see Lionel there, I'm thankful for his willingness because there are a lot of walls to paint. I put the bolt of striped fabric on the couch and think maybe it can work. Then I take the other bolts of fabric upstairs to Mollie. Fortunately, she knows how to sew and seems to understand as I explain my general plan to make seat cushions for the wicker and some pillows. "But you are banned from the basement," I firmly tell her.

"I told the guys I'd order some food," she says as she rolls out some fabric, smoothing her hand over it. "I like this."

With that encouragement, I head back down to the basement to attack the couch and chair, which I plan to "slipcover" with the help of scissors, a lot of strategic folding, and a big box of safety pins.

"You guys are doing a great job," I tell them. "The paint looks awesome."

"This is some really good paint," Blake says as he dips his roller into the tray.

"The guy promised me it would cover in one coat," I tell him.

Lionel nods. "It's a real time saver."

By the time we break for dinner, the basement is about two-thirds finished, and the section where I want to start arranging furniture into a living space is completely done. But when Mollie begs to see it, I tell her to forget it. "You can't go down there until tomorrow." I plan to spend the night to make sure she doesn't—and to make sure I complete this project.

The guys finish up the painting around ten. "Thank you so much," I tell them. "I think this is really going to encourage Mollie."

Blake looks around the room. "Yeah, it's a huge improvement."

Lionel nods over to where I'm now setting up the living area. "Looks like you have a knack for this, Erin. Maybe you should take some set design classes when you come back to UCLA."

"That'd be fun."

"You mean *if* she goes back to school," Blake teases. "From where I'm sitting, Erin's got a pretty good setup without college."

Lionel looks skeptical. "But that gig won't last forever."

"You're right," I tell him. "It won't." I thank them both again and invite them to come back tomorrow if they want to see the finished product. But I'm barely back to work when I hear their voices again.

"We thought we should move Mollie's bedroom stuff down while we were still here," Blake tells me. "Those stairs are kind of scary."

It takes them less than an hour to finish, and I go up to check on Mollie, who has now taken over her parents' bedroom. I can't help but laugh when I see her parked in the middle of their king-sized bed with a bag of microwave popcorn. "Oh, if your mom could only see you now," I tease.

Mollie laughs. "Yeah, she'd have a fit. But don't worry, I'll clean it all up before she gets home. She'll never know."

"I'm going to keep working downstairs," I tell her.

She frowns. "It's kinda late, Erin."

"I'm spending the night."

"Oh." She pats the bed. "Feel free to join me if you like."

"Or I'll just sleep down there."

She makes a face. "Ugh. That sounds horrible."

"It's steadily getting better," I assure her.

And by the time I call it quits, it really is better. Much, much better. It's also around three in the morning when, feeling like a zombie, I put fresh sheets on Mollie's bed. Then I crash.

It's around nine when I wake up, and it takes me a moment to figure out where I am. Then I make the bed and putter around and finish up a few things. I finally look around the basement with a very pleasant sense of accomplishment. The striped couch and chair are actually pretty cool. I've combined some of Mollie's interesting antiques and things with the wicker chairs and cushions and some of the new accent pieces, and it really does look like shabby chic. And, with the windows being open all night, I think the paint smell is pretty much gone too. It's time, I decide, to bring in Mollie.

I actually blindfold her before I slowly and carefully guide her down the stairs and into the basement. "Ready?" I ask.

She nods and I remove the blindfold. But she just stands there. Without saying a word, she looks around. It's like she's not having any reaction. She just keeps looking and looking. Then she turns to me and I see there are two streams of tears pouring down her cheeks as she grabs and hugs me, sobbing, "*Thank you! Thank you! Thank you!*" Then she lets go and dances around the room exclaiming about everything and how much she loves it. Now *that's* the reaction I was hoping for.

"It's so amazing," she tells me. "I absolutely adore it. I could live here forever. My baby and me . . . forever."

Okay, I'm glad she loves it, but I'm not so sure about that last bit. I mean, it's not that I don't want her to keep her baby, but I don't like feeling that I may have encouraged her to do something that's not in her best interests. Then I remind myself—only God knows what's in her best interests. I pray that he shows her what that is.

"Now to thank you, I'm going to go fix us breakfast," she tells me.

We decide to bring our breakfast back down to Mollie's basement and, as we eat, I point to the area by the bathroom. "Right where the washer and dryer used to be . . . wouldn't that be a great place for a small kitchen?"

"Yeah. Maybe I can get Dad to help me with it." Then she points to an open area near her bed. "And the baby's furniture could go right there," she says happily. "Maybe I could get a rocking chair too."

I bite my tongue and nod. "You should be pretty comfortable down here, Mollie. I'm almost starting to feel jealous."

She laughs. "Yeah, right. I'm sure you'd love to trade lives with me."

"Speaking of lives, I should probably get back to my own." I glance up at the French-looking clock that I hung over by the window and stand up to leave.

"But what about practicing for your show?" she asks eagerly. "Don't you want me to coach you?"

"Yes, of course."

"And, don't forget, I still need to pay you back for the stuff you got. Did you save your receipts?"

"I have an idea," I tell her. "Let's just call it an even exchange. You coach me for a while and this will be your payment."

Her eyes grow wide. "You're definitely getting the short end of the stick in that deal."

"Not if you really help me."

"Okay." She nods with a serious expression. "I'll do my best."

So, for the next several hours, with my camera set on the tripod and running, Mollie plays director and I pretend I'm hosting *On the Runway*. We start with me doing a commentary on shabby chic and how it works both in the bedroom and on the catwalk. After this practice episode, we replay what we just filmed and Mollie gives me some fairly blunt but honest critique.

"Pretend the camera is your best friend," she tells me. "You need to relax and smile more."

"That's easier said than done," I point out. "My comfort zone is the *other* side of the camera."

"But how would you like to be filming someone who's treating you like the enemy?"

I consider this. "Good point."

"And quit taking yourself so seriously. Lighten up. Remember that anything can be cut."

"You're really good at this," I tell her. "Do you think you'll continue in film school after the baby comes?"

She sighs. "That's my plan ... but sometimes it feels overwhelming."

Next I do a mock interview with Mollie's old Barbie doll,

which actually turns out to be pretty hilarious. I think it would be fun to try something like this when I do the show about fashion's impact on body image.

We watch this segment, and then Mollie makes me do it again. And then again. By the end of the day, I think I'm either getting better or I'm too tired to know the difference.

As I'm leaving, Mollie thanks me again for her basement makeover and I thank her for coaching me. "We're not done," she reminds me. "But you really made some good progress."

The question is—am I progressing enough to make the cut and help host our show? I'm fully aware that I am not Paige. But as Mollie keeps reminding me, *they don't want me to be Paige.* They want me to be me. But what if me is not good enough?

Chapter

6

Fran schedules the Chanel boutique for our wedding shopping show at the end of the week. Because we shoot it early in the day, before the store opens, Mom is able to come too. But as we're filming, Paige seems a little uneasy about the way that Fran is trying to bring me onto center stage. It's almost like Paige didn't really think we were going to go through with it.

For the sake of the show, we're pretending that Mom hasn't already purchased her wedding clothes. I have a feeling Paige is hoping that she can get Mom to rethink her choice, as she leads her in a completely different direction.

"Look at the soft, flowing lines of this design," Paige tells Mom as she removes a pale peach chiffon number from the rack. "The tea-length skirt would be just perfect in a garden wedding." She holds the dress up in front of Mom, like she's wearing it. But as Mom studies the image in the three-way mirror, her expression is uncertain.

"That doesn't really seem like Mom's style to me," I say as I step next to her.

"And I don't really care for that color," Mom adds.

"Oh, we can see about a different color," Paige insists. "But imagine this dress in a garden wedding. Isn't it sweet and romantic?"

"I don't think I'm really the romantic type." Mom chuckles. "I mean when it comes to fashion."

"I have to agree with Mom," I say. "She's more of a classic."

"Yes." Paige nods. "I'm fully aware of this, but this is for her wedding. What better time to be romantic than at your wedding?"

"But I'm so used to wearing suits and business wear." Mom frowns. "I think I would feel a bit silly in a dress like that."

I pull out a satin two-piece ensemble in a silvery shade of white. "Now I can see you in something like this," I say to Mom as I hold this dress in front of Paige's recommendation. Naturally, Paige tosses me a look—like *why are you show-ing Mom something that's similar to what she already has?* But I ignore her. "It's sophisticated and classic," I tell Mom. "But this beaded detailing gives it a soft feminine look too."

Mom touches the fabric and smiles. "It's beautiful."

"Why don't you try it on?" the manager suggests.

Mom looks slightly uncomfortable.

"It appears to be your size," the manager tells her.

"Yes, Mom," I urge. "Go try it on while Paige and I look around for bridesmaid dresses."

After Mom goes into the fitting room, Fran suggests that Paige and I split up in the store, each with our own camera-man and doing our own commentary as we look for dresses. JJ follows me, and Alistair trails Paige. Remembering what Mollie said about treating the camera like my best friend, I pretend that JJ is Mollie and just start chatting away.

"I know that Paige wants something softer and lacier," I say quietly to JJ. "Something *romantic*. I realize that would look fabulous on Paige, but Mom and I would probably look silly. And since this is Mom's wedding, I want her to look her best—and to feel comfortable too. You see, my mom and I are really more the classic type. We're just not into frills or lace too much." I finger through the rack, commenting on the various styles and fabrics and colors until I come to one with some good potential.

I pull out the periwinkle satin dress, holding it up for the camera to see. It has cap sleeves and a gently scooped neckline. "See the simple lines, the princess seams ... it's a very classic style. Now some people might think that's boring—kind of the way some people think vanilla ice cream is boring. But I happen to love vanilla ice cream. It tastes good with almost anything and it has a timeless appeal. Kind of like this dress." I chuckle. "Of course, most people wouldn't compare dresses to ice cream."

I go over to the three-way mirror again, holding the dress up as if I'm wearing it. "It's really nice. And even though it's a classic, I can imagine it in a garden wedding."

"Would you like to try it on?" the manager asks me.

"Sure." I nod and head over to the fitting room. Paige had us wear the right shoes today so that the dresses we tried on would look better. Before long I have the periwinkle dress on and zipped. It's about a size too big, but close enough to get the picture. When I come out of the fitting room, Mom is dressed in the silver-white suit and standing in front of the mirror with JJ filming her.

"You look beautiful," I tell her as I go and stand beside her. Just then Paige comes back with another saleswoman. Paige is holding a white dress which resembles the earlier one she showed us with a flowing layered skirt, as well as several others in various shades of pink and rose.

"You're already trying dresses on?" she asks me.

"Only this one," I admit.

"I thought you were going to get several," she says as she holds the white gown up for Mom to see. "Now, I know you *think* you want to stick to classic," Paige tells Mom. "But you should at least give this one a try." She smiles brightly. "Just for fun and to make me happy." Then she hands me a rose-colored dress, which again has the soft, layered, romantic look. I have to admit that it's a beautiful dress, but I don't think it'll be beautiful on me.

"What do you think of this one?" Mom asks Paige as she holds out her arms.

"It's nice." Paige nods. "But kind of expected . . . a bit conservative. Plus it's missing any wow appeal."

"Wow appeal?" I echo.

"It's a very safe dress," Paige says with fashion authority. "It would be appropriate for the *mother* of the bride to wear . . . if she wanted to be cautious. But, Mom, you *are* the bride. Don't you want to feel special? Like *wow*."

I can't help but laugh. "What if Mom doesn't want to feel *like wow*?"

Mom laughs. "Okay, Paige, I'll give your dress a try."

"You too," Paige tells me. Then she's literally pushing Mom and me back toward the fitting rooms. I want to protest and ask her why we can't give these other dresses more of a chance, but it's too late. For now that is. As I try on the rose-colored chiffon dress, I decide that I will insist we give the classic styles a second look. Then I get an idea. Maybe we can invite the viewers to vote.

Before long the three of us are standing in front of the mirrors. Naturally, Paige looks stunning, although a bit too princess-like for my taste. But Mom and I both look uncomfortable.

"See," Paige beams. "Isn't this a romantic-looking scene?"

Mom looks like she's trying to be a good sport. "I'll admit the dresses are very pretty, Paige."

"But . . . ?" Paige looks disappointed.

"But this just isn't me." Mom makes a weak smile.

"And it's sure not me," I add. "Although if Mom wanted me to wear this dress, I would do it. Remember, this is Mom's wedding . . . not ours."

"Yes, of course." Paige presses her lips together and nods. "If Mom wants to do classic, then classic it will be. But perhaps we can try some different versions of classic."

So Mom and I cooperate, trying on several more dresses, but we are running out of time and so far I haven't seen anything that everyone can agree on. So, while Paige is out looking again, I decide it's time to step in. "I think we should give the dresses we first tried on another chance," I say to Mom. "The silvery two-piece for you and the periwinkle for me."

Mom smiles. "Yes, let's do that." She turns to the manager. "Perhaps you can find something similar to the periwinkle dress for Paige to try on."

"I know just the one," she tells Mom.

It's not long before Mom and I are standing in front of the mirrors again. "This is more like it," I say.

"I really do like this dress," Mom says as she examines herself in the mirror. She tosses me a glance like maybe she's having second thoughts about the dress she has at home.

"You should get married in the dress you like the most," I assure her.

She smiles. "I love that on you, Erin. It's perfect. I know brides always tell the bridesmaids that they can wear the dresses again, but I actually think you could wear that one again."

I nod. "I think so too."

Paige emerges from the fitting room. Her dress is lilac satin and cut similar to mine, but not exactly the same. Wearing a hard-to-read expression, she joins us. "What do you think, Mom?"

Mom is beaming. "I think it's perfect."

Paige frowns slightly. "Really?"

"What do you think?" Mom asks hopefully.

"Honestly?"

Mom nods. "Yes. You are, after all, the fashion expert, Paige. What do you honestly think?"

"I think it's a bit bland."

Mom looks disappointed. "Oh . . ."

"I disagree," I say. "If we carry the right flowers and—"

"You can't expect flowers to eradicate the blah factor," Paige says.

"I have an idea," I say to the camera. "How about if we let the viewers decide?"

Paige laughs. "You want the viewers to tell our mother what to have for her wedding?"

"I'm not saying that Mom has to make her decision based on the viewers' choice. But it might be fun to hear what they think." I glance over at Fran and she is nodding eagerly. "So . . ." I step closer to the camera. "We want to hear from you. At the end of this show, we'll give you our two best choices and you can let us know what you think."

Fran is signaling to us to wrap it up and I turn to Paige. "Well, this has been fun, hasn't it?"

Paige takes the cue and delivers her traditional line, and then Fran yells cut.

"That was fun," Mom says as we go back to change into our own clothes. "I'll be curious to hear what the viewers think."

"Well, this show won't run for a couple of weeks," Fran tells her. "You might not want to wait that long."

Mom laughs. "No, and that's okay because I've already made up my mind."

Then, to my surprise, Mom actually buys the silvery white satin two-piece dress, as well as the lilac and periwinkle bridesmaid dresses for Paige and me. And because we'll be using today's filming on our show, we get a very nice discount. After we leave, Mom tells us that she will return the other dress.

She sighs. "I suppose high fashion is a bit contagious. After wearing that Chanel dress today, I just knew I couldn't be as happy in the other one."

"You're going to look gorgeous," I tell her.

Paige says nothing as we walk back to our cars. But after we part ways, since Mom has to go to work and I'm riding with Paige, my sister opens up.

"I realize that Helen and Fran are encouraging you to take an active role in the show," she says calmly. "But I hope you know what you're doing."

"What do you mean?"

"The reason the show works is because it's about fashion." She says this like she thinks I'm an idiot.

"Yes . . . I know that."

"And the reason that works is because I am the fashion expert."

"Meaning there can be only *one* fashion expert?"

She nods with a confident smile.

"Okay, I realize I'm not an expert," I admit. "But I do have some opinions. And there's more than one kind of fashion. Not everyone is into your expensive forms of haute couture."

"I'm aware of that, Erin." Paige scowls. "What you seem to forget is that real style begins with excellent design. Excellent design translates into haute couture and that does not come cheaply."

"Don't forget that beauty is in the eye of the beholder."

"Don't forget that great designers and haute couture are the foundation of beauty in the fashion arena."

"But what if I happen to think that Granada Ruez is a great designer?"

Paige looks slightly horrified. "Oh, please, Erin. Don't tell me you want to get back on the Granada Greenwear bandwagon."

"Hey, you said you liked her designs after Granada showed you how to wear them."

"I was simply being a good sport. We had a show to do and I wanted to make it a good one."

"Well, Helen wants our show to be broader now," I remind her. "That means more than just high design and haute couture and clothes that only a few can afford."

"You still don't get it, Erin. Good design trickles down from Paris to Wal-Mart. Eventually everyone can afford it. My job is to help them recognize it."

Okay, that actually makes a tiny bit of sense, but I'm not willing to concede just yet.

"I want to help our viewers," she continues. "I care about those fashion-challenged girls who want more style in their lives. What's wrong with giving them what they want?"

"But how do you know what they want? My guess is that our viewers are more like me than you."

She laughs. "See, that's my point. That's why they watch a show like *On the Runway*. They need to be educated about what is and what is not good style."

I groan and lean back. This is so not going to be easy.

"I'm not trying to pick on you, Erin. It's just that the show is working. It's a success and the viewers love it. If we start reinventing it midstream, well, it might hit the rocks and sink."

I consider this. "You could be right."

"I am right."

"So are you saying that Helen Hudson is wrong?"

"No … not exactly. I think she wants to try something different, because that's the way she is, always thinking of new ways to do things. But I'm saying if it's not broken, why fix it?"

"Because it could be even better?"

She firmly shakes her head.

"Well, what about the episode that I was promised about body image and how it's damaged by stick-thin fashion models? Are you suddenly against that?"

"No … not exactly. Because I do feel sorry for girls who think that fashion only comes in one size. That's wrong. But, on the other hand, I wouldn't want us to do too many issue-based shows, like how high heels are bad for feet, or which designers are polluting the planet. It's not as if we're a social documentary program. Or like we think we can fix everyone. I mean, like it or not, we're a show about fashion. We're *On the Runway*, Erin. Not *Dr. Phil*."

I decide it's time to keep my mouth shut about the other show ideas I've been noodling on lately. I should probably run them past Helen and Fran first. And, who knows? Paige could be right. If the show's not broken, maybe it's crazy to attempt to fix it.

Chapter 7

"*I thought you said that Paige and Ben* were history," Mollie says as I drive her home from fellowship group on Saturday night.

I shrug. "Well, that's kind of what she said a couple weeks ago."

Mollie holds up her phone. "I just got a tweet saying the two were spotted at OurHouse this evening."

"At *our* house?" I frown at her. "Huh?"

"OurHouse is a new club in town."

"Oh." I nod.

"Do you think it's serious?"

"I honestly don't know, Mollie." I say this, but I'm starting to feel apprehensive.

"The tweet said they were kissing."

I let out a little groan. "Well ... it's her life. Not much I can do about it."

"It could be a publicity stunt."

I cringe. I'm not even sure which is less appealing ... that Paige is back with Ben because she really likes him, or that she's back with him for the publicity. And, really, what kind of publicity would that be anyway? I know the old saying that any publicity is good publicity. I just don't happen to agree.

"Although I don't think Paige needs publicity as much as Benjamin does," Mollie continues.

"Seriously?"

"Oh, yeah. Paige is all over the place. You can hardly look at any of the Hollywood gossip sites without seeing Paige's pretty face."

"What kind of gossip is it?"

"The typical stuff—love triangles, secret engagements, fashion tidbits, pictures of Paige around town. Nothing terrible." Mollie laughs. "So you still don't even peek at it?"

"It's just not my thing."

"You've got to be the most reluctant reality TV star out there."

"I'm not a star," I protest.

"Says you."

"Well, I'm not a star like Paige is a star. The truth is I've been rethinking my role as Paige's costar."

"Why would you do that?" Mollie demands. "You were just starting to get good at it. Don't give up before you even begin."

"It's not that I'm giving up, exactly."

"What do you mean?"

"I'm only questioning whether it makes sense or not."

"Why wouldn't it make sense?"

"It's like Paige keeps saying—the show is a success as it is. Why change it?"

Mollie doesn't respond and I hope she's getting it.

"And even though Paige and I have our differences … she's my sister and I love her. I don't want to ruin a show that's already working. You know?"

"Yeah, that makes sense."

"Anyway, I have a meeting with Helen and Fran this Monday. I'm supposed to run my ideas past them … and we'll see."

"I'm sure they'll do what's best for the show, Erin. It's not like they'll want to mess it up."

"I know."

I'll admit I'm disappointed that I might not get to do the shows I've been planning. But at the same time it might be a relief to be free from all the pressures. Maybe there'll be another way to share my opinions about style and fashion.

But at the meeting on Monday, to my surprise both Fran and Helen seem totally open to my ideas.

"The key to good reality TV is to be open to shaking it up a bit," Fran tells me.

"Shake it but don't break it," Helen adds.

"So we'll play with some controversies," Fran tells Helen. "If they don't work, we can always cut them later." Then she explains her plan to us. "As you know, Paige will continue in the lead, but we'll introduce a seven-minute segment that I'm calling 'Sibling Rivalry' where the girls will go head-to-head over fashion." Fran turns to me. "You'll gather your facts as well as some footage of interviews or fashion shows or whatever you can use to back up your opinions. We'll let you both have at it, then do some editing and see how it works."

"Excellent!" Helen claps her hands together. "I can just imagine."

"Seven minutes isn't much time," I point out. "I thought

that I was going to get a whole show to focus on body image and fashion." I hold up the proposal sheet I put together for "Killer Style: What Happens When Fashion Turns Lethal?"

Helen frowns. "I know you wanted to do that show, Erin. But the more I thought about using an entire *On the Runway* episode to cover this issue, the more concerned I got. Fans expect the show to be upbeat and fun. We need to maintain that general feeling."

"Upbeat and fun with a little edge," Fran says. "Just like the 'Sibling Rivalry' segment will add."

"We want you to take the lead in deciding what the controversial topics can be, Erin. But we can't let the show become too negative. Do you get that?" Helen studies me.

"I get it," I tell them. "And I guess I'm not that surprised."

"Who knows …" Helen gives me a sly smile. "Maybe the 'Sibling Rivalry' segment will catch on and you'll have your own spin-off show."

"It happens." Fran looks down at what appears to be a schedule. "The plan is to film some of these segments before we go to London. We'll insert them into some shows and see how viewers respond."

"In the meantime," Helen tells me, "we still expect you to act as Paige's costar during the other filming. Be yourself."

"That's right," Fran tells me. "Feel free to mix it up like you did at Chanel last week."

Helen nods. "I saw outtakes this morning. It looked good. So keep it up, Erin. Express yourself and your opinions."

"I'll go over these ideas," Fran tells me as she puts my stack of possible show topics into a folder, "and see what we can line up to shoot between now and London. We have only ten days before we have to leave."

As we exit the room, I think about what Fran and Helen proposed. It's not exactly what I had imagined, but I'm open to it. And maybe I'm actually relieved ... some of the pressure is off. I'm sure Paige will be happy too. She'll probably love the idea of arguing fashion with me. Not that she's been talking to me much lately. I'm not sure if it's because she thinks I'm infringing on her fame or if she's simply feeling guilty for "secretly" dating Benjamin again. Whatever it is, I decide it's time to find out. Now if I can only think of a non-confrontational way to bring it up.

Paige is watching TV when I come into the house. But when I see she's watching *Britain's Got Style*, I realize this is about work, not entertainment. "Doing research?" I ask.

She nods as she takes a drink of iced tea. "Fran sent these DVDs over last week."

I want to ask why no one told me about this, but I realize that might ignite a feud. Instead, I sit down and watch with her. The main host of this show, Chloe Brinkman, used to be in a music group and then did some modeling, but now she's best known as Brit's number-one fashion diva. And she's very opinionated. However, I find that I agree with much of her take on fashion and modeling. In fact, by the time the show ends, I find I rather like Chloe Brinkman.

"She's really good," I say as I get a glass of iced tea for myself.

"Who?" Paige calls.

"Chloe Brinkman." I return to see Paige slipping in another DVD.

"Oh ... she's okay."

"Just okay?" I sit down and wait.

"She's not as much of an expert as she wants everyone to

think." Paige points the remote at the TV and the next DVD starts playing.

I'm tempted to argue this "fact," but decide to save it for one of our "Sibling Rivalry" segments. "I met with Fran and Helen this morning," I say offhandedly.

"How'd that go?" She turns the volume down slightly.

I study her for a few seconds. I can tell by her expression that this isn't a surprise to her. "Okay."

"So they told you about the 'Sibling Rivalry' thing they want to do?"

"You knew about it?"

She pauses the DVD then turns and blinks at me. "Of course I knew about it. Did you think they would've told you before they told me?"

"Well . . . no . . . not really." Okay, I actually did think this. Not that I plan to admit it.

"I told them I think it'll flop, but it's worth a try."

"Right . . ."

"Did Fran tell you that we're set to shoot more film for our bridal episode?"

"I thought we were done with it."

"No. We need to fill out the show with a few more designers."

"But Mom already made up—"

"This isn't about Mom, Erin." She lets out an exasperated sigh. "It's about our show."

"Oh . . . okay." I try to sound positive. "So what do we do? Pretend to still be shopping for bridesmaid dresses?"

She nods. "That's the general plan. First we'll look at the Vera Wang collection and then we'll head over to check out a new designer—a guy who used to design for Badgley

Mischka and is trying to set up a studio in LA. Fran just heard about him."

"Fran said we'll shoot some 'Sibling Rivalry' segments this week too."

"That should be fun." Paige makes a face.

"Are you okay with it?" I ask a bit tentatively.

She smiles, but it looks slightly forced. "Yeah, sure. I think it'll be fun."

"Also, just so you know, I've been thinking about what you were saying the other day — about how the show already works, and how we don't want to mess that up."

"And?"

"And I think you're mostly right."

She looks relieved.

"I mean, I can still have my opinions," I add quickly. "We don't have to agree on everything."

"That's what Helen and Fran are hoping for."

"So we should be okay ... right?"

She nods. "Yes. I'm sorry if I bit your head off the other day. I think I was kind of stressed."

"Speaking of stressed ... Mollie mentioned that you and Benjamin have been a topic on Twitter and some of the Hollywood gossip shows."

Paige just smiles.

"So are you guys dating?"

Her smile fades. "No, of course not. Remember, I told you that I gave that all up."

"But you're seeing him?"

She nods with a catty smile. "And the media is eating it up."

"You're only doing it for publicity?"

"It's a win-win for everyone, Erin."

I frown at her. "How is that even possible?"

"Benjamin needs publicity right now ... and a little more face-in-the-news time doesn't hurt us either."

"But hasn't Ben kind of been *bad* news lately? I mean, the whole thing with Mia was only a couple of months ago. I don't see how you being photographed with him can help our show much."

"You'd be surprised, Erin. Plus it's ratings sweeps next month. We need to keep this thing rolling." She gives me a perturbed look. "It's not like you're doing anything to help in that regard."

I'm not sure how to react to that one.

"But that's okay," she says in a slightly patronizing tone. "We don't expect you to get out there and get your hands dirty."

"What's that supposed to mean?"

"You know what it means." Paige gives me her devious grin. "You're the good sister ... and I'm the wild one."

"I thought we were *both* good sisters."

She nods. "We are. But I have an image to maintain. I have fans to amuse."

"I so don't get that."

"I know." She clicks the remote, causing the DVD to play again. "I didn't expect that you would."

I watch the show for a while, but I find myself getting more and more aggravated at my sister. It gets to the point where I can't even focus on Chloe Brinkman anymore. And yet, when I sneak a glance at Paige, she's calmly watching, like she's totally oblivious to what she just said or how it might have sounded. Then I wonder if I'm overreacting. Finally, I get up and leave. But once I'm in my room, I call Mollie and tell her what happened. "It's like Paige doesn't care what people think of her," I say finally. "Like it's no big deal that she's going to clubs with a guy who came very close to being prosecuted for manslaughter, and still hasn't stopped drinking. I mean, he could be behind bars right now. Instead, he's running around with my sister, making the front pages of the gossip rags."

Mollie simply laughs. "And that's called publicity."

"If I hear that word again—I think I'll scream."

"It's what sells things like reality TV shows, Erin. Surely you know that by now."

"I know it," I seethe. "I just don't like it."

"Then you are in the wrong business."

I consider this. "Yeah, you're right. I probably am."

"Okay . . . sorry not to sound more sympathetic," she says. "But I'm sitting here feeling the world is passing me by and you're complaining about publicity. Man, I'd love to have your problems, Erin."

"Sorry." I shake my head and wonder why I'm apologizing to her.

"Hey, in happier news, my parents got home last night and couldn't believe what you did to the basement."

"They were okay with it?"

"Yeah. They were almost *too* okay with it. Suddenly my mom was rethinking her plan to take over my old bedroom. Like she might rather set up her writing studio in the basement now."

"No way. That's *your* basement."

Mollie laughs, but I can hear a trace of sadness mixed in. "Yeah, that's what I told them. It's my basement . . . for now anyway."

We talk awhile longer and I begin to feel guilty for complaining about Paige and her recent publicity stunts. Really, it's a small thing compared to what Mollie is dealing with right now. After we hang up, I think about Tony's role in all this, and how he was so into Mollie — until she got pregnant, that is. Now he's pulled this amazing and mysterious disappearing act. I'd almost like to hunt him down and give him a piece of my mind, not that he would listen. In fact, I'm starting to suspect that no one wants to listen to any of my strong opinions.

Chapter
8

"So are you girls okay with these?" Marty
Stuart asks as he hands us the revised contracts that he's been
negotiating with Helen Hudson.

"I am," I tell him as I pick up a pen and get ready to sign.

"I'm not." Paige pushes her contract back across his desk.

"Huh?" I study her expression. "What's wrong? You want
more money?" I actually thought the pay increase was pretty
generous.

"No, it's not about the money."

"What is it then?" Marty looks perplexed too.

"I don't like the 'Sibling Rivalry' idea. I think it will only
slow down the show and bore the viewers. Besides that, I
want creative sign-off on the show. And I want the assurance
that I will continue as the host—the *only* host. And I want it
in writing."

Too stunned to respond, I just stare at my sister, curious
as to whether I can actually see her head increasing in size.
What is going on with her? And what's up with this prima
donna act? She can't be serious.

Marty looks slightly nervous. "The *only* host?"

"Yes. I don't want to share that spot with anyone."

"Not even Erin?" He glances back and forth between us.

"I'm happy to see Erin moving beyond Camera Girl in the show," she says carefully. "I'm fine with that. But I do not want the 'Sibling Rivalry' segment and I do not want to share my host position with anyone. Not even my sister." She turns and smiles sweetly at me. "Surely you understand that, don't you?"

I nod slowly, trying to think of a way out of this mess. "I do … understand." And this is true; in a strange and slightly twisted way I do understand. And in a way, I'm not completely blindsided by this either. Hurt, yes; surprised, not so much. I mean, this is Paige. "But what about Helen?" I ask carefully.

"Oh, I think Helen will understand too."

"Meaning what?" Now I realize my sister is full of herself, but I can't believe she thinks she can overstep Helen. I mean, how can she be so nonchalant? She's about to tell Helen that she plans to take over the show, and it's like she honestly thinks Helen is going to just say "no problem."

"Don't worry, Erin. Helen will get this."

"But what if she doesn't? What happens then?"

Paige presses her lips together.

"Erin poses a good question," Marty tells Paige. "What if Helen *doesn't* agree?"

Paige shrugs. "In that case, maybe I'll just walk."

"Walk?" I stare at Paige, wondering who this girl is and what she's done with my sister. "You must be kidding. You love this show."

She sighs. "I *used* to love the show."

"So what are you saying then?" Marty asks. "You're done with it? After a few months?"

"I'm simply saying *On the Runway* isn't the only show in town."

"Seriously? You think you can get another show as good as this?" I shake my head doubtfully.

"Maybe even better."

Marty grabs a pencil and starts jotting on a notepad. "So you're sure this is what you want, Paige? You really want to make a demand like this to Helen?"

"I do."

"*Paige?*" I want to shake her. Like *wake up*—why is she nuking her show and her career like this? At the same time, I think why not let her—get it over with. It's bound to happen; the sooner the better.

"What, Erin?" She looks evenly at me.

"What if you do this and it blows up in your face? Are you seriously going to go looking for another show after less than six months on this one?"

"Erin has a point." Marty continues writing. "You haven't even done a full season on your show. The industry won't take that sort of thing lightly."

Paige holds her head high. "I'm not worried."

"How can you not be worried?" I ask. "I'm worried and this show isn't as big a deal to me as I know it is to you. How can you be so calm about this?"

"Because I know I will land on my feet."

A little light goes on in my brain. "So ... who have you been talking to?"

"No one." But her eyes betray her. I can tell she's been talking to someone. And I have a pretty good idea who.

"*Benjamin Kross.*" I pound my fist on the desk. "What's he been telling you, Paige? That you're a big star now? That you can get more money somewhere else? That you should pull the prima donna act and make your demands, stomp your designer shoe and get your way?"

She shrugs.

"Is Benjamin offering you something specific?" Marty persists. "A new reality show perhaps?"

"Let's say this . . . I have my opportunities."

"So, just for clarification's sake," I say, "if Helen *doesn't* agree . . . that means you really plan to walk away from the show? Is that right?"

"I can't predict the future, Erin. I don't know which way this will go. I honestly don't expect Helen to balk at this."

"But you would walk if she did? You would, wouldn't you?" I can't believe she's so cool about this.

"Probably."

I'm so frustrated I feel close to tears. "Do you know how selfish that is, Paige?"

"Selfish to look after my own future?" She looks honestly confused, like the idea of selfishness never even occurred to her. "If I don't take care of my career, who will? Don't forget that I'm the one who wanted to do this in the first place. You know that you've been reluctant from the get-go, Erin."

"I may have been reluctant, but I did give up film school to do this show with you, Paige! I put my life on hold and dropped everything just to—"

"And look at the experience you've gotten from it!" she shouts back. "Do you honestly think you'd have learned this much in school?"

"Time out!" Marty says loudly. "Both of you take a big deep breath and chill for a minute. Okay?"

His office grows quiet and all I hear is the scratching of

his pencil on paper as he continues to write notes. Then he punches his phone and calls in his assistant, tapping his pencil on the desk as he waits for her to come. When she arrives, he hands her Paige's contract along with his notes, and asks her to make the revisions and new copies. After she leaves he folds his hands on the desk in front of him and shakes his head. "I can't say that I approve of this decision, Paige, but I do understand. And as your agent, I am willing to do my best to get Helen Hudson to agree to this."

"Thank you." Paige reaches for her bag.

Marty looks directly at me now. "It would probably help if you agreed to it as well, Erin."

"In writing?"

He smiles. "I mean more of in spirit . . ."

I shrug. It's weird, but I think I'm relieved. Maybe this crazy ride is about to end. Maybe I can part ways with Paige without feeling guilty now. Maybe I can have my life back. And yet it hurts. "I guess I can agree. I mean, it's not like I have much of a choice." I hold up my contract. "Do you still want me to sign this?"

"If you're still okay with it. Paige's revisions don't really impact your contract."

"Well, other than the fact that it might make my contract worthless."

"I'm not doing this to hurt you," Paige says in a flat tone.

"Yeah . . . right." I don't even look at her as I sign my name and the date.

"But you're still mad at me, aren't you?"

I take in another deep breath, trying to hold back tears as I open another copy, looking for the right line to sign on. I'm not even sure why this hurts so much. Other than the fact it feels like my sister just knifed me in the back. But, really, I should be relieved. Maybe this will end this insane sister act once and for all. Because, honestly, I don't think I can take anymore of this. With a tightened jaw and imagining that I am signing divorce papers—to divorce my sister—I sign the last copy and slide it all back over to Marty.

"If my work here is done, I'd like to go," I tell him as I stand. Thankfully, Paige and I took separate cars here today. I'm ready to make a quick exit.

He nods. "Thanks, Erin."

"Thank you," I say with a lump in my throat.

With a sad expression, Marty stands and reaches out to shake my hand. For some reason it feels like a farewell gesture. Like he's telling me this is it—time to kiss *On the Runway* adios. Then, without saying a word to my sister, I leave.

I get in my Jeep and just sit there. Really, I don't know why I'm taking this so hard. Paige is right ... the show was never my dream in the first place. I've been dragging my heels since day one. And, while it hurts a little to see everything just vanish, that's not the most disturbing part of this.

The hardest thing is feeling like my own sister has dismissed me. Like she's been using me all along and now she's done and ready to move on ... like see ya later, little sister.

I remember other times like this. Not as hurtful perhaps, but painfully similar. Paige always had a hard time getting and maintaining friends. Of course, I have my own suspicions as to why this happens. I still recall a number of times when Paige, between friends, would solicit me as her "little buddy." I'd usually try to accommodate her. Of course, this usually meant getting stuck in some inane activity like playing Barbies or dress-up, or sneaking into Mom's makeup and taking the blame once we were found out.

What I remember today is how Paige and I would be in the middle of some crazy Paige-directed activity and I'd be try-ing to "cooperate" (which meant doing things her way), and out of the blue one of her friends would call and invite her to do something. And—just like that—Paige would dump me like last year's bell bottoms.

I feel just as horrible now. Since I don't want to go home, because Paige will probably end up there too, I drive over to Mollie's. But she's at a doctor's appointment.

"She should be back in about half an hour," Mrs. Tyson tells me. "At least she better be back since she borrowed my car and I have a meeting to go to at two."

"Oh." I step back. "Okay."

"But you can wait for her if you like."

Normally I wouldn't care to do this, but right now I'd like someplace to just lie low. "Okay," I agree. "I guess I'll do that."

"I'm sure you can find the way to her new room," Mrs. Tyson says in a way that's hard to decipher.

"Right." I glance at her. "Was the makeover okay?"

"Oh, sure." She folds her arms across her front. "We'd been encouraging her to move down there. And it looks very nice. But ..."

"But?" I pause and look directly at her.

"But Mollie's father and I were hoping she'd fix up the room herself, Erin. We didn't want anyone to help her."

"You didn't want anyone to help her?"

She shakes her head.

"Why not?"

"Well, as her father says, she got herself into this mess and she should have to get herself out of it."

I frown at her and it takes all my self-control not to say something totally regrettable. I guess I should've known better. Mollie warned me that her dad was not taking her pregnancy well. It seems clear he has influenced her mom now too. "I'm sorry if helping Mollie offended you," I say in a stiff voice. "But it seemed like she needed some help."

Mrs. Tyson makes a look like *duh*, but says nothing.

"I know you guys are Christians." I push this a bit further. "And Jesus tells us to treat others how we want to be treated ... so I guess that's what I was trying to do."

"Yes. I suppose that makes sense ... to you."

"But not to you?"

"You know I love Mollie, Erin." She frowns. "But I have to agree with her father on this. If Mollie doesn't step up and own her problems—in this case a child—well, then she'll never grow up ... will she?"

"I think she's growing up."

She chuckles. "Well, I suppose we're both just looking at Mollie from two different places now, aren't we?"

"I guess so." I can't help but get the implication here that I, like Mollie, am young and have a lot to learn still. And maybe it's true. But maybe parents forget that it takes time to get this stuff. Maybe they don't remember how things were when they were younger. Or maybe growing up just came easier to them.

"But I'm glad that Mollie has some good mature friends like you," Mrs. Tyson says as I open the door to the stairway.

I force a smile. "Oh, I'm not sure that I'm all that mature," I say lightly. "Just a few minutes ago I wanted to take a swing at my sister. That's not terribly grown up."

She looks slightly horrified. "You wanted to hit that beautiful sister of yours?"

I nod. "Yeah ... actually I did."

"Oh, Erin. She's been so good to let you be on her TV show. I would think you'd be more grateful."

"I guess we're both just looking at Paige from two different places," I say to her.

She frowns and then smiles in a slightly condescending way. "Well, I'm sure you and Paige will work it out."

"Yes. I'm sure we will." Then I go downstairs, pick up one of the pillows that Mollie and I re-covered a few days ago, and soundly punch it.

When Mollie gets home, we commiserate over our problems together. I can tell it's a consolation to Mollie to hear that all is not smooth sailing with Paige and the show. But she has the sense not to say that.

"You know Paige will come around," Mollie says with confidence. "If Helen doesn't agree to her demands, Paige will cave. She loves that show, Erin. She's not about to let it go. You know that old saying, 'A bird in the hand is worth two in the bush.'"

"But what if Paige's other birds aren't in the bush?" I protest. "What if she's got one bird in the right hand and two in the left?"

Mollie laughs. "I guess that wouldn't surprise me."

"I'll bet Benjamin has something brewing," I speculate. "Something he wants Paige to be involved in so that it will help his ratings."

Mollie opens her laptop. "How about if I check out the gossip sites and see if I can find something?"

I sink down onto her re-covered sofa and sigh. "I'm not sure I even want to know. Or that I even care."

"Don't forget that knowledge is power, Erin. You shouldn't keep your head in the sand as much as you do."

"Really, I should be happy that this crazy ride is over," I say, mostly to myself since Mollie seems absorbed by the computer now. "I mean, now I can go back to school." I shake my head. "Although it'll be like starting over again. Everyone else will be ahead of me now."

"Hey, here's something about Benjamin Kross talking to someone at Bravo."

"Bravo? What's that?"

"Man, Erin, you really do live under a rock, don't you?"

"Okay ... I remember now. It's the high-end reality TV channel."

"Something like that."

"So what does it say specifically?"

"Not much. There's also something about his movie deal ... like it's still a possibility. Especially after last week's episode of *Malibu Beach*. Did you see that?"

I groan. "No, thanks, I'm not really into that."

"Well, it was actually pretty good. I mean it seemed genuine and heartfelt. Benjamin even cried."

"Good for Benjamin."

Mollie looks up from her computer now. "Sometimes it sounds like you hate him, Erin."

I press my lips together and try to examine my feelings.

"Do you hate him?"

"I don't know exactly. I hope that I don't hate him. I mean, it's wrong to hate anyone, no matter how twisted they are."

"Yeah." She nods soberly. "And, trust me, I know how that feels whenever I think about Tony."

I consider this. "That has to be a lot harder," I admit. "It's so much more personal. When I think about you and Tony, I even feel like I hate him."

"You need to get over this, Erin. Hate isn't good for you."

I smile at the irony. "Seems like I was just telling you that."

"I know. But my obstetrician told me that my blood pressure seemed a little high today."

"Your blood pressure?"

Mollie nods. "She said I need to keep things calm."

"Did you tell your mom about this yet?" I'm recalling her parents' attitude about how Mollie needs to grow up and take responsibility for things.

"No . . ."

"You better let her know, Mollie."

She looks back at her computer screen. "Here's another juicy piece about Benjamin and your sister."

I groan. "I'm not sure I want to hear it."

"It says here that they were rumored to have had a secret rendezvous in Paris."

"I can only imagine who leaked that one. It's not like the paparazzi were trailing us."

"You think Ben leaked it?"

"Use your imagination."

"So what if he and Paige really did get serious?" Mollie asks me.

I shrug. "Not much I can do about that."

"Besides lose the attitude?"

"Hey, I'm working on it."

She laughs and closes her computer. "Yeah, I can tell."

I lean back and sigh. "Do you remember when life was simple?"

"Was it ever simple?"

I frown to think about how my life feels slightly out of control lately ... How my mom's getting married and moving out to live with Jon. How my sister seems intent on blowing up our show and going in her own direction, which might include a guy I don't respect. Plus, I've only got one term of college under my belt when most other kids my age are finishing their first year.

"You know, like back when we were kids," I tell her. "Do you think we'll ever get to live like that again?"

"I think we had our chance," she says glumly.

"Too bad we didn't appreciate it more, huh?"

She shakes her head as she rubs her rounded stomach. "Yeah. Like they say, you don't know what you got until it's gone."

I guess that's pretty much true. The sad part is I can remember being so eager to grow up—like I couldn't get there fast enough. Now I'm suddenly old enough to supposedly manage my own life, and all I want is to go back and be a kid again. It just figures.

Chapter
9

My cell phone rings just as I'm leaving Mollie's house, and my caller ID informs me it's Helen Hudson. I get inside my Jeep to answer, trying not to sound too nervous. "Hi, Helen."

"Erin." Her deep voice has a chilly calmness to it. Almost like the hush before the hurricane. "What is going on with your sister?"

"What do you mean?"

"I mean I've got a revised contract here with Paige's name on it and I want to know *what's going on.*"

"Maybe you should ask Paige about—"

"Have no doubts, I definitely plan to speak to Paige, but I wanted to hear your thoughts first."

"Oh."

"I'm curious as to how you feel about big sister trying to shove you back into the corner."

I take in a deep breath and carefully consider my answer. Maybe it was talking to Mollie . . . or maybe it was just taking time to chill, but I no longer feel so enraged at my sister. "I don't think Paige is actually trying to shove me back into the corner."

"You don't?"

"No ... not exactly."

"Well, maybe you didn't see this revised contract."

"I have a pretty good idea of what's in it."

"And you're okay with that? No 'Sibling Rivalry' segment. Paige has creative control. You are relegated to ... well, pretty much to where you've been before."

"I know that Paige has a need to be in the spotlight," I say slowly. "I'm used to this."

"Yes, yes ... I know you don't mind playing second fiddle, Erin. But I think your sister wants to be the *only* fiddle — in fact, she seems to believe she's the entire orchestra."

"I don't disagree ... but isn't that why you hired Paige in the first place?"

"Producing a successful reality TV show requires more than one star, Erin."

"But hasn't the show *been* successful?"

"Yes, but this is the result of a team effort. I assumed that you, more than most, might understand this, Erin. After all, you were going to film school. Don't they teach that sort of thing anymore?"

I consider reminding her that I barely even started film school, but have a feeling it wouldn't do much good. Besides, she's right. Good production is the result of a good team. "If it's any consolation, I was pretty mad at Paige to start with," I say carefully. "I couldn't believe that she wanted to change her contract like that, especially since she told me privately that she was okay with the 'Sibling Rivalry' segment. But at the same time I understand her need to protect her position as the one and only host of the *On the Runway*."

"Even if the producer wants to go in a new direction?"

"I didn't say that I agree with her, Helen. I already warned her that I thought she was taking a risk."

"And?"

"She didn't seem concerned."

"Does she not understand that the way shows like ours remain hot and viable is that they are able to shift gears and change directions quickly—reality TV is like a living, breathing art form. It needs room to grow and adapt—to be able to catch the next wave. I feel that Paige's new contract will cut us off from that kind of flexibility. *On the Runway* will become stale and stagnant."

"Not as stale and stagnant as it would become without her," I counter.

"Touché. Your loyalty to your backstabbing sister is moving."

I force a small laugh. "Thanks."

"Erin, be straight with me. Is someone offering Paige another show? Is your sister looking for greener pastures? Because if she is, she's not only incredibly naïve, but she is going to be in a mountain of trouble too. I'll have my attorneys on this so fast that Paige's pretty little head will look like she should be starring in *The Exorcist*."

I honestly don't know how to respond to this. Part of me wants to protect and defend my sister, but another part gets Helen's anger. I don't say anything.

"I have two questions for you, Erin."

"Yes?"

"One, do you think Paige is trying to leave the show? And, two, do you feel ready to step up and take her place?"

"Wow ... I don't know."

"You don't know the answer to *either* question?"

"I honestly don't, Helen. As far as Paige goes, she's not exactly communicating with me and I'm not a psychic. You'll have to talk to her. As for me hosting the show ... well, the truth is that's flattering, but totally overwhelming."

"Yes. I expected you'd say something like that, but I appreciate your honesty. Now one more question."

"What?"

"Will you be terribly disappointed if we go back to the original format for the show—with Paige acting as the one and only host, the diva of divine style, the goddess of good taste, the final say in fashion?" She laughs in a sarcastic tone, although I suspect she knows that's not much of an exaggeration since the media sources have been saying pretty much the same thing.

"Not at all. It's your show, Helen."

"Really? You're not just a little disappointed to be shoved back into the corner away from the limelight?"

"I still wish we could address some of those tough topics that concern me, like how anorexic models impact the rest of us. But maybe Paige is right. Maybe that belongs on a different show."

"I have an idea, Erin."

"What's that?"

"Another avenue you might take. Tell me ... are you a good writer?"

"I guess I'm okay."

"Why don't you start a blog or something on the Internet to get your opinions and information across?"

"A blog?"

"Or a website or some other kind of media access."

"Do you honestly think anyone would read it?"

"You don't seem to appreciate that you have a platform now, Erin. Because of your role, albeit small, on a hot reality show like *On the Runway*, people are interested in you. They want to hear what you think. If your selfish sister won't let you get your opinions onto the show, you can always get them out through other means." Helen laughs. "I know you believe in God, Erin. Haven't you heard that saying—when God closes a door, he opens a window. Remember the line from *The Sound of Music*?"

As I'm chewing on this, Helen says she has to take a call. "Now don't tell Paige we talked," she says quickly. "And don't mention this to Fran either. I'd just as soon keep Fran removed from the sticky negotiation side of things. Don't want to sour her against our Princess Paige." She laughs, but I can tell she still doesn't think this is too funny. Then she says good-bye.

By the time I get home, Paige is pacing in the kitchen like a nervous cat. I can tell by the twist of her mouth she's starting to get worried. I know I could try to console her a bit, but I decide to just let her brew for a while. Without saying a word, I head straight to my room, but I've barely closed the door when my phone rings and I'm surprised to see it's Blake. I think this is the first time he's called me since I told him I wanted to cool it after the Paris trip.

"Hey, Blake," I say in a friendly tone. "What's up?"

"That's what I'm wondering ... *what is up?*"

"Huh?"

"Well, I was just with Benjamin and it sounds like he and Paige have been going out ... and I thought you said that you and your sister made some kind of sisterly agreement to have a non-dating pact so that you could focus on your show without the distraction of guys." His tone sounds frosty.

"Yeah ... well, that agreement has been steadily deteriorating." I quickly explain how Paige seems to have cheated on me. "But, trust me, that's only the tip of the iceberg right now."

"What do you mean?"

"Oh, it's just some messed-up stuff in regard to our show. I probably shouldn't even say anything."

"Unless you need to talk. Because you sound frustrated, Erin. You know me—I don't always have answers, but I think I'm a pretty good listener."

It's so good to hear Blake's voice again. So I just open the gates and the whole story spills out about the revised contract and Helen's reaction and how Paige might want to be on a different show. "But please don't tell anyone."

"You know you can trust me."

I think I can trust him ... I *believe* I can trust him. Yet he did break my heart once. Although, to be fair, that was a year ago and for the past six months he's been rock solid. Still ... I should probably keep my guard up. "Most of all, please, don't mention it to Benjamin," I say finally. "The last thing we need is for him to know more about what's going on than Paige."

"You have my word, Erin."

"Thanks ... and thanks for listening."

"So, tell me ... what's the deal now? On dating, I mean."

"For me?"

"Yeah. I don't want to pressure you, and I'm willing to go back to the just friends thing as long as I know that I'm still on your short list—hopefully a really short list—of guys you might potentially go out with."

I think about this. "Well, absolutely, I want you as my friend, Blake. I've missed going out with you. But regardless of how Paige handles her love life or keeps her promises, I still kind of feel that I'm not ready to get seriously involved—and I mean with anyone."

"But if you were?"

I laugh. "Well, of course, you'd be on my very short, short list, Blake. Don't you know that?"

He laughs too. "I had hoped that was the case ... but sometimes I feel a little insecure. It's not easy being infatuated with a star."

"A star?" I laugh even louder now. "Did you suffer a recent head injury? Because it sounds like maybe you're seeing stars."

"Hey, I'm serious, Erin. You don't seem to get that your popularity has steadily increased since the makeover segment in Paris. Don't you ever pay attention to this stuff?"

"If you mean tweets or social networks or tabloids or the polls or the gossip shows, I honestly *don't* pay attention. In fact, I get most of my information from Mollie—usually whether I want to hear it or not."

"See ... and that's just one more thing I like about you. This stuff never seems to go to your head. So back to whether or not you'll go out with me—and I don't mean so that we can get seriously involved—I get that. But, how about it—do you want to go grab a burger or something with me tonight?"

"That actually sounds good." The truth is, I wasn't looking forward to being stuck at home with my mixed-up sister this evening. After we set a time and hang up, I get ready to go, waiting in my room until I hear the doorbell. Paige is still pacing in the kitchen as I hurry to answer the door.

"I'm going out with Blake," I call to her, not waiting for a response, then I slip out and close the door.

"I'm starting to feel a little bit sorry for her," I admit as Blake drives away from the condo.

"Why?"

"I don't know ... but sometimes it feels like Paige is her own worst enemy."

He nods like he gets this. "Maybe it's because she almost always gets what she wants."

I think about this. "You know, you could be right. She does almost always get what she wants. But sometimes it turns out that what she wants isn't necessarily the best thing for her."

"That's why it's kind of cool to turn things over to God ... to wait when he says wait, or to trust that him saying no might turn out to be a good thing."

I study Blake as he drives, and it might just be me, but I think this boy is growing up.

"I thought we'd made an agreement," Paige says to me as soon as I come into the house.

"Huh?" I set my bag on the table by the door and study her. She's wearing warm-ups and her face, devoid of makeup, harbors an expression that reminds me of our childhood. Not exactly pouting, but slightly hurt.

"We agreed we weren't going to date."

"Oh, that." I wave my hand. "Rumor has it you already broke that agreement. And now I'm following your fine example."

Her eyebrows shoot up. "What do you mean?"

I shake my head. "Seriously, Paige, you follow that stuff. You know exactly what I mean."

"Do you mean Benjamin?"

I give her my best *duh* look and wait for her to explain.

"Well, that's nothing."

"Nothing?" I stare at her, wondering if she honestly expects me to swallow that.

"Of course it's nothing, Erin. Surely you knew that."

"How would I possibly know that?" I kick off my shoes. "It's not like you talk to me."

"I talk to you," she says indignantly.

"Right. You tell me one thing and then you do the opposite. That's a great way to communicate."

"What do you mean?"

"Are you serious?" I stare at her. "You know what you've done, Paige. Don't act like you don't."

"You mean by protecting my career?"

"By throwing your sister under the bus?"

"I never did that."

"Right." I shake my head. "And I'll never write a book called *Sister Dearest* either."

"Huh?" She looks honestly clueless and this makes me want to just shake her.

"Where's Mom?" I ask as I go into the kitchen to escape her.

"With Jon." She follows me. "Besides, you're the one who doesn't talk to me, Erin. I know you've been avoiding me."

"I'm talking to you now." I fill a glass with water.

"So, tell me then, why is it okay for you to go out with Blake?"

I am determined to remain calm as I look evenly at her. "Why is it okay for you to go out with Ben?"

"You honestly don't know the answer to that? You don't know why I go out with Benjamin Kross? Are you really that dumb?"

I give her a blank look.

"It's about *publicity*, little sister. Haven't you noticed how much I've been in the spotlight this past week?" Her eyes twinkle and I can tell how much she loves this—being the center of attention. It makes my stomach hurt.

"You seriously think Ben is good publicity?"

"You know what they say about publicity, Erin."

"But you're already in the spotlight," I try to reason. "You have that without Ben. You don't need him."

"You really don't get it, do you?"

I frown. "No, apparently not."

"It's like this ball is rolling, Erin. But I need to help keep it rolling. It won't just roll by itself."

I set my empty glass in the sink. "Really?"

She firmly shakes her head. Judging by her expression, she believes herself. "No. It's up to me to keep it going. And that means getting attention when and how I can."

"So you're saying that you and Benjamin aren't really dating?"

"Not in the romantic sense."

"Says you."

Paige takes a small bunch of grapes from the fridge and pops one into her mouth.

"But you can't speak for Ben, can you?" I persist. "What if he's serious?"

"Oh, Erin, you know it takes two to tango." She laughs and pops another grape into her mouth.

"Well, just so you know, I told Blake that I'm not going to

get seriously involved with him or anyone for a while. And I plan to stick to my guns. But I don't think it'll hurt to go out with him occasionally." I flash her a snide smile. "You know, for publicity."

She rolls her eyes. "Whatever."

"Not that we'll need much of that if our show shuts down."

"Our show is not shutting down, Erin."

"What makes you so sure?"

"Because I just got off the phone with Helen Hudson."

"Oh ...?"

"Don't act so innocent. I know she already talked to you."

"So."

"So we've reached an agreement."

"Which is?"

"Which is I will be the sole host and star of the show, but you will be my supporting costar."

"Supporting costar as in playing Camera Girl?" Although I should be relieved to go back to this role, I'm still mad.

She seems to study me, like she's taking some kind of inventory or maybe even about to critique my outfit, which is more my style than hers. I'm ready to defend myself.

"No ... I mean supporting costar as in playing yourself and my little sister. If you feel the need to lug your camera around, well, it's okay with me. Although Helen might disagree. But I will draw the line at you trying to upstage me. Either I remain the star of *On the Runway* or I will walk."

I give her a blasé look. "And that's supposed to surprise me?"

"I wasn't trying to surprise you ... I was simply trying to make myself clear."

I nod and, trying to keep from saying or doing anything I'll be sorry for, I begin making my way toward my bedroom.

"We're still on for the morning," she calls out.

"On for what?" I pause with my hand on my doorknob.

"You know, we need to get some more film for the wedding episode."

"Oh ... right." I nod, suddenly feeling sleepy. Or maybe I just want to escape this craziness.

"Fran will meet us in the studio at eight."

So I promise to be ready to leave here by seven, then go into my room and close the door. And, okay, I guess I should be happy that this thing has been resolved ... or sort of resolved. But I still feel seriously irked. And hurt. I feel like my sister should apologize to me. Okay, I realize that, in her weird twisted way of thinking, she might actually believe she's done nothing wrong. But the way she's treated me was insulting and selfish and hurtful—and unless she figures it out, I don't really see how we can work together. At least without some horrible sisterly catfight, which the viewers might like.

As I get ready for bed, I realize that I probably need a slight attitude adjustment myself. Perhaps even a big one. But as I open my Bible—part of my adjustment strategy—I'm still resenting that I'm the one who always has to make these amends. I wish that Paige, the "older" sister, would take more responsibility for maintaining good relations with me for a change. Of course, I know that's not likely to happen anytime soon. And, not for the first time, I'm reminded of how God always takes the first step toward us ... he's the one who initiates reconciliation. I know I should be honored to be able to do the same. But the truth is, I'm going to need some help. A whole lot of help!

Chapter
10

"This is from Helen," Fran hands me an envelope as Paige and I are getting makeup and hair done at the studio.

"Uh-oh," Shauna says in a teasing tone. "Hope it's not a pink slip."

I frown as I open the envelope.

"Stop making that nasty scowl," she scolds as I unfold the note from Helen. "You'll ruin your eyeliner. Not only that, but you'll need Botox before you're thirty."

My face muscles relax as I begin to read the memo.

Dear Jiminy:

As you know, we've settled on the contract. I wanted to call you this morning, but I have an early appointment, so this must suffice. This is what I want from you: Be yourself on the show. Fran will support this direction. But it must also come from you. We understand that Paige is the star, but you are the costar and we want you to let your personality shine. Don't be afraid to push

*things—even if big sister doesn't like it. This is what
makes for good TV. If I have not been clear, please feel
free to call me later in the day.*

Best,

Helen Hudson

Executive Producer, On the Runway

I refold the memo and return it to the envelope with a smile. So this is Helen's open invitation for me to be both seen and heard. I'm glad she actually put it in writing.

"Good news?" Shauna asks as she brushes on some blush.

"Kind of."

"Let me guess . . . you're getting a raise?"

"Something like that," I tell her. And in a way it's true. It's like Helen is trying to raise my position in the show. I have to appreciate that.

Naturally, I don't mention my memo to Paige, and she seems oblivious as we ride over to our first appointment. It's with the new bridal-wear designer Fran said is supposed to be so great, but unfortunately it turns out to be a bit of a disappointment. Not that his designs are bad. In fact, I think some are rather nice. But the poor man has absolutely no camera appeal, and despite the fact that our show would give him some good, free publicity, he pretty much blows it and I suspect his footage will end up on the cutting-room floor.

Next we head over to Vera Wang. Then, with cameras rolling, Paige and I start checking out Vera's gorgeous designs. This designer definitely gets it when it comes to high-fashion weddings.

I don't mind trying on some bridesmaid dresses, but I draw the line at wedding gowns. Call me old-fashioned or a stick in the mud (like Paige is doing today) but I am not about to try on a bridal gown. Not until I'm planning my own wedding, and I don't see that happening any time soon. But Paige has no problem trying on several gowns, like she wants to test fate. And, of course, she looks absolutely amazing in them. I wouldn't be surprised if someone doesn't invite her to pose for a cover of a bridal magazine after our show airs.

"You'll make a gorgeous bride!" The woman assisting Paige adjusts a short veil that is supposed to be reminiscent of the fifties.

"Who's the lucky guy?" I tease my sister.

"Wouldn't *you* like to know." Paige tosses me a sideways glance, which I know is meant for the camera but still feels like a personal jab.

"That's right." Ignoring the prick, I speak confidentially to the camera. "Sister of the bride and I don't even know who the groom is." I hold up my hands and look down at the pale blue dress I'm modeling. "Chances are I won't even be invited to participate in the wedding."

"Not if you're wearing *those* shoes anyway." Paige turns up her nose at my sensible sandals. Naturally, I neglected to pick up some wedding-appropriate footwear from the studio this morning and Paige is not letting me, or the viewers, forget this.

"At least I can walk in these shoes," I tell her. "I mean without injuring myself anyway." I turn to the camera again. "I wonder if our viewers realize that high heels are a real health threat. Besides the possibility of broken ankles or serious foot injuries, high heels can cause chronic back and knee problems and—"

"But that all depends on the design of the shoe," Paige

injects with a confident smile. "You see … there's a perfect high heel for everyone."

"Says who?" I ask a bit defiantly. After all, Helen told me to be myself and Fran seems to be looking on with approval.

"Every foot is different," Paige explains to me. She turns to the camera. "Seriously, fashion friends, unless you're over forty, you don't need to switch over to orthopedic shoes just yet. Don't let my little sister scare you into sacrificing style for boring sensibility." She points to my shoes, which I must admit do look a bit odd with the gown, and the cameras follow. "Seriously, do you want to go around looking like that?" She laughs.

So I hunch over, acting like I've injured my back. "Or would you rather go around like this?" I ask as I limp about, acting like I'm really messed up, and groaning with each step. "Because this is what could happen if you keep wearing overly tall high heels."

Paige laughs louder now. "Oh, that's a good look, Erin. Maybe our viewers will understand that good posture is essential to good style. You're making a perfect example of fashion don'ts today."

I stand up straight and force a smile. "I just wanted to give our viewers a visual aid—something to take with them the next time they're tempted to buy four-inch heels."

"Speaking of harmful foot health." Paige turns her attention back to the cameras. "I'll bet you don't know what can really mess up your feet." She looks back at me. "Do you know, Erin?"

"Besides high heels?"

"Yes." She has that catty smile again. "In fact, I'll give you a clue. This is one of your favorite forms of footwear."

"What?"

"*Flip-flops.*" She looks smugly back at the camera. "That's right, girls and boys, I said flip-flops. I just read an article about it." She chuckles. "Not only are flip-flops a big fashion flop, they are very bad for your feet."

"How's that?" I ask.

"For starters, unless you wear these fair-weather friends only in your home, you are literally exposing your feet to hundreds of thousands of germs and bacteria." She makes a face. "Eww. Imagine all that crud accumulating on your sweet little tootsies. I am talking about some serious germs too — some that are too nasty to even mention on this show."

"Oh, come on," I challenge her. "What could be that bad?"

"Think about it, Erin. Where do you walk in flip-flops? Bathrooms and parks and beaches and all sorts of places where disgusting things happen. You carry those things in the soles of your flip-flops and on your feet. I'm not kidding. They are seriously gross." She makes a face.

And, okay, I'm feeling a little speechless. Not that it matters, since my sister's gift of gab is fully kicked into gear.

"Not only that, but I want you to think about what some of you do with those flip-flops ... think about where you store them when you're not wearing them. Some of you — and you know who you are — actually tote them around in your *handbags.*" She firmly shakes her head. "Unless you have them sealed safely in a plastic bag, that is a great big no-no. Trust me, you so do not want those nasty flip-flop germs residing right next to your favorite lip gloss."

"Are you serious?" Now I'm wondering where she finds this stuff.

"Absolutely."

"So maybe everyone should start washing their flip-flops," I suggest. "I mean, what's so difficult about that?"

She shrugs. "Well, here's some more breaking news. Did you know that besides the germ factor, flip-flops are dangerous in another way too? Are you aware that flip-flops are responsible for thousands, maybe millions, of falls that result in serious injuries?"

"Serious injuries?" I question.

"Do the research. Besides that, flip-flops are not good for your feet in general. They offer no support and are really hard on arches. So no matter how you look at it, flip-flops are a big flop." She shakes her finger. "And, in this girl's opinion, they are a big fashion *don't*."

I hold up my hands, making an incredulous face. "Who knew?"

"Now you do." Paige smiles brightly as Fran gives us the sign to wrap this up. "And that is why you tune into my show, because I'm your style expert. This is Paige Forrester for *On the Runway*, and I want to remind you to put your best foot forward—not in flip-flops either. As for me, that would be Prada today! I'll see you next week in London, England, where we will be enjoying Mayfair in May!"

After we've changed from the bridal wear and are walking back to our cars, I ask Paige what "Mayfair in May" is supposed to mean.

"Don't you do any research for our show?" she asks with a dismayed expression that I'm sure is for Fran's sake.

"I try to do some," I assure her, "but as you just told the viewers, this is *your* show. I don't see the need for me to be the expert."

"Mayfair is the fashion district in London," Fran tells me.

"It's where we'll be staying—in fact, we're booked in the May Fair Hotel, which actually makes for a pretty good story, not to mention a great place to stay."

"And since it's May," Paige says smugly, " 'Mayfair in May' seemed appropriate. Do you get it now?"

I let out an exasperated sigh. "Why don't you save your denigration of me for when the cameras are rolling?"

Fran chuckles. "Too bad they're not rolling now."

The remainder of the week was spent going to planning sessions for the London trip, previewing episodes for the next couple of weeks, and generally avoiding conversations with my sister. I tell myself that Paige and I are just having one of those sisterly snits, and that we will get past this, but the night before we're scheduled to fly out of LAX, a part of me is starting to get worried. When I go to tell Mom goodnight, I mention it.

She nods sadly. "I've noticed you two seem a little out of sorts."

"I'm sure it'll blow over," I say. "Well, unless it just blows up."

She pats her bed. "Want to talk?"

I sigh as I sit down. "I'm so frustrated," I admit. "I mean, I feel like I'm trying, but it's like Paige always wants to do the one-up thing with me. Like she thinks I've suddenly turned into her key competitor."

"Maybe she does."

I nod. "Yeah, maybe so. She kind of reminds me of this model we've had some run-ins with." I tell Mom a little about Eliza and how everything with her is a big competition. "That gets so old."

"I know what you mean. There's a woman at work who's like that. It can be exhausting."

"Exactly."

"I usually tell myself that it's because Arden is having some self-esteem issues," Mom confides. "But the truth is that Arden is gorgeous and smart and, as far as I can see, she should be nothing but confident."

"But she's not?"

Mom shakes her head. "No. And, unfortunately, she often has the need to boost her confidence at the expense of others."

"Why is that?" I look at Mom, hoping she has the answer or maybe some kind of magic button.

"I wish I knew."

I frown. "You don't?"

"All I can say is that there's one thing that usually smoothes over the rough spots."

"What?"

"Just being extra nice to her, giving her compliments, commending her for a job well done . . . you know the drill."

I stare at Mom now, trying to make sense of something that I've been exposed to for as long as I can remember—a game of sorts that I was taught to play long ago. Sometimes it feels as if I'll be playing it all my life. "So . . . what if you're only contributing to her bad behavior?" I ask.

Mom looks surprised. "What?"

"What if being nice and giving compliments is simply a form of enablement?"

Mom looks amused. "Enablement?"

I nod. "I've read about this. Enablement is doing something that allows another person to continue in a harmful or destructive behavior. It's a form of codependency."

Mom laughs. "I thought your major was going to be film, not psychology."

"Psychology and film are related, don't you think?"

She nods. "Yes. I'm sure you're right."

"Anyway, what if you've done such a good job enabling Paige, as well as your friend at work, that they get stuck in some bad habits? Do you feel any responsibility for that?"

Mom's brow creases. "I suppose I should."

"But you don't?"

"Okay." She looks at me. "I will take some responsibility for your sister. I realize that your dad and I both probably spoiled her some. But we did it for the welfare of the family, Erin. And for you."

"Really?"

"So many times it was just not worth it to allow Paige to throw a fit that would ruin something for everyone. I know you understand this."

I'm feeling a little irritated. "So the princess throws a fit and everyone comes running to make it better, and this helps the princess how?"

Mom smiles. "To become even more spoiled?"

"Bingo."

"You do the same thing with Paige, Erin."

"Because I've been trained to do the same thing."

Mom makes kind of a helpless little sigh. "Here's the truth, Erin. Your dad and I never claimed to be child-rearing experts. We figured if we took care of your basic needs, loved you, and tried to offer forms of enrichment, you girls would be okay." She smiles as she runs her hand over my hair and then rests it on my cheek. "I'd say we didn't do half bad either."

For her sake, I force a smile. "Yeah, you guys did great."

Mom hugs me now. "Oh, Erin. You were always such a serious little girl. Unfortunately, you probably got that from me." She holds me out and looks at my face. "That's why I think you should understand that people like us—ones who tend to take life a bit too seriously—actually need others like Paige. We need their brightness . . . their lightness. And sometimes we have to take a little bit of selfishness with it. It's a package deal."

I nod like I get this. And, okay, I mostly get it. But I still think I'm right about the enablement thing. Paige has been enabled and encouraged to be fairly self-centered and spoiled. And, sure, she might be Little Miss Sunshine when she gets her way, but like the weather, she can turn on you. So, once again, I suppose it's my job to help make sure that things continue to go her way during our stay in London. What's new?

Chapter 11

Why am I not surprised when Benjamin insists on driving Paige to the airport? Since they arrive right before Fran and me, we get to witness the scene as paparazzi swarm Benjamin's SUV. Because the photographers are on foot, I have to wonder how they got there so quickly. Did someone tip them off? Or do they just hang out at LAX twenty-four/seven, waiting for a celeb to show so they can snap something? It reminds me of sharks in a feeding frenzy. Even though Paige Forrester and Benjamin Kross aren't the hottest Hollywood couple to be caught together, I'm sure that some of these photos will score some fairly big bucks when the paparazzi sell them to whatever gossip magazine is currently buying.

Paige and Benjamin are acting oblivious as he helps her unload her sleek Louis Vuitton bags. I have to chuckle to myself as I remember her old set of pink luggage, which was donated to Goodwill when she replaced it a few months ago. Of course, she wouldn't be caught dead with those Malibu Barbie bags now that she's a star.

Paige, impeccably dressed in Armani, removes her Gucci shades and poses for the cameras, making a sparkling smile that I'm sure she hopes will grace the cover of something. Benjamin acts a bit more subdued, almost as if he's embarrassed by this attention, which I seriously doubt. Then Paige actually pauses to answer questions.

"Where are you two going?" someone calls out.

"It's only me going," Paige answers sweetly. "Ben just offered me a ride today. I'm on my way to London to tape some *On the Runway* episodes and to make a guest appearance on *Britain's Got Style.*"

"But you two are back together?"

"We're good friends," Paige says innocently. "Ben's been through a rough patch and friends help each other." She turns and pats Benjamin on the cheek. "Don't they?"

He flashes one of his famous "Hollywood" smiles and nods. "Yeah ... good friends stick together."

Fran and I are joining them and Ben kisses Paige on the cheek. He tells her to have a good time as the paparazzi take a few more shots of us going into the terminal.

"That was fun," Paige says lightly as we go to check our bags.

"Fun?" I glance at her curiously.

"Oh, come on," she says to me. "Don't tell me you don't enjoy the attention just a little, Erin?"

I shrug. "I guess I see it as a necessary evil."

Fran chuckles. "I see it as free advertising."

It's not long before we're checked in and waiting for our plane to board. Paige, as usual, purchases an armload of the latest fashion magazines at the newsstand, which she will skim through and then leave on the plane. As we're sitting at the gate, I can feel eyes on us. Several girls have spotted Paige and they approach hesitantly, asking for autographs. When she complies, they also take photos with their phones and I can see one girl is already sending a picture—to who knows how many people. I suspect Mollie will soon be spying these same shots on whichever social network is most popular these days.

I can see that Paige, who acts nonchalant as she patiently smiles for the shots, is totally eating this up. It's like she never gets tired of the attention. I just don't get it. Yes, I understand the need for publicity and being polite to fans. But doesn't she care about privacy? Doesn't she have any boundaries when it comes to being approached by strangers? Yet again, I wonder how we can be sisters and be so totally different.

Finally, and thankfully, first class is boarding and I'm relieved to escape the little fan club. Paige blows them kisses as we head on our way and reminds them to tune in to the show.

"I won't miss that," I say as I find my seat by the window.

"What do you mean?" Paige asks as she arranges her carry-on and then sits down beside me.

"I mean in London. I won't miss the fans or the paparazzi."

She frowns. "Are you serious?"

"Huh?"

"You honestly thought there would be no paparazzi in London?"

"There weren't any in Paris. Not much anyway."

She gives me a patronizing smile. "Little sister ... you have so much to learn."

"You honestly think there'll be paparazzi in London who want to follow us?" I question.

She nods. "I'd be disappointed if there weren't."

I just shrug, then open my Birkin bag to retrieve my book, a biography of the famous director John Ford. But as I search the spaces of the bag, I realize that it's not here. I must've left it on my nightstand at home. I let out an angry growl and close my bag.

"What is it now?" Paige asks me.

"My book." I scowl. "I forgot it."

"Here." She hands me one of her fashion magazines. "Read this. It'll probably do you more good anyway."

"Right …" But I take the magazine and begin to flip through the glossy pages, frowning at the perfectly airbrushed images of overly thin models and wondering—for the umpteenth time—how I managed to get pulled into an industry like this. A few minutes into the flight, I finally manage to find an article between some ads, and I'm actually rather intrigued by the title: "Are You an Attention Junkie? What Will You Do to Win Praise from Others?"

I glance at Paige then continue to read. Honestly, it's like they know my sister and are writing about her. The more I read, the more I realize that Paige could be seriously at risk.

"You should take this little quiz," I tell her after the flight attendant serves us coffee and scones.

"A fashion quiz?" she says with interest.

"Kind of," I say.

"Okay." She nods. "Give it to me."

I grab a pen and begin to read through the questions, circling the answers as she gives them to me. But after several questions, Paige catches on. "I thought you said it was a fashion quiz," she tells me.

I hold up the cover of the publication. "It's a fashion magazine," I say. "I just assumed it's somehow related to style." I continue, reading the next question, which is about where a person might stand in a crowded room of strangers.

"That would be C," she tells me. "In the center, of course,"

"Of course." I nod as if I'd do the same, although I know I would pick D, 'near an exit'.

Finally we are done and I'm tallying up her score.

"So how did I do?" she asks.

"Pretty much like I expected," I confess as I figure out which category she's fallen into.

She leans over to see, but I close the magazine. "Come on, Erin," she pesters. "What kind of test was it? How did I score?"

"It was just for fun," I tell her.

"Okay, that was fun. Now explain."

"It was a test about whether or not you might be an attention addict."

"You mean like ADD?" she asks. "I was evaluated for attention deficit disorder as a kid, you know, but they didn't think I have it. They decided I was restless and energetic."

"No, it's not that kind of attention," I explain. "It's not a deficit disorder. It's more like an addiction."

"An addiction?" She frowns. "What do you mean?"

"The psychologist who wrote the article claims that some people can be addicted to attention."

"What?"

"It's like a drug for them. They can't get enough. They'll do anything to get praise and approval from others."

She makes a face. "That sounds desperate . . . and pathetic."

I don't know how to respond to this, so I just nod.

"So, how did I score?"

"Well, the author had five categories . . ." Now I'm wishing

I hadn't done this. What good will it do? Most likely it'll only aggravate her.

"What were the categories?" Paige breaks off a piece of scone and nibbles on it.

"I, uh, I can't remember." My fingers curl around the edges of the magazine and I'm wishing I could open the window and just chuck it out.

"Oh, come on, Erin." She gives me an irate look. "It's my magazine anyway. Do I have to pry it out of your fingers?"

"No."

"Then *tell* me. What are the categories, and how did I score?"

"But it might make you mad."

She gives me a sugary smile. "I promise I won't get mad at you, Erin. Now you've got me really curious. I want to know what kind of pathetic people get addicted to attention."

I take in a deep breath and open the magazine, deciding to read them to her backward. "The five categories are: One, the Hermit Crab—you stay as far away from others as possible and if they come your way, you snap at them. Two, the Mole—you use false humility to pretend you don't like the limelight, but you secretly crave it. Three, the Cat—attention is no big deal, you can take it or leave it, but mostly you just want to live your life. Four, the Dog—you adore attention and eagerly pursue it with tail a-wagging." I pause to clear my throat. "And five, the Peacock—you live for attention, you can't get enough, and you will strut your stuff until your feathers fall off to obtain it."

"And . . . so?" Paige waits.

"So what?"

"Which one am I?" She smiles sweetly.

"You mean you don't know?"

She glares at me now. "Do you know how aggravating you can be sometimes?"

"You're the peacock," I say quickly. "A perfect score."

She frowns. "The peacock?"

I nod and continue reading the article.

"Well ..." She sighs. "At least peacocks are the prettiest ones in that quiz. I wouldn't want to be a hermit crab or a mole."

I can't help but laugh since that's exactly a peacock sort of response.

"So which one are you?" she asks.

"I didn't take the test."

"Well, take it then because I'm sure you're the hermit crab."

I roll my eyes. "I'm pretty sure I'm the cat. But if it makes you happy I'll take it."

"No, you'd probably just cheat. So does it say anything else about the peacock?"

"Yeah, most of the article is aimed at the peacock."

"Why?"

"Because the peacock is the serious attention addict."

Paige shakes her head. "No ... I don't think so."

"You don't?"

"No. I think whoever wrote that article didn't understand peacocks. Peacocks get attention simply because they can. It's the way they're made. I mean, you wouldn't expect a peacock to go around hiding in a hole or trying to keep people from looking at her beautiful feathers. The nature of the peacock is to be the center of attention. Everyone enjoys looking at a peacock."

"Right." I nod and return to reading. Fortunately Paige returns to her magazine too. And, although I'm surprised at how dense my sister is, I begin to realize as I continue to read the article that it's like a blind spot with her. She doesn't have any idea that she's an attention addict. And it sounds like she won't get it either—not until certain things happen.

The article lists various circumstances that might help an addict move toward recovery—things like suddenly being shoved out of the limelight due to unfortunate circumstances like illness or injury or financial difficulties. Or she might literally exhaust herself and her resources while seeking the limelight. Last but not least, she might come to the realization that all the attention in the world will never satisfy her. It seems that, like with other addictions, the first step to getting better is to admit you have a problem. Since I don't see that happening with Paige anytime soon, I won't be holding my breath.

But after I finish the article I realize that peacocks like Paige don't get there alone. Their hunger for attention combined with their narcissistic nature drives them to surround themselves with friends, fans, and even the occasional stalker. They crave for their followers to adore them and constantly shower them with praise and attention. Without those faithful admirers, a peacock will perish.

It's not that I want Paige to perish. But I wouldn't mind if the peacock in my sister turned it down a notch or two. This is for Paige's sake as much as for mine, because it sounds like peacocks eventually suffer from serious burnout. The article lists a number of celebrities who've gone to desperate measures to keep the spotlight on them even though their careers were clearly over. It's not pretty. I hate to think of my sister ending up like that.

Yet it seems the only thing I can do to help her—and it's not much—is to make sure I'm not one of those people that constantly feeds her addiction with my praise and adoration. Not that I want to do that, but I know I've often fallen into that pattern simply because it's my easy way out. But lately it seems like I don't care anymore, like I'm rubbing Paige the wrong way on purpose.

So maybe that's it; maybe I'm the antidote for Paige's attention addiction. Or maybe I'm only fooling myself. For all I know I could be the mole—the one who secretly craves attention almost as much as a peacock. Just to be sure, I take the test. To my relief, unless I cheated (and I tried not to), I am the cat. Attention is no big deal … I can take it or leave it. Of course, like a finicky cat, I want attention when I want it … and I don't want attention when I don't want it. And, as the article points out, life is seldom like that. Especially mine.

Chapter
12

It's the next morning when we arrive at Heathrow. Although I slept somewhat during the flight, I feel frazzled and frumpy as we walk through the terminal, but Paige looks like she just stepped out of makeup and hair, which is handy because the camera crew arrived in London yesterday. Right after we pick up our bags and pass through customs, they start filming us.

As always, Fran hangs behind the scenes as the cameras roll, but I don't get that luxury as Paige and I (just two American girls) casually stroll through Heathrow making our official arrival in London look like we think we're Brad and Angelina. I try not to feel conspicuous as a crowd of curious onlookers watches our progression. But I wish I'd thought to check my hair ... not to mention my teeth. I obviously did not study my schedule carefully because I really thought we'd have time to go to our hotel and freshen up a bit before launching into shooting today.

"Here are my tips for arriving fresh and lovely after an overnight flight," Paige says to the cameras as we pause near the exit. "First off, drink plenty of water to avoid puffy eyes." She points to me and giggles. "Apparently somebody forgot to do this. Next, remember to remove your makeup and apply moisturizer before falling asleep so your skin will wake up looking refreshed. Then be sure to give yourself time to apply some fresh makeup before the plane lands." She looks at me and dismally shakes her head. "Notice these raccoon eyes from yesterday's mascara. Well, a little moisturizer and tissue could've cleaned that right up."

"Thanks for telling me now," I say with a stiff smile.

"And here's a tip for avoiding this little disaster." She actually turns me around so the camera can see the back of my head. "Oh, my!" She giggles. "To prevent serious bed head like this, try wrapping a silk scarf loosely around your hair before you fall asleep on the plane. It will keep your hair in place and looking coifed when you make your arrival."

As I turn around and touch the back of my head, I can feel that it's flat and messy. Big surprise there. Then as we head outside to the passenger pickup area, Paige is telling the cameras about how she packed a couple of extra clothing items in her carry-on. "So I could do a quick presto change-o and not have to stand here on this lovely sunny morning looking like I slept on the street." She turns to me. "Unfortunately my sister was not as well prepared." She shrugs and smiles for the camera. "Oh, well. Maybe next time." Then she waves her arms dramatically. "Welcome to London, England, where we will soon discover what makes Brit fashion sizzle."

"That's a wrap," Fran calls out. "Nice work, Paige."

Paige grins at me. "Thanks for being such a good little example of the fashion-on-the-go don'ts. You make my work so easy."

I suppress the urge to growl. "I'm sure your fans will appreciate seeing your true colors, Paige. The way you treat your sister must endear yourself to them ever so much."

She gives me a puzzled frown.

"There's our limo, girls." Fran points to a black car, then goes over to consult with the crew. With relief I hurry over to the car, but Paige is suddenly besieged by the small crowd that has been watching her. Naturally, she is in her element as she cheerfully poses for photos and signs her name on whatever pieces of paper are shoved her way. Eventually Fran pulls her away from her adoring fans and ushers her over to the limo.

"So you thought there'd be no paparazzi in London," Paige says as she slides in next to me.

"I wouldn't exactly call curious onlookers paparazzi," I point out.

"Don't be too sure," she says as she removes a compact from her bag, opens it, and checks out her already-immaculate appearance. "A couple of those cameras looked fairly serious to me."

I'm looking over my notes for our trip now and I realize that there really isn't anything in here about being filmed upon our arrival, but when I point this out to Fran she tells me it was a last-minute change. "Didn't Paige tell you before we left?" Fran asks.

"Obviously not."

Fran laughs. "Oh . . . I think I see why."

"So this was a little set-up to make me into your fashion don't?" I glare at my sister. "Real nice."

"Hey, I could've told you to fix yourself up," she says, "but would you have given up your precious sleep to do it?"

I consider this. I had finally been sleeping soundly just before the flight touched down.

"Besides, according to that survey, you're the one who doesn't care about being in the spotlight, right?"

I just shrug as I search in my bag for something to improve my appearance—like that's even possible.

"Why should you care about how you look then?"

"Oh, Paige." Fran shakes her head with disapproval. "That's not very nice of you."

"But it's true."

"I'm sorry you were caught off guard," Fran tells me. "Paige thought our viewers would enjoy hearing some tips about how you can travel and arrive in style. I had no idea she didn't tell you."

"Don't forget," Paige holds up her index finger, "this is a reality show. I was merely trying to keep it real for the sake of the viewers."

I carefully measure my words now, trying not to lose my temper as I respond to my sister's trickster ways. "Well ... for the sake of the show, and since it *is* a show about fashion and style, I would think you'd want your own sister to put her best foot forward too. After all, if your costar looks bad, doesn't it reflect poorly on you as the queen of style—like, oops, you missed something?"

Fortunately this seems to stump my sister. Without saying a word, she turns away from me, looking out the window as I continue to forage through my bag. Finally I find a scruffy-looking tube of lip gloss and smear some on my chapped lips.

"I spoke to Shauna and Luis at the airport," Fran tells me. "They'll meet us at the hotel and we should have plenty of time to work you over before our next shoot so that you'll be perfectly presentable."

"Thanks." I run a hand through my messy bed-head hair and sigh. "It's nice to know that *someone* in the show cares."

"Okay, girls," Fran begins in a firm voice. "This is a reality show. We do want you to be yourselves, including sisterly squabbles if necessary, but you also need to bear in mind we have a number of shows to film in London. That means *everyone* does their part to make them a success. Right, Paige?"

Paige turns to us with what seems a pleasant expression, except that I can see a glint of mean in those big blue eyes. "Of course. You know I always deliver my very best for the show."

Fran nods. "Yes. I just wanted to be sure we were all on the same page now."

"Meaning no more surprises?" I aim this to Paige and she smiles like she's got all kinds of clever things tucked up those designer sleeves.

"Oh, there should always be some surprises," she says in a catty tone. "What would be the fun if there weren't?"

Fran chuckles and I look out the window, taking in the British scenery and hoping there will be time to shoot some photos myself. As we drive, Fran points out some places of interest, including several museums. "And that's Harrods," she points out my window.

"What's Harrods?" I ask as I peer out on what looks like a castle.

"*What's Harrods?*" Paige repeats sarcastically as she leans over to see better. "Just the most magnificent department store in the world." She sighs. "We are going there, right?"

"Yes, definitely. It's on the schedule."

I blink in disbelief at the huge castle-like structure. "*That* is a department store?"

"Nearly five acres of lovely shopping all under one amazing roof." Paige looks smitten. "Oh, it'll be like dying and going to heaven."

I make a face. "I sure hope heaven is better than a humungous department store." I shake my head. "How can one store be nearly five acres? That's just crazy."

"Crazy good." Paige sighs again and I wonder if she's about to swoon.

A few minutes pass and Fran is pointing out where Hyde Park is and then explaining how we are now on Piccadilly and coming into the fashion district. "If this were actually Fashion Week," she says, "it would be packed. As it is, we were able to get a pretty great suite with adjoining rooms in the May Fair Hotel."

"Will we be able to stay there during the next London Fashion Week too?" Paige asks hopefully.

"Leah is working on it." Fran checks her phone now. "Fortunately September is still a ways off. Let's just focus on this London trip, okay?" She points to the right. "That's Green Park," she tells us. "Buckingham Palace Gardens are just beyond."

"So is Buckingham Palace there too?"

"No," Paige tells me in her most sarcastic voice. "They only have a garden, Erin. No palace. The queen has to camp out there when she's in town."

Fran laughs while I roll my eyes and wonder if Paige took mean pills this morning. A drizzly rain is starting to fall as our driver meanders through the heavy traffic, but it's coming down hard by the time Fran points out the hotel down the street.

"I thought you said this wasn't the busy time of year," I say to Fran as our limo pulls onto the end of a fairly long line of cars, which are dropping guests off at the front entrance.

"Well, there are a few fashion shows this week," she admits. "I suppose that might account for the traffic. That and the weather. Everyone probably wants to be dropped off at the door."

I stare at the non-moving line of cars ahead of us. "This looks like it could take awhile. Do you think we should just get out and make a run for it?"

"Seeing that we're due at Burberry at two thirty and we still need to get you through hair, makeup, and wardrobe — that's not a bad idea." Fran turns to Paige. "I suppose you can ride on up to the front door if you want to make a queenly entrance and stay dry, but Erin and I will hoof it. I wish I had taken my umbrella out of my suitcase."

Paige frowns. "You're going out in the rain?"

"The entrance is like fifty feet from here," I tell her as I scramble to grab my purse and carry-on. Fran shoots the driver some instructions for dropping off our luggage and picking us up at one o'clock, and then pops out and starts running toward the entrance.

"Okay," Paige says reluctantly. "I guess I'll come with you too."

I wait for Paige to gather her things and then we both spurt out of the limo, dashing through the rain until we reach the protection of the portico, which is crowded with other guests trying to emerge from cars and gather bags as they avoid the wet weather. Fran seems to have already made her way inside.

"There's Paige Forrester," someone calls out, and the next thing we know several people, as well as some cameras, are clamoring around us. I cannot believe the British paparazzi are here — or that they even know who my sister is. Naturally, Paige's eyes light up and, in one movement, she gives her head a quick shake and fluffs her damp hair to instant perfection, breaking out into a smile so sunny I almost expect the clouds to part.

"I'm Claire Kelly of *London Star Watch.*" A pretty dark-haired woman hands Paige a card. "Do you have a moment for a quick interview for tonight's show?"

"Certainly." Paige nods congenially. She doesn't even look surprised and I almost wonder if she might've been the one to tip off the press. But why should they care?

"I understand you're here to appear on *Britain's Got Style,*" Claire says to Paige. As her camera guy begins filming, several others draw in closer, snapping photos or holding up mics like this is the story of the year. It must be a slow day for the London press if these people have no more-newsworthy items to cover.

"That's right," Paige tells her. "Our show *On the Runway* was invited to participate in a *Britain's Got Style* episode, and I am honored to assist as a judge."

"And what qualifies you, a relatively young American girl, to judge British style?" a middle-aged woman asks in a snooty tone.

Paige lets out a tinkle of a laugh. "Oh, that's a great question. I realize I am rather young, but I seem to have an innate sense of style that our American viewers can relate to. Our show has experienced a growing popularity both in the States and abroad." She ignites her most engaging smile. "I guess it's hard to explain ... *je ne sais quoie.*"

"How long will your show be in London, Paige?" Claire

asks pleasantly, as if she wants to apologize for the other woman.

"We expect to wrap up—"

"Never mind that," a man behind Claire interrupts. "What Brits really want to know is—are you and Benjamin Kross in a relationship?"

"Benjamin and I are friends and I've—"

"But isn't it true that you were seen *shopping for wedding gowns?*" another woman calls out. "Are you planning to *marry* Benjamin Kross?"

"What about the criminal charges against Benjamin Kross?" the earlier guy persists like a bulldog. "Isn't he going to go to prison for the murder of Mia Renwick, his deceased costar from *Malibu Beach?*"

"The charges against Benjamin have been dropped," Paige says in a stiff voice that's quickly losing its warmth. "The investigation revealed that a number of factors contributed to the—uh—the automobile accident."

"And there's been a settlement." I offer this morsel of information to relieve a bit of the pressure from Paige and hopefully to get us out of here. "Mia Renwick's family agreed to drop the civil charges. I'm surprised you haven't heard about this by now. A special *Malibu Beach* episode aired recently with Benjamin explaining what actually happened that night." I'm tugging on Paige's arm, trying to move us toward the entrance and out of this British media feeding frenzy.

"That's the younger sister," someone else says and—great—the cameras are all pointing at me now.

"We need to go prepare for a show," I say loudly. "Please, excuse—"

"So what about those wedding plans?" The bulldog guy

steps in front of Paige. "Are you and Benjamin planning to marry now that Mia is out of the picture?"

"Yes, please tell us *why* you were trying on wedding gowns!" a female voice calls out.

"Seems a bit hasty to be tying the knot with a young man barely cleared of murder charges," someone comments.

Without answering, Paige looks at me with worried eyes, like she's blanking out or about to have some kind of panic attack. So, still holding on to her arm, I go ahead and field this question too.

"We tried on wedding gowns for an upcoming episode of our show," I yell above the crowd that's getting noisier, tugging on Paige's arm, which is futile since we're enclosed on all sides now. "The show will air in early June and—"

"I want a word with Paige Forrester," a short man with a dark beard yells as he muscles his way through the crowd. He steps up and shakes a newspaper at Paige. "So you're the Yank who thinks she's going to tell us Brits how to have style?" He holds up what appears to be a British tabloid. "Have you seen this? It's hot off the press and something that should interest everyone here."

I stare at the grainy photograph, which appears to be of me and Paige, but I cannot for the life of me remember when or where it was taken. In the picture I'm standing by a white baby crib, holding a teddy bear, and Paige is on the other side of the crib with a startled expression on her face. The headline reads: "A Pregnant Paige Forrester Arrives in London to Teach Brits about Style."

"Pregnant?" I turn and stare at Paige.

Her face pales and she slowly shakes her head. "That's not true."

"Who's the father?" a woman calls out. "Benjamin Kross?"

"That baby should be some looker then," someone comments with laughter. "Paige Forrester and Benjamin Kross having a baby together! There'll be good money for whoever captures those baby pictures."

I grab the tabloid and stare closely at the photo. Something about it is familiar, but then I realize it's not what it seems. "This photo has been tampered with," I yell out over the new flood of baby comments and questions. "Yes, that's me standing next to a baby crib, but I was shopping with a friend—*not Paige*. I was with my friend who actually is pregnant. But someone must have taken a photo of Paige and stuck it on right here to make it look like a big story." I shove the paper back at the man now. "Why anyone believes this kind of trash—or spends money on it—is beyond me."

"I am not pregnant," Paige says stiffly.

"You heard her," I yell at them. "Now, please, excuse us before I call for security. Thank you for this very warm British welcome and this very lovely press conference!" And, with my hand still wrapped around Paige's arm, I drag her along behind me as I push my way through the crowd and into the hotel where Fran is standing in the middle of the lobby just shaking her head.

"Good grief," she tells us. "I thought I was going to have to call for backup. How did you manage to get caught by that group of media thugs?"

"That's what I'd like to know." I turn to look at Paige who still looks fairly rattled.

Fran's looking at Paige too. "Do you have any idea where they came from or how they knew you were staying at this hotel?"

"Well . . . it is the May Fair Hotel," Paige says meekly as we proceed through the lobby. "The fashion hot spot."

"Yes, but it's not the only hotel in this neighborhood." Fran looks suspicious. "How did they know what time you were arriving?"

Paige looks nervously over her shoulder as we wait for the elevator. "I . . . uh . . . I thought a little publicity . . . might be good."

"You really did set that up?" I ask as we step inside.

"Not exactly." She sighs.

"What do you mean not exactly?" I persist.

"Well, I suppose it kind of leaked out onto one of the social networks."

"You mean you announced to the whole world what time we were arriving in London? And where we were staying?" I stare at my sister in wonder.

She gives me a blank look that says it all.

"No more giving out specific information," Fran says as we ride up.

"But I thought publicity would be a good thing," Paige says as we emerge on our floor.

"Tabloids saying that you're pregnant with Benjamin Kross's baby and picking out wedding gowns?" I demand. "That's a good thing?"

"*What?*" Fran looks at Paige with a shocked expression.

Paige holds up her hands in a helpless gesture. "I didn't know they would take that direction . . . or go that far. I didn't know they would make up vicious lies about me!"

"Don't you get it?" I ask her. "Paparazzi and tabloid reporters are like a runaway train—why would you even want to get on board?"

"Maybe I don't … not anymore." Paige makes a weak smile. "Let me off at the next stop, please."

"It might be too late to get off." Fran hands us our room keys. As I go into my room, which adjoins Paige's, I think Fran might be right. This train has left the station. Hopefully we're not heading for a serious wreck.

Chapter
13

The May Fair is a very fashionable and contemporary hotel. *Quite posh*, as Brits might say. Now some people might think "posh" simply means stylish. And people might assume it's thanks to Victoria Beckham, who went by Posh back in her Spice Girl days. But I looked up the meaning of posh and was surprised to learn the word originated in the early 1900s. The initials P.O.S.H. were used on ships traveling between India and England, standing for "Portside Out and Starboard Home," and this would be stamped onto the first class passengers' luggage so that their luggage could be switched to the appropriate side of the boat ... because first class passengers always occupied the shady side of the ship. If the story is true, this must mean that regular folks like me got to bake in the sun. But when I told Lionel my piece of trivia, he laughed and told me the story was an urban legend. True or not, I still like it.

Anyway, I'm completely pleased with my swanky hotel room and thankful I'm not sharing it with Paige. Of course, when I see Paige's digs—a large comfortable suite—I do feel a tiny twinge of jealousy. I remind myself, however, that she is the star of *On the Runway*, and I agreed to let her stay that way. After her grilling downstairs, I think she's paying dearly for her fancy accommodations.

It's not long before Luis and Shauna show up and go to work on me while Paige changes her clothes and picks out an outfit for me to wear today. Meanwhile Fran has ordered room service and when we get the chance, we take turns getting a bite to eat. Finally, I change into the somewhat conservative outfit of a khaki wool skirt and black cashmere sweater and black ankle boots. Actually, I'm pleased with the outfit, but I'm surprised Paige was okay with it since we're shooting today. Even the accessories are fairly low-key. Just a silver chain necklace, stud earrings, and a simple clasp bracelet.

"Here," she says as she hands me a khaki Burberry trench coat, complete with their trademark plaid lining.

"You look nice," I tell her as I slip on the new coat. "Is that Burberry too?" She has on a pale gray jacket and pencil skirt with a pink silk scarf tied loosely around her neck, as well as perfect accessories that, as usual, make a bit more of a statement than mine. And her shoes, gray suede ankle boots, are very chic.

She smiles and strikes a pose, then slips on a really gorgeous pale gray trench coat. "All thanks to Christopher Bailey."

"Who's that?"

"Just the reason Burberry is selling a lot more than raincoats these days."

"Well, we picked a good day to go to Burberry," I say as Fran hands us our umbrellas. Mine is plaid and Paige's is that same soft gray.

As we go down the elevator, Paige dons her oversized Gucci sunglasses and even rearranges her pale pink scarf to cover her hair, like she thinks she's disguising herself. If anything, it makes her even more striking as we walk through the lobby and I notice that a lot of heads turn to watch as she strides toward the entrance. Fortunately the throng of media freaks has disappeared, probably off to torture some other unsuspecting celeb. And, because our car is waiting, we don't even need our umbrellas.

"Chris Bailey started with Gucci," Paige informs us as we drive through town. "He's been with Burberry about ten years. He's taken some heat too."

"Taken some heat?" I question.

"Several years ago, Chris's designs, particularly the ones with the Burberry plaid, became so popular that knock-off companies started reproducing them. For some reason British gangs and street kids couldn't get enough. Their designs became part of what was called 'chav' culture, and Chris had to scramble to protect the Burberry image."

"How did he do that?" I ask as I watch London scenery flashing by. I want to ask Fran if she knows what we're passing, but Paige seems to be on a roll and I think it's probably going to help her to get into gear for this next interview.

"Mostly he had to pull way back on the plaid," she says as she checks something on her phone. "In fact, Burberry threatened to sue some automaker for producing a car that was painted in the plaid."

"You're kidding." I look at the lining of my trench coat and try to imagine a whole car painted like that.

"They called it a Chavrolet." She chuckles.

We're going over a bridge now. "Is this the Thames River?" I ask as I peer at the rather gray-looking water, which merely seems to be reflecting the gray dreary day.

"It is," Fran confirms.

"But, please, Erin," Paige says to me, "don't mention a word about the chav business when we're at Horseferry House."

"Horseferry House?"

"That's Burberry headquarters," Fran tells me as she looks up from her map. "It looks like we're almost there."

"Now, remember," Paige directs me as the car pulls up to a large structure. "This is Great Britain, where good etiquette is expected."

"What are you saying?" I ask as I reach for my Birkin bag.

"Just that manners matter."

I frown at her, but refrain from voicing my thoughts. But, seriously, does she think I'm going to pick my nose or belch or something?

This time we need to use our umbrellas, but soon we're inside where our crew is already set up and ready to go. Soon we are given the tour of what seems a never-ending building, and during a brief lull I inquire as to the size of Horseferry House.

"We're about twenty thousand square meters," our guide tells me.

"Oh ..." I nod as I attempt to convert that to square feet in my mind.

"Or for you Yanks, about one hundred and sixty thousand square feet."

"Wow, that's huge."

He just smiles in that understated British sort of way, but I can tell he likes the idea that we're impressed.

We finally wind up in the showroom and I must admit that I really do like Burberry's style. "These are exactly the kinds of clothes that I feel comfortable wearing," I say as we wait for one of the designers to join us for Paige's final interview. "Stylish but sensible."

"I like that," says a British voice from behind me. "Stylish but sensible."

I turn to see a good-looking guy coming in. Lanky and thin, he has serious eyes and his hair has that mussed-up look, but it only adds to his overall attractiveness.

"Christopher Bailey," Paige says, and with a bright smile, she moves past me to where she takes his hand. "Thank you for allowing us to visit Horseferry House today. And thank you so much for taking time to meet with us now."

"Ah, the renowned Paige Forrester." He returns her smile. "I heard we're having the American Fashion Invasion."

Paige looks slightly off guard, but quickly recovers. "Oh, we've simply come over to study British design." She tilts her head coyly. "I think we could learn a lot about style here."

He chuckles. "So you're not actually here to educate *us* then?"

"No, of course not." She shakes her head.

"I think your style is brilliant," I tell him, still trying to figure out my role in this new little game we're playing. "I was just telling Paige that you design the kinds of clothes I like to wear."

He nods. "Stylish but sensible."

"This is my sister, Erin Forrester," Paige takes the reins again.

"Tell me, Erin Forrester . . ." He studies me with curiosity. "What brought you into the world of fashion?"

"I . . . uh . . . mostly my sister," I admit.

He looks amused.

"She's the true fashionista of the family," I continue. "But

I do have some interest in fashion." Okay, this is probably an overstatement.

"Such as?"

"Well ... I care about environmentally conscious fashions," I begin. "And I appreciate creative designers who come up with new ways to communicate fashion." I glance at Paige, hoping she'll jump in now.

But he nods as if he appreciates my slightly lame contribution. "Perhaps you've heard of our foundation then ..." Naturally, I am blank.

"Oh, yes," Paige says quickly. "The Burberry Foundation." She turns to me now. "Christopher was instrumental in setting up this foundation. The purpose is to dedicate global resources to help young people realize their creative dreams. It's really a wonderful program with a focus on the future of fashion."

He looks both intrigued and impressed. "Someone's been doing her homework."

"I always appreciate hearing about designers who give back to the community," she continues, "whether local or global. Burberry does both."

Again, I can't help but be impressed with my savvy sister. Also, I'm relieved to have her back in the driver's seat. I can tell that she's pleased with herself too. She and Christopher chat amicably for a few more minutes, and then when it's time for him to go, she gracefully wraps it up.

"Nice work," Fran tells her as the cameras shut down.

"Thanks."

"You too," Fran tells me.

"Thanks," I say with less enthusiasm. "But I have a feeling that I should follow my sister's example and start doing my homework."

Paige laughs. "Oh, that's okay, Erin. You keep being your-self and I'll be me, and I think we'll be just fine."

In other words, I think she's telling me to watch out — warning me that she wants to remain in control of the show and, hey, I'm okay with that.

"Next stop is Stella McCartney," Fran informs us almost apologetically. "Sorry to pack so much into your first day but, as you know, the payoff is a free day tomorrow. The only time we could tour Stella's was after-hours today, so we decided to jump on it."

"Now here's someone I know a little about," I admit as we ride through London, where the rain has stopped and the city seems to be shining in the sunlight.

"Do tell," my sister says in a challenging tone. "I suppose you've heard of her famous father."

I give her a *duh* look. "Yes, I'm sure everyone has heard of Sir Paul McCartney from the Beatles. But not everyone knows that Stella's mother, the late Linda McCartney, was an animal rights activist and probably the reason Stella is a strict vegetarian and uses no fur or leather in her designs."

"Bravo." Paige nods. "Tell me more."

"Uh ..." I'm trying to remember what else I read about her when I was doing a bit of research at home. Apparently not enough. "Stella also designs sportswear for Adidas and someone else ... I think."

"Yes, as well as her own full line of clothes," Paige supple-ments. "She used to work for Chloé and Gucci. She designs for icons like Madonna and Gwyneth Paltrow and she even has a skin-care line called CARE."

"Bravo," I say back to her.

She nods in a queenly sort of way.

"You know we have a bit of time to kill before six," Fran tells us. She glances down at her map and notes then calls up to the driver. "Let's stop at Bar Italia in Soho."

"We're going to a bar?" I ask.

"A coffee bar," she tells me.

"Yes, this *is* London." Paige uses a tutorial tone. "If we wanted something more than coffee, we would go to a pub."

I roll my eyes. "Oh, yes, wise one," I say with sarcasm. "Thank you for straightening me out."

Bar Italia turns out to be an interesting place. According to Fran, it's the most popular all-night coffee bar in London. Why anyone wants to drink coffee in the middle of the night is beyond me, but I suppose some might come for the food. I'll admit it smells delicious, but since we only have about forty minutes to spare, we settle for coffees and pastries.

Then we clean crumbs from our faces and freshen our makeup, and we're off to Stella McCartney. The shop is very chic and impressive. While Paige, in top form, does a quick interview, I mostly just listen, somewhat in awe of this woman who seems much younger than her late thirties. Not only is she pretty and creative, it's like she has a youthful spirit. And, once again, I'm surprised at how much I like most of her designs. Maybe I am secretly a British fashion freak and I just never knew it before now.

But as Paige is wrapping it up, I can tell that we're all feeling pretty tired. When we return to the hotel it's past seven and all I want to do is order some room service and crash. But, once again, we are met by some media thugs as we attempt to enter our hotel.

"We don't have time for this," Fran says as they literally block the door.

Paige is back in her Gucci shades and pink scarf disguise. Very effective. I'm controlling myself from yelling at them to get out of our way.

"Just a quick question," a guy says to Paige.

"You and Benjamin Kross were —"

"Benjamin is just my friend," Paige practically shouts at him.

"But photos of you two kissing are already circulating the Internet," he continues. "And rumors of your pregnancy are —"

"I am not pregnant!"

Fran is waving to a doorman over by a taxi. "Please, call security," she yells at him.

"When is the wedding date?" another paparazzo calls out.

"Get out of our way," I shout as I push past the rude man.

Just then the doorman rushes over and takes charge, threatening the paparazzi with legal action if they don't leave. Suddenly we are free of them and inside the lobby.

"If this doesn't stop we might have to change hotels," Fran says with irritation.

Paige groans. "I'm sorry."

"Hey, maybe we can spread a new rumor," I say as we get in the elevator. "That we've switched hotels."

"Or maybe I can get a better disguise," Paige suggests as she removes her scarf and shades. "Like a long black wig."

Fran nods. "You know, that's not a bad idea."

"I suppose that means I'll need a wig too," I say without enthusiasm.

"Or else we just come and go separately," Paige says dismally.

I consider this. In some ways, I wouldn't mind separating

myself from my sister a bit. Fending off paparazzi and hearing those kinds of accusations isn't exactly fun. Especially when I'm not totally sure what is and is not actually true. I wouldn't be surprised if there really are photos of Ben and Paige kissing circulating on the Internet right now. Really, for all I know, they may be secretly planning a wedding. Not that I plan on asking Paige about this. Because, the truth is, I'm not sure I totally trust her right now. I get the feeling that not only is she protecting her place on the show, as she clearly showed me this morning with her airport ambush (and possibly her choice of clothing for me today), but that she's not being totally honest with me either.

Chapter
14

We agree to go our separate ways on our day off. Paige wants to sleep in and then do some shopping, and I want to do some typical sightseeing that she's not interested in. I decide to get an early start, but once I'm down in the lobby, I have no idea what I should do. So I consult with the concierge, a middle-aged man with wire-rimmed glasses and a neat bowtie. He reminds me of the stereotype of an English butler.

"How much time have you got?" he asks me quickly, studying his computer screen as if it's of more interest to him than I am.

"All day," I tell him.

"What are your primary interests?" He looks up from his screen and studies me closely as if trying to determine who I am and where I came from.

"I'm not sure. I do like to take photos."

"Have you any interest in Shakespeare?" he asks suddenly.

"Yes," I say eagerly. "Absolutely."

"Have you a car?"

I shake my head no.

"Are you are on your own?"

"Today I am."

"But you say you have all day?"

I nod, wondering where he's going with this inquisition.

"Then, if I were you, I'd nab a seat on the Gray Line tour of Stratford-upon-Avon."

"Gray Line? Is that a bus?"

"Yes. But I promise you, it's a good tour. You'll see Shakespeare's birthplace and Anne Hathaway's cottage. If you're at all interested in literature, I think you'll find it charming."

I'm still not sure. "It's an all-day tour?"

"Yes. If you decide right now there's a chance I can get you on it."

I'm thinking about it. Do I really want to spend the day on a bus?

"Of course, there are some Shakespearean sights one can see right here in London," he says offhandedly. "The Globe Theater and such. You can easily catch those on another day. But truly, if you want to experience Shakespeare, to walk where he walked, to see the sights that the great Bard saw, you should capitalize on this tour. Also, you might snatch some brilliant photos this time of year. Stratford-upon-Avon is spectacularly beautiful in May."

"All right." I nod. "Please see if you can get me on this tour."

He looks back down at his computer screen, clicks a few times, then picks up the phone, has a quick conversation, and finally hangs up. "You're in luck," he announces.

Soon we have it all squared away and he tells me the bus will be by to pick me up in about an hour, which gives me just enough time to sample the "full English" breakfast. I'm guessing it is rarely served in this hotel because the waiter seems delighted when I order it. This traditional meal comes complete with grilled tomatoes, mushrooms, eggs, sausages, and "rashers," which is actually bacon and rather tasty. Of course, I can't eat the whole thing and I suspect the reason they call it the "full English" breakfast is because you become quite full upon consuming it.

By the time I'm stuffed and making my way through the lobby, telling myself that now I had better skip lunch, I see the concierge waving toward me.

"Your chariot awaits," he calls out, pointing to the entrance. I thank him and wave, hurrying out the door and onto a bus that is full of — old people. Not terribly old-old, like one foot in the graveyard old, but around my grandma's age. To my surprise, they all cheer when I step onto the bus. Feeling conspicuous and wondering if I've just made a huge mistake, I give them a feeble smile and take a seat near the front.

"I hope you don't mind," a middle-aged woman seated opposite me says, "but I took the liberty to tell everyone that we've got a real celebrity on board."

I blink. "A celebrity?"

She glances down at a notepad. "You *are* Erin Forrester, correct?"

"Yes."

"That's what the concierge told me." She sticks out her hand. "I'm Harriet Barstow, your tour guide."

"Nice to meet you and thanks for waiting."

She peers curiously at me. "Now is it true that you're a star of some American television show?"

"Not exactly a star," I say quickly. "My sister, Paige Forrester, is the real star. I'm just her costar. Our show is called *On the Runway*."

"Because the other tourists, also Americans, were eager to have a young star in their midst, they tolerated your lateness just now." She smiles patiently. "But I hope you won't make a habit of it." She stands as the driver pulls out into traffic, getting her microphone ready.

"I'll do my best to keep you from waiting." I assure her.

"So, we're off now," she announces to the rest of the bus. "We welcome Erin Forrester to our group. She has informed me that her television show is called *On the Runway*. We will be traveling northwest for a bit. For our entertainment, I have a little quiz for you. Since I know you are mostly retired school teachers, I will attempt to make the questions a bit more challenging than usual." She begins to ask questions about Shakespeare, his history, his works, and even some quotes. Several of the retired teachers seem to be serious Shakespeare buffs. I even get one right when she asks who the main character's daughter was in *The Tempest*.

"Prospero's daughter was Miranda," I call out before anyone else, which wins me a Cadbury chocolate bar. I stick this in my bag for later—just in case I ever get hungry again.

It's around eleven when the bus stops in the quaint-looking town of Stratford-upon-Avon. As we get out and mill around, waiting for our tour guide, I learn that the retired teachers are all from Madison, Wisconsin. It seems they are mostly women, and for the most part seem very chatty and friendly. A few, to my surprise, have actually seen *On the Runway*.

"My granddaughter Elsie loves your show," a woman who told me to call her Mildred informs me as Harriet shepherds us across a street. "She lives with me and we've been watching it together. I can't tell you how pleased I am that your sister is such a good example to these young girls." She shakes her head. "I would get so tired of some of the trashy shows that Elsie used to watch. Shopping with her used to be a nightmare. It seemed the poor girl was determined to look like a call girl." She chuckles as we get in line again. "Although I have to admit Paige's influence comes at a price."

"What do you mean?" Suddenly I'm worried that Mildred has already seen the latest tabloids.

"Now Elsie wants expensive designer clothes. I finally had to put her on a budget before she drags me to the poor house." She laughs. "But I must say I'd rather spend money on those nice clothes then the horrid rags poor Elsie used to wear. That is an improvement."

The line is moving again and I put my focus on the words of our tour guide and the charming buildings. After we've seen the home of Shakespeare's birth and Nash's, the place where he died in 1616, we visit Hall's Croft, the house where his daughter and her wealthy husband lived. It has a lovely photogenic garden where I get a number of good photos. Then we visit Holy Trinity Church, and finally get on the bus and continue on to the cottage of Anne Hathaway, Shakespeare's wife.

By the time we finish it's not even one and I'm wondering how this can be an all-day tour, but to my surprise Stratford-upon-Avon is just the beginning. We also stop in Oxford where I take a full card's worth of photos, and then we stop at Windsor Castle, which is perfectly lit by a gorgeous dusky sky, translating into another card's worth of photos. Finally we return to London around eight and I tell all my new teacher friends good-bye. Okay, it wasn't exactly the kind of day I would brag about to anyone my age—I mean, hanging with a bunch of retired teachers probably sounds pretty lame. But I actually had a good time. I feel like I experienced more of England than I thought would be possible on this trip.

Of course, as I go into the hotel, which is thankfully free of paparazzi, I am exhausted. I'm barely in my room and am just getting ready for bed when Paige comes rushing through the adjoining door and falls onto my bed, sobbing.

"What's wrong?" I ask in horror as I pop my head out of my nightgown.

"Everything," she cries.

"What?" I demand, sitting down next to her. "Is it Mom?"

She sits up and looks at me with a tear-streaked face. "Where have you been all day?"

"On a bus tour—but tell me, is it Mom? Did something happen?"

"No . . . it's not Mom. Mom is fine, although she was a bit miffed at you. She'd tried to call you—and so did I—but it seems your phone was turned off."

I shrug. "I didn't see any reason to leave it on."

"Well, except for the fact that you are here with me and here with our show and I was in the midst of a crisis!"

"What crisis?" I demand. I look closely at her now. "I don't see any broken bones, no bleeding wounds. What are you talking about?"

"I had the worst day ever."

"And . . . ?" Okay, I hate to seem totally unfeeling, but what am I supposed to do about it?

"And it would've been nice to have had you around . . . for moral support, you know?"

"But all you wanted to do was sleep in and do a little

shopping," I remind her. "I can hardly see how you'd need my help to do that."

"Except for the paparazzi."

"You had paparazzi following you while you were shopping?"

She nods. "They were horrible. And being by myself—well, they just kept hammering away at me. They all seem certain that Ben and I are going to be married, that I'm pregnant, that Ben is a dirty rat, as they called him. It's all getting bigger and bigger." She sighs. "It's like the blogs' and networks' stories have taken on a life of their own and no matter what I say or do, no one is listening."

"Welcome to celebrity." I hold up my hands in a helpless gesture. "I mean ... what did you expect, Paige?"

"A little more respect."

"Are you serious?" I study her and wonder if she's really as naïve about this as she sounds. "You used to follow all the tabloids and Hollywood gossip yourself," I remind her. "Remember how obsessed you were when Brad Pitt dumped Jennifer for Angelina? You totally hated Angelina for almost a year."

"Well, I was young and silly."

"And you were reading the tabloids and believing everything you read, Paige. Exactly what some people are doing right now."

"But how do I stop them?"

I shrug. "I have no idea. How did Angelina get you to stop believing that she was the devil and had destroyed Jennifer Aniston's life?"

She makes a sheepish smile. "I'm not sure she has stopped me."

"Oh, Paige." I shake my head.

"I'm kidding." She lets out a long sigh.

"It's the price of fame," I tell her. "You know what they say—if you can't take the heat ..."

"But it's so unfair ... and mean." She looks at me. "I would think you, of all people, would see how wrong it is. I would think you would be outraged, Erin."

"I'll admit that it really aggravates me. When I'm with you, I'll try to speak out, like I've been doing. But I don't think we can really stop them. Short of a lawsuit, and I'm not sure that even works."

"What were you doing today?"

So I tell her about my bus tour with a bunch of old schoolteachers, and she actually looks envious. "That sounds like fun."

I can't help but laugh. I mean, seriously, go figure!

Chapter

15

As exhausted as I was, once Paige got done unloading on me I was wide awake. Now I can't sleep. Something about this whole thing gets me. So I take out my computer and begin to write. My goal is to just get some of these thoughts down, at least for now. Maybe someday I'll do like Helen has suggested and start my own blog. Or not.

Other than snickering over the occasional sensational headline while waiting in a checkout line, I've never paid much attention to tabloids and gossip rags. Mollie used to buy them sometimes, until she discovered she could find her dirt for free online. But I've always kind of stayed away from the smut. It never interested me before . . . and it wouldn't interest me now except that suddenly it's feeling personal.

Being in London has really opened up my eyes about this business. I've concluded that, although tabloids cover—and oftentimes create—a variety of stories (including bizarre alien abductions and UFO sightings), they seem to favor one particular sort of "breaking news event."

And that is anything that involves the public humiliation

of a popular celebrity. Of course, if the person weren't a celebrity—a person of interest—there would be no point in public humiliation. Because everyone knows that writing embarrassing stories about ordinary people will not sell newspapers.

I've decided that tabloids thrive on celebrity downfall—or anything that can be portrayed as downfall. Their list of favorite topics include divorce, arrest, unwed pregnancy, bad parenting, rehab treatment, weight gain, arrests, or any negative experience that a public figure might prefer to keep private. And, naturally, the bigger the celebrity, the bigger the story.

But it seems to me that it wasn't until this London trip that Paige became such a big focus of this mean-spirited mudslinging. Why is London so interested in tearing my sister to shreds in their tabloid papers? To answer that question, I go to the lowest common denominator—money. Of course, those papers are all about making money. If consumers didn't buy those smutty tabloids, they wouldn't get printed. So apparently, there are people out there who enjoy reading bad things about my sister.

Again, I have to ask myself *why?* Why does the average person enjoy reading unkind and often untrue stories about a celeb? What makes men and women plunk down their hard-earned money to read what are mostly lies about someone they don't even know?

After much deliberation, I have come to the conclusion that some people are just plain jealous and as a result they're willing to buy into gossip and slander to make themselves feel better.

And so, even though I still think misleading tabloids are wrong-wrong-wrong, I guess I get why they're so popular. It's a human way of compensating. Some might go as far as to say this is how the playing field gets evened—a chance for the haves and the have-nots to be equal. The secret cost of fame, and a way celebrities pay their dues for being idolized, is by being victimized by tabloids. Blah, blah, blah . . . finally I even put myself to sleep.

Of course, morning comes and I have to shove my philosophical and slightly judgmental musings aside and get ready to "perform" with my star sister. The irony of this does not escape me. Fortunately, and probably because it's early, we manage to exit the hotel without any fanfare.

"Where do you think they went?" Paige asks as the car pulls away.

"You sound like you miss them," I point out.

"No," she says quickly. "It's more like noticing that a toothache stopped."

"Well, I spoke to hotel security," Fran says. "They promised to do what they can, but they also reminded me that there are other fashion personalities staying at the hotel who appreciate being pursued by paparazzi."

Our first appointment is with Vivienne Westwood, the designer responsible for bringing punk into the mainstream, and I can't believe how easily Paige converses with this woman who must be almost fifty years her senior. Of course, I have to give much of that credit to Ms. Westwood, who seems like she's about our age and masquerading as an older woman.

"You are what I would call an extreme designer," Paige says finally. "Years ago you were instrumental in the punk trend in fashion and most recently your designs were featured in the movie *Sex and the City*." Paige smiles as if remembering. "I must say that wedding gown was exquisite and I wasn't a bit surprised when Carrie picked it to wear in her wedding."

Then Paige wraps up this interview and we head on to the next appointment, which amazingly enough is with former supermodel Naomi Campbell. Paige is ecstatic because she believes Naomi is one of the most beautiful women in the world. But when we get there, it seems that Naomi has changed her mind and her assistant informs us that Naomi only wants to do a one-on-one interview with Paige and one camera guy. Naturally, Paige agrees. Paige and JJ remain behind while Fran, the rest of the crew, and I go out for coffee.

"What was up with that?" I ask Fran as we sip our java and kill time.

"I'm guessing that Naomi wanted to be sure she had control of the interview."

"Why?"

"She's experienced some publicity issues."

"As in bad publicity?"

Fran nods.

"So does she think we're going to give her bad publicity?"

"I hear it's happened. Frankly, I was surprised that Leah was able to line up the interview in the first place." She frowns and looks at her watch. "I just hope it's going okay."

"Meaning what? How could it not go okay?"

"Hopefully Paige won't ask any incendiary questions."

"Such as?"

Fran rolls her eyes. "Such as some alleged assaults."

"You mean Naomi's been assaulted?"

"I mean Naomi's been accused of assaulting others."

"Oh . . . well, hopefully she and Paige won't start smacking each other around." I laugh to imagine my sister putting up her fists against anyone—especially someone as gorgeous as Naomi Campbell.

Fran laughs. "Yes, I suppose that's unlikely."

And when we go back to pick up Paige, she seems completely pleased with her interview, telling us that Naomi Campbell couldn't be nicer. "She even does some great charity work with children in sub-Saharan Africa," Paige tells us as we drive back to our hotel for a little break.

"So why was she so worried about having the crew at the interview?" I ask.

"She's seen some of the bad publicity I've been getting," Paige admits. "She thought I might be out for revenge in my own interviews."

"Do people even do that?" I ask.

Paige shrugs. "I guess so."

Fortunately, we are able to get into our hotel without any unwanted fanfare. Then we meet with the crew in Paige's suite to look over tomorrow's appointments, making some game plans. While we're meeting, a room service lunch that Fran previously arranged for is delivered.

"What is this?" Alistair asks as he picks at a veggie platter. "Model food?"

Fran laughs. "Maybe so."

"Where do we go to get some real food?" JJ teases.

"Or is this a hint?" Shauna shakes a celery stick at Fran. "Are you saying we need to lose some weight?"

"No," Fran tells her. "I just ordered from the menu. I can't help it if they cater more to anorexics. Consider their usual clientele."

"Speaking of anorexics," I glance at tomorrow's schedule. "Kate Moss is our first appointment." I look at Paige. "I don't want to point fingers, but some people have. Are you going to ask her about her eating habits?"

Paige laughs then shakes her head. "No way."

"Why not?" I demand.

"Because that's not the point of my interview."

"Why isn't it?"

Paige looks at Fran, but Fran just shrugs.

"I was promised a show about body image and eating disorders," I remind both of them. "Kate Moss would be a great place to start. Do you realize that she started the waif look?"

"That's a matter of opinion." Paige picks up a carrot stick.

"Hey, maybe I should get the camera out," JJ suggests. He's already on his feet, going for his bag.

"Not a bad idea," Fran says. "Are you girls okay with that? Taping your candid conversation about this subject?" She points to me. "We could use this in your segment, Erin."

And so we agree. The next thing I know Paige and I are seated on the swanky sofa in her suite, going head-to-head about models and how they influence the average American woman.

"So are you telling me that you think Kate Moss had nothing to do with the stick-thin model craze that took hold during the nineties, or that her influence on fashion hasn't impacted the way the average American teen girl views her body?"

"That's a lot to pin on one person," Paige counters. "I don't see how you can blame Kate Moss for every eating disorder in America."

"I'm not trying to blame Kate Moss personally," I point out. "After all, it was the fashion industry that hired Kate to model in the first place. The industry helped to make her a star. She was pretty young so maybe she couldn't help that she was skinny. She probably had no way of knowing what a health hazard she would become to the average American woman."

Paige laughs. "Health hazard? Don't you think that's blow-ing it a bit out of proportion, Erin?"

"No, I don't. Not only was her lifestyle of under-eating a bad example, she may have used drugs too."

"Allegedly."

"Where there's smoke there's fire," I say and then wish I hadn't. "What I mean is that a lot of models use drugs to stay thin. Cocaine, amphetamines. It's no secret, Paige. Let's not pretend it doesn't exist. Okay?"

She shrugs. "Okay. What's your point?"

"My point is that Kate Moss is a huge influence in the fashion industry. I would think she could take some respon-sibility for that influence. Like it or not, she's a role model in the industry for young women. She needs to own up to some things and help others make better choices."

"Why?" Paige frowns. "Why should Kate Moss suddenly take responsibility for the choices we make? She's a fashion model—not a life counselor."

"Think about the word *model*," I say suddenly. "What does it mean?"

Paige actually looks stumped.

"Model, just by nature of the word, means something we look to as an example. Or it can be an imitation. It can even be an ideal. So women who work as fashion models should know that they are examples. Examples that others will want to imitate and that they might even be perceived as an ideal."

"But they're simply modeling the clothes."

"You can say that, Paige, but I know you don't believe it. Even you follow the personal lives of some of your favorite models. And someone like Kate Moss, who is still in the spot-light, has followers too. Women, especially young ones, want to look like her. Even to the point were some will resort to bad choices like eating disorders and drugs to accomplish it."

Paige seems to be considering this. "But models have always been thin, Erin. Everyone knows clothes look better on thin models."

"That's not true. I did some research and both actresses and models used to weigh more. Yes, there were a couple of short eras when the stick-thin models were popular for a while. But for the most part, models have been tall and slender, but not anorexic—at least they didn't *look* that way. Before Kate Moss's influence, the most popular models were women like Cindy Crawford, Claudia Schiffer, and Naomi Campbell."

Paige nods. "I can see you've done some research."

"I have. What I want to know is why we can't get back to that. Why can't we accept that the female human body is supposed to have curves, or that women are meant to carry more body fat than men, or that starving yourself or taking drugs to lose weight is a big mistake?"

Paige sighs. "Good points."

We continue sparring for a while longer, and finally I get Paige to agree to bring up this subject with Kate Moss tomorrow. "I'll put it in a non-confrontational way," she says as if thinking out loud. "I'll ask Kate to speak a bit about body image and health . . . and what kind of influence she thinks the fashion world in general has on women. That shouldn't be too intimidating." Paige looks at me. "Will that make you happy?"

I smile. "It's a start."

"And that's a wrap," Fran says. "Now we need to get ready for our last appointment of the day."

I feel like I gained a bit of ground this afternoon. Okay, maybe it's only a tiny bit of ground, and it remains to be seen whether or not my sister will be true to her word tomorrow. But I've decided that if she just happens to forget her little resolve to ask Kate her non-confrontational question ... well, I might have to help her out a bit. After all, I am supposed to be costarring in this show.

Chapter
16

Our next appointment is with Jenny Pack-
ham, a popular Brit designer. To our surprise, she actually has
set up a mini fashion show for us. I have to say her evening
gowns are stunning. She uses a lot of beads and adornments
along with interesting fabrics, and the end result is truly beautiful. My only complaint, which I keep to myself, is that her
models—while pretty—look a little hungry. I wished I'd
thought ahead to sneak some pastries into the changing area,
although I'm sure I would've been raked over the coals for
such a subversive attempt.

"Wasn't that fantastic?" Paige says as we're riding back
through London. "I don't know when I've seen such gorgeous
gowns. You could take me to her showroom, blindfold me,
and let me pick out any one of them and I'd be happy."

"That's high praise. But I have to admit Jenny's designs
were magical," I say. "She reminds me a little of our designer
friend Rhiannon, in New York, although Jenny's designs are
more sophisticated."

"I can't wait to see her wedding dress collection," Paige says. "That show is on Saturday."

"So what do you girls think?" Fran says. "Want to eat out or go back to the hotel for room service?"

Remembering our "model" lunch, I opt for going out and, thankfully, Paige agrees. As we drive Fran calls ahead and finds a popular place in Soho where the wait will only be fifteen minutes.

"Do you think any paparazzi will be around?" Paige asks quietly.

"I don't see why," Fran tells her. "Unless you're sending information onto one of the social networks."

"Of course not." Paige firmly shakes her head. "And I spoke to Benjamin last night — told him that he'd better not do anything else to fuel this fire."

"Has he?" I ask.

She shrugs. "He hasn't helped to put any rumors to rest."

"I'm sure he's enjoying the free publicity," Fran says.

"Free at my expense, you mean."

When we're dropped at the restaurant, we go in without any sign of paparazzi. I do notice a few heads turn as we're being seated, but I remind myself that's always been how it is with Paige. She turns heads and she enjoys doing so.

"Maybe the paparazzi have found bigger stories to follow," Paige says as we're browsing our menus.

"You sound like you miss them," I point out.

She shrugs. "No. But no one wants to be ignored either."

I can't help but laugh at how flaky that sounds. "I don't mind being ignored," I tell her. "At least by paparazzi anyway."

We eat our dinner in peace and quiet and exit the restaurant with no unwanted fanfare. Unwanted from me that
is … I'm not so sure about Paige. But when we get back to
our hotel, there seems to be a fair number of people clustered
around the entrance again.

"Oh no," Paige says in alarm. "I guess our little reprieve
is over."

"Want me to go ahead?" I offer, "and act as a smokescreen
so you can slip in the side door?"

She seems uncertain, but Fran agrees to this plan. When I
get to the door, however, I see that the spotlight is shining for
someone else. It turns out that Tyra Banks and her entourage
have just arrived. It seems they're here for the taping of her
show and the upcoming fashion events next week. I laugh to
myself as I go back to inform my sister that she is no longer
the hottest fashion story in London.

Paige seems disappointed as she gets out of the car, and
strides toward the entrance of the hotel like she's a superstar.
Seriously, she's like *look at me, I'm so hot. Don't you want a shot
of me?*

And to my dismay her persona works. It seems that Tyra
and her crew have gone inside now, and since the paparazzi are
already gathered, they turn their cameras onto Paige. Just as I
expected, these "journalists" show how small-minded they are
since their questioning goes straight to the Benjamin Kross relationship again: is Paige pregnant and when is the big wedding?

"Really," she says in a tone that might be interpreted as
haughty. "Can't you come up with anything better than that?
Why don't you write a story about how a flying saucer full of
fashion-conscious aliens from Venus brought me here so that
I could spy out fashion trends on Earth and—"

"Why are you always avoiding the questions?" a guy interrupts her. "There's no crime in being in love with a man — even if he has broken the law. In this day and age, it's not a big deal to be pregnant when you're not married, Paige. People do it all the time. Just own up to it and we'll let you be."

"That's right," yells another, "own up to it and we'll be on our merry way."

"All we want is the truth," a woman calls out.

"The truth?" she shouts at them. "You want the truth?"

No one responds. It's as if they're waiting for some choice morsel of gossip.

"The truth is I'm sick of you Brits posting bogus photos and printing lies about me. I don't know how you can look at yourselves in the mirror when you get up in the morning. If you keep this up I will be speaking to my attorney." She turns around and nearly stumbles over the woman standing behind her. I grab Paige's arm, steadying her, and the two of us push our way through the grumbling throng, who apparently didn't appreciate Paige's comments. We find Fran standing in the lobby with an I-told-you-so look on her face.

"Happy now?" Fran asks her.

Paige smiles. "As a matter of fact, I am."

However, she is singing another song the next morning. "Look at how they're maligning me now," she says as we're standing in the lobby, waiting for our car to arrive and take us to our Kate Moss interview.

"Where did you get that?" I frown as I spot one of Britain's most popular tabloids in her hand.

"Here in the gift shop." She thrusts the paper at me. "This morning's edition. Look what they said about me."

As Fran joins us, I scan the headline — "Paige Forrester

Blasts Britain." For Fran's sake, I read the words out loud. "'Miss Forrester, star of America's *On the Runway*, in an angry outburst against Great Britain said, "The truth is I'm sick of you Brits, and I don't know how you can look at yourselves in the mirror." Apparently Miss Forrester, a self-proclaimed fashion diva, is under the impression that no one in Great Britain has any fashion sense whatsoever, and it seems that she plans to make this clear on her reality TV show. Miss Forrester went on to say that she planned to seek legal counsel to sue any paper who printed her statement. Miss Forrester is a guest in Great Britain, with plans to make an appearance on our popular reality show, *Britain's Got Style*, but the question on many a Brit's mind this morning is whether or not Miss Forrester has any style herself. Not to mention class. Miss Forrester is reputed to be pregnant with—'"

"*Stop!*" Paige rips the paper from my hands. "I can't take another word!"

"Oh, dear." Fran shakes her head. "This is not good."

"How can they print such lies?"

"I don't know," Fran says in a grim tone. "But the car is here. Let's go."

I take the rumpled paper back from Paige and as we're riding, I reread the opening sentence of the article again— silently this time. "Actually, it's not all lies," I say quietly.

"Not lies?" Paige looks like she's on the verge of tears now. "How can you, my very own sister, say that?"

"Because it's true. I was with you last night and I heard you talking." I point to the paper. "You *did* say you were sick of the Brits, Paige. You also said you didn't know how they could look at themselves in the mirror. Maybe you didn't mean it in the context that they took it, but you did say those words."

Paige lets out a low animal-like growl. "They twisted it, Erin. You know they did."

"They twisted your meaning to make a story," I tell her. "But you did say those words."

"Quiet," Fran tells us. "I can't hear this message."

So we both sit quietly as Fran listens to her voicemail with a severe frown.

"Who is it?" Paige asks.

"Kate Moss's spokesperson."

"And?" I wait.

"Kate has cancelled this morning's interview and has no intention of rescheduling."

Paige makes two tight-balled fists. "Why?"

"Sounds like she's been following the press and she doesn't want to be linked with you."

"This is so unfair!" Paige slumps back into the seat, her head hanging.

"It is unfair," I admit. "But you opened yourself up for it again when you spoke to the paparazzi last night. You could've easily slipped past them, you know."

"Please. Do. Not. Lecture. Me." Paige looks like she's about ready to blow and so I decide to be quiet as Fran tells the driver to take us back to the hotel. Fortunately, it must be too early for the paparazzi because the entrance is still pretty empty. We all quietly go inside and without anyone saying a word, we ride back up the elevator and walk into our rooms.

So now I'm pacing in my room, and thinking, *this is great. Just great.* We're over here to record episodes and suddenly, because Paige has stuck her foot in her mouth, it looks like we're being shut down almost before we're even started. Seriously, if Kate Moss doesn't want to talk to us, why would anyone else? And why would *Britain's Got Style* still want Paige on their show?

It's like Paige got off on the wrong foot with this country as soon as we got here. I can't really blame her for anything specific in regard to the paparazzi—well, before last night anyway. At first she was actually polite to the rabid reporters. But I can blame her for blabbing on the social networks and for tweeting before we even got here. I can also blame her for her indiscretion with Benjamin. I never thought that was a good idea. Benjamin has always had a bad-boy image with the press and with Mia Renwick's death, his image has only gotten worse. I'm frankly surprised that he still has a movie offer—if that's even true.

"Erin?" Paige sticks her head through the open door between her suite and my room.

"What?"

"I need to talk."

Okay, I'm not sure I'm ready to talk to her yet. The fact is I'm feeling a little mad at the moment. When I think of how I've sacrificed most of my first year of film school to get to this point ... well, it's a little disturbing.

"Will you come in here?" she asks.

Without answering, I follow her back into her suite then collapse on the sofa and let out a big deep sigh.

"I don't know what to do," she says quietly. "Fran is mad at me, which means Helen is mad at me." She looks up with moist blue eyes. "Are you mad at me too?"

I just frown.

"Okay, I'll take that as a yes."

I fold my arms across my front and sit there.

"I don't know what to do ..." she says again.

"I don't either."

"But you're the one who usually has the answers," she tells me.

"I'm fresh out at the moment, Paige."

So we both sit there in silence. While I'm sure I could think of something if I tried hard enough, I'm just not willing to try. I'd rather let her stew in this mess she's helped cook up. Savor the flavor. I keep sitting there, simply looking down at my lap, until finally I glance up, to see that she's gone.

So much for coming up with solutions. I'm about to return to my room when I hear the sounds coming from her bedroom. I go in there to find her stretched out on the bed, quietly crying. Something about this gets to me. Maybe it's because she's not being a drama queen. This is real.

I sit down beside her and wait for her to stop. But the crying goes on for quite some time and I finally reach over and touch her hair. "Crying isn't going to fix this," I say quietly. "When you're ready to listen, I think I have some ideas."

She keeps on crying and now I don't know what to do. I mean, I know my sister and I know she can overreact and get wildly emotional sometimes, but this seems like honest-to-goodness despair. So I go over to Fran's room and explain what's going on.

"I suppose I was kind of hard on her after we got up here," Fran admits. "But Paige knows that a lot rides on her. Helen has made it clear that she expects Paige to keep a relatively clean reputation. Our sponsors expect it too."

"But most of the stuff that's being printed about her isn't even true," I remind Fran.

"Perception can be stronger than truth." Fran shakes her

head. "Now I'm finding out that Kate Moss isn't the only one to cancel on Paige."

"Oh ..." I let out a sigh. "I was worried about that."

"British people don't take kindly to being insulted by a twenty-year-old fashion diva."

"No, I expect they don't."

"Anyway, I'm glad you came over to talk. Helen has a new plan." She waves me to a chair to sit down. "She thinks that her little Jiminy Cricket might be able to save this sinking ship."

"How?"

"First of all, both you and Paige will hold a press conference. Helen wants a repentant Paige to stay in the background while you step up and make a very sincere and intelligent apology. Do you think you can do that?"

"I guess so."

"Helen said it's important that you don't make this an attempt to clean up your sister's smeared reputation. Just let that go for now. Mostly you have the challenging task of winning back the Brits." She actually laughs. "Now that sounds easy, doesn't it?"

"Right." I roll my eyes. "Easy breezy."

"Okay. I'll set up the press conference." She looks at my outfit. "You change into something that looks British and slightly serious." She chuckles. "Kind of like your usual clothing."

"I happen to really like British style," I admit.

"Make that work for you."

I stand now. "So that's it."

"That's it for now. I'll admit it's a long shot ... but it's worth a try."

"Do you want me to tell Paige?"

She nods as she picks up her phone. "Sure. I'd appreciate that."

I go back to Paige's suite and attempt to tell her about Helen's plan, but I'm not sure she's getting it. She still seems to be a basket case. So, once again, I sit on the edge of her bed. "Paige," I say gently. "Is there more going on here than this bad publicity?"

She sits up now, wiping her wet face with her hands. "What do you mean?"

"It just seems like an overreaction. I mean, we've been through some really difficult stuff before. It seems like you're taking this especially hard. What's really going on?"

Paige takes in a long breath. "I miss Dylan."

I blink and stare at her. "Huh?"

"I know. It sounds really dumb. But I think I'm in love with him."

I want to agree—this does sound really dumb, especially right now—but I control myself. "I don't get it. What do you mean you miss him . . . that you think you're in love with him? I thought you guys broke it off. That you were going to just be friends. Did I miss something?" She nods and now fresh tears are coming down her cheeks. And, okay, I'm totally bewildered. Like how is this breakdown about Dylan? But she's crying so hard again that I doubt I can get to the bottom of it. I'm not even sure I want to.

Chapter
17

"First of all, I want to apologize on behalf of my sister and myself," I say after Fran introduces me at the press conference that's being held in one of the hotel conference rooms. The audience looks grim and although Paige and Fran are standing nearby, I feel very much on my own. It's some comfort to spot our camera guys in the back of the room, acting like they're part of the press.

"Yesterday, my sister made a statement that was misconstrued." I glance at my notes—notes that Fran read and approved. "Paige spoke out in frustration last night. Her comments were in reference to a misrepresentation in some tabloids. She said she was sick of Brits, but not all Brits, only *Brits who had been printing false stories and bogus photos to smear her name.* But as for everyone else in Great Britain, we have nothing but the highest praise. We love your country." I break away from my notes now, hoping to make this seem more personal. "I enjoyed taking a bus tour of the countryside. I couldn't believe how beautiful it is here. And your amazing buildings and Windsor Castle—well, let's just say we don't have anything like that where I live." I pause for a few chuckles and hope that they're warming up a bit. "I've enjoyed the food and I had my first rashers. I've enjoyed meeting people and I love the way you guys talk. And I have to say—I adore British fashion." I smile at the faces, noticing that some seem softer now.

"There are so many things about your country that I love that I'm thinking maybe I'm actually British at heart." I pause for the laughs that follow. "But I mostly want you to understand that Paige was misquoted. I was there when she made the statement about not knowing how British tabloid reporters can look at themselves in the mirror in the morning. She wasn't talking about Brits and fashion." I shake my head. "She was simply referring to how a dishonest reporter might feel after writing an article that slandered Paige's name." I pause again. "I'm sure you can imagine how it feels to have someone reporting malicious and untrue things about you. It hurts. Paige's outburst was a result of the libelous things that have been said about her. But because we are guests in your country, we feel it's our responsibility to apologize and attempt to set the record straight. Thank you for your graciousness." I smile and nod, and as I step away from the podium I'm surprised to hear several people clapping. They are joined by more and I feel hopeful.

Fran steps back up to the podium again. "And Erin is happy to give honest answers to your questions now." As I step back up, Fran and Paige exit and I am left on my own with reporters. But for the most part, the questions are relatively polite and I do my best to answer them.

"No, my sister is not pregnant," I say slowly. "The photo you saw a couple days ago was taken when I was shopping with my best friend who happens to be pregnant. Then someone photoshopped the photo of me by a baby crib with a photo of Paige to give the impression she was pregnant."

"But what about her relationship with Benjamin Kross?" someone shouts from the back. "Are you saying those photos were tampered with too?"

I firmly shake my head. "No. Those photos are legit. Paige and Benjamin have dated in the past." I pause now, wondering how much to say. "Okay, I'm going to be very honest with you and I hope my sister doesn't get mad." I take in a slow breath and I can tell the reporters are eagerly waiting. "Paige just confessed to me that the main reason this whole thing has been so stressful is because she is, in fact, in love with someone. But it's not Benjamin Kross." Okay, even as I speak, I'm wondering if I just made a huge mistake. Of course, I have no intention of revealing who that someone else is. Naturally a whole new set of questions follow and now everyone wants to know about the mystery guy.

"All I can say is that it's not Benjamin Kross," I say with an air of finality, like this interview is over. "Paige was only spending time with Benjamin as a friend. I can't speak for his interest in my sister, but take it from me Paige Forrester is not romantically interested in Benjamin Kross."

"How about you?" someone calls out. "How's the little sister's love life?"

I laugh. "Well, I've got several guy friends, but I'm not ready for anything serious."

Fortunately the rest of the questions are fairly innocuous and mostly in regard to the show. As the crowd dwindles and interest fades, I thank them for their time, remove the microphone, and excuse myself.

"Why did you tell them that?" Paige demands when I join her and Fran in a little side room where they've been sitting and listening to all that I said. I can tell she's nervous, and probably more scared than she'll admit.

"I wanted to lead them off the Benjamin trail," I tell her.

"That's a good idea," Fran agrees. "It's okay to stir some curiosity about Paige's love life. After all, we don't want to cut the press loose from us. Publicity is publicity."

Paige sighs with a sad expression. "I guess."

"I told Paige that she's going to take the rest of the day off," Fran tells me.

"What about our interviews?"

"They're fairly small ones." Fran smiles at me. "I think you can handle them."

"Alone?"

Fran nods. "You just handled the London press alone. Surely you can handle a couple of small-potato interviews."

"I appreciate it, Erin." Paige makes a weak smile. "I'll get it back together by tomorrow. I promise."

I study her and wonder what happens if she *can't* get it back together. But then I remind myself that she always gets it back together. She's the queen of bounce-back.

The first interview turns out to be just the sort of thing I really like. Ashley Amberly is only twenty-seven and a relatively new designer who is refreshingly green. She only uses fabrics made from renewable resources in her designs — like bamboo, wood fibers, hemp, recycled plastic, polyester, organic cotton, and linen. But she has a huge British following.

"Most of my customers are young people," she tells me as we're winding down. "So I try to keep my designs affordable.

Although I've been encouraged to create a couture line for next year's London Fashion Week. I'm thinking about it."

"What would be the advantage of participating in Fashion Week?" I ask her. "I mean, since you already have a solid consumer base of environmentally conscious customers."

She frowns as if thinking. "You know ... that's a good question. On one hand, it's flattering to be invited to the ball, but on the other hand it might be offensive to some of my green groupies." She smiles. "Not to mention PETA."

"I know Stella McCartney is a strong supporter of animal rights."

Ashley nods vigorously. "I'm a huge fan of Stella McCartney."

"Have you heard of Granada Greenwear?"

"Oh, yes. Granada's been an inspiration too."

"Has anyone ever considered doing a Green Fashion Week?" I ask.

Ashley's eyes light up. "That is a brilliant idea, Erin."

"Thanks." I smile. "I know I'd want to attend it."

"If you don't mind, I might steal that idea and attempt to run with it."

"You're more than welcome. Just promise to keep me posted. Maybe *On the Runway* could participate with you."

We talk for a while longer and Ashley's enthusiasm is contagious. But finally Fran gives me the wrap-it-up sign and I thank Ashley for her time.

"That was great," Ashley tells me as we're removing our mics. "You do a fabulous interview, Erin. Your big sister better watch out."

"Thanks. But I don't think she has too much to worry about."

"Nice work," Fran tells me as we drive to the next appointment.

"Ashley was just my cup of tea," I admit. "That made it easy."

"The next one should be fairly straightforward too." She looks at her notes. "Gregory Maxwell is a popular British jewelry designer, but since he's in Thailand, his assistant Valerie will show us his studio."

"Do we know anything about his style?"

"Just that he's quite popular in the UK." Fran shrugs. "Let's wing it and hope that this Valerie is a talker."

Thankfully Valerie, who turns out to be Maxwell's daughter and not much older than me, *is* a talker, as well as an apprentice jewelry maker. And her dad's work turns out to be absolutely lovely. Again, I think I got lucky because his nature-inspired designs are just the kinds of things I like. He imitates the beauty of flowers, plants, birds, fish, and small animals, combining his graceful designs with precious and semi-precious gems to create some absolutely charming pieces.

"I love this," I say as I examine a silver vine-like necklace with seed pearls posing as pussy willows.

"Our designs are primarily sold in the UK, but we've also expanded into a number of international markets," Valerie tells us. "We've recently become rather well liked in Asia. My father's work became internationally known in the nineties when some of his pieces were worn by Kate Holloway."

So for the most part, and to my relief, Valerie plays both tour guide and narrator. Finally we're done and I'm thanking her.

"I must've seemed like such a chatterbox," she says as she

hands back her mic. "I was just so thrilled about this opportunity. I hope I didn't muck anything up for your show."

I smile. "No, you were perfect. We'll send you a DVD of the show when it airs. That way your father can see what a great job you did today."

It's nearly six by the time we get back to the hotel. As we're walking through the lobby, I'm surprised to see that I have a phone message on my iPhone. And even more surprised when I see it's from Dylan Marceau.

"I'm going to swing by the gift store," Fran tells me. "Need anything?"

"No. I'm fine." As she heads off, I find a quiet corner and I listen to the message.

"Erin, you're probably wondering why I'm calling you. A little British bird just told me something this morning . . . and I was hoping you could give me a quick call." Then he leaves his cell phone number and I glance around, worried that someone might be around to eavesdrop on my conversation if I return his call. But I seem to be the only one here. And if I go to my room to call, the connectivity is sketchy at best, plus Paige might walk in on me. I'm pretty sure this is going to be about her. I decide to just get this over with.

"Erin?" he says happily. "How are you?"

"Okay."

"I heard about your press conference."

"Seriously? Who told you?"

"A Brit fashion friend. But never mind that. I'd seen some of the other stories about Paige and Benjamin in the news lately . . . and I think it was very nice of you to help your sister out of that mess."

"Well, it was kind of turning into everyone's mess." I tell him about Kate Moss's cancellation.

"Maybe I could give Kate a call," he says. "She's an old friend."

"You seem to have a lot of friends."

He laughs. "Well, it's helpful in this business. I consider you a good friend too, Erin."

"Thanks, Dylan. Same back at you." I glance around again, but I still seem to be alone.

"So ... my friend told me you said that Paige is romantically interested in someone else ..." His voice trails off.

"Uh ... right."

"I don't want to twist your arm to tell me about this mystery guy. But I want you to know you can trust me. I really care about Paige. Even though she broke my heart in Paris, I still want the very best for her life and—"

"She broke up with you?"

There's a long pause. "Well, it's not a tale I want everyone to hear. No guy likes getting dumped. But since you're her sister ... I assumed this would be old news to you anyway."

"Let me get this straight. You're saying Paige dumped you?"

"That might be an overstatement. As I recall I saw the writing on the wall that night. But, being a guy with a fair amount of pride, I probably acted as if the breakup was mutual."

"But it wasn't mutual?" I'm trying to wrap my head around this.

"So what are you saying, Erin? Did Paige tell you a different version?"

I try to remember now. "Well, to start with she told me it

was mutual. Back when she and I agreed to give up any serious relationships with guys and just focus on the show."

"Yes, that's about what she said that evening ... or what I refer to in my mind as the last supper."

"But you're saying she broke up with you?"

Another long pause. "What do you know? What is Paige saying to you, Erin?"

I consider this. Upstairs my sister is pining away. She's missed a whole day of work ... she cried for more than an hour this morning ... she admitted that she misses Dylan, that she thinks she loves him. But what am I supposed to do about it?

"Who is this guy, Erin? You can trust me. I swear I won't breathe a word to anyone."

"Oh, Dylan ... maybe you should talk to Paige."

"Really?"

"Yes," I say eagerly. "You really, really should talk to Paige. In fact, I have a very strong feeling she'll be extremely glad to hear your voice."

"You really think so?"

"I know so. I just think this is something I need to stay out of, you know?"

"I understand."

"She's probably in her room right now. You might want to call the landline though, since our cell phone service is a little sketchy in the hotel."

"You're sure it's a good idea?"

"Pretty sure."

"Thanks, Erin."

"Sure. But maybe you shouldn't tell Paige you talked to me, okay? I don't want her to think I'm meddling."

"You got it. I'll just start out the conversation low-key. Like I'm just calling to say hey . . . and see where we go from there."

"Sounds good." Then I give him Paige's room number. But after I hang up, I wonder what I've done.

"Hey, you still down here?" Fran comes around the corner and takes me by surprise.

"Oh, yeah," I say quickly. "Just using the phone down here since it doesn't work that well in my room."

"Everything okay at home?" she asks as I walk with her to the elevators.

"Sure. Everything's fine."

"You really did a good job today, Erin," she says as she pushes the button to our floor.

"Thanks. It was actually kind of fun. But I'll be relieved to have Paige up and running again."

"Do you think she's going to snap out of it?" Fran looks at me curiously. "She seems to be in quite a slump. I didn't know this publicity crud would get to her like this."

"I'm sure she'll be fine tomorrow." I give Fran a hopeful smile. "She's pretty resilient."

"I hope you're right. We've got several great appointments back-to-back tomorrow, starting first thing in the morning. And the opening fashion show is tomorrow evening. After that we're booked with style shows throughout the day Saturday clear into Sunday night. If Paige doesn't kick it into gear and if we miss out on these opportunities, we'll be short on material when we get home next week. And Helen will not be pleased."

"I don't think you need to worry about Paige," I tell her as we get out of the elevator.

"I hope you're right." She looks at her watch, then covers

a yawn. "I plan to order in my dinner tonight. I've already arranged for breakfast to be delivered to Paige's suite tomorrow. The plan is to meet there for hair and makeup by eight o'clock sharp."

"Gotcha." I make a mock solute then turn toward my room. As I unlock and open the door, I try to imagine Paige's surprise when Dylan calls her out of the blue. Will she be happy, or shocked? Or will she figure out that I've been involved and get mad for my interference? With nothing else to do, I shoot up a silent prayer and tiptoe into my room where I'm tempted to lean my head against the adjoining door. Instead, I grab up my iPod, slip in the earbuds and, crossing my fingers, fall backward onto my bed where I intend to crash until hunger takes over.

Chapter
18

"*What a gorgeous day,*" *Paige says cheer-*fully as I come into her room through the adjoining door. I'm still in my pajamas and barely awake. But in here, all the drapes are pulled open and bright morning light is pouring in. The hair and makeup people have also arrived, and are milling around.

"Uh-huh," I say sleepily.

"What is wrong with your hair?" Luis frowns at me.

"It's clean," I say sheepishly. "I washed it last night."

He shakes his head, pointing toward the kitchenette. "Go wet yourself down like a good girl. I'll bring you a towel."

I nod and pad into the kitchen, turn on the water, adjust the temperature, then stick my head under the flow. I know how much Luis hates it when I wash my hair at night. I wake up looking like a scarecrow and it takes him longer to style it. But I like showering at night. At least my hair is short so it dries quickly.

"Here you go." He drapes a towel around my soggy head, then leans over and whispers in my ear. "What or who do you think is responsible for our Little Miss Merry Sunshine this morning?"

I wrap the towel tighter then stand up with a grin. "The sunshine perhaps?"

He rolls his eyes. "If only the sunshine were capable of such miracles . . . the whole planet would be deliriously happy most of the time."

"We have a busy morning," Paige chirps as Shauna works on her makeup. "By the way, Erin, Fran said you did great yesterday. Thanks for covering for me!"

"You're welcome." I stop by where some food is set up and help myself to a muffin and a yogurt, which I plan to munch on while Luis does my hair. "It was actually kind of fun. Where is Fran anyway?"

"Getting some decent coffee downstairs." Luis wraps the styling cape around my shoulders. "Shauna and I threatened to go on strike if we had to keep drinking the stuff that's in our rooms."

"I offered to make them some here," Paige says, "but Fran said we need to hurry and get ready. I laid out an outfit for you on my bed, Erin. Business casual for the day, and then we'll come back and switch into something more festive for the fashion show tonight."

"You seem extra happy this morning," I say a bit cautiously.

"Oh, I am." She turns to me with a sunshiny face. "I really, really am."

"Care to share with the class?" Luis teases as he aims the blow dryer at my head.

"Not yet." She gives him a catty smile. "But maybe in time."

Well, I have no doubt that her change in mood is thanks to Dylan. I can't say I'm not appreciative, but this sudden act of secrecy is an interesting twist. Although, I can't say that I blame her after all the questionable media coverage she's had lately. Even though I'm sure we can trust Luis and Shauna, loose lips might still sink ships. *On the Runway's* ship is barely back to floating again as it is.

"It's such a nice day," I say as Luis rubs some product into my hair, "I think I'll get a hop-on, hop-off pass."

"A what?" Paige asks.

"It's a day pass for the double-decker buses," I explain. "The concierge told me about it. If you get one, you can just hop onto a bus and ride for a while, then hop off when you reach your destination."

"That sounds fun," Paige says. "Why don't you get me one too?"

"Get you one what?" Fran asks as she comes into the room with a cardboard carrier full of coffees.

"A double-decker bus pass," Paige tells her.

Then I explain the on and off concept. "I thought if we had a break or two today, which looks possible according to the schedule I studied last night, it might be fun to play tourist today. Especially since the sun is shining."

"I asked Erin to get me one too," Paige tells her.

"Really?" Fran looks surprised, and I am too. Because this does not sound like Paige to me.

"I plan to ride on top of the bus," I warn Paige, "out in the open air so I can really see things. You sure you want to do that?"

"Yeah. Why not?"

"You girls better take a scarf for your hair," Luis warns us.

"Oh, we can do touch-ups before each event," Shauna tells him. "Let the girls have some fun."

"Maybe we should send a camera along too," Fran says. "That would be a fun snippet to have on the London shows. I think I'll call down and get us several passes. This sounds like a great idea, Erin."

Now I'm feeling even more enthused. "I already checked the bus route map," I tell her. "It runs right through some of the areas we'll be in today. So I think it's doable."

"And tomorrow, before the first fashion show, we should get some shots of you girls in front of Buckingham Palace ... some flirting with the Beefeaters."

"What's a beef eater?" Paige asks as Shauna removes the makeup bib and gives it a shake.

"The guards in front of the palace," Fran tells her. "The ones with the tall furry hats."

"Actually, that's not quite right," I correct her. "The Beefeaters guard the Tower of London."

"How do you know that?" Fran questions.

"I learned it on my tour the other day. A lot of people mistake the palace guards for Beefeaters, but that's not accurate. Although the palace guards do wear those tall bearskin hats."

"So what's up with the hats?" Paige comes over to wait for Luis to finish up on me.

Luis gives a final misting of spray to my hair. "There, maybe that will stand up to riding around on top of busses."

I stand up and let Paige take my place. "The tall hats were designed to make the soldiers look taller for battle. More intimidating."

"Ah-hah," Paige says. "You see, there are many reasons for various fashion statements."

Paige's sweet spirits continue on throughout the morning. She is gracious and kind to everyone—from the doormen to the CEOs. Her compliments flow like a river and yet each one sounds genuine and unique. Whether designers, models, or assistants, they all just warm right up to her aura of happiness. Every interview seems to go as smooth as butter. Really, it's like she can't say or do anything wrong. It appears the magic is back and everyone seems to adore her.

And, naturally, I am getting suspicious. What exactly did Dylan say to her last night? What could he have possibly done to bring about this miraculous transformation?

When we hop onto the double-decker bus, Paige is still full of sunshine and joy. Her mood is contagious as other tourists begin to laugh and joke with her, and she even manages to snag some interesting conversations which JJ catches on camera. Meanwhile I enjoy the London scenery, take a few photos myself, and actually listen as the guide explains what it is we're seeing.

Finally, the hardest part of our shooting for the day seems to be done, and after one more hop-on, hop-off bus ride we're back at the hotel with enough time to relax for a couple of hours before tonight's fashion show.

"I know," Paige says as we're riding up in the elevator. "Let's eat downstairs in the hotel restaurant tonight. We can dress up for the fashion show and then we'll walk into the restaurant and see how many heads we can turn. Jenny Packham was supposed to send over some dresses today."

I'm considering this. The truth is it's been a long day, and because this place is already crawling with models, I'm sure heads will be turning in every direction—not just at Paige.

"Come on," she urges me, "it'll be fun."

"Count me in," Fran tells her. "I'm willing and hungry."

"Erin?" She looks hopefully at me.

"Sure. I'm in."

"I'll call down for a reservation," Fran says as we're going into our rooms. "Let's say six. That should give us time to get to the show."

"Come on into my room," Paige calls to me. "I'll help with your hair and makeup and then we'll pick out a sizzling outfit."

It takes less than an hour until Paige and I are both dressed to the nines. As promised, Jenny Packham came through and sent over several fantastic-looking cocktail dresses. "Are you sure this isn't too much?" I ask Paige as I check out my image in the mirror. My dress is a black and hot pink number that reminds me a little of the Roaring Twenties with its beaded fringe and beautiful corset belt. Paige looks elegant in a silky dress of peacock blue with touches of beading around the neck and the waist. We're both wearing dark hose with a bit of sparkle to it—compliments of Jenny—and some very cool platform shoes.

"I feel like a grandma with you two," Fran says when she meets us in the suite. She has on a two-piece black dress that is actually quite nice.

"You look great," Paige tells her. "Sophisticated chic."

"Or middle-aged frump?"

"No way," Paige assures her. "You are hot, Fran."

I nod. "You always look great. Very director-like ... with authority and class."

She smiles. "Well, no one will be looking at me tonight anyway. You girls look stunning."

I suppose I was wrong about not turning any heads tonight. As we walk across the lobby, I notice a number of people looking. Some seem to know who we are, while others look curious. But everyone is rather nonchalant too, like no one wants to be caught looking.

We enjoy a nice dinner and as we're finishing up, I tell Paige thanks for coming up with a good idea. "This really was fun. Much better than eating in our rooms."

"See, you just need to trust me sometimes."

"I must commend you on your amazing comeback today," Fran tells her as she sips her coffee. "I already left a message for Helen telling her what a brilliant job you did today. Both you girls."

I shrug. "I didn't really do much."

"But I am curious, Paige. What made you able to pull yourself out of the depths like that? What's your secret tonic? Is it something we can bottle? Legal, I hope."

Paige just laughs.

"Maybe it was the sunshine," I say quickly. "It really was a pretty day."

"Yes," Paige agrees. "The sun came out and that makes everyone happy."

Fran looks a bit skeptical. But then she glances at her watch. "I better tell the driver to bring the car around if we want to get there in time to film some of the behind-the-scenes stuff. I'll bet the crew is already there."

"Do we need to check our hair or makeup?" I ask.

"No, you both look great."

"We'll touch up our lips in the car," Paige says.

As Paige and I are doing our last-minute primping, Fran's iPhone chimes. She lets out a little groan when she checks to see who's calling. "Hello, Mark," she says in a falsely cheery tone. "What's up?" As she listens, two sharp frown lines crease her forehead, and I can tell something is wrong.

"What happened?" I ask as she slides her phone back into her bag with a low growl.

"That was Mark McCall." She presses her lips together and folds her arms across her chest.

"The producer of *Britain's Got Style*?" Paige asks with a worried look.

Fran nods grimly. "He called to inform me that your presence is no longer needed on their show."

Paige's shoulders droop and she looks down into her lap. "Because of me."

"Or because Mark McCall is a great big chicken."

"I just don't get it," I declare. "I thought reality shows loved controversy and any kind of publicity. Mark should be grateful for all the press Paige has gotten recently. Viewership should be higher than—"

"Unfortunately, there seems to be a lot of pride involved here," Fran says crisply. "Maybe it's the old Brits-versus-Yanks competition, or maybe it's something more. I don't know. But I'm not eager to report to Helen."

"Is there anything I can do?" Paige asks meekly.

Fran lets out a long sigh. "Just do your best for the rest of this trip. Be a professional."

Before long, we're behind the scenes and Paige is interviewing models as they get ready. I'm sure no one but me could possibly guess how bummed she's feeling about being shut out of *Britain's Got Style* right now, because she's like her old self, smiling, passing out the compliments, and doing a magnificent job of saying the right thing to put others at ease. However, I suspect that if Paige acted like this all the time, our show would either be a huge hit or viewers would get tired of Pollyanna. Okay, I can't believe I actually just thought that. But, hey, I'm a realist.

Finally, it's time for the style show to start and we head

for our seats in the front row. But as I'm about to sit down, I notice a familiar name on the placard that's sitting on the empty seat next to Paige's chair. "Dylan Marceau is coming here tonight?" I exclaim as we sit down.

Paige gives me a nervous smile, then nods. But she looks too much like that proverbial canary-eating cat, and this makes me curious.

"How is that possible?"

She turns and peers at me. "What do you mean—how is *what* possible?"

"I mean why would Dylan be here?" Even though I'm confused, I realize I don't want to blow my cover. "He's not a British designer."

"Not all the shows this weekend are British designers," she reminds me.

"But he doesn't have a show here, does he?"

She shakes her head no. "But it's not out of the ordinary for a good designer to hop over the pond to check out the competition, Erin. London Fashion Week isn't that far away. Maybe Dylan wants to do some spying."

"Right . . ." I slowly nod, still taking this news in. "So where is he then?" I whisper as the lights go down and the music begins.

She shrugs then looks straight ahead. "I have no idea."

Then the show is about to begin and the amazing runway, which is actually multiple runways that resemble a maze, is suddenly flashing with colored lights and smoke and other special effects that make me feel slightly dizzy. The music is booming so loud it's like I can feel it pulsing through my veins. As I watch model after model parading some pretty extreme designs and strutting up, down, and all around this runway, I totally forget about Dylan's empty seat next to Paige.

Finally, the show ends and with my ears still ringing, I glance over to see that Paige looks disturbed.

"Are you okay?" I quietly ask. "Are you still upset about *Britian's Got Style?*"

She shrugs. "A little." Then she points to the empty seat next to her.

"Oh …" I nod. "Dylan didn't make it?"

With troubled eyes, she holds her chin up. "His flight was probably delayed."

"Yes." I nod in agreement. "Or he got stuck in London traffic."

Then, almost like magic, Paige puts on her sunny face, which has just a trace of sadness in it, and with JJ trailing her through the crowd, she launches into some off-the-cuff interviews with some of the glitterati in the British fashion world. I can't help but question Mark McCall's judgment. Can't he see that Paige is still a hot item over here? Our camera guys are hard-pressed to stick with her, so many fashionistas are glomming onto her. After about an hour, right as she's just finishing up with tonight's designer, I see Paige's eyes light up — like she's just spotted something over the designer's shoulder. Something I can't see. But Paige remains professional, wrapping up her interview with high praises to the designs and tonight's show. And that's when I see Dylan waving as he pushes his way toward her.

The next thing I know, Paige is in his arms and I'm just watching what looks like a scene in a movie — a final scene. Our camera guys are watching too — through their lenses. Although I suspect this is a scene that will end up on the cutting-room floor … or maybe not.

Chapter
19

I wasn't too surprised when Paige opted to let Dylan give her a ride back to the hotel. I didn't stay awake to make sure she got back at a decent hour either. Dylan is a good guy. He cares about Paige, and he's mature and trustworthy. Especially compared to Benjamin Kross. Really, compared to Benjamin, Dylan is a white knight in shining armor. And if his presence in London, if only for a few days, picks up Paige's spirits like this, well, who am I to complain?

But when Paige wakes me up at 6:48 on Saturday morning— a day when we weren't scheduled to go to "work" until noon— I feel a bit grumpy. "What's up?" I ask groggily, blinking at the light that's coming in through my opened shades.

"Sorry to wake you." Paige sits down on the edge of my bed ... and suddenly I feel worried.

I sit up now and, rubbing the sleep from my eyes, I frown to see that Paige is still wearing that pretty peacock blue dress from last night. "Did you stay out all night?" I demand.

"Don't worry," she says with a smile that's even sunnier than yesterday's. "We didn't do anything you wouldn't approve of."

"How do you know what I would or wouldn't—"

"Never mind." She stands, strutting across the room like she's walking on a cloud.

"What is going on?" I ask as I crawl out of bed and walk over to look at her face. "Why are you so happy?"

She holds out her left hand and I feel a wave of shock and disbelief rush through me as I stare at what appears to be an engagement ring. "Please, Paige," I whisper, "tell me that's not what I think it is."

She nods and giggles. "It is!"

I sit down on the chair by the window and can only shake my head. How is this possible? Paige is barely twenty—how is it possible she is engaged? I feel slightly dizzy.

"I know you're shocked, Erin. But just be happy for me, okay? Last night was the most romantic night of my life. First of all, Dylan had hired a carriage ride that took us all through London—it was amazing and wonderful. And then he had arranged a midnight dinner, which was like something out of an old movie. Dylan has such a sweet old-world spirit." She sighs. "Then just after dessert was served, he pulled out a little blue box. Tiffany's blue." Paige sinks down into the chair across from me. "I thought I was going to faint when I saw it."

"And?" I try to make my face look happy, expectant, pleas-ant . . . but I feel like such a fake.

"And Dylan got down on one knee and told me that I was the love of his life and that he knew I was a little young, but that I would make him the happiest man in the world if I would agree to marry him."

"And you said yes." My voice sounds way too flat, but it's the best I can do.

"Of course." She holds out the ring again — like evidence. "Aren't you happy for me?"

I take in a long, slow breath. "I think I'm just in shock, Paige. It's a lot to take in. And it's so early." I stare at her in wonder. "Did you really stay out all night?"

"After he asked me, we were both too excited to call it a night. So we went dancing and had another carriage ride, then we walked along the river and talked and talked, and finally right after the sun came up, which was incredible, Dylan brought me back to the hotel."

"Wow . . . you must be tired."

She sighs and nods. "I guess I'm tired . . . but I might be too excited to sleep."

"You need to sleep, Paige. Today will be a long day." I take her by the arm, leading her back to her room and, as she continues to babble on about Dylan and how happy she is and how perfect this is, I help her out of her dress and into bed. "Just close your eyes," I say quietly. "Dream about Dylan."

She nods and smiles. "Yeah . . . that's what I'll do."

After she's safely snuggled in, I go and put the Do Not Disturb sign on her door. Then I write a note that I slip under Fran's door explaining that Paige needs extra sleep this morning and shouldn't be awakened until noon. Today's first fashion show isn't until two, but there are three altogether and the last one won't be over until after ten. So if Paige wants to be in top form, she will need some rest. I'll leave it to Paige to tell Fran her news. How this will impact our show is anyone's guess. I'm just hoping that I still have time to secure a place in film school this coming fall. Because as I get dressed — and not very carefully — I am telling myself that I am almost finished with this rollercoaster ride called *On the Runway* with Paige Forrester.

With sunglasses on and a hat pulled low on my head, like I'm worried that I'll suddenly be the target of paparazzi—which is ridiculous—I walk through the hotel lobby and over to the restaurant where I had the good English breakfast a few days ago. Was it only a few days ago? But as I sit down and look over the menu, it occurs to me that I'm not really very hungry, and so I only order coffee and toast.

"No rashers?" the waiter asks hopefully.

I realize this is the same guy who waited on me before, the one I raved about the rashers to. "Sure," I tell him. "I'll have some rashers too."

He grins. "I saw you on television. Nicely done."

I smile and nod. "Thanks." *Yeah, nicely done*, I'm thinking. My big mouth about Paige's love life ignited this whole thing. As I eat I'm longing to talk to someone about what's going on. I consider Mom, but know that Paige should be the one to tell her. Then I think of Mollie, but I don't totally trust Mollie not to go public with this. Finally, I decide to tell Blake. He's been a good one to keep confidences before.

So after I leave the restaurant, I go outside and hit speed dial for Blake's cell phone. I have no idea what time it is in LA, but I'm desperate.

"Hey," Blake says in a congenial tone, "How's London, Erin?"

"Oh, it's so good to hear your voice." I tell him about how Paige was uninvited from *Britian's Got Style*. "She took it pretty hard."

"That's too bad," he says. "So how's everything else going? You girls have sure been getting a lot of press."

"Even back home?" Maybe I should pay more attention to this gossip thing.

"This is LA, Erin."

"Oh, yeah."

"So, really, what's the story on Paige's mystery man?"

I take a second before I respond. "You heard that too?"

"Oh, yeah . . . it's the talk of the town."

"Well, can I totally trust you?"

"Of course. But hang on a minute, okay?"

"Sure." So I wait for what is actually about a minute, then Blake is back.

"Sorry about that," he tells me. "I was with Ben."

"You were with Ben?"

"Yeah. He's kinda bummed about Paige. He asked me to hang with him. And, hey, at least I'm keeping him from a bad night of clubbing."

"What time is it there, anyway?"

"A little past midnight."

"Oh . . . right."

"So what's up?"

In one long rambling sentence, I tell him about Paige's engagement.

"Wow." He lets out a long sigh.

"I know . . . wow. I'm still in shock. I mean, she's not much older than me. And there's the show. I just can't believe it."

"Is she happy?"

I consider this. "Yeah, she's like over-the-moon happy."

"Good for her."

"Really?" I consider his point. "You think this is a good thing?"

"Well, if she's happy, how can I not be happy for her? Dylan is a good guy."

"Yeah . . . I guess."

"But you're not happy for her?"

"I just feel caught, Blake. Like I've been so jerked around in this show. I've given up a lot. Now it's like the show is going to go straight down the drain."

"Just because Paige is engaged?"

I think about that. "Yeah, maybe I am overreacting."

"Seriously, you don't think they'll run off and get married and just give up their careers, do you?" He chuckles. "I'm guessing they'll have a long engagement."

"You could be right." Suddenly I feel a bit hopeful.

"And, really, what good does it do for you to be bummed, Erin? It's Paige's life, right? As her sister all you can do is support her and love her. You, of all people, should know that she makes her own choices."

"You're right, Blake." I let out a relieved sigh. "I knew I would feel better talking to you."

"Really?"

"Yeah. You almost always make me feel better."

"I like the sound of that."

"Okay, now remember to not breathe a word of this to anyone yet."

"I promise."

"I'm sure Paige will break the news soon enough." I wince at the thought.

"Poor Ben."

"I know. But I'm sure he'll get over her."

Blake doesn't say anything in response.

"Anyway, like you said, there's nothing we can do about it," I add, a bit awkwardly.

"Yes. That's right. I'll be praying for Paige and Dylan ... and you too. Although I was doing that anyway."

I thank him and we hang up, and I realize that he really is right: There's nothing I can do about this anyway. I might as well be happy for Paige. And really, isn't this better than seeing her all depressed over the *Britain's Got Style* rejection? Then I remember how Jesus said we should rejoice with those who rejoice, and right now my sister is rejoicing. So I will join her!

I decide to stop at a bakery not far from the hotel and buy a chocolate torte for my sister. (Hopefully, in her happy state, she won't think about the calories.) The baker uses pink frosting to write Dylan & Paige and frames it in a heart. Then I go back to my room and prepare myself to wait until noon. But as I wait, I pray. I ask God to help me to be supportive and positive about this new era of Paige's life. I ask him to help me to trust him more for my own life—knowing that no matter what my sister does, it's God's direction that should lead me. And finally I ask him to bless my sister and Dylan.

It's about eleven thirty when I hear a tapping at the adjoining door. I go and get my celebratory cake and open the door with a big smile.

"Is that for me?" Paige asks happily.

"Yeah. I thought we should celebrate."

"Oh, Erin." Paige takes the cake, sets it on a side table, then gives me a big, hard hug. "Thank you!"

"I'm sorry I wasn't more excited earlier," I say as I get the cake and follow her into the suite. "I was in shock and not quite awake."

"I know," she says as she gets out plates and forks from the kitchenette and I start a pot of coffee. "I should've broken it to you a bit more gently. But I was so excited. I couldn't wait another minute."

"I understand. I mean, I saw how much you brightened up yesterday . . . after Dylan called."

"So you knew he called?"

I chuckle. "Yeah. He and I had a little chat yesterday—after he heard about my little press conference."

"It's funny—I was mad at you for saying that. But now . . . well, I'm so happy."

I slice into the cake, putting a big piece on Paige's plate. "So when are you guys going to announce this publicly?"

She forks into the torte. "Probably today. No sense in waiting . . . because with my luck, someone probably knows now anyway."

We talk about the logistics of this new development as we eat our chocolate torte. Then as Paige is pouring us some coffee, she turns to me. "I'll need you more than ever now, Erin."

I laugh. "You'll need me?"

"Dylan and I talked about this. He thinks I need to share more of the show with you, Erin, and I think he's right."

Dylan is growing on me more and more. "So you plan to continue with the show?"

"For now I do."

I slowly nod. "Do you have any idea when you'll actually get married?"

"Of course, we haven't set the date. If Dylan had his way, which he says he won't push for, it would be next week."

"Seriously?"

Paige nods with sparkling eyes.

"But how about you?" I ask.

She shrugs. "I'm not really sure. I definitely need at least a year to plan a fantastic wedding."

"And you'd continue with the show throughout that year?"

"Well, we are under contract, Erin."

"But we both know contracts can be broken."

"Yes, Dylan pointed that out." Her smile gets even bigger, if that's possible. "Which reminds me of something."

"What?"

"Fran called this morning. It seems Mark McCall is rethinking his decision about having me on his show."

"Really?"

"Fran said that Helen is putting some pressure on his boss. Now there's a possibility we will do his show after all."

I look at the clock and realize we were originally scheduled to start the show today. "Then we better get busy to make it there—"

"Not here in London, Erin."

"Huh?"

"In the Bahamas."

"The Bahamas?"

Her eyes sparkle as she grins. "Yes. How cool would that be?" Then she explains that the Bahamas trip will be scheduled after we get back home.

"So we are going to be busy." I study her closely. "And you're okay with that . . . I mean, in light of this engagement biz?"

"I think so. I think I'll take Dylan's advice too."

"What advice?"

"Remember I told you that Dylan thinks you should be more involved in the show, Erin? The more I think about it, the more I think he's right. If you stepped up more . . . I might be able to step back a little."

Okay, I've been down this road before, but I'm not going to say that. "So you think you're really ready to share the spotlight with me now?"

She nods. "I really do. I was silly and selfish to try to hog it all to myself. Look where it got me — I almost had a complete breakdown."

"It's not like they can ever use me to replace you," I remind her. "*On the Runway* is what it is because of you, Paige. But I could help to share the load a little more."

"And you don't mind?" She sets down her fork and looks into my eyes. "I mean, I'm not stupid, Erin. I know this was never your dream. I don't want to feel like I'm dragging you along against your will."

"I'll admit I've been kind of grumpy ... especially when I'm not quite sure what my role is. But I actually enjoyed doing those interviews after you broke down. When I'm allowed to be myself, it's kind of fun."

She looks relieved. "So maybe we can do this? I can be engaged and we can still do a first-rate show?"

"I don't see why not."

"Because I really do love Dylan, Erin. If I had to choose between him and the show, I would choose Dylan."

I smile as I raise a forkful of chocolate torte in a toast. "Here's to you and Dylan, Paige. May God bless you both!"

She has tears in her eyes. "Thanks." She lifts her fork again. "And here's to sisters sticking together through thick and thin." She looks down at what little is left of her cake and giggles. "And if I keep eating this, I'll be more thick than thin."

I laugh and hold up my fork. "Here's to sisters! Sisters forever!"

We click forks and as I take a bite I know that somehow, some way, and with God's help — despite obstacles of competition, jealousy, misunderstanding, and all the other challenges of sisterhood — Paige and I really will be sisters forever.

ON THE RUNWAY

GLAMOUR

A Novel

Bestselling Author
Melody Carlson

Chapter

1

After nearly six months of the drama and chaos connected to it, I hoped we'd finally left the reality show *Malibu Beach* behind. Far behind. And really, it seemed a natural assumption. Especially after Paige permanently distanced herself from one of the show's ex-stars, Benjamin Kross, by getting engaged to brilliant young designer Dylan Marceau last month in London. Apparently I was wrong.

It turns out that *Malibu Beach* is the reality show that keeps on giving. And now they want us to "give us the opportunity" to devote an entire *On the Runway* episode to one of their popular stars, Brogan Braxton. Brogan, who is only nineteen, recently declared herself a fashion expert, and is now coming out with a new line of beach clothing called The BBB (aka Brogan Braxton Beachwear).

"But these are awful," Paige tells our producer, Helen Hudson, as we all lean forward to peer at the images on the screen of Fran's laptop computer.

"I have to admit I'm with my sister on this one," I tell

them. "What made Brogan Braxton suddenly decide she was a designer?"

"You mean besides Daddy's wallet?" Paige teases.

"I think you're missing the point," Fran says as she closes the laptop.

Helen adjusts her glasses and clears her throat. "Brogan is still one of the hottest commodities in the teen market."

Fran waves a piece of paper. "According to this, Brogan has almost as many Facebook friends as Ellen DeGeneres."

"Yes, and they're *real* friends too." I roll my eyes. I may be the last person on this continent to join Facebook, but I'm still holding out.

"I consider my Facebook friends to be real," Paige says to me in a slightly wounded way.

"Yes, and I'm sure they'd still be your friends if you didn't have a show, right?" I turn back to Helen. She's encouraging me to take a bigger role in our show and I am trying. "But I thought we were talking about fashion, and I still don't get Brogan Braxton, or The BBB ... which, by the way, also stands for the Better Business Bureau, and I wonder how they feel about—"

"You're missing the point," Fran says with a bit of aggravation.

"Remember the *R* word, girls?" Helen asks in a slightly bored tone.

"Ratings." Paige sighs. "Never mind whether it's fashionable or not, as long as the viewers tune in."

"Wait a minute," I say. "Just because we feature a fashion designer doesn't mean we have to approve of their style, does it?"

"That's true." Paige nods. "And my fans expect me to be honest. Do you have a problem if we do the show and I express my candid opinions about The BBB?"

Helen shrugs, then pushes her chair away from the conference table. "Just keep the fans happy, Paige. Keep the ratings up." She stands and peers down at her. "And keep it clean."

"Oh, you know I always keep it clean, Helen." Paige flashes her best smile.

Helen reaches down and pats Paige's cheek. "Yes, darling, but you know what I mean. Keep it polite and respectable. You have an image to maintain. One element that makes *On the Runway* different from the other shows is that Paige Forrester, for the most part, is a lady. And the sponsors seem to appreciate that."

"You don't ask for much," Fran says to Helen. "Just keep the ratings up and play nice. That's so easy to do."

"Yes, well, our Paige is quite expert at it." Helen laughs as she heads for the door. "Sorry to meet and run, girls, but I have a major appointment with the network in about ten minutes. Ta-ta!"

Fran shuffles some papers into a stack, then slides them over to her assistant, Leah. "Brogan's show is scheduled for this Saturday at two." Fran gets a worried look. "That's not your mom's wedding date, is it?"

"No, that's the following weekend," Paige says. "You are coming, aren't you?"

"Yes, of course, I already RSVP'd. I just blanked it." Fran takes a long drink from her bottle of water.

"The crew is scheduled already," Leah fills in for her. "You girls can come to wardrobe around ten then we'll head over to the site and do the pre-show shoot. After the fashion show, we'll do the wrap-up." Leah smiles. "The usual stuff."

I'm curious as to why Leah is telling us this ... since it's what Fran usually does. Maybe Leah, like me, is trying to take a more active role in the show.

"Brogan wants to do an interview before the show," Fran says, then looks at Leah. "When was that scheduled?"

"She asked for Wednesday afternoon," Leah tells us. "Two o'clock ... on *Malibu Beach* turf."

"So Brogan called us and asked us to interview her?" Paige frowns.

"Her people called us," Leah clarifies.

"We thought we might get something to use for the show," Fran says.

"And the interview is just with Brogan?" Paige asks. "Not any of the other cast members or the *Malibu Beach* crew, right?"

"I'm not totally sure about that," Fran tells her. "In fact, it sounds as if their crew will be filming this too. Just in case it's show-worthy."

"You mean in case they want to *make* it show-worthy." Paige groans. "Something about this whole thing is starting to smell fishy. It's not some kind of setup to get me, is it?"

"No, of course not." Fran shakes her head.

"Because I know Brogan was pretty close with Mia Renwick. I mean, they weren't *best* friends. But when Mia died in that car accident after the Oscars, it was like everyone in the cast suddenly decided they had been her very best friends. And I can understand that. But I also understand that some of those girls seriously hate me, Fran."

"At least you're not with Ben now," I remind her.

"And I hear he's getting back with Waverly Stratton,"

Leah says in a somewhat-gossipy tone. "I saw it on *WWW* last weekend."

"The world wide web?" I ask.

Leah laughs. "No, that new entertainment show, *Who's Who and Why*. Haven't you seen it?"

I shake my head, thinking maybe it should be called *Who's Who and Who Cares?*

"Really, Erin," she tells me, "you need to keep up. Anyway, they showed some pics of Waverly and Benjamin at a club, and in the interview Waverly said that they were together."

Paige looks skeptical. "That was a stretch on Waverly's part."

"So back to the topic at hand." Fran taps her pen impatiently. "What exactly are you saying, Paige? That you don't want to work with Brogan?"

"I just don't want to be sabotaged and end up on their show looking like an evil backstabbing witch, like the time Mia and Ben set me up on their show after the dating scandal."

"Seriously, Paige, what could they actually do?" I ask her. "If it starts to go sideways, we'll just walk out." I turn to Fran. "Right?"

She nods then takes another sip of water.

"Speaking of walking out ..." Leah holds up her Black-Berry. "Don't you need to get moving, Paige? I have you scheduled for that spot on *ET* this afternoon, remember?"

Paige suddenly stands. "That's right."

"Why don't you let me drive you?" Leah offers. "That way you can get ready on the way over there. And we'll be on time."

"Great idea." Paige reaches in her bag and then tosses me her car keys. "Guess I'll see you at home." And just like that they are gone.

I turn to Fran and study her for a moment.

"*What?*" she says in a slightly cranky tone.

"Are you . . . *okay?*" I use what I hope is a gentle voice.

She shrugs and reaches for her bag. "I'm fine." We both get up, but before we leave the conference room I decide to try again.

"Really, Fran, you don't seem like yourself. Is something bothering you?"

And just like that, like I pressed the wrong button, she starts to crumble. Tears are coming and her hands are shaking and I wonder if I should've kept my big mouth closed. Just the same, I go over and close the blinds on the glass door and ask her to sit back down. "What's wrong?" I ask.

"I didn't want anyone to know — to know — that — " She chokes in a sob.

"Know *what?*" I'm seriously worried now. Something is really wrong.

She looks at me with watery eyes. "My cancer is back."

I blink. "You had cancer?"

"Had . . . and now I have it again."

I reach out and put my hand on her arm. "Oh, Fran."

"I was diagnosed with leukemia in my early thirties. I went through all the treatment and it seemed to have worked. I thought it was gone. And now I have it again."

"I'm so sorry."

She nods as she opens her bag and retrieves a packet of tissues, pulls one out, then wipes her eyes. "I'd been in remission for almost six years. Six years!" She blows her nose. "And five years is considered cured. I really I believed I was cured."

"But you're getting treatment?"

"I started chemo last Friday."

"Does Helen know?"

Fran shakes her head. "No one knows. Today I told Leah I was feeling under the weather so that she could help me out in the meeting."

"I wondered why she was so involved."

"But I don't know if I can hide it for the whole time ... I mean, while I'm doing chemo."

I don't know what to say. I've never known anyone with cancer before.

"Promise me you won't tell anyone," she begs. "I wouldn't have told you, Erin, except you pushed me. And I trust you. Just promise you won't tell."

I nod. "Sure, it's not my place to talk about your personal life to anyone."

"I want to be realistic, and if I can't do my job ... well, I will deal with that when the time comes." She gives me a forced-looking smile. "But my oncologist was quite positive. She says the new drugs are better than before. And she really thinks the chemo will wipe it out again."

"But doesn't chemo kind of wipe a person out too?" I ask. "I mean, how can you expect to work while you're going through treatment?" I don't point out that, even today, she seemed wasted—and she's barely begun her chemo.

"My doctor seemed to think it's a possibility. A lot of people continue with their jobs during treatment. There are some new anti-nausea meds that are supposed to work. I just have to take it easy, get lots of rest, drink water, eat the right foods."

"Oh ..." I'm trying to absorb this. But it just doesn't make sense. I always assumed if a person had cancer, they needed time off ... to get treatment and recover.

"I *have* to work, Erin." Her eyes look desperate now. "Not just financially, because I know insurance will help. But work is my life. And without it, I wouldn't have a chance of surviving this. Can you *understand* that?"

"I guess so." Although I silently question how or why work should be anyone's life. "But, as your friend, I want you to do whatever it takes to get well. That's the important thing. Can you understand *that*?"

Fran smiles. "You're such a good kid, Erin."

I kind of shrug. "Yeah, well . . ."

"Not that you're such a kid. You're mature for your age, and you have a really good head on your shoulders. And I know I can trust you with this."

"Of course."

"And I want to go to the Bahamas with you girls on the upcoming shoot. I've really been looking forward to it. And I don't know what I'd do if I missed out on that . . ." She looks close to tears again. "It would feel like . . . like the cancer had won."

I take in a slow breath. "Then you have to do everything you can to get well." I think about the timeline. "But that gives you less than four weeks. Can you be healthy enough to travel by then?"

"That's my goal."

"And you wouldn't go if your doctor recommended against it?"

She pauses as if considering. "No, of course not. That would be foolish."

"If there's anything I can do to help," I offer, "please, feel free to ask. And I mean that, Fran. I wouldn't say it if I didn't mean it."

"Thanks, Erin. I believe you. And I'll keep that in mind."
She turns to me with a funny grin. "So, how are you at holding a girlfriend's hair back while she worships at the porcelain throne?"

"Huh?"

She chuckles. "You never were a party girl, were you?"

"Not so much."

Now she pats my shoulder. "One of the things I admire about you. You are *so you*." She slowly stands. "I think I need to get home now ... I need to get some rest."

We walk out to the parking lot together and, although Fran is quiet, my brain is buzzing like a mosquito on caffeine. And whether it makes sense or not, I am suddenly feeling very responsible. Not only for Fran's wellbeing and medical treatment, but for how it might impact our show if she's trying to direct us when she really should be home in bed. It's got me very worried and I really think Helen should be informed. And yet I know I have to keep my promise to Fran.

"You take care now," I say as I wait for her to get into her car. "Promise you'll call me if you need anything."

She gives me a weak smile as she puts her window down. "Yeah. And you promise not to worry about me. Okay?"

I nod, knowing that's a promise I might not be able to keep.

"Leah will call you with the details on the interview with Brogan. And I'll see you on Wednesday."

"Get some rest," I say as her window goes up. She makes another weak smile, then drives away. And suddenly I feel like crying. *Poor Fran!* Why is this happening to her? But instead of breaking down right here in the parking lot, I slowly walk over to Paige's car, and as I walk, I pray. I ask God to do a miracle in Fran's life. I'm not exactly sure what kind of a miracle I have in mind; I'm trusting that God knows what's best. But that's what I'm expecting—a real true honest-to-goodness miracle.

DISCUSSION QUESTIONS FOR
SPOTLIGHT

1. In this story, Erin is thrust further into the world of fashion and the drama that surrounds it. How would you handle the pressures of navigating this unfamiliar world and dealing with a high-maintenance sister?
2. Erin goes from being behind the camera to taking a more prominent role on the show. If you were Erin, would you have gladly accepted this role? Or would you have tried harder to stay behind the scenes? Why?
3. If you were Erin, how would you treat Paige in this book? Do you think Erin sacrifices too much for her sister? What do you think of their relationship?
4. Mollie goes through a tough time accepting the prospect of being a single mother and has parents who don't always support her. If you were her friend, what would you have done or said?
5. Paige and Erin make a pact to swear off boys at this point in their careers, yet Paige publicly breaks the pact several times. If you'd made this pact with Paige, what would be your reaction to her behavior?
6. Erin is promised a segment on On the Runway that will deal with body image and eating disorders. If you had a chance, would you do a segment on this topic? If not, what topic would you choose for your segment?
7. Mollie follows the tabloids and Internet gossip while Erin does not. Which person do you most relate to? Why?
8. In the quiz Erin and Paige take on the flight to London, which animal do you think you would be? Why? Do you

have any "peacocks" in your life? How do you tend to treat them?

9. When Erin is on the Shakespeare tour in London, a woman named Mildred claims she would "rather spend money on those nice clothes than the horrid rags" her granddaughter used to wear, even though the "nice clothes" cost a lot. Do you agree with Mildred? Is good fashion worth the high price?

10. Paige craves publicity throughout most of the book, until she realizes there is such a thing as bad publicity, and then panics. If you were Paige, how would you have reacted to all the negative comments?

11. Much of the book focuses on body image and the thinness of models, and at one point both Paige and Erin agree the fashion industry promotes thinness as the best way to look good in clothes. Do you ever feel the pressure to look a certain way? How have you dealt with this pressure?

12. Erin gives a very detailed description of how Barbie would look if she were real. Describe your reaction after reading that segment. Do the facts make you look at Barbie—and our culture—differently?

13. Has this book affected the way you look at the fashion industry? If so, how?

14. What was your reaction to Paige and Dylan's sudden engagement? Do you think Paige is ready to get married? Why do you think Paige is in love with Dylan?

15. Erin discovers she really likes British style. What are your favorite styles or designers? Does anyone influence your own style? If so, why do you think that is?

16. Have your feelings toward Benjamin changed since the first book? How?

On the Runway Series
from Melody Carlson

When Paige and Erin Forrester are offered their own TV show, sisterly bonds are tested as the girls learn that it takes two to keep their once-in-a-lifetime project afloat.

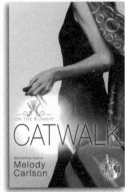

Premiere
Book One

Catwalk
Book Two

Rendezvous
Book Three

Spotlight
Book Four

Glamour
Book Five

Ciao
Book Six

Available in stores and online!

Carter House Girls Series
from Melody Carlson

Mix six teenage girls and one '60s fashion icon (retired, of course) in an old Victorian-era boarding home. Add boys and dating, a little high school angst, and throw in a Kate Spade bag or two ... and you've got the Carter House Girls, Melody Carlson's new chick lit series for young adults!

Mixed Bags

Book One

Stealing Bradford

Book Two

Homecoming Queen

Book Three

Viva Vermont!

Book Four

Lost in Las Vegas

Book Five

New York Debut

Book Six

Spring Breakdown

Book Seven

Last Dance

Book Eight

Available in stores and online!

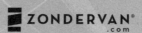

WRONG

Joshua Rabb was defending the wrong man in court. He had a nasty feeling that Franklin Carillo was guilty of unspeakable crimes, and using a legal loophole to free him would be a monstrous perversion of justice.

Rabb was sleeping with the wrong woman. Diana Thurber was the kind of well-bred young lady who seemed too good to be true and too torrid to resist, even though her passion might come with a hidden price tag.

Rabb was on the wrong side of a sadist on the wrong side of the border. At first Agostino Diaz just tried to shake Rabb down and lock him up. Then the corrupt cop took off the kid gloves.

Everything was going wrong for Rabb in a labyrinth of law, lust, and larceny—and he'd have to muster all his smarts as a lawyer and veteran if he didn't want to wind up on the wrong end of a gun. . . .

**"SEX, VIOLENCE, SUSPENSE . . .
PLENTY OF SURPRISES!"**
—*Phoenix Magazine*

"SEX, MURDER, BETRAYAL."
—*Kirkus Reviews*

VERSIONS OF THE TRUTH

RICHARD PARRISH

AN ONYX BOOK

Dedicated to Jerome and Pearl Parrish
and, of course, to Pat

ONYX
Published by the Penguin Group
Penguin Books USA Inc., 375 Hudson Street, New York, New York 10014, U.S.A.
Penguin Books Ltd, 27 Wrights Lane, London W8 5TZ, England
Penguin Books Australia Ltd, Ringwood, Victoria, Australia
Penguin Books Canada Ltd, 10 Alcorn Avenue, Toronto, Ontario, Canada M4V 3B2
Penguin Books (N.Z.) Ltd, 182–190 Wairau Road, Auckland 10, New Zealand
Penguin Books Ltd, Registered Offices: Harmondsworth, Middlesex, England

Published by Onyx, an imprint of Dutton Signet, a division of Penguin Books USA Inc. Previously published in a Dutton edition.
First Onyx Printing, December, 1994
10 9 8 7 6 5 4 3 2 1
Copyright © Richard Parrish, 1994

REGISTERED TRADEMARK—MARCA REGISTRADA

ACKNOWLEDGMENTS

Technical information about cement and concrete was supplied by Chet Miller and Craig Starkey of Arizona Portland Cement in Phoenix. With their help, I have attempted to simplify the bafflingly complex chemistry of concrete.

Three friends of mine have been very good sports, lending their names to me to create three fictional characters who help to give real life to Joshua Rabb's world. My sincere thanks to Pima County Superior Court Judges Robert ("Buck") Buchanan and Bernardo Velasco, and to former Chief Criminal Deputy Pima County Attorney and now Assistant U.S. Attorney W. Randolph Stevens.

"Fear came upon me, and trembling, and all my bones ached. . . . An image was before my eyes, there was silence, and I heard a voice say, 'Shall mortal man be more just than God?'"

—Job 4:14–17

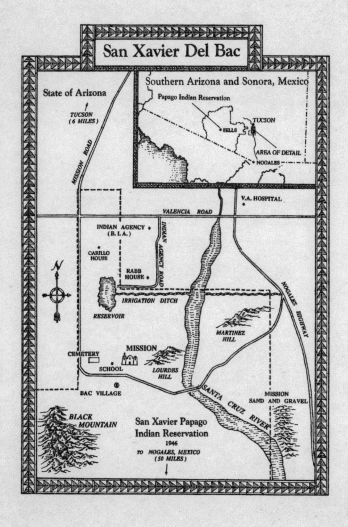

San Xavier Del Bac

Southern Arizona and Sonora, Mexico

Papago Indian Reservation

State of Arizona

TUCSON
(6 MILES)

SELLS • • TUCSON

AREA OF DETAIL

• NOGALES

MISSION ROAD

V.A. HOSPITAL

VALENCIA ROAD

INDIAN AGENCY
(B.I.A.) •

INDIAN AGENCY ROAD

CARILLO
HOUSE •

RABB
HOUSE •

NOGALES HIGHWAY

N

IRRIGATION DITCH

RESERVOIR

MARTINEZ
HILL

CEMETERY

MISSION

SCHOOL

LOURDES
HILL

SANTA CRUZ RIVER

BAC VILLAGE

MISSION
SAND AND GRAVEL

BLACK
MOUNTAIN

San Xavier Papago
Indian Reservation
1946

TO NOGALES, MEXICO
(50 MILES)

CHAPTER
ONE

A red-tailed hawk circled slowly in the topaz sky. It screamed raucously, *kee-ahrrr, kee-ahrrr*. The sound dissipated quickly into the vast open space over the Sonora Desert. Again it screamed, harsh and piercing, and two more hawks darted upward to meet it and join the circling. One of them swooped down suddenly and snatched a pocket gopher in its talons, swept off to a skeletal mesquite tree, and landed on an outstretched dead limb. It held the gopher clenched in one clawed foot and tore at it with its hooked, razor-sharp beak. It chewed ravenously and stared alertly at the people walking slowly along the dirt road thirty yards away. Sunlight glinted off one of the Papago Indian's silver concho hatbands and startled the hawk. It dropped the remnants of the gopher and hurtled away from the dead mesquite tree to join its companions in the endless sky.

There was sepulchral silence in the processional of 350 people walking slowly from San Xavier Mission toward the Papago cemetery a half mile away. Heading the funeral processional, as always, was the old pickup truck that the Papago tribe used as a hearse. Just behind it walked two elderly Indian men carrying six-foot-tall whitewashed wooden

crosses, crafted crudely of rough-hewn two-by-fours
bolted together at the cross joint. Chief Francisco
Romero carried one of them, which was kept in the
mission and carried by the chief of the tribe at all
funerals. The dead man's father carried the second,
which would be the only grave marker.

Joshua, Hanna, and Adam Rabb walked with the
Indians. When they had arrived in Tucson four
months ago on a scorching June day, they had been
shocked by the arid landscape, as though they had
arrived in an inferno. But the monsoon rains fell in
July and August and nurtured the parched Sonora
Desert and transformed its dull sepia hills into a
storm of color—forest-green mesquite trees and
glaucous palo verdes, white-flowered saguaro cactus
and yucca with cadmium-yellow blooms and cholla
and prickly pear with gleaming amethyst and vermil-
ion clusters of waxy blossoms. It was October now,
cool, even pleasant. The desert around the Franciscan Mission of San Xavier Del Bac, six miles south
of Tucson on the Papago Indian Reservation, was
covered with dense wild grasses resembling coyote
fur. The flat lands around the Santa Cruz River
were flooded by wildflowers. The colors melded like
a Monet painting of an Argenteuil field in spring,
blurry and radiant and beautiful. But today the
beauty went unseen.

Tears fell from Hanna Rabb's gray-hyacinth eyes
and streamed down her cheeks. Her long brown hair
glowed reddish in the sun. She was dressed, as were
virtually all of the Indians, in a multicolored cowboy
shirt, faded Levis, and dusty cowboy boots of ser-
viceable harness leather. Just ten days ago everything had been so much better. She'd celebrated her

fifteenth birthday, surrounded by her Indian friends from the Reservation as well as her new friends from her tenth-grade class at Tucson High School. That same afternoon, her father had received a letter from the Arizona Bar Association that he had passed the bar examination and would be admitted to the practice of law the following Monday at the County Courthouse at ten o'clock in the morning. Of course, he had practiced for ten years in New York City, but that didn't seem to count. He still had to pass the Arizona Bar. Hanna and Adam had gone with him to the swearing-in by Judge Fran Rooks, who didn't seem to like daddy for some reason. Then daddy had taken them to McClellan's for ice cream. But the last ten days had made a difference. No one was happy now. Samuel Santos wasn't supposed to die. The doctor had told them that he was getting better. And then he died, just like that. . . . It frightened Hanna. She held Magdalena's hand tightly.

Magdalena Antone had been in tears since Samuel's skull had been fractured by an assailant nearly three months ago. But now she was cried out and her tears were gone. Sam's attacker had been killed in the middle of August, and Sam's soul was now free to ascend to his Father's open arms.

Magdalena's lovely chocolate face and obsidian eyes showed the ravages of months of grieving. Sitting by Samuel's hospital bed waiting for him to awaken from the coma, she had slowly come to grips with the inescapable fact that he would never awake again in this world. Father Boniface from the Mission had come to Samuel's bedside and administered last rites just two days ago, late at night, in the murky darkness of the hospital room, which was eerily illuminated only by an anemic night-light plugged into a wall socket. And then Magdalena had gone into the hospital chapel with the priest, who had taken her confession in the tenebrous stillness. She was pregnant with Sam's child. What would she do? She could not have Sam's child, because a bastard could not be baptised into the Church, and its eternal soul would be in jeopardy.

Father Boniface's eyes had filled with tears and he rubbed them hard with his fists. He looked sorrowfully at her. He had no answers. He made the sign of the cross and told her to say ten Hail Marys and perform an act of contrition. It would cleanse *her* soul. But what about the new life in her womb? There was no absolution for *it*.

"Could you marry us, Father?" she had murmured.

The priest had shaken his head glumly. "It's against canon law. Someone in a coma cannot enter into the sacrament of marriage." So he had refused to join them together as husband and wife, refused to give the baby legitimate parents. Father Boniface's eyes twitched and his cheeks sagged, making him look much older than his fifty years. But what was he to do? Was he to abrogate a thousand years of papal dicta for the sake of one wretched Papago girl who had sinned? It was not in his power.

For yet another day, Magdalena had sat by Samuel's side, holding his motionless hand, watching as his breathing slowed. Then it stopped and his body grew rigid. The color drained quickly from his lips, leaving them an ugly pale purple. She rang for the nurse and rose up slowly, crossed herself, and left the room.

Now she was clinging to Hanna Rabb's hand, walking behind the pickup truck that carried Samuel's body. Magdalena was the Rabbs' "acculturation" girl. She had lived with the family for four months now, ever since Joshua Rabb had brought his family here from Brooklyn and become the part-time legal officer for the Bureau of Indian Affairs as well as the head of the local Federal Office of Land Management. All of the employees of the Bureau of Indian Affairs were required to house a girl from the Reservation. She acted as the family servant, and—as the theory went—would thus be acculturated to the white man's ways. But she didn't need much acculturating, since she had studied for two years at the University of Arizona in Tucson and had lived there with white girls in a dormitory. Now she spent long hours with Joshua and Hanna and Adam, teaching them Papago customs and history and the history of the Sonora Mexicans with whom the Papagos had for centuries been intimately entwined.

Joshua was not using his cane today. He had lost four toes of his left foot to frostbite a little less than two years ago in the Battle of the Bulge, but he concentrated on walking without a limp. He still had his big toe, and it gave him balance. The left sleeve of his white dress shirt was pinned to the yoke of the shirt. He didn't like wearing his mechanical arm when he had to walk long distances. It made his left shoulder ache. His face was drawn, and his usually brilliant blue eyes were dulled with sadness. He was taller than most of the hundreds

of Papago Indians in the funeral processional, and
his height was accentuated because he was walking
with his eleven-year-old son, Adam.

Adam had grown a little during the summer, and
now he was a couple of inches taller than Jimmy
Hendly, walking next to him. Jimmy was cute, with
shaggy blond curls and an impish smile, and he
would probably grow up looking like his father
Edgar, short and overweight. Adam already resembled Joshua, tall and slender with a rich shock of
brown hair and sparkling blue eyes the color of the
wild penstemon that grew all over Black Mountain,
a hundred yards to their left. Adam and Jimmy held
back their tears, sniffling repeatedly. Real men don't
cry, Edgar had told them. Joshua told Adam the
opposite, that real men cry sometimes. Adam didn't
know whom to believe. But Jimmy wasn't crying,
although he looked very sad. So Adam resolved that
he wouldn't cry either.

The superintendent of the Bureau of Indian Affairs, Edgar Hendly, and his wife Frances and their
son Jimmy usually skipped Indian funerals. But this
one was different. It was for Samuel Santos, Magdalena's boyfriend, and Magdalena was the Rabbs' acculturation girl. Even more important, Magdalena
was Macario Antone's granddaughter. Macario had
been chief of the Papago tribe until he retired just
over a year ago. Magdalena must be twenty-two or
-three years old now—Edgar couldn't remember.
She was as pretty as a picture. So this wasn't just
any funeral for a run-of-the-mill Papago.

As usual, Edgar was dressed in a rumpled gray
wool suit and white dress shirt buttoned tightly
around his thick neck. He was short and fat. His

florid face perspired heavily despite the fact that it was only eighty degrees. He had an oddly effeminate mannerism of always smoothing a few wisps of gray hair over his sweat-glistening bald pate, like a vain actress nervously adjusting her coiffure with fluttering fingers.

The 350 people in the funeral processional scuffed up puffs of dust like Indian smoke signals on the unpaved rutted road. Lupine and wild Mexican primrose lined the sides of the road. They were of a robin's-egg blue so delicate and translucent that they matched the pellucid sky. The processional entered the front gate of the cemetery, which was enclosed by barbed wire, and walked past rows of mounded graves marked by whitewashed wooden crosses, faded by the unpitying sun and turned gray by time. The Mission bell rang mournfully in a dirgelike rhythm. The graveside ceremony was short and simple. Samuel Santos was laid to rest wrapped in a gray and black hand-woven rug, surrounded by his clothing and books and other possessions he would need in the world to come. The six-foot cross carried by his father was pounded into the dirt at the head of the grave as its marker. "Samuel Santos, 8/20/20 – 10/14/46" was hand-painted in black on the cross stave. Father Boniface sprinkled the grave with holy water, and Indian diggers began shoveling dirt over the body. The mourners walked silently away.

▼▲▼

Two hours later, Joshua sat absorbed in thought in his overstuffed armchair. Finally he could prac-

tice law again. As a member of the Arizona Bar, he
no longer needed a judge's dispensation to try law-
suits. Now he could make money to supplement the
measly $2.13 an hour he made with the BIA and
OLM. Of course, the job had been very interesting
so far—eventful, to say the least—and it also provided him a rent-free house. He looked around the
dingy plastered walls of the tiny adobe house and
grimaced.

"Something wrong, Dad?" Hanna asked. She was
looking at him with concern.

Joshua stirred himself from his reverie and gave
her a reassuring smile. "No, honey, just this day."

Hanna frowned and nodded. She was sitting on
the floor in front of the big radio, and Adam and
Magdalena were next to her in their usual spots.
The radio was on low, playing some big band music
from New York or Atlantic City. Macario and Ernestina Antone, Magdalena's grandparents, sat on
the threadbare couch. Macario was dozing, his straw
cowboy hat pulled low over his eyes. He was sev-
enty-six years old and had been chief of the tribe
until a little over a year ago, when the Japanese
surrendered to MacArthur on the battleship *Mis-
souri*. As the men had trickled back to the Reservation after the war, Macario knew that it was time
to turn over the tribe to a younger man.

He let out a loud snore, and Ernestina gouged
him in the ribs with her elbow. He snapped awake
and rubbed his russet leathery jowls with his hand.

"Come, we go," he said to his wife. He stood up
from the couch slowly and arthritically and nodded
to Joshua.

Magdalena called out something in Papago. Her

grandfather responded with a few staccato grunts, and he and his wife left the house.

Joshua sat silently in the armchair and pulled absently at the tuft of batting sticking through the worn tan burlap upholstery. He stared at the carved wooden harp that covered the brown mesh fabric of the radio speaker.

"I'm going over to Jimmy's," Adam said. Joshua nodded, and Adam left through the back door.

"Magdalena and I are going to take a walk down to the reservoir," Hanna said. "It's too hot in here." She looked hard at her father. "You sure you're okay?"

"Yes, honey, I'm sure," Joshua said absently.

"What are you going to do? Just sit here all day?"

"Quit worrying about me, honey. I'm okay. I'm just thinking. I've got to go back to my office"—he glanced at his watch—"and I'm just a little preoccupied. Don't worry." He gave her a reassuring smile.

She leaned over and kissed him on the cheek. "Okay, Daddy, we'll be back by five-thirty or six."

Hanna and Magdalena left through the front door. Joshua remained in his chair, motionless and pensive.

▼▲▼

Early that afternoon, Joshua sat in his office in the BIA looking over the construction contract for the repair of the highway and a box culvert for Coyote Creek on the road to Sells on the Big Reservation. Everything seemed legally proper, and he signed it as legal officer for the BIA. Martinez Concrete and Asphalt Company had supplied the low bid, lower by $6,000 than its nearest competitor, and the bid had been approved by Edgar Hendly and Francisco Romero, chief of the Papago tribe.

Edgar came into Joshua's office looking frightened. His brown cow eyes were wide open and he was breathing quickly and wheezily.

"Three Indians are dead down the river about four miles."

Joshua looked up and studied Edgar. "Murdered?"

"Dunno yet. Just got a call from Father Boniface at the mission. One a the three is a old lady named Rodriguez. She was a regular at the masses. When she didn't show up for a week one a the nuns went down to see her. Just this morning after Samuel's funeral. There are two men dead with her. I called the FBI and the Indin Police in Sells. FBI has a new special agent named Collins. He'll meet us over there."

They drove down the Nogales Highway to where it crossed over the Santa Cruz River on an old wooden bridge. Then they turned west on a rutted dirt cart path that wound for a mile through heavy thickets of creosote bushes and desert broom and rabbitbrush. They drove slowly past a cotton field that had just been picked almost clean. There were about a dozen Papagos going through the waist-high plants gleaning the leftover white fluff into burlap sacks. They saw a nun in a full habit and broad white wimple standing in front of a tumbledown wooden shack with a tar-paper roof. Edgar pulled into the yard in front of her. Cackling chickens scattered in all directions.

"Hello, Sister Louise," Edgar said, getting out of his car.

The nun's face was pinched and pale, and her voice came out thinly. "I've never seen such a thing before, Mr. Hendly. Three of them just lying on the floor, all puffed up and bloated and foam coming from their mouths. And the stink . . ." She put her hand to her mouth and looked away.

"You gonna be sick, Sister?" Edgar asked.

She breathed deeply and put her hand down stiffly by her side. "I'll be all right."

Joshua and Edgar walked inside the small one-room shack. The odor of the decomposing bodies was cloying, and Joshua took the handkerchief out of the breast pocket of his gray sharkskin suit and held it over his nose. It didn't help much. He breathed as shallowly as he could.

One of the corpses was an old woman. Another was an old man. The last was a middle-aged man. They were fully clothed. One was lying on the floor next a rickety card table with a cardboard top and thin tubular folding legs. The two others were lying on mattresses on the floor. On the table were the remnants of a meal: three dishes of dried-up beans and rice and a bowl of shriveled flour tortillas.

Joshua heard footsteps behind him. He turned and a man in a seersucker suit came up to him. He was about Joshua's age, shorter than Joshua and a little bit stout. He wore a baggy seersucker suit and had a blond butch haircut and soft brown eyes in a round, boyish face. He extended his hand toward Joshua.

"Hello, Mr. Rabb. I'm Roy Collins, the new Special Agent here."

Joshua shook his hand. "Nice to meet you. Call me Joshua."

Edgar stared at the bodies and shook his head. "Way bodies been turnin up on the Res lately, best we open our own funeral parlor. 'Pears to be a growth industry."

"Has anyone touched the bodies?" the FBI agent asked.

"We haven't," Joshua said, "and I doubt the nun did."

Collins took a small jar of Vicks out of his baggy coat pocket and dabbed a little gob of it directly under his nose. He offered the jar to Joshua. "Helps some," he said.

Joshua put some on his upper lip and handed the jar to Edgar.

"I got a better idea," Edgar said. "I'll just wait outside for you boys. Too many cooks and all that." He left the house.

Joshua handed the Vicks back to the agent. Collins bent low over the old woman and studied her closely. Then he scrutinized each of the other bodies.

"Well, no signs of violence. Must have been poisoned. We better get an ME out here to check them out, and this food also." He pointed to the table. "You have a medical examiner, don't you?"

"Yes, sure," Joshua said. "Damn good one. Stan Wolfe. I'll go back to the Agency and call him."

"No need. I have a radio in the car. I can call into my office and they'll telephone him."

Joshua nodded. "Okay, I've had about enough. Edgar and I will be back at the Agency if you need us." He shook hands with the FBI agent. Collins stared at the shiny steel prongs of Joshua's mechanical arm emerging from his left coat sleeve.

Edgar was very pensive. The big Chevrolet sedan bounced uncomfortably over the rutted road toward the highway. "You think they're at it again?" He gave Joshua a grim glance.

"I can't imagine it," Joshua said, shaking his head resolutely. "That's all over with the Sand and Gravel Company, I'm sure of it."

"Shit," Edgar muttered. "Cain't go a gott damn week around this place anymore without havin to bury someone. And now *three* of em." He frowned and shook his head slowly.

Could it be the Sand and Gravel Company again? thought Joshua. No, how could it? That was taken care of. Wasn't it? He gritted his teeth and stared out the window, seeing nothing.

▼▲▼

Joshua sat on the porch steps of his house. It was three in the morning and a lovely sixty degrees. A beautiful starry night, silent except for the crickets sawing away somewhere on the porch. A cat had adopted the Rabb family about a month ago. It was skinny and young, gray with big white spots, and it had come to the door meowing pitifully. Hanna had given it a bowl of milk, and the cat knew a good thing when he found it. Adam named it Billy the Cat. It slept all day on the porch, its head up like one of the lions guarding the entrance to the New York Public Library. But at night it came to life and prowled around hunting gophers, rats, and birds.

Billy came up to Joshua and rubbed himself against Joshua's leg. He picked the cat up and hugged him and set him down on his lap, and Billy kneaded Joshua's thigh lovingly with his needle-sharp claws. Joshua put him down beside him, and Billy purred contentedly.

It can't be the Sand and Gravel Company, Joshua thought. That's over. But something crazy is going on again around here. This Reservation is the most dangerous place I've experienced since the war. It attracts death.

Penny couldn't take it. Who can blame her? I don't. But I miss her. Doesn't love conquer all? Apparently not. Damn, if only she'd have told me she was leaving, I would have been able to persuade her to stay. We would have made love until she couldn't walk anymore. The thought of her made him hard and he touched himself. He had on no shirt and was wearing only the thin cotton athletic shorts he wore as pajamas. The front of them bulged.

He heard footsteps coming and stood up abruptly.

"Well, I see you ain't doin no better sleepin than I was," Edgar Hendly drawled. "I saw your porch light on, figured you'd be out here."

Edgar saw the bulge in Joshua's shorts. "Whattaya gonna do, fuck the cat?"

"I already did," Joshua said, sitting down and feeling relieved. "That's why he's purring so happily."

Edgar chuckled. "You oughta put that weapon to good use with that gal up on Mount Lemmon. You two gonna get married?"

Joshua shrugged his shoulders. "She's gone back to New Jersey."

Edgar shook his head and grimaced. "Yep, I reckon she had her fill a good old Tucson this summer. Cain't rightly blame her none." He sat down on the porch steps next to Joshua.

"Hey, I ever tell ya 'bout the priest and the cat?" he asked, his voice serious.

Joshua shook his head.

"Well, this priest is hearin confessions and a guy says to him, 'Father, Father, I have sinned before Thee. I screwed a cat and enjoyed it.' So the priest says to hisself, 'Jesus, this guy's some kinda pervert,' and he tells him to say a hundred Hail Marys and not to flog his pecker for a month and to think pure thoughts. So the priest goes home, and he's real lonely as usual, and he gets to lookin at his cat lyin on the couch. And he thinks to hisself, well, maybe it ain't so bad. So he strips down and grabs the cat by the hind legs and tries to stick it in, and the cat scratches the hell outta him. I mean practically rips the skin off his arms and legs. And the priest finally has to let go so he can go the hospital emergency room and get a hundred and fifty stitches all over his body."

Edgar paused and rubbed his arms and legs and grimaced with the priest's pain. Joshua was smiling broadly.

"So the priest is in the confessional a month later, and in comes the same guy and says, 'Father, Father, I have sinned before Thee. I screwed the cat again and I really enjoyed it.' So the priest cain't help hisself, he's gotta find out why the guy didn't get clawed to ribbons. So he says to him, 'Just how did you accomplish it, my son?' And the guy says, 'Well, I took a shoe box and cut three holes in it and stuck the cat's rear legs through the two outer holes and held em tight and screwed it through the center hole.' So the priest thinks for a minute and

says, 'For your penance, my son, I want you to do
it without the box.' "

Edgar laughed so hard that tears trickled down
his cheeks. Joshua also laughed appreciatively.

Edgar's face turned grave. "Whattaya reckon is
goin on around here?"

Joshua shook his head. "I can't figure it. Maybe
food poisoning. There were no injuries found on
the corpses."

Edgar breathed deeply. "I hope to God that's all
it is. I can deal with a salmonella germ. But the
gott damn murders, I cain't deal with much more
a them."

Joshua nodded.

"Well, have a good time with yer cat," Edgar said,
standing up heavily. "Reckon I'll take another shot
at gettin some shut-eye. Gotta go to work in the
mornin." He walked away into the darkness.

Joshua stood up slowly and went into the house.

CHAPTER
TWO

Erma Carillo was a short, scrawny woman. Her pallid parchment skin hung loosely and jiggled from her arms and cheeks and neck. She had long shiny strawberry-blonde hair tied in a loose ponytail. She had cupid's-bow lips and high cheekbones and wide-set pale gray eyes. She must have been beautiful once, Joshua thought. She came into the living room of the Rabb house walking with the help of two long metal canes. She was in obvious pain. She slowly descended to the edge of the couch and teetered there breathlessly, holding both canes for support.

"Thank you very much for seeing me, Mr. Rabb. I hear you're an excellent lawyer. You don't think the Papagos are just a bunch of animals like most white men do."

"That's true," Joshua said. "But you don't look Papago."

"I'm not. My husband is. He was born on the Big Reservation, near Topawa."

Joshua nodded.

"You did real good for Chief Antone's grandson," she said. "We need your help."

She had a young torch singer's voice, throaty and rich, emerging from a shriveled throat and emaciated face. It seemed almost as though her voice were being thrown by a ventriloquist into a repulsive dummy. To complete the incongruous picture, she was wearing a yellow sundress with a string-tie top tied behind her neck.

"What can I do for you, Mrs. Carillo?"

"My husband Franklin was arrested a few weeks ago, and I'd like to hire you to represent him."

Joshua put the name together with the newspaper stories he had read recently.

"You mean the man that was arrested for the rape and the murders?"

"He didn't do it, Mr. Rabb, not my Franklin. My Franklin is a wonderful man."

Joshua nodded and kept his face expressionless. He had learned over the last ten years of law practice not to register shock or disgust or disbelief to potential clients. They would just go somewhere else and hire a lawyer who wore an eager, interested look. You can't make a living as a lawyer if all your potential clients walk out the door with their wallets still in their pockets.

"Well, Mrs. Carillo, one of the newspaper stories I read said he was positively identified by the first woman and that someone picked him out of a lineup as being around the laundry room the night the second woman and the baby were kidnapped and murdered."

"I know what they're saying, Mr. Rabb, but it's just not true. Franklin was with me the night that poor woman was murdered. And I know he didn't rape that first girl. He doesn't have to get sex anywhere else, Mr. Rabb, he has me, and we're very good in bed."

Joshua's eyebrows must have raised just a bit, because she immediately shook her head and smiled and began to cajole him like a child.

"Now I can see you don't believe me, Mr. Rabb, but that's just because you probably don't know about muscular dystrophy. I'm only twenty-nine years old, and my arms and legs are becoming hard to control, but there's nothing wrong with my sex parts. I still make Franklin very happy, and frequently, too."

Joshua didn't know quite what to say. At times like this it was always best to exude your most scholarly, detached air.

"Well, Mrs. Carillo, I'm certainly not knowledgeable enough about your relationship with your husband to make any particular judgments. But I'm sure you're aware that rape is not a sex act by men desiring sex, it's a crime of violence. It really has nothing to do with a man's normal sexual desires."

"Listen, Mr. Rabb." Her voice became imploring. "I don't know about all that psychological stuff. All I know is Franklin Carillo. We've been married nine years. He works hard, makes a good living, and he loves me. When I was diagnosed with this disease five years ago, he stood by me. A lot of men would have snuck out the kitchen door and kept on walking. But Franklin stayed. I'll be dead in maybe three, four, five years. Franklin will have the house and twenty-five thousand dollars life insurance on me. But right now, while I still have the strength to love him, I need him with me, not rotting away in a jail cell."

Tears began streaming from her eyes into the numerous tiny gullies of the shriveled skin on her face and dripped off her flaccid chin. She pulled her withered arms out of the canes and laid the canes against the arm of the couch. She reached into her purse and took out an envelope. Her fingers quavered and she moved very slowly. She pulled a check out of the envelope and handed it to Joshua.

"I took a loan on all the cash value of the life insurance, Mr. Rabb. Will you be Franklin's lawyer? Do you believe what I say about Franklin?"

Joshua took the check. It was a Hartford Insurance Company check made out to Erma Carillo in the sum of $2,732 and endorsed by her on the back. What's that great line from *The Maltese Falcon*, Joshua thought inanely. Miss Wonderly hires Sam Spade to find her runaway kid sister and tells him a cock-and-bull story about the innocent sister being seduced by an evil married man. She pays Spade $200. Sam's partner is murdered doing the job, and Sam tracks down Miss Wonderly and demands the truth. She admits to him that what she had told him was just a story. Whereupon Sam says, "Oh, that. Well, we didn't exactly believe your story. We believed your two hundred dollars." Joshua knew exactly what Sam Spade was talking about.

"Of course I'll represent your husband, Mrs. Carillo. I'll go see him today."

"Oh, thank you, thank you, Mr. Rabb. You'll discover that Franklin couldn't have done those terrible things."

She stood up slowly, grimacing, grunting, and propped herself on the two canes. "Can you get him out on bail?"

"Probably not," Joshua said, rising from his armchair and coming to the couch to help her up. She put her hand on his mechanical arm, looked suddenly shocked, and pulled it quickly away. She struggled to her feet.

"It's a first-degree murder case," Joshua said, "and the judge is entitled to hold him without bail. I probably can't get bail set. And even if I did, it would be a hundred thousand dollars or something crazy like that. You don't have a hundred thousand dollars, do you?" He heard himself ask the question, and he detected eagerness in his voice that made him feel a little guilty. She shook her head sadly. He walked her to the door. She clumped awkwardly onto the porch and down the steps to a shiny black Ford roadster. An old woman wearing a flowery bonnet was sitting in the driver's seat reading a *Life* magazine.

▼▲▼

The Pima County Men's Jail was a place that instilled in you the intense desire never to get thrown into jail. You walked up a barbed-wire-enclosed ramp and through two steel doors to enter a large room with a shiny, heavily waxed green linoleum floor, the corners of which were filled with cobwebs and inches of crud where the round floor buffer couldn't reach and no one had cared enough for decades to bend over and clean them. Three sheriff's deputies sat in a steel-mesh-enclosed booth and operated the various doors. On the right was a large cell door that led into two hallways. In the hallway on the left was a small cubicle for lawyers to interview their clients.

Joshua sat uncomfortably in the interview room. It was six feet square and had two folding metal chairs on a bare gray cement floor. A single dim light bulb burned behind wire mesh in the nine-foot ceiling. There was no door on the cubicle, one thing for which Joshua was grateful. It was claustrophobic enough in here without a closed door.

Franklin Carillo shuffled into the cubicle. He was handcuffed and footcuffed. Joshua shook his hand. He wore jail issue: a white T-shirt, green surgical pants, and white rubber thongs. He was one of the handsomest men Joshua had ever seen, tall, six foot one or two, slender, with black curly hair and frightened ebony eyes. Joshua felt himself relaxing. He was no rapist-murderer.

"Hello, Franklin. Your wife came to see me and asked me to represent you. I'm Joshua Rabb."

The prisoner sat uneasily across from Joshua. "Yeah, she told me she was going to try to hire a real lawyer. That other guy they appointed to advise me hasn't been out to see me but a couple times."

"Well, I'm here to talk about your case, see what I can do for you. Why don't you tell me where you were on September 11 at about three in the afternoon, when the first girl was raped."

"I didn't rape her, Mr. Rabb," Carillo said pathetically, and his handsome eyes twitched. "I swear to you I didn't rape her."

"I believe you, Frank. Just tell me where you were and whether there's anyone who can help prove it." Joshua patted him on the knee with a brotherly gesture.

The prisoner slumped into his chair, and his voice softened. "I work for my mother-in-law. She's a real estate agent. She mostly deals with the Mexicans in South Tucson. She owns a few small rental houses, just junk on the south side. I'm the handyman/rent collector. So on that day, it was a Wednesday I think, well, maybe a Thursday, well anyway, I had been way down on Nogales Highway fixing a toilet in a house my mother-in-law has there, and I finished about two o'clock or so and was driving back to the real estate office. It's over on Ajo Highway near Mission. So just after the light on Ajo, there's this really pretty girl hitchhiking, so I stopped and gave her a lift. She was wearing a kind of halter top, you know, tied by a knot in the middle, and she's got a great pair of jugs, and she says she's going over to her boyfriend's house down by the University. So I says, well, why are you fooling with schoolboys, you know, a girl like you can find herself a man, you know. And she giggles real cute, and I know I can score with her. So I do a U-turn and head back out toward the Santa Cruz River."

"She did want to go with you, didn't she?"

"Yeah, sure, man, what do you think?" Carillo looked imploringly at Joshua.

You always want to believe your own client, Joshua thought, but experience teaches you differently. Anybody in jail will lie to get out. Yet there was something about Franklin Carillo that drew Joshua to him and made him believe that Carillo was telling the truth.

"Okay, go on with the story," Joshua said.

"Well, she was acting like she wanted out, you know, grabbed the door handle, but I tapped her a little in the face. Then she settled down." He smiled at the apparently pleasant memory.

"So anyway, we go way out past the riverbed into the desert, you know, and I pull off. And she's putting out this phony bullshit act, you know, some tears and shit like that. But I know better, I can see through all that bullshit. So I unbutton my Levis and pull them down and give her a good look at heaven, you know what I mean, and then I undress her and she goes down on me, but I don't know, I just can't come for some damn reason, and she was sucking me like a pro, you know what I mean, so then she sat on me for a while, but it still wasn't happening, and then she starts crying, you know, and she says all she wants to do is go home and all that kind of shit, so I had a Ruger .44 Magnum single-action under the seat of my truck, you know, and I pulled it out and showed it to her and I pushed her head out the passenger window and shot the gun off by her ear. And that quieted her down a good bit, you know, and she jacked me off—I guess the gun kind of turned her on or something— kind of did me too, you know. And then I just drove her by the University and dropped her off. She wanted to know how to get hold of me 'cause she wanted to see me again, so I gave her my name and phone number. Now that's no rape, huh, Mr. Rabb?" He looked hopefully at Joshua.

Joshua was speechless.

"Then this other thing that happened, Mr. Rabb, you know, the mother and baby they say I murdered? Well, I didn't murder them. You can bet your ass on that."

Joshua's voice came out a little thin, distant, as though he were listening to someone else speak. "That was a week later, right?"

"Right."

"Weren't you arrested on the first one?" Joshua tried to make his voice sound normal, conversational.

"Nope!" Carillo shook his head resolutely. "Couple of detectives came over to the house to talk to me that night, and they had the piece of notepaper I gave her with my name and number. Then they just left, said they were going to turn it over to the County Attorney's Office. Said any guy who rapes a girl don't give her his name and phone number, you know."

"Did they ask you about the gunshot?"

"Yeah, sure. But I told them it was bullshit. And it was, you know. I didn't do it to hurt her or nothing. But anyway, I told them it was a lie." He looked imploringly at Joshua. "It ain't no rape when you give them your phone number, huh, Mr. Rabb?"

"Wouldn't seem to be," Joshua murmured.

"Then a week later or so, I went over to some new duplexes on Valencia near where I live. They got a big laundry room with a couple of new machines—you know, the kind that don't need no wringers—and I sometimes do our laundry there. You know, you saw my wife, she don't do so good on housework no more. So it was real late, and I had my stuff in a washer, and I see this woman go in there, it was probably about midnight and I was sitting by a palm tree having a cigarette, and she leaves again and about a half hour later she comes back down. I went into the laundry room, 'cause my clothes were about washed, but hers weren't quite done, and she was just sitting there in a chair and had her bathrobe open and a tiny little baby breast-feeding. So she turns away from me, you know, so I wouldn't see her tits. So I says to her, you know, how my wife and I sure would love to have a little baby of our own and all, and how sweet it was to see a mother nursing, you know, and she gets a little more talkative and says she just had a fight with her husband and so she's down here doing the laundry instead of being in bed, and it served him right. And she looked me over, kind of, you know how they do that, and I could see that she was interested and I asked her would she like to go for a ride, and she said no, so I took her baby away from her and she started to scream and I told her if she screamed I'd drop her baby on his head. But I wouldn't have done that, Mr. Rabb, I mean I'm not a bad guy, you know, so anyway she starts crying and saying everything's okay, just don't hurt her baby, so I give the baby back to her and take her out and put them in my truck. We drove a couple miles down to the wash and I pulled onto the bank there about a mile up, and I laid the baby on the floor, and I tell the mama to get undressed. She has a great body, I mean really something, and I sit her up on me, but damned if I can come, you know, hard as I try, and after a while she said I was so big I made her sore and she needs to rest, so we both laid back and took it easy, and I'll be damned if I don't fall asleep, would you believe it, and I don't know how long later I woke up, couldn't have been more'n a couple of minutes I guess, and she ain't in the truck anymore, and I start up the truck and turn it around and start down the bank to look for her and bang, I hit something, and I threw the truck in reverse and turned on the lights and I saw her and the baby lying sprawled on the ground and I knew I'd hit them by accident, and she sits up and is rubbing her legs and crying and all, and I got real scared, you know, 'cause if anybody thought I did it on purpose they'd arrest me, you know, and she'd be telling everyone that she was raped and all, 'cause she wouldn't want her husband to know she was out cattin' around, looking for it, so I backed up the truck to talk to her and it was so damn dark I didn't see her and I must've run over her by accident, but I didn't do nothing to the baby, and I got the hell out of there fast. I went back and got my laundry, and some old cunt was walking a poodle smoking a cigarette and says she saw me. A day or two before they arrested me, I saw the old bitch and the two detectives who had come to see me the week before, and they followed me around and I pretended not to see them. Then the day they arrested me, they searched my bedroom closet and found the Ruger. But I didn't do nothing so terrible. I gotta get outta here and go home and take care of my wife, Mr. Rabb. She's real sick."

Franklin Carillo's voice trailed off, and he looked away from the wide-eyed, shocked stare of his lawyer.

Joshua stood up and felt a little unsteady. He thought he was going to vomit and breathed deeply to stave off the hollow sickness gnawing at his stomach. He walked out of the cubicle and banged on the cell door to get back into the lobby. A deputy in the enclosed booth pressed a button and the door rattled open on its tracks.

Joshua went into the men's room in the entry area. He stepped to the urinal and started to unzip his pants, but suddenly stopped, holding his hand in front of him. How could he touch himself with a hand that had touched Franklin Carillo? He went to the wash basin and shook the handle on the soap container. It was empty. He held his hand under the water. He banged on the empty soap container.

Nothing. He smashed it with his fist. It fell to the floor with a clatter.

"Goddamn you!" he screamed at the soap container. "Goddamn you incompetent assholes can't fill a shitty little container with soap!"

He swung the door open and lurched out of the bathroom. The three deputies in the booth were already standing, staring at him.

"Can't you bastards put some soap in the bathroom? I gotta wash my goddamn hand!"

The deputies looked quizzically at each other. Then one of them walked to the back of the booth and bent over and picked up a bar of Boraxo. The electrically controlled steel sliding door ground open, and he brought the soap to Joshua.

"Take it easy, pal," he said, handing Joshua the Boraxo. "This'll take care of you."

Joshua went back into the bathroom and scrubbed his hand for five minutes, until all of his cuticles were bleeding.

▼▲▼

He returned home from the jail at a little after six. He parked the wheezing old De Soto in front of the rickety wooden porch steps and wondered for an instant what a new Ford roadster would cost, like the one Erma Carillo's mother was driving this afternoon. Two thousand dollars, twenty-five hundred? He walked into the house.

Hanna and Adam were at their usual places on the floor in front of the radio.

"Where's Magdalena?" Joshua asked.

"She went over to the Reservation to spend the

night with her grandparents," Hanna said. "She's worried about Chief Macario."

"Yeah, he looked real tired." Joshua wrinkled his brow. "Well, what do you say to eating dinner over at the Dixie tonight? That way nobody will have to cook or do dishes."

Adam nodded vigorously and his face brightened.

"Sure," Hanna said. She stared at her father's hand. "Gee, what happened?"

Joshua glanced at his still-bleeding cuticles, then thrust his hand nonchalantly into his pants pocket. "Had to change a tire. Kind of hard with just one hand. Scraped it real bad."

They got into the DeSoto. It took several turns of the key to start the ten-year-old car, and it wheezed jerkily down Indian Agency Road.

"I think we need a new car," Joshua said.

"Yeah, me too," Hanna said. She turned toward him and studied his profile. "You get the new case today?"

Joshua nodded. He glanced at his daughter and allowed a small smile.

"Gee, that's great, Daddy," she said. Adam was sitting in the back seat staring out the side window, not listening.

"What kind of case?" Hanna asked.

"It's a murder, a Papago Indian named Franklin Carillo."

Hanna thought for a moment. Then she squinted at her father and screwed up her face. "Isn't that the guy they arrested for murdering the mother and her baby?"

Joshua nodded.

"How can you defend an animal like that? It isn't right."

"I'm a lawyer, honey. That's what I do for a living."

"But gee, Dad, not somebody like that. He deserves to be shot."

"How do you know he's guilty? What gives you the right to decide?" He chided her gently.

"*Daa-aad,* the paper says he did it, and everybody knows he did."

"The paper said that Ignacio Antone killed Sister Martha, but we didn't believe it, did we?"

She shrugged and pondered that for a moment. "Did Carillo tell you he did it?"

Joshua pursed his lips and breathed deeply. "That's privileged information, honey. You know I can't talk about what my clients tell me."

"Aw, come on, Daddy, that's a crummy excuse. I'm your daughter. I won't tell anybody."

Joshua was tensely silent for a minute. "Yes, he told me he did it."

Hanna stared at her father accusingly. "Well, then why are you defending him?"

"Because that's the way our legal system works. That's what I do for a living."

Hanna looked shocked. "Sounds dishonest to me," she mumbled.

"It's not, honey. It's just my job."

She looked at him a little incredulously. "You mean a guy tells you he murdered a woman and a baby and he gives you money and then you go buy a new car and try to get him off. That's your job?"

Joshua raised his eyebrows and shook his head. "When you put it that way, it sure doesn't sound very noble."

"It sounds pretty shitty to me."

"Honey, I told you not to use that kind of language. It's not nice."

"*Daa-aad*, it isn't very nice to do what you're doing, and I'm not a little girl anymore, I'm fifteen."

Joshua looked tiredly at his daughter and then back at the road. "Okay, let's change the subject. I've had a real shitty day."

She looked at her father and grinned.

They rode in relaxed silence for a few minutes. The sunset to their left was a spectacular orange-red over the jagged crests of the Tucson Mountains. Hanna pulled a letter out of the back pocket of her Levis.

"This came for you today," she said, her voice a little reluctant. She laid it on the seat next to her father.

"Who's it from?" Joshua asked, not paying much attention.

"Mrs. Chesser."

He looked at Hanna and then glanced at the letter. "Where's it postmarked?"

"Matawan, New Jersey," Hanna answered slowly.

Joshua breathed deeply. "Then she really did leave," he murmured.

"I guess," Hanna said quietly. "Sorry, Dad."

"It's not your fault, honey. Just too much happened." His voice trailed off, and he switched on the headlights and concentrated on the darkening road ahead of them.

When Penny hadn't come to the funeral at noon, he had known that something was wrong. But of course it was a school day, and her son Danny was in the second grade at the elementary school in Summerhaven, and maybe she'd had car trouble or

something. But all of that was just wishful thinking.
He realized the truth deep inside. She had really
left. Their last night together, last Saturday night in
her cabin on Mount Lemmon, had been strained,
and she had been cool. It wasn't their lovemaking.
That was always the best. They seemed to have the
perfect fit together. But she was somehow stiff and
very troubled. They didn't talk about it anymore, the
night she'd been arrested back in July, but it obviously preyed on her mind. She had suffered sexual
humiliation and physical abuse from the sheriff, and
there was nothing that could be done to make it
better.

Joshua's mother used to "make it better" when he
was a kid. He'd scrape his knees or cut a finger and
his mother would kiss it and say in Yiddish, *"Ez
zy gezint, kenna hurra,"* and then she'd knock her
knuckles on the closest piece of wood she could
find, and everything was sure to be better.

But when you are thirty-seven years old, and the
injured girl is twenty-eight, and it isn't just a little
wound that you can kiss away, well, it's a whole lot
harder. And it apparently hadn't worked. The evil
eye had won, soured her on this place and its people, and finally took her back to more familiar sur-
roundings, to her parents' home. Maybe they could
make it better.

He felt like crying. He didn't even want to read
the letter, because he already knew what it said. He
gritted his teeth and swallowed hard and kept his
eyes on the road so that Hanna would not see the
pain in them.

CHAPTER
THREE

Edgar was his usual mellifluous, poetic self.

"Y'ever hear of anythin more fuckin outrageous?" He shook his head gravely and looked hard at Joshua, who sat in the armchair in front of Edgar's broad desk in the BIA. "Seven cases a cholera so far because a them Meskins down in Nogales. They been told a hundred times to put in sewers or dig leachin pits, but no, they're too fuckin dumb for any a that, they just pipe the sewage right into the Santa Cruz River so it can get into the underground water table and poison our wells for fifty miles! Helluva thing this, Joshua. Helluva thing."

"You sure that's what caused the deaths?" Joshua asked. Despite the obvious dangers from an epidemic, he felt relieved that it wasn't murder.

"Hell, yes! I got the report from Stan Wolfe just ten minutes ago. He tested two wells down past the Sand and Gravel Company, and they're both contaminated with cholera. No doubt about it. And it can only come from raw sewage. They ain't no other cause for it, Stan said. Hell, I went down to Nogales with him and that FBI man Roy Collins yesterday, after the last two bodies were found in a shack right next to the river, and you could see the turds floatin by right on top a the water. It was downright shitty." Edgar paused long enough for his double entendre to bring forth a tiny grin on Joshua's face. "There's been twenty-six more cases a cholera reported on the Reservation just since noon yesterday. Lucky nobody else died of it yet."

"It's just a matter of time," Joshua said grimly.

"So anyways, here's what we gotta do," Edgar said. "Well, actually it's you gotta do it 'cause it's outta my bailiwick, but you got authority through the Office of Land Management—I checked with Herman Schultz in Washington, D.C.—you gotta negotiate a joint U.S./Mexico sewer system and a sewage treatment plant that'll span the Santa Cruz at the border. It's the only way we're gonna be able to keep our water supply clean."

"That shouldn't be so difficult. As long as our government is willing to pay for the construction, the Mexicans will jump on it."

Edgar snorted sarcastically. "I can see you never worked with no Meskin government officials before." He rolled his eyes. "By the time you're done negotiatin a deal, the sewage system and plant'll cost ten million and you'll need twenty million more for *mordida*."

"What?"

"*Mordida*, baby," Edgar rubbed his thumb and forefinger together. "Bribes."

"Why the hell would we have to bribe anybody to put in sewage treatment? It would benefit the Mexicans as much as us."

" 'Cause them Meskin politicians don't give a hoot in hell about benefitin their people. The only benefit they understand is greenback dollars in their pocket."

"So why don't we just build a plant on the U.S. side of the border?"

"Well, that'd be awful nice if it could be done thataway, but unfortunately most a the Santa Cruz River is underground twenty, thirty, forty feet. So we gotta make sure that a sewage system is put right into Nogales itself to trap waste before it gets to the river. Otherwise, the treatment plant by itself ain't worth a shit." He cracked a smile.

Joshua nodded. "Who am I supposed to talk to first?"

Edgar shrugged. "I 'magine the Office of Land Management gotta publish a solicitation for contracts for the sewage system with preliminary specifications. Then you bring it to the Meskins and tell em we'll fund a sewer system for Nogales. I think they'll get bids from one a their own contractors— you know, the mayor's brother or the governor a Sonora's son-in-law or horseshit like that—and we'll get it done."

"How do I get the specifications?"

"Well, I done thought a that too, Joshua." Edgar smiled broadly, pleased with his command of the situation. "I got Harry Morland comin down from Phoenix. He's the head of the Corps of Engineers office for Arizona. He's gonna bring along a couple of his boys, and they'll go down to Nogales with ya and put together some specifications."

Joshua nodded. "All right. Sounds like you've thought of everything."

Edgar beamed at him.

"How about our water supply?" Joshua asked. "It

all comes out of wells off the Santa Cruz, doesn't it?"

"Yep, sure does," said Edgar. "We gotta boil it. I sent a couple bucks through the Res to pass the word. Don't drink no water that ain't been boiled first."

Joshua nodded. "When will the Corps of Engineers men be here?"

"By noon or thereabouts, I guess," Edgar said. "It'll take a couple days down there. Is Magdalena back with you?"

"Yes. She's doing a lot better."

"Good. Frances will look in on em now and then, make sure everythin's okay." He winked at Joshua. "You'll have a good time down in Nogie. It's a different world." He laughed maliciously.

▼▲▼

The fifty-mile ride to Nogales was pleasant. The highway had just been asphalted all the way to the border, and Harry Morland drove fast. The elevation rose steadily as they passed the Santa Rita Mountains and neared Nogales. With the rise in elevation, they reached the point where the waters of the Santa Cruz were above the ground once again as well as below. The valley along the river became increasingly lush with cottonwood trees and live oaks. On the American side of the border, the little town of Nogales was no more than two square blocks of shops, a granite-block courthouse of territorial vintage, a couple of gas stations, and a Customs House at the border. The river flowed just thirty feet east of the highway here, and they could see the raw sewage and garbage floating in patches of scum on the surface.

Harry Morland had been with the Corps of Engineers for over twenty years and had spent two of them in England and France and Germany rebuilding bridges that had been destroyed first by the Nazis and then by the Americans. He had been reassigned to Phoenix just over a year ago and said that he had never been this far south in Arizona. He was about fifty years old, studious and serious-looking, thin, tall, and almost completely bald.

The other two men were not bureaucratic types like their boss. Ferdie Molina was thirty and had spent three years in the Seabees as a heavy-equipment foreman on Wake Island, Guadalcanal, and Tarawa. He was of average height, a dark and wiry Mexican, and he spoke fluent Spanish, an indispensable asset in Nogales.

Mike O'Leary was twenty-eight years old and had a chemical engineering degree from the University of Arizona in Tucson. He was very good looking, blond and green-eyed, muscularly built, six foot three or four, and 225 pounds, an inch or so taller than Joshua and twenty-five pounds heavier. He had spent two years as a civil affairs officer in the Army, one of them in a small town in southern France that had been Vichy, and another in Naples, Italy. He spoke neither French nor Italian, but he said with feigned regret that his pioneer Arizona family had had the clout to keep him out of a combat assignment. Of course he had wanted to be a paratrooper or in the Rangers, he assured the men in the car with him, but his father's reach was long enough to prevent his frequent combat applications from being honored.

Joshua studied him in the rearview mirror and saw an effete, almost too handsome rich man's son, painfully hungry for the admiration and approbation of the other men.

Mike literally bubbled over with stories about his exploits in the French town, where he had been the senior "Amgot" officer, even though he had only been a captain. "There was this one broad, Nannette, who danced at a little place called 'L'Eglise'— honest to God, it was called 'The Church'—and she was completely bareass nude right on stage, I swear to God, and she puffed on a cigarette with her pussy, I mean stuck the end of the Lucky Strike right up her and puffed and blew out smoke. That was one lucky cigarette! Man, I never saw anything like it in my whole life, and the first time she saw me there, you know, one of the guys had found out about it and I went with him one night, well she took one look at me and fell in love and I didn't spend a night alone from then on. If she was working, she'd line up one of her friends for me, and I swear to God, it's true what they say about them French broads, I mean, man oh man, they can suck the chrome off a tailpipe and still be begging for more. And Nannette always said, 'Michel'—she always called me Mee*shell*—'Michel,' she says, 'you 'ave a *peestol* like a pine log,' " he mimicked her French accent. "And sometimes her and a couple of friends of hers would jump in bed with me and I'd have my dick up one and my tongue up the other."

He laughed happily and slapped his leg. Ferdie

snorted and shook his head in disbelief. Harry Morland just plain shook his head. "Jesus," he muttered under his breath. Joshua watched the landscape rush by, hardly listening.

They crossed the border at two checkpoints. An American border patrolman in a square steel guard shack waved them past without challenging them. A Mexican wearing a filthy tan uniform shirt, sweat-soiled and stained, threadbare Levis, huarachis, and a shiny new-looking black leather belt and holster with a Colt single-action revolver, was standing beside an adobe guard shack fifty feet inside Mexico. He listlessly waved them past.

Nogales, Mexico, didn't look at all like its twin sister on the American side. Here there was nothing but unrelieved squalor. They drove slowly on a narrow dirt road with craters that reminded Joshua of mortar holes. The tourist shops on both sides of the main street, three blocks long, were simple wooden stalls with corrugated tin roofs. Barefoot children sat near the shops. Eight- and nine-year-olds smoked cigarettes. Boys no older than Adam carried wooden shoeshine boxes slung over their shoulders and called out as the car of Americans passed by.

They drove out of downtown Nogales. The hills on both sides of the road were pocked with tiny hovels made of tin and tar paper and flimsy slats from fruit crates. The shacks were brightly painted and looked incongruous against the barren rocky slopes of the hills.

Canal Street was an open sewage ditch that ran from the hills on the west through the center of town, picking up the raw sewage from the rivulets of runoff trickling in front of or beside the houses, collecting at least some of it and depositing it into the Santa Cruz River flowing beside the hills to the east.

"What do you think?" Harry said to Ferdie.

He shrugged. "No worse than the islands. It'll take some piping on the streets where the open ditches are, bring down a grid of pipes to a central collection point, no reason why we can't use Canal Street, put a little bridge over it on the main street here, run an open culvert along the river to the treatment station we put in on the border."

"Why an open culvert?" Joshua asked.

"If you do a closed one, you'll more than double the price. And trucking the preformed conduit down here is practically impossible. You'd bust up half your tubes right on the truck, and you'd need cranes and skilled operators on this end, or you'd lose the rest of the tubes." He shook his head. "The only practical way is an open culvert."

"How about the smell?" Joshua asked.

"Well, they don't seem to mind it now," Harry said. "Anyway, they can treat it, throw some cheap chemicals in it every day. It'll smell a whole lot better than it does now, and it'll cost only a couple of dollars a day."

Harry pulled the car to the side of the road and turned off the engine. He pointed up the hill on the west. "I'd say four lines of horizontal pipe, maybe ten coming down the hill. And on the other side, where there are a lot fewer houses, probably three horizontal and five coming down. We'll have culvert coming down both sides of the river to the plant." He paused a moment and turned to Mike, who was jotting notes on a pad and making calculations with a slide rule. "How much?" Harry asked.

"Well, we'll need about eighty-four thousand feet of eight-inch for the grid on the hills, and about five thousand feet of twelve-inch pipe coming down. The culverts will be maybe four miles on this side, three on the other. There's plenty of surplus eight- and twelve-inch pipe in the Corps' storage center up at Hoover Dam, but the culverts will have to be poured concrete, four-foot radius." He did some calculations on his slide rule. "I'd estimate 2,225,000 cubic yards of concrete." He looked up and smiled at Harry. "It's a damn good time to go into the concrete business, wouldn't you say." He turned back to his slide rule. "At Arizona wholesale price, which is seven sixty-one a yard, the material cost for the concrete culverts over here is about seventeen million dollars."

Joshua raised his eyebrows. Somebody could get phenomenally rich off this contract.

Harry Morland turned to Ferdie. "How many man-hours do you estimate?"

Ferdie pondered it a moment. "We have to put a hundred men on this side, sixty on the other, they'll dig trenches and lay the pipe, I'd say sixty days, ten-hour days over here at a dollar a day for each man." He hesitated while Mike O'Leary did the calculation.

"Ninety-six hundred for the labor," Mike said.

"We'll need a dozen qualified pipe-fitters," Ferdie continued. "I doubt we can find them on this side. We'd better make that part of the American contractor's job. We can probably get a pipe-fitting subcontractor for about twenty thousand for the job. Then we'll need carpenters to make the frames for the concrete pouring. The culverts can be poured a hundred feet at a time. The forms can be removed and reused the next day. Probably take a crew of twenty men about four to four and a half months, depending on the weather."

Mike O'Leary calculated quickly. "Another five thousand for labor, max, total of thirty-five thousand dollars for the labor, seventeen million dollars for the materials. How about the treatment plant?" he asked, turning to Harry.

"A fair estimate is about a million and a half," Harry said. "We'll need to build a suspension bridge over the river. It looked to be about forty-five feet across at the border. We'll put the plant right under the bridge." He paused and directed his attention to Joshua. "What we got here is roughly an eighteen-and-a-half-million-dollar project. If the Mexicans will let us, we'll supply the labor for the treatment plant and all the materials except the wood for the concrete framing. They'll supply the labor for the piping on the Mexican side."

Joshua was surprised. "You mean out of an eighteen-and-a-half-million-dollar sewage system in Mexico, the Mexicans get a labor contract worth about fifteen thousand dollars and American contractors get the rest?"

Harry Morland chuckled. "It's a starting point for negotiation. That fifteen grand for Mexican labor is going to turn into a *hundred* fifteen grand when you talk to the mayor. And if they insist on supplying the concrete and the pipe, we're looking at having to award the whole contract to them. That means twenty-five million bucks, garbage quality, rusted leaky pipe, concrete that dissolves in the rain, and a whole system that doesn't work, except to pump money into some fat politician's pocket. They'll have *our* twenty-five million and we'll still have *their* shit floating in our river."

Joshua nodded. "How long will it take you to get me a set of specifications so I can publish for a contract?"

Harry looked at the other two men. "What do you think? How long to measure the hills?"

"A day," Ferdie said. Mike nodded.

"Okay," Morland said, "it'll take me a day to lay out the treatment plant and the bridge. I brought a sonar rebounder with me to sound the depth of the underground river. That'll take another half day." He looked at Joshua. "We'll be done day after tomorrow."

"Good," Joshua said. "Anybody know a nice hotel down here?" He laughed.

"Hell, yes," Ferdie said. "The Fray Marcos de Niza, a block from the border. And we can eat at the Caverns, best damn turtle soup and abalone steak you'll ever eat. They truck it up fresh from Guaymas."

▼▲▼

Hanna had given her father a book about the history of Arizona for his birthday. He had read about the expedition of the Jesuit missionary Father Marcos de Niza in the mid-1500s after the Spanish conquest of Mexico. He had also read a little of Mexico's contemporary history in Henry Parkes's *History of Mexico,* which Magdalena had checked out of the Carnegie library.

In the early sixteenth century, Cuba was becoming overpopulated with newly arriving Spaniards from Europe. The governor of Cuba sent an adventurer, Hernando Cortés, on an expedition to Mexico to subdue the Aztec Indians in the center of the vast country. The first Spanish expedition two years earlier, in 1517, had resulted in death to most of the invading mercenaries. But Cortés proved equal to the task, and his army of five hundred soldiers of fortune and cutthroats subdued the Aztecs and pacified their capital city, Tenochtitlan, a few miles from the present capital of Mexico City.

It was Cortés's novel idea to avoid the annihilation of the local population and expropriation of their lands, which the Spanish conquistadores had practiced in Haiti and Cuba. So instead of sending forth expeditions of conquest under the aegis of brigands or soldiers, the expeditions were led by Catholic priests whose genuine primary purpose was to convert pagan souls to the service of the one and eternal God.

Twenty years later, such an expedition was led by Friar Marcos de Niza. He quested in vain for Cibola's legendary cities of gold. And a hundred and fifty years after Fray Marcos, in 1687, a Jesuit missionary named Eusebio Francisco Kino began building churches along the route of the Sonora, Altar, San Pedro, and Santa Cruz rivers through northern Sonora and southern Arizona, the same route that had been followed by Fray Marcos. Padre Kino erected two dozen missions in Indian villages from Opodepe, Mexico, all the way north one hundred and eighty miles to San Xavier Del Bac, on what was now the Papago Indian Reservation just below Tucson.

This vast domain in the heart of the Sonora Desert was the *Pimeria Alta*, the homeland of the Papago Indians, and they were converted to Catholicism by the Jesuit priests and the Franciscan friars who followed after them. Among themselves, the Papagos were known simply as *"O'odham,"* "people," but it meant more than that. It meant "dry earth with human qualities," just as the Indo-European words "humus" and "human" stem from the identical concept of "earth." But the Spanish missionaries dubbed the *O'odham* *"Papagos,"* "the bean people," because of their dietary staple, and by that name they had come to be called by all white men.

It seemed to Joshua as though the Fray Marcos Hotel might indeed have been built by the legendary priest himself. It was a ponderous two-story box with a two-foot-high foundation of rough-hewn granite blocks and forty-foot-high walls of plaster, once a gaudy yellow, now cracked and streaked and blemished like the skin of an old banana.

They went to the front desk to check in, and the clerk stared at the stainless-steel hand protruding from Joshua's suit coat. Joshua moved his left shoulder jerkily to operate the two stainless-steel pincers, and he clicked his hand toward the clerk's nose. The young man jumped backward and then looked fearfully into Joshua's smiling face. His fright swiftly turned to humor, and he smiled and laughed and pointed at the hand and mimicked the movement of the pincers with his own fingers, snapping the four stiffened fingers of his left hand against his thumb. Joshua laughed.

His room had a ceiling at least fifteen feet high
with a motionless fan in the middle and a bare light
bulb in the center of the fan. The room was huge
for a hotel, probably twenty feet square, with a double bed, a small desk and wooden chair, a lamp with
no bulb, and four chairs around a small round table.
The chairs were leather slings with ocotillo rib
frames, the kind that are lovely to look at and impossible to sit in comfortably. The window faced
south into the town and was three feet square, covered by a thin curtain of multicolored chintz. Joshua
opened the curtain and lifted up the sliding window.
It stuck after it opened less than a foot. A pleasant
breeze wafted into the room. He stared through the
spotlessly clean window. It was almost six o'clock,
and the sun was disappearing below the hill to the
west, leaving a lavender and orange haze over the
hilltop. The town was still and quiet. Hardly anyone
could afford the luxury of a car in Nogales, and the
narrow streets and alleys were uncluttered.

From somewhere deep in his mind came the
words to "O Little Town of Bethlehem," and he
found himself singing quietly, ". . . how still we see
thee lie, above thy deep and dreamless sleep the
starry skies go by." He walked into the bathroom,
struggled out of his jacket, and removed his tie. He
rolled up his right sleeve slowly and methodically,
having spent hour after hour patiently learning the
exact movements to make with his left shoulder to
work the thin steel cables that opened and closed
his pincers. He didn't roll up the left sleeve. The
steel hand was shocking enough to strangers without exposing them to the flesh-tone-painted pickaxe
handle that was his arm.

He splashed water on his face, opened his Dopp kit, washed his hand with the bar of Ivory he had brought, and brushed his teeth. He toweled his face with the thin hand towel and felt refreshed. He changed out of his gray wool trousers and black wingtips into Levis and tan loafers.

In the expansive lobby of the hotel, the other three men were standing and waiting for him impatiently when he finally came down.

"Hey baby," Ferdie Molina said, "gotta hurry up and grab us a handful of pussy down at the Caverns. There ought to be a slew of maidens just waiting for us." He had changed from his work uniform of gray cotton twill work pants, long-sleeved shirt, and gum-soled half boots into a cowboy shirt, cowboy boots, and Levis. Harry Morland still wore the baggy brown wool suit he had worn all day. Mike O'Leary had replaced his white shirt and tie with a tightly fitting pink polo shirt, rippling over his well-muscled chest and arms. He wore a pair of western-style beige cotton slacks and shiny new brown cowboy boots.

"We're going to let this guy catch them for us," Ferdie said jerking a finger at O'Leary, "and then we'll eat them up." He laughed.

They walked out of the hotel into the dark evening. The Caverns was two blocks away, a long cave hewn into the heart of the granite hill that bounded Nogales on the east. They walked into the restaurant, and the first room was a bar forty feet long. Each of the barstools was taken by a woman. Thirty heavily mascaraed eyes turned toward them as they came into the bar. Joshua got the sudden sensation that he was being scrutinized by a herd of raccoons.

"These are the *maidens* you were talking about?" Harry asked maliciously.

"Well, I didn't mean in the biblical sense," Ferdie drawled.

"The Bible ain't much in vogue around *this* joint," Mike said.

They walked down the bar and one of the women got off her stool and gestured toward it.

"Don't mind if I do," Ferdie said, sitting down.

Two other women next to him promptly stood up and Mike and Harry sat down, smiling at the solicitous attention being paid to them. The women were dressed in variations of Mexican cotton sundresses, low bustlines and a frill around the bodice, long flouncy skirts in bright colors, the same pinks and blues and yellows they had seen on the hovels on the sides of the hills. The women all had long glistening brown or black hair pinned back with hibiscus or rose blossoms. Their perfume was thick and sweet, like the cheap junk you could find at McClellans in Tucson.

A maiden from the end of the bar walked up to Joshua and took him by his good hand with both of hers, rubbing her ample breasts against his arm. Despite the very heavy makeup, she was pretty, young—perhaps twenty or twenty-two, tall, willowy, and buxom.

"Wanna buy me a drink?" she purred in a thick Mexican accent. "My name is Lucy."

"Sure," Joshua said.

They moved up to the bar behind the other three men. It seemed that everybody was drinking whiskey sours, and Joshua ordered two. They came in a moment, and Lucy drank the entire tumblerfull in two swallows. She smiled exultantly at Joshua and held up her empty glass. He ordered another one for her and watched the bartender pour the whiskey from the same bottle of Canadian Club as he had been pouring the others. Well, at least I'm paying for real booze, Joshua mused to himself.

By the time they were ready for dinner, Joshua had finished his second drink and Lucy had polished off four. They were only twenty cents each, so it was easy for Joshua to be generous. She looked none the worse for wear, and she walked steadily into the dining room in front of him. She was really quite lovely, with pretty pink skin and long brown hair falling to the middle of her back. She had a voluptuous figure.

The eight of them sat at a large round table in the center of the restaurant. A small band was playing American dance music at the far end of the restaurant. Almost all of the forty or fifty tables were full, some with American couples, others with American or Mexican men with maidens from the bar.

"Turtle soup and abalone steak," Ferdie said to the waiter. "Best food in the world, right here," he said, looking resolutely from Mike to Harry to Joshua.

Everyone around the table except Joshua ordered the same thing. He sat pondering the menu.

"Hey baby, tacos you can get anywhere," Ferdie said, "but you can't find turtle soup and abalone."

"Okay," Joshua said. "You convinced me."

The waiter collected the menus.

"I'm in love," Mike said, his arm around the maiden next to him. His long arm hung over her shoulder and his fingers were under the frilly elastic band of the bodice of her sundress. She was obviously accustomed to liquor. Her eyes were glazed and her smile was fixed, and she snuggled close to Mike. She had her hand in his lap, rubbing.

"Yeah, well, don't do it right here on the table," Ferdie said, slurring his words a little. "They'll add the price of a hotel room to the meal." The men laughed. The maidens sat quietly smiling, dulled from the liquor.

They ate dinner avidly, cracking jokes and laughing and drinking heavily. Mike and Ferdie and their maidens danced for an hour after the waiter cleared away the dishes. Joshua was drowsy and tired, unused to all the drinking. Harry was asleep in his chair, his grizzled chin hanging down on his chest, his mouth open. His maiden smoked cigarette after cigarette. Otherwise she didn't move.

Lucy reached under the table and rubbed Joshua, making him hard. "That's my big man," she whispered in his ear.

Joshua called for the check. It was only twenty-seven dollars for eight of them. He stood up and pulled his wallet out of his back pocket, pressed it against his stomach with his mechanical arm, and awkwardly counted out eight dollars and laid the bills in the center of the table.

Lucy looked up at him. "I come your room?"

"No, honey, I'm too tired." He walked out of the restaurant, leaving her pouting at the table.

It was a deliciously cool evening, with a starry sky like sparkling snowflakes. He walked languorously to his hotel room and undressed slowly, laying his clothes on a chair. He lay back on the soft bed and soon fell asleep.

▼▲▼

Joshua jerked his head up from the pillow. There was a pounding on the door that exacerbated the painful pulsing in his temples. He swung his legs over the side of the bed and sat there a moment until his head stopped twirling. He stood up tentatively, got his equilibrium, and looked at his watch. Both of the luminous hands were close to the top of the dial. The pounding continued on the door. Joshua opened it a crack. The person in the dimly lit hallway immediately pushed the door open. Joshua stumbled backward. The door closed and the person switched on the overhead light. He was a short heavyset Mexican, dressed in a pale blue silk suit with a crimson silk shirt. It was a "zoot suit," a baggy jacket with trousers that narrowed toward the ankles, the kind of clothes worn by the Mexican *pachuco* gangs in Tucson. He was thirty years old or so. His straight black greasy hair was combed flat to his skull and hung below his collar. One eye was opaque white, and the eyebrow and cheek around it were heavily scarred.

"Hey, motherfucker, you owe me money," he growled at Joshua in unaccented English.

Joshua was frightened. He stood there silently, breathing fast, and the Mexican pulled a knife out of his pocket and flicked out a four-inch switchblade.

Joshua backed up. "What are you talking about?" he squeezed out through his constricted throat.

"You take up my Lucy's time, but you don't wanna fuck her. You *maricon* bastard. You owe me twenty-five dollars."

Weird thoughts danced through Joshua's alcohol-enriched brain. Maybe five dollars I'd give you, just to get you out of my room so I could go to sleep. Maybe even ten dollars if you asked a little more politely, but twenty-five? Now that's really over-reaching. After all, she's only a whore. I mean, it isn't as though I spent an evening with Betty Grable. Or Vivien Leigh. Jesus! She'd be worth every dime in my pocket!

The pimp came toward Joshua waving the switchblade. Joshua parried the knife with his right arm, but the tip of the long razor-sharp blade cut him on the cheekbone an inch from his eye. It was a small cut, but it immediately started to bleed copiously, and blood dripped from his chin. The pimp stepped back, preparing to make another thrust. Joshua lunged forward and brought his right foot up hard between the man's legs. He fell to his knees groaning and holding his groin. Joshua kicked him hard in the face. He sprawled backward and lay still, blood flowing from his smashed nose and mouth. Several teeth spilled out with the blood. Joshua picked up the switchblade from the floor and slashed long tears in the man's suit jacket and pants and shirt. He reached in the man's back pocket and pulled out his wallet. He took a wad of bills, about a hundred dollars American and twice that much in pesos, walked to the window, and threw the bills and the wallet as hard as he could through the window.

The pimp moaned on the floor and his legs moved slightly. Joshua walked over to his bed, put on his loafers, walked back to the man, and kicked him hard in the ribs. The pimp was unconscious now,

motionless, breathing with gasps through his
bloody mouth.

Joshua opened the door, dragged the pimp with
difficulty out of the room and down the dim hallway, and tumbled him down the stairs to the lobby.
The night clerk ran over to the man and looked up
the stairwell fearfully.

"He tried to rob me," Joshua called down.

He walked back to his room and locked and
bolted the door. He wet a towel and wiped up the
blood from the linoleum floor. He wet another towel
and wiped the blood off his cheek and chest. The
cut was closing, and the heavy bleeding had
stopped. He pressed the towel hard against it for a
few minutes to stop the bleeding completely. Then
he folded the switchblade, put it under his pillow,
and laid back slowly on the bed. Alcohol was crashing through his temples and his forehead, and he
forced himself to lie still so that the pain would
stop.

▼▲▼

The plump orange orb of the sun low over the
hills cast sparkling beams of light into Joshua's
room. He awoke again to pounding on the door,
and his head ached dully. He rubbed his eyes hard.
He decided not to open the door this time. Whoever
it was would get tired of knocking.

The bolt slid open. The night clerk pushed the
door open and retreated quickly down the hall. A
Mexican in a dark green uniform walked casually
into the room. He was of medium height and build,
and his uniform looked clean and new, an oddity in

this town. He wore a .45 U.S. Army automatic in a brown leather holster on a matching Sam Browne belt. He was about sixty years old, with thick wavy graying brown hair and a brown leathery joweled face pocked with acne scars. He smiled broadly at Joshua, revealing too-even, too-white teeth.

Joshua swung his legs over the side of the bed and sat up slowly. "You're in the wrong room," he said with a gravelly voice. "This is my room. It's against the law to come into my room without an invitation."

The Mexican laughed deeply. "You some tough guy. You beat the shit outta Juan Iturbe. Not everybody could do that." He paused and studied Joshua. " 'Specially not with just one arm." His English was fluent but accented.

"Mr. Iturbe pulled a knife and tried to rob me," Joshua said, looking gravely at the Mexican. He pointed at the cut on his cheek. The bloody towels lay on the floor by the bed. "Who are you?"

"I am Agostino Diaz, chief of the Federal Police here, Mr. Rabb."

Joshua nodded. "So, what now?"

"So I just wanted to see you, apologize for your problem. Juan is a *pendejo* sometimes. I know. He married to my niece Josefina." He shook his head and frowned. "Pity. He not be able to work for a while. Maybe some asshole try to take over his girls. You know, is much competition out there. Josefina be mad like a wasp at me." He gritted his teeth and shook his head at Joshua.

Joshua stared balefully at the ugly man. "What now, you bastard? You want money too?"

"I think I gonna have to fine you fifty dollars for

fighting," the policeman said thoughtfully. "I can't let this stuff get out of hand in my town."

Joshua shrugged his shoulders. "I don't have fifty dollars. I'd better go downstairs and call the American Consul."

The man looked shocked. "What for, the Consul? He all the way down in Hermosillo, two hundred mile from here. This is just a little thing between you and me, amigo."

"Well, I just want to make sure it's all done properly." Joshua stood up slowly and slipped on his loafers.

"That is not how we do here, amigo," the Mexican said gruffly. "You don't got money for a fine, I throw you in jail. Five dollars a day. You get fucked in the ass every day by drunk *maricons*. You like that?" He looked at Joshua and winked. "Maybe is better you borrow the money, huh?"

Joshua studied the chief of police and then nodded. "Okay, there are three other men here with me. Let me talk to them."

"That's good, *amigo*. You a smart guy."

They left the room. Ferdie Molina was in room C on the first floor. Joshua pounded on the door. Ferdie opened it a crack, then wider. He squinted sleepily at Joshua.

"What the hell you doing?" Ferdie asked. "It must be three in the morning."

"It's after seven," Joshua said. He pointed his thumb over his shoulder to the policeman and quickly told Ferdie what had happened and what the policeman wanted. Ferdie opened the door wide and walked to a chair and put on the same clothes he had been wearing last night. He came back to the door and started screaming at the policeman in Spanish.

Agostino Diaz looked shocked, then angry, then venomous. He turned to Joshua. "Okay, tough guy. You some kinda big shot, gonna see the mayor and the governor. I'm gonna forget the fine this time. But you watch your step here, señor *beeeeg* shot. I rip your fucking throat out you hit anybody again." He jabbed a stubby forefinger at Joshua and walked quickly down the hallway.

Ferdie looked at Joshua and shook his head grimly. "Wouldn't it just have been a whole lot easier to let her suck your dick and give her a few bucks?"

Joshua rolled his eyes and shrugged and walked back to his room. The fear that had seized him seven hours ago, when the pimp had tried to rob him, had been muted by his drunkenness. But now he suddenly had goose bumps all over, and he started shuddering. It was a balmy sixty-five degrees, but he felt chilled to the bone. He stood under a hot shower for fifteen minutes trying to get warm.

▼▲▼

The day passed uneventfully, save for sarcastic remarks. But Joshua just laughed them off and tried to bury it all in the alcoholic blur of last night. Worse things had happened to him and he was still alive and kicking.

They had dinner at the hotel that evening, and while the maidens were as ubiquitous as honeysuckle blossoms everywhere in Nogales, the men steered clear of them. At the restaurant table, they

worked for almost three hours on the specs for the
sewage system.

The next day was devoted to the projected treatment plant, and they were done by two o'clock.
They drove to the border and stood by the car as
the Mexican policeman searched it. Then they had
to endure another search on the U.S. side by a Customs inspector. After that delay of almost fifteen
minutes, they drove back to Tucson and dropped
Joshua off at his house. The others returned to
Phoenix.

▼▲▼

Joshua was sitting in the living room, staring dully
at the radio, when Hanna came home from school
at four-thirty. Usually she walked from the bus stop
at Valencia Road through the mile-long mesquite
field to Indian Agency Road and then down to the
house, which was just across from the irrigation
ditch that marked the northern boundary of the Papago Indian Reservation. But this time Joshua heard
a car door slam, and Hanna walked into the house
a moment later.

"Hi, Daddy," she said. "Did you have a good
time?" She stopped in front of him and saw the
inch-long scab on his cheek. "What happened to
you?"

"Nothing," he answered. "Just cut myself
shaving."

She frowned. "Daddy, I'm fifteen. Do you really
want me to be that gullible?"

"It's really nothing," he persisted, making his face

bland and shrugging his shoulders. "Who gave you a ride?"

"Oh, just a boy." She smiled a little embarrassedly.

"*Just* a boy?" Joshua said. "I'd like to hear a little more than that."

"Well, he's on the football team and he's real big like you and he's got brown hair and hazel eyes and he's a senior and he's seventeen years old and all the girls think he's gorgeous and he has his own car, a new Dodge convertible, and he asked me to go to the dance Friday night after the football game with Phoenix Union."

Joshua nodded slowly, absorbing all the information gushing excitedly from Hanna. "Isn't the game in Phoenix?"

She beamed at him. "Yes, but I'm going on the bus with the team because I made the cheerleading squad and we get to go to all the games with the team."

"That's great, honey. I'm really happy for you. Are the whole team and all the cheerleaders going to the dance?"

She looked a little sheepish. "Well, not exactly. Mark is going to drive up in his own car and then he'll drive me home."

"From Phoenix?"

She nodded.

"Over my dead body."

"Daddy," she pleaded, "you can't treat me like a kid anymore. I'll be okay. Nothing will happen."

"Honey," he cajoled, "one of the tragedies of being my daughter is that you'll always be my kid, and I'll always worry about you. You're not driving back from Phoenix in his car. You can go up on the bus and come back on the bus."

She scowled at him and sighed.

"Understand?"

"Yes, daddy, I understand," she said sulkily.

"What's the boy's name? Have you met his family?"

"His name is Mark Goldberg and his father owns the big department store downtown."

Joshua's face brightened. "You mean you got a date with the only other Jewish kid in all of Tucson?"

"Come on now, Daddy. There are a bunch of Jewish kids in school." Her eyes lit up hopefully. "*Now* can I go to the dance with him?"

"Hell no," Joshua said. He smiled at her. "There's plenty of time left in your life for everything you want to do. You'll survive."

She frowned at him and went into her room and slammed the door shut.

Joshua sat back on the couch and tried to relax. He stared at the radio and barely heard the music coming softly from it. He remembered the first dance he had gone to with Rachel, so many years ago, when he was a junior at Columbia and she was a freshman at Barnard. They'd met at a mixer after the Columbia–Yale football game, and Joshua had been instantly smitten. And like Rachel's namesake in the Bible, she was the kind of woman for whom a man would happily work a lifetime. Hanna was her mother's perfect twin, beautiful, mink-brown hair, gray-hyacinth eyes, porcelain skin, and a gorgeous figure.

He could think about Rachel now without feeling

the penetrating, paralyzing pain that used to grip him for hours. She had died in an automobile accident in Brooklyn in early 1945, and he hadn't even been told of it at the time, because he was recuperating in an Army hospital in Antwerp, Belgium, from a leg wound and frostbite he'd suffered in the Battle of the Bulge. The doctor had told him about Rachel just before he was released from the hospital, and he had wept for hours. The pain of loss, the frustration of not being able to be home with Hanna and Adam at such a terrible time. It had overwhelmed him. Then he had been promoted to major and attached to Patton's 3rd Army as it rumbled eastward to conquer Germany and free Czechoslovakia and Austria. He had lost his arm in Czechoslovakia, by a little river in a forest near a town with an impossible-sounding name, after his company had liberated a concentration camp.

The heavy baggage of memories had long blended into one parcel by now, a package that was small enough that Joshua could carry it around with him and not be crushed by its weight or thrown off balance so that he stumbled and fell. He could think about these events now without being disabled. He breathed deeply and gritted his teeth. How proud Rachel would have been of Hanna. She would have exulted in her daughter's coming of age, her beauty and her intelligence and her sweetness. Joshua rubbed his mouth hard and blinked away the moistness in his eyes. He stood up and went into his bedroom to change out of the blue serge suit he had been wearing all day.

CHAPTER FOUR

Franklin Carillo sat fidgeting in the jury box in Judge Toby Vatter's courtroom. Vatter was only about thirty years old, but he had the sallow skin and watery eyes of a sick old man. He breathed shallowly and with little gasps like an asthmatic or an emphysemic. He was thin and had a bony face and dark brown hair slicked straight across. He lifted his face from the file in front of him on the bench, lowered his half glasses on his nose, and scowled at the prisoner.

"State versus Carillo," the judge said. "Preliminary hearing. Announce your appearances."

A stocky man with thinning blond hair and very pale blue eyes stood up at the prosecutor's table next to Joshua's defense table. "William Randolph Stevens, Chief Deputy County Attorney, for the State."

Joshua stood up and announced his name. The courtroom was high ceilinged and spacious, paneled entirely in dark walnut, with a terra-cotta tile floor. The acoustics were poor, and the voices echoed hollowly off the ceiling. Several dozen spectators sat behind the railing. Usually a preliminary hearing would attract no attention, but Franklin Carillo's case had caused a stir of hatred in the community.

The door to the courtroom slammed open, and Erma Carillo banged slowly down the tile floor on her metal canes. Her mother was with her, wearing the same old-fashioned flowery bonnet that Joshua had seen her wearing last week. She had pulled it low over her face, like a shabby, overaged movie star protecting her anonymity. Erma clacked into the first row of spectator pews and smiled at her husband.

Well, thought Joshua, sympathy from the judge won't hurt a bit.

"Randy, call your first witness," the judge said, giving the prosecutor a friendly smile.

Isn't that nice, thought Joshua. It looks like Stevens and Vatter are drinking buddies. This preliminary hearing will be over in a hurry.

Under Arizona state law, a person accused of a felony could be made to stand trial only after he had been given a preliminary hearing before a justice of the peace. The justice was an elected official who presided over criminal misdemeanor trials as well as civil disputes involving less than five hundred dollars. All felony trials and civil cases of higher value were the jurisdiction of Superior Court judges. But the preliminary hearing for felony cases was held before one of Tucson's two justices of the peace. At the hearing, the County Attorney's office would present just enough evidence to establish probable cause that the defendant had committed the crime he had been arrested for. If probable cause was established, the justice of the peace would bind the defendant over to stand trial in Superior Court.

A girl walked into the courtroom behind the bailiff. She stood self-consciously in front of the court clerk and raised her right hand, put her left hand on a Bible, and swore to tell only the truth. She sat down in the witness chair to the right of the justice of the peace. She cast frightened, twitching eyes around the courtroom, and when they focused on Franklin Carillo, she looked quickly away.

"State your name and age and occupation," Randy Stevens said.

"Arlene O'Donnell." Her voice was thin and tremulous. She was attractive, though not pretty. She wore her long blonde hair in a pageboy and was wearing a simple white long-sleeved blouse, a Wedgwood-blue loose skirt, and bobby sox and white and black saddle shoes. "I'm nineteen and I'm a sophomore at the University of Arizona."

"Do you see anyone in this courtroom whom you recognize?"

"Yes, sir."

"Point him out, please."

She pointed a shaking finger toward Franklin Carillo without looking at him.

"Tell the Court where you first met the defendant."

"Object, Your Honor," Joshua said, standing up at the table. "No foundation, assuming facts not in evidence. There's no evidence yet that she 'met' Mr. Carillo, only that she 'recognized' him."

The judge waved off Joshua with an annoyed backhanded gesture. "We're not in trial here, Mr. Rabb, just looking for probable cause. Go on, Randy."

"Arlene, where did you first meet the defendant?"

"I was hitchhiking to the University near the corner of Ajo Highway and Mission. He picked me up in his truck."

"What happened then?"

"He does a U-turn on Ajo Highway after we went over the bridge on the Santa Cruz River and drives down along the bank of the river."

"Did you ask him to do that?"

"No, I wanted to go to the University. I had a history class."

"What did he do then?"

"He parks the truck and tells me to get undressed." Her voice broke and she started weeping. The courtroom was hushed. She slowly stopped crying.

"Did you?"

"No. I tried to get out of the truck, but he hit me in the face. Then he pulls out a big gun from under the seat and points it just in front of my face and pulls the trigger—" she gasped and wept for a moment, then sniffled and wiped her eyes with a pink handkerchief "—and tells me he'll blow my brains out if I don't do like he says."

"What did you do?"

"I got undressed," she said quietly, looking down.

"I know this is embarrassing and painful for you," said the prosecutor, "but we need to do it to convict this animal." He pointed at Carillo.

"Your Honor, this is outrageous," Joshua said, rising up from his chair.

"Go on, Randy," said the judge. He fixed Joshua with a reproachful stare.

"Please continue, Arlene," Stevens said.

"He pulled his pants down and he sat me on him and hurt me real bad."

"Were you a virgin, Arlene?"

Joshua stood up immediately. "Objection, Your Honor, irrelevant. The rape statute makes no distinction between virgins and any other women."

The justice of the peace leaned forward on the bench and snarled, "It's all *res gestae,* Mr. Rabb. Objection overruled. Now you're beginning to try my patience."

"But Your Honor, I—"

"Sit down, Mr. Rabb."

Joshua sat down.

"Were you a virgin?" the judge asked.

The girl nodded her head, and her chin wrinkled up and she cried for a few minutes.

"Okay, Arlene," Stevens said, "then what happened?"

"He lifted me off him and pushed my face down and made me suck him." Her last words were barely audible.

"Did you do any of these things voluntarily?"

"No."

Randy Stevens sat down at his table.

Joshua stood up and faced the witness.

"Actually, Miss O'Donnell, you told Mr. Carillo that you were going over near the University to visit your boyfriend, isn't that so?"

"No." She was no longer weepy. She looked at Joshua belligerently.

"You weren't a virgin, were you?"

"Objection, Your Honor," Stevens said. "Irrelevant."

"Sustained," said the judge.

"But Your Honor," Joshua said, "the prosecutor

asked the same question on direct, and I'm entitled to inquire into the alleged victim's sexual history to establish her proclivity for sexual misconduct."

"Not in this courtroom you're not," Judge Vatter said. "Proceed."

"Mr. Carillo drove you over to the University, isn't that so?"

"Yes."

"You asked him for his name and telephone number?"

"Yes."

"If you had just been raped by this vicious animal, why would you do that?"

The judge sat a little stiffer in his chair and glanced at Randy Stevens, then back at the girl.

"Because I was scared. I thought he might kill me with that gun. I tried to make it seem like I liked him and wanted to meet him again."

"Where did he drop you off?"

"Around Euclid and 5th Street."

"Does your boyfriend live there?"

She hesitated. "Near there," she said.

"When did you first contact the police?"

"That night."

"Where were you?"

She hesitated again. "I was at my boyfriend's house. I had a bruise on my cheek. My boyfriend asked me how I got it. I was ashamed to tell him, but I had to tell someone. He called the police."

"Did the police examine you?"

"Yes."

"Do you know if they found any evidence of rape?"

"Well, I don't think so. I had taken a shower at

my boyfriend's, to wash him off of me." She pointed a finger at Carillo. This time her finger was steady and her look was vicious.

"No more questions, Your Honor," Joshua said and sat down. He hadn't accomplished very much at all. There was more than ample probable cause to establish rape. But Arlene O'Donnell was just for openers. Randy Stevens called his next witness.

"State your name and occupation, please."

"Dr. Stanley Wolfe, Pima County Coroner." He had a round pink face with bloodhound jowls and big dark blue eyes magnified by glasses. He was short and pudgy.

"In your official capacity, did you come into contact with Victoria and Alicia Grant?"

"Yes, I did."

"Tell the court how that occurred, Doctor."

The coroner opened a file and laid it on the desk in front of him. He perched the round rimless glasses on the end of his narrow nose. "In the early morning of September 19, 1946, I was called by Deputy Sheriff Paul Wheaton—he's my assistant—and was told that there were two homicides on the bank of the Santa Cruz River near the Ajo Highway bridge. I went over to my office right here on the first floor of the County Building and Paul had already brought the bodies in. One was a woman whom we later determined to be Victoria Grant and the other was her four-week-old daughter Alicia."

"How was the ID made?"

"The husband, John Grant, reported his wife and baby missing. He was brought in later that morning to identify them."

"Did the decedents have any identification on them, tags on their clothing, anything at all?"

"No, they were both found nude, no clothing or wallet or purse or anything in the area."

"Could you determine a cause of death?"

"Well, with the baby, it isn't entirely clear. The baby was shot through the head with a large-caliber weapon, right here." Wolfe pointed to the middle of his forehead. "It exploded out the entire posterior cranium and the brain as well. But the baby had also been raped, practically torn in half." Dr. Wolfe paused for a moment, looking pained, and cleared his throat. "The vagina was torn all the way through to the rectum and the penetration of the penis or whatever object was used ruptured the obturator artery and vein, the uterine artery, the iliac artery, and virtually all of the mesenteric vessels, causing heavy extravasation. In other words, she may have bled to death, or the gunshot may have killed her. Whichever came first."

Joshua gulped, and it was so loud in his ears that he hoped no one else had heard it. He looked around at the spectators. Several of them were weeping, men and women alike. Probably the family of the victims, Joshua thought. Others were staring in shock and disgust at the defendant.

Erma Carillo smiled reassuringly at her husband. He wore a bland look of detachment. Joshua felt only hatred for him. What a prince of a human being this Franklin Carillo was. Joshua suddenly felt dirty, immoral, for sitting here at the defense table, for taking money to try to discredit a nineteen-year-old girl who had been brutally raped and fellated. And now he was supposed to do what, stand up and proclaim the innocence of Franklin Carillo? Was he supposed to try to prove that good old Frank didn't do it because he was in Timbuktu at the time? Joshua knew better. Carillo had admitted to kidnapping the victims. What do you do ethically, Joshua Rabb? Oh, come on, quit being so whiny and self-righteous. You learn what to do in the first year of law school: You force the *state* to prove its case. That's what you do. You don't lie for your client or create a false alibi or bring him home to dinner so he can wave his dick at your children. No, you just do what the Constitution tells you to do, you see to it that the state proves its case against your client beyond a reasonable doubt with legal and properly obtained evidence. Hold on to that thought, Josh baby, you are a member of an august profession performing a noble task in the service of democracy. He heard the coroner's voice through the torrent of his own inner voices.

"As for Victoria Grant, the cause of death was loss of blood from a large-caliber bullet. She was shot in the upper chest and the projectile shattered the left clavicle and severed the subclavian artery. Her body was also run over by a vehicle. Tire-tread injuries were on her abdomen. It was flattened, all of the organs of the abdominal cavity were crushed, and the skin of both of her flanks was ruptured to permit the forced extrusion of the large and small intestines."

Joshua breathed deeply and slowly to make sure that he didn't gulp audibly. Remember, this is a noble deed you are doing, he said to himself. This is the cornerstone of democracy. The courtroom was deathly silent.

"Your witness, Mr. Rabb," the judge said.

"Do you have any evidence which positively links Mr. Carillo to these terrible crimes, Doctor?" Joshua asked, performing his role nobly.

"Yes, we believe so," the coroner answered. "One of the bullets we found is testable. It weighs 242 grains. A .44 magnum. Half of it is completely intact and still bears rifling marks. I sent it to the FBI lab in Washington, D.C. for ballistics testing, along with several test firings that we made with the Ruger revolver belonging to Franklin Carillo. We haven't gotten the test results back yet."

"Thank you." Joshua sat down. He turned around, and Erma Carillo frowned at him. *I wonder how she's going to feel about me when her husband gets executed at Arizona State Prison,* he thought.

The state's next witness was Wanda Tucker, a small hunchbacked old woman of seventy-eight with short white hair like ermine fur and rheumy eyes. She was gaunt and wrinkled like a raisin. She testified in a squeaky high voice that she had been walking her dog around the duplex where she lived and she had seen "that man over there"—she pointed at Carillo—at about midnight sitting under a palm tree smoking a cigarette. Victoria—"she was such a sweet girl, always had a few minutes to chat with an old lady like me, I'm all alone, got no one"— Victoria was doing laundry. Then a few minutes later they were all gone. She assumed that Victoria had finished her laundry and had gone back to her duplex with Alicia.

"Are you sure it was this man?" Randy Stevens asked, pointing at the defendant sitting all alone in the jury box, handcuffed in his jailhouse green pants and white T-shirt, with "PIMA COUNTY JAIL" stenciled on the front.

The old woman wrinkled up her nose, squinted at Carillo, and said, "Oh yes, that's the one I saw. He was right outside the laundry room where Victoria was nursing Alicia."

"Thank you, ma'am," Stevens said and sat down.

"Questions?" Judge Vatter asked, looking at Joshua.

Joshua knew that there was overwhelming probable cause to bind Carillo over, and the justice of the peace was not about to dismiss any charges no matter how thoroughly Joshua might be able to discredit the old woman's identification of Carillo.

"No questions, Your Honor," he said.

Randy Stevens held a revolver up at his table. A tag hung from the trigger housing. "The only other evidence at this time is this Ruger .44 single-action that was found hidden in the closet of the defendant's bedroom." He handed the weapon to the bailiff, who brought it to the judge.

Without hesitation, Justice of the Peace Vatter said, "Franklin Carillo is bound over for trial in Superior Court, November 18, 1946, Count One, armed rape, Count Two, assault with a deadly weapon, Count Three, murder in the first degree, Count Four, armed rape involving a minor, Count Five, murder in the first degree." He banged his gavel and walked off the bench through a rear door into his chambers.

Two sheriff's deputies led Franklin Carillo down the aisle. He shuffled with short jerky steps because of the ankle cuffs attached to the belly chain. His wife called out something to him that Joshua didn't catch. Franklin nodded and forced a fleeting smile.

"You gonna get him off, right, Mr. Rabb?" Erma Carillo said, standing up slowly with the help of her two canes. "You ain't gonna let them convict an innocent man." She sounded more threatening than entreating.

"I'll do my best, Mrs. Carillo. The rest is up to a jury and God."

She crossed herself and kissed her fingertips. "He's all we need, Mr. Rabb. He'll protect my Franklin." She hobbled slowly down the aisle and out of the courtroom.

"Yeah, right," Joshua said.

CHAPTER
FIVE

Sealed bids began arriving at the BIA office within a week after the publication for the contract. Joshua kept them in the middle drawer of his metal desk. By the ten-day deadline, seven envelopes had come in marked on the outside "CONFIDENTIAL: CONTRACT U.S. 4732/46."

Mike O'Leary came down from Phoenix on Thursday morning to evaluate the bids. Joshua opened the seven manila envelopes and laid the bids out on his desk. The important elements of the bids were conformity with the concrete specifications, the completion dates, the overall raw material price, and the labor total for the pipe-fitting and the construction of the suspension bridge and treatment plant.

A national contractor based in Phoenix had bid $18,986,000, with a five-month completion date. Another contractor with an office in Tucson had underbid that by $63,000, but it had a one-month-longer completion. The only other bid in the ballpark was from Avra Valley Concrete Contracting, Inc., an enterprise that was unknown to Joshua and Mike. Its bid was by far the lowest, $17,900,000, although it had bid for a slightly different composi-

tion of the concrete than called for in the specs. Its
concrete had a higher ratio of water to cement, .52
instead of .45. Mike said that he didn't think it
would make a significant difference in the density
and hardness of the finished product. And for a
project of this magnitude and a bid of almost a million dollars less than the others, and even below
what Mike thought was the best wholesale price for
concrete, they couldn't just throw it aside without
answering the question.

"How do we determine if it's good quality?"
Joshua asked.

"I'll go out and take a look," O'Leary said. "The
plant's located about twenty-five miles north of
here, right on Rillito Creek on the west of Highway
87 to Phoenix. You can see the rock crusher from
the road. I'll stop off there and get a sample of the
concrete and bring it up to Phoenix for testing."

"When will you know?"

"I'll wet it down this afternoon and slump test it.
Then I'll give it twenty-four hours to dry and do a
compression test. I'll call you by five o'clock tomorrow afternoon."

"Okay, go for it," Joshua said. "I want to be able
to get a contract signed by Tuesday at the latest.
Then I can airmail it back to the OLM in Washington and have it approved by the end of next week."

The men shook hands, and Mike left Joshua's
office.

Edgar Hendly came in a few minutes later. "You
gettin the contract squared away?" he asked.

"Yes. We'll have it done by the end of next week.
Then I'll have to take it down to Nogales and see
the mayor."

"I read Harry Morland's report. He says you had a run-in with the head of the *Federales*."

Joshua nodded. "Straight out of one of those movies they're showing now. Lowlife bastard of a lawman and a vicious Mexican pimp, perfect stereotypes."

"Except this really happened," Edgar said.

"I guess that's what makes stereotypes, that these things actually do happen enough times to make them clichés. Anyway, the cop won't bother me again. All he wanted was fifty bucks. He didn't have the imagination to ask for fifty thousand."

"Maybe you'll get lucky. Next time he'll ask for a million."

Joshua laughed.

"Anyways, reason I'm here is I just heard some news on the radio, thought you'd be interested. Judge Fran Rooks died last night of a heart attack."

It would have been tasteless to smile or to cheer, so Joshua suppressed the sense of pleasure that leapt up in him. He looked blandly at Edgar. "Well, too bad. And such a young man too."

"Yeah, I knew you'd be emotionally shattered."

A small grin turned up the sides of Joshua's mouth.

"I hear tell that the Governor'll appoint Bernie Velasco," Edgar drawled.

"A Mexican?"

"Yep."

"I thought nobody around here had much use for Mexicans, except maybe as farm hands or ditch diggers."

"Well now, there's Meskins and then there's Meskins. Some of em been here longer 'n alla us.

They was here when this part a Arizona was still Mexico, before the Gadsden Purchase back in 1853, 1854, whenever it was. Bernie's family's one a them. They been livin here long 'fore any a us. Got a ranch up north a ways. His daddy works at the copper mines in Winkelman when the price a cattle goes down. Bernie is old Arizona."

"Old enough that the Governor will appoint him to a judgeship?"

"Shit, yeah! Them pols are finally figurin out that if the Meskins ever realize they got the vote, they can control half the elections in the state. Anyway, Bernie's a good ol' boy, done his politickin, slapped the right guys on the back. He's damn well liked. He goes over to the Mountain Oyster Club most lunch times, grabs hisself a shot or two a moonshine and shoots the shit with the boys. I'll take you down there for lunch today, you oughta meet him." He glanced at his watch. "In fact we can go over now. It's almost noon."

Joshua shrugged and nodded. "Sure, sounds good."

They drove in Edgar's car downtown to a Mexican style house on Stone Avenue, just two blocks from the courthouse. They went through a wrought-iron gate in an adobe arch and came into a lovely flowered courtyard. A flagstone walk led into the M.O. Club. The first room was a bar, but no one was in it except the bartender polishing glasses. They went into a spacious restaurant with a high ceiling covered by a trellis with some kind of lime green vines woven thickly into it. The tables were covered in fresh bright pink tablecloths and set with what looked to Joshua like real china and silver. Several waiters in tuxedos walked solicitously around the room ministering to the twenty or so diners.

"There he is," Edgar said, pointing to a man sitting alone at a corner table reading a paperback book. Edgar led the way to him.

"Bernie," he said, holding out his hand, "how's the boy today?"

"Fair t'middlin, fair t'middlin," Velasco said, shaking Edgar's hand.

"Like you to meet Joshua Rabb. He just got admitted to the bar, been workin over at the BIA with me."

Joshua extended his hand. "Nice to meet you."

Velasco had on a pair of "readers." He lowered the half glasses on his nose and studied Joshua and shook his hand. He had a bushy black mustache and only a fringe of graying hair around a completely bald crown. He appeared to be in his mid-forties. "I've heard a little about you," he said.

Joshua nodded. "Well, I hope it wasn't too bad."

"Not bad at all. Buck Buchanan is a good friend of mine. He says you did a damn fine job for that Indian."

"Thanks," Joshua said.

"Sit down, boys, where's my manners," Velasco said.

Edgar and Joshua sat at the table, and a waiter immediately brought them menus.

"Have the M.O. omelette," Edgar said.

"What is it?" Joshua asked.

"Bull's balls and eggs."

Joshua narrowed his eyes at Edgar. "Are you serious?"

"As God is my witness," Edgar said, holding his right hand over his heart.

"Steak and a baked potato," Joshua said to the waiter.

Edgar guffawed loudly. "Same here," he said, handing the waiter his menu.

"So what's the good word, Bernie?" Edgar asked.

Velasco shrugged. " 'Bout what?"

" 'Bout you know what. Don't be coy now."

Velasco shook his head. "Don't know yet. Creighton called me an hour ago. But it isn't definite yet."

Edgar turned toward Joshua. "Henry Creighton is the governor's right hand," he said in a low voice, as though he were imparting secret information.

"Well, I reckon it won't take long," Edgar said.

"Too bad about Fran Rooks. Fifty-seven is too damn young to die," Velasco said.

Edgar shrugged and rolled his eyes. Joshua sat comfortably in the thick padded armchair and said nothing.

A tall elderly man in a high gray felt cowboy hat and an elegant cream linen suit and gleaming black alligator boots came to the table and held out his hand. "Congratulations in order yet?"

"Not just yet, George," Velasco said, shaking the man's hand. "You know Edgar, don't you?"

The man shook Edgar's hand. "Sure do. Edgar'n me go back a ways."

"George Callan, this is Joshua Rabb," Edgar said. "Joshua's workin over at the BIA as legal advisor and also runnin the Office of Land Management."

"Oh yeah, sure," George said, shaking Joshua's

hand. "You got pretty famous back there a couple of months ago. I read about you."

"None of it is true," Joshua said.

"Oh hell, I know that. If the newspapers only printed the truth, nobody'd buy the papers!"

The men all laughed.

"Well, good luck to you, Bernie. You'll do a damn good job," George said. He walked to another table close by and sat down with a girl who looked to Joshua as though she might be his daughter or even his granddaughter. She was very pretty, in her early twenties, with rich auburn hair in a ponytail, brown eyes, and spectacular alabaster skin like a marble statue. She smiled softly at Joshua.

"You oughta get to know George," Edgar said to Joshua. "He owns half a the gott damn county. From the Cortaro farms all the way up past the Rillito River and Avra Valley to Marana. A good ten, twelve miles, and then on west maybe twenty-five miles. He's got cattle, cotton, God knows what all."

"He's got one hell of a pretty girlfriend too," Bernie Velasco said. "Must be forty years younger than he is. His wife died of consumption a year or two back, and talk is he met the girl in Kansas City a couple of months ago. Her daddy is one of the big cattle buyers for the stockyards."

Joshua looked at her again, and she was staring back at him. She looked quickly away.

"Yep, she could bring a little color into a old fart's cheeks, no doubt about it," Edgar said quietly.

Velasco laughed. Joshua smiled and nodded. A young man's cheeks too, he thought.

They exchanged small talk over lunch, and they

left at one o'clock. George Callan waved to them, and the girl cast Joshua an unmistakably sultry look.

The look did not go unnoticed by Edgar. "Seems you made a friend there, Josh boy." He chuckled.

Maybe so, Joshua thought, maybe so.

▼▲▼

When Joshua and Edgar got back to the Bureau, Frances Hendly jumped up from her little reception desk behind the smeary window in the lobby and came running through the door to her husband.

"Edgar, Charger's down in the shed. He's groanin and don't seem to be able to get up. I called Doc Forelli."

"Take it easy now, Frances. Charger's 'bout twenty-five years old, awful old for a horse, and he ain't been lookin too spry lately. I figured it wouldn't be long." He patted his wife on the back.

Frances's small yellowish-gray eyes were wet, and she sniffled. She pulled a soiled handkerchief out of the pocket of the dun-colored plain shift she was wearing and dabbed at her pinkened nose. Her light brown hair was lined with gray and pulled back severely in a bun.

A short skinny man in denim overalls and muddy cowboy boots came through the front door of the Bureau carrying a large carpet bag. He doffed his soiled cowboy hat, revealing a glistening bald head, pink, speckled with dark splotches. He was at least sixty years old and walked with a limp.

"Afternoon, Miz Hendly, Edgar," the man drawled. "Old Charger down?"

"Yeah, Doc," Frances said. "Come on through the

back door here. He's in the shed." She led the veterinarian through the door into the receptionist's office and out the back door of the Bureau. Edgar
and Joshua followed.

The horse shed was small, only about ten feet
square, and Charger, lying on his side, had most of
the floor covered. He flailed his head and tail as the
people crowded around him, but he couldn't stand
up. The vet put on a large stethoscope and held it in
various places about the horse's bloated abdomen.

"Impaction colic," said the vet standing up. "I can
relieve the bloat, and that'll take care a most of his
pain, but it sure ain't worth oilin him and trying to
get him up and walkin for two days. He's too old
and tired. If he doesn't get up by himself after a
bit, it's best I put him down."

Edgar nodded gravely. Frances sniffled and blew
hard into her handkerchief.

The vet took a long needle that looked like a knit-
ting needle out of his bag. He knelt at the horse's
belly between his outstretched legs and applied the
stethoscope at various places, listening intently.
After a few minutes, he laid aside the stethoscope,
picked up the needle, worked the sharp end through
the horse's thick chestnut hair, and punched the
flat end of the needle hard with his open palm.

Joshua jumped at the shock of it. The horse didn't
even flinch. The vet drove the needle about eight
inches into the horse, leaving four or five inches of
needle exposed. A loud rush of fetid gas immediately
began to hiss through the hollow core of the needle.

"Got it," Doc Forelli said, his hand wrapped
around the top of the needle just under the flat
head. He held it there steady for several minutes

until the horse's bloated belly had shrunk noticeably and there was no more hissing of gas. The vet pulled the needle out and stood up.

"Well, let's wait a few minutes and see if the old boy feels good enough to get up," he said.

They all stood there, shuffling their feet, chatting idly. After ten minutes, the vet walked to the horse's head and lifted it. "Come on now, Charger, get on up here and you'll feel a whole lot better."

But the horse seemed grateful just to lie on the ground, unmoving, relieved of the gas pain.

"Help me try to roll him up," the vet said. He pointed to the horse's back.

Joshua and Edgar and Doc Forelli knelt side by side at Charger's back and tried to push him up. The thousand-pound horse just lay there, breathing hard. The vet stood up and shook his head. "Gotta put him down, Edgar. He's only gonna suffer. It ain't no use."

Edgar grimaced. "Do what's right, Doc," he mumbled.

Frances walked out of the shed. The vet walked to his bag and took out a syringe kit. He put it together and filled the barrel with amber liquid from a small bottle. He plunged the syringe into the side of the horse's neck.

The men walked outside. Joshua felt queasy.

The vet took a small notepad out of his pocket and wrote on a sheet of paper. He tore out the sheet and handed it to Edgar. "Here's the number of Tucson Tallow Company. John Haugh will get a truck out here as soon as you call him."

Edgar nodded and put the notepaper in the pocket of his rumpled gray suit jacket. He reached into his pants pocket and took out a money clip. He counted out a five and five ones, most of what was in the clip, and handed the money to the veterinarian.

"Nuff?" Edgar said.

"Plenty," Doc Forelli said putting the bills in his pocket. "Sorry."

Edgar nodded. The vet walked to his pickup truck and drove away. Edgar and Joshua walked glumly back into the Bureau.

▼▲▼

Four hours later, the Tucson Tallow Company truck arrived. Jimmy Hendly and Adam Rabb stood slump-shouldered and watched two men attach the horse's legs to chains and winch the horse into the back of a horribly smelly stake truck. Edgar laid his arm lightly on Jimmy's shoulders. Joshua held Adam's hand. No one spoke. They watched the truck drive off down Indian Agency Road.

"You think we could get another horse, Dad?" Jimmy asked, turning his teary-eyed face up to his father.

Edgar shook his head. "Dunno where."

They all stood silently outside the shed, having no strength or desire for words.

Magdalena walked up to them. She took Adam's free hand and pressed it in both of her own, like the surrogate mother she had become. "You ready for a little supper?" she asked softly.

Adam sniffled and nodded. "See ya," he said to Jimmy.

Joshua and Adam and Magdalena walked down

Indian Agency Road to their house at the end of it. Hanna was inside the chicken coop attached to the west side of the house. She threw several handfuls of corn on the ground for the sixty-five fluttering White Rocks. She came out of the coop, latched the rickety chicken-wire door, and set the bag of feed on the ground.

"You okay?" she said to Adam. He shrugged.

"Poor old Charger just died of old age," Joshua said. "He didn't suffer."

"Let's go in and eat supper," Magdalena said softly.

▼▲▼

The next afternoon, Edgar came into Joshua's office. "Damnedest thing just happened," he said, his face beaming with pleasure. "George Callan just called me and said that Doc Forelli was over there at his dairy takin care of a coupla milk cows, and he told George about Charger, and George said we should all come out to the main house tomorrow afternoon and Jimmy and Adam can pick out a horse. Free a charge. George says he's got three of em out to pasture, just waitin for a coupla kids to adopt em."

"That's terrific," Joshua said. "Adam will be thrilled."

"We'll go over 'bout two o'clock," Edgar said.

"Great."

The phone rang on Joshua's desk. Edgar waved and left the office.

It was Mike O'Leary. "I wet down the concrete yesterday and let it set twenty-four hours. It didn't have the hardness required by government specs. So I called the plant in Avra Valley and talked to the guy who made the bid. He says that if they lower the water/cement ratio to .45 to meet our specs, that'll increase their bid $520,000 to a total of $18,420,000. That still makes Avra Valley Concrete's bid $503,000 lower than the nearest competition, and they'll bring it in with a five-month cap on completion."

"Are you getting it in writing?"

"Yeah, sure," Mike said. "A messenger will deliver a revised bid to you before five o'clock."

"Okay," Joshua said. "Good job."

▼▲▼

Joshua and Magdalena drove to Tucson High School at 10:30 that night and waited for Hanna to return from Phoenix. The games were played at five o'clock in the evening and were over by seven-thirty at the latest, when it was too dark to play anymore. So Hanna would be at the school by eleven o'clock. There were numerous other parents waiting as well, many chatting together in groups, others sitting idly in their cars. It was a fabulously balmy fall night.

Joshua and Magdalena had lived together for over four months and were as comfortable together and as unconscious of each other's presence as family. But tonight she was uncharacteristically silent, even a little brooding, and Joshua began to notice.

He looked over at her, and she was staring vacantly out the front windshield. "Something wrong?" he asked.

"Jesus Leyva asked me out," she said slowly.

"The new Reservation policeman?"

"Yes."

"That's fine," Joshua said. "I met him the other day, when he first came in. He's going to be assigned here permanently. That way there'll be an Indian policeman at San Xavier at all times, and we won't have to call over to Sells whenever there's trouble and wait two or three hours until they get here."

She nodded.

"He's a good-looking guy."

She nodded.

"So what's wrong? Still thinking about Samuel?"

She turned her face to him. "I just can't help it. Chuy saw me on the Reservation—"

"*Chuy?*"

"Yes, *Chuy* is the nickname for Jesus. Anyway, he saw me yesterday at my grandmother's *vato*, I was grinding corn, and he came over and introduced himself, and we talked for a while, and I kept feeling guilty."

"I know what you mean," Joshua said. "I felt that way about Rachel at first. But you just have to come to grips with the truth. They're dead. We're still living. And we have to go on living normal lives."

"I know." She nodded her head, but her face remained taut. "I'm going out with him tomorrow night."

"He's from a really nice family. He has a couple of years of college up at Arizona State, and his father was on the Tribal Council."

"Yes, my grandfather knew his father well. He's known Chuy since he was a boy."

"Well, I hope it works out," Joshua said.

She sighed deeply, but her expression remained grim. Her lips were clenched together tightly. She gritted her teeth and her cheek muscles bunched up like little ribbed apricot pits.

A bus pulled into the parking lot. Its windows were down, and no sound came from the passengers.

"They must have lost the game," Joshua said. "Otherwise they'd be singing and dancing."

Teenagers piled out of the bus quietly, and Hanna flopped into the back seat of the DeSoto.

"Tucson 7, Phoenix 24," she said.

"Can't win them all," Joshua said. "How did Mark do?"

"Fumbled the ball on the eleven-yard line. Phoenix recovered and scored."

"Oops," Joshua said. "Did you have fun being a cheerleader?"

"Oh yeah." Hanna's voice became brighter. "It's really neat."

"Well, we'll all come to the next home game and watch you."

They drove silently for a while. "I think tomorrow morning we'll go buy a new car," Joshua said. "I looked at one of those new Chevy convertibles yesterday. Pretty snazzy."

"Wow, Daddy, that's neat!"

Even Magdalena's sour look evaporated. She smiled.

When they got back to the house, Magdalena and Hanna went into their bedroom. Hanna was tired from the long day and all the cheerleading. Magdalena slept on a four-inch-thick foam-rubber pad on the floor next to Hanna's bed.

Joshua switched on the radio low and sat on the couch listening to it for a while. There was deep silence in the house, and Joshua thought that he heard crying from the girls' bedroom. But it was only for a moment, and then the silence again carpeted everything.

▼▲▼

"I'm gonna feel like a rich tourist ridin in this thing," Edgar said, looking very impressed.

Joshua stood beside him in front of the Rabb house and grinned like a new father at the shiny yellow car.

"How much did it set ya back?"

"$2360," Joshua said.

"Whew," breathed out Edgar respectfully. "Crime sure does pay!" He looked at Joshua and winked. "As the Good Book says, 'Ye shall know a man by his delights.'"

"Where's it say that?"

Edgar shook his head. "Don't rightly know. But if it don't say it, it should!"

Joshua laughed.

"Yep, I sure didn't know you was such a spunky devil, buyin a pussy wagon like this." He looked at Joshua and chortled knowingly. "You can take em out and park over at 'A' Mountain and recline them seats and put on the radio and ball em in the moonlight."

"Where are all these willing ladies coming from?"

"You'll find em. They seem to be attracted to ya like mares in heat to a stallion."

"Well, I didn't do so well with Penny. She ran out on me."

"Yeah, there is that episode for sure. It don't say much for yer *prowess*." Edgar cackled maliciously. "But then there's that little girl that was with old George Callan. She'd jump you like a alley cat, you give her half a smile. I'll spot you ten to one she's right there today when we go to look at the horses."

Joshua shrugged. "Thou shalt not covet thy neighbor's wife, nor his maidservant, nor his ox, nor his ass, nor anything that is thy neighbor's."

"Well, don't get me wrong. I didn't say nothin 'bout old George's ass!"

Both men laughed. They got into the car and drove down the road to the fort that Adam and Jimmy had built in the mesquite field across the road from the BIA. The boys ran to the car and got in the back seat.

"Wow, this is really neat," Jimmy said.

Adam didn't say anything, just smiled broadly.

They drove for forty-five minutes, enjoying the cool breeze. When they crossed the bridge over the Rillito River they passed an old plywood sign by the side of the road that read AVRA VALLEY CONCRETE COMPANY. Big faded black letters on a cracked and weathered white surface. The plant was about a mile west, a long building on the north bank of the river. A high conveyor crane reached from the bed of the river to a tall round cement stack.

"That belong to George Callan?" Joshua asked.

"Wouldn't be surprised," Edgar said. "He owns just about everything around here."

They neared a turnoff, and Edgar told Joshua to take it. It was Tangerine Road, and they drove just east of the highway through a grove of tangerine trees for about a mile. The trees were heavy with their orange fruit almost ripe for picking. Past the grove they drove through a wrought-iron arch, fifteen feet high and thirty feet across, the top of which was two curved rods two feet apart with a name in cursive wrought-iron letters welded between them: LAZY G RANCH.

Past the arch, the dry rocky fields of creosote bushes, mormon tea, and maroon Santa Rita prickly pear cactus abruptly ended at a three-board white painted fence that ran as far as the eye could see on both sides of the road. The fence enclosed pastures of thick emerald green ryegrass and an occasional live oak tree. Hundreds of cattle grazed stolidly. A few of them, near the fence on the right, became skittish at the sound of the car on the dirt road and loped deeper into the pasture.

The car topped a small rise and the ranch house came into view. It was huge, built of red brick on the bottom four feet and white boards the rest of the way up to a high mission-tile roof. A white picket fence surrounded it. Two Mexican gardeners were clipping the honeysuckle bushes that nestled behind the fence, thick with orange bell-shaped blossoms.

Joshua drove toward the group of a dozen cars and trucks in a parking area to the right of the house. Beyond it was a round corral of split logs that looked woven together around a dirt arena. At the far end of the corral stood three horses asleep on their feet in front of a watering trough and hayrick.

"This place is somethin, ain't it?" Edgar said. "Right out of a pitcher book."

Joshua nodded. The boys appeared awestruck. As they parked, George Callan and the girl came through the front door of the house and walked quickly toward them as though they were welcoming arriving royalty.

"It's a real pleasure to have you boys out here," George said, extending his hand in turn to Edgar and Joshua and Adam and Jimmy.

"This is my niece Diana Thurber from Kansas City. I think you boys saw her over at the M.O. Club."

"Yep, I sure do remember," Edgar said. "Howdy, ma'am."

This is a scene right out of a Roy Rogers movie, thought Joshua. "Nice to see you again, Miss Thurber," he said and smiled. She smiled back at him. God, she could light up a room, he thought. What a beauty. "This is my son Adam," Joshua said, putting his hand on Adam's shoulder. "And this is Edgar's boy Jimmy." He pointed with his stainless-steel hand at Jimmy. Joshua's red-, blue-, and yellow-checked long-sleeved cowboy shirt covered all of the mechanical arm but the prongs on the end.

"Hells bells, boy!" George said, looking at Joshua's steel hand. "I gotta put you on as foreman for the roundup in the spring. With that contraption you can castrate a bull in about two seconds flat!" He laughed and slapped his thigh, and Edgar let out a bellow of laughter. Diana smiled demurely. Joshua chuckled, a little self-conscious. Niece? Is she really his niece? thought Joshua. That would sure be a nice surprise.

"Come on over to the corral here, boys," George said to Adam and Jimmy. "I got three old geldings back there that are just dyin for a coupla boys to play with. You can take your pick."

The boys smiled excitedly.

"Can we have all three of em, Dad?" Jimmy asked, looking earnestly at his father.

"Well now, Jimmy, I hardly think our little shed is gonna hold more'n one."

"How about me, Dad? Can I have my own horse?" Adam gave Joshua a look of ineffable hope.

Joshua shook his head. "We have nowhere to keep a horse. Can't put him in the coop with the chickens."

George stopped walking and turned to Joshua. "Well, maybe I can help you out a bit. I can have a couple of my boys bring out some lumber and tin and tar paper this afternoon. Won't take them two hours to slap together a little shed for you."

"I couldn't let you do that," Joshua said, embarrassed.

"*Pleeeease*, Dad," pleaded Adam.

"Listen, you don't have to give it a second thought," George said to Joshua. "I'm a horseman, and these three guys over here mean a lot to me. They've worked long years for me and they deserve a nice retirement. You'd be doing me a favor. Honestly. If I can make one of them happy and make your boy happy at the same time, why hell, it's worth a lot."

He was so earnest, and Adam's look was so hopeful, that Joshua couldn't refuse. "Well, I just don't know what to say. I'm really overwhelmed."

"Think nothing of it, son. It's my pleasure,"

George said. He unhooked the rope tie over the corral gate and they walked up to the horses. The horses snorted a little and tossed their tails, but they didn't walk away.

"Now this here's Geronimo," George said, patting a short pinto on the withers. "He's just about seventeen years old. Got run a little too hard a few months ago and got winded, but he's still a damn fine animal."

George walked over to a tall fat bay. "This is my pal Mesquite. He's nineteen and sound as a dollar. Loves carrots." He reached into the back pocket of his Levis, pulled out a stubby thick carrot, and gave it to the horse. The horse munched.

"Now this is my favorite," George said, patting a tall stocky buckskin on his pink nose. "I rode him for years. Then he got a bowed tendon and couldn't work anymore." He ran his hand down the back of the horse's right foreleg. "But he's okay now, he just can't work real hard. His name is Golden Boy, and he's sixteen."

Jimmy was in paradise. He was rubbing his cheek against the pinto's neck. Adam walked up to the buckskin and patted his nose.

"Here, give him some of this and you've got a pal for life," George said, handing Adam a couple of sugar cubes from his back pocket. Adam held them in his palm under the horse's drooping lower lip, and in a second Golden Boy had taken the sugar in his mouth, hardly touching Adam's hand.

"Isn't that sweet," Diana whispered to Joshua. He hadn't noticed that she had come up next to him and was pressing her breast against his right arm. Joshua wished he had some sugar cubes to hold out for *her*. She was dressed like a cowgirl in a tight pink shirt and tight Levis and gray and black snakeskin boots. She looked like she belonged in these clothes, not like a Brooklyn tourist at a dude ranch.

"Yes, I've never seen Adam look so happy," Joshua whispered.

She sidled even closer to him, whispering confidentially, "You just don't know how happy you're making Uncle George, giving two of his horses a good home. He's a real old-time rancher. He cares more about his livestock than most people care about their kids."

"Can I have him, Dad?" Adam asked, his face grave.

Joshua nodded.

Adam's face burst into a radiant smile. "Oh wow! This is the best day of my life."

"Well, that does it, then," George said. "I'll get Chico and some of the boys over to your place right now, and Alfredo will deliver Geronimo and Golden Boy to you in a couple of hours."

"I'm very grateful," Joshua said. "I just don't know how to thank you."

"Don't give it a second thought," George said. "At my age with all I got for a blessing, just watching the smiles on these boys' faces is thanks enough for me. I'll be seeing y'all. I better go find Chico and get him in gear." He walked away.

"I hope I'll be seeing you real soon," Diana purred.

Joshua nodded. "Me too," he said. He still didn't know if she was Callan's niece or lover, and he couldn't ask her for a date until he knew. He walked back to the car and waved to her as she went through the picket-fence gate to the ranch house.

That evening, when Alfredo brought the horses, Joshua asked him casually if George Callan owned the Avra Valley Concrete Company.

"Hey, man," Alfredo answered, "I dunno all what the boss got, but he got plenty."

"When did Diana Thurber first come to the ranch?"

"Well, Miss Diana been comin out here summers during school break for years, long as I can remember. She was real close to her aunt and uncle. Then Mrs. Callan died from cancer, and Miss Diana came and stayed on with her uncle. He's gettin old, needs someone to look after him, take care of the house, you know." Alfredo was about sixty years old, tall and paunchy, with graying wavy black hair and dark brown eyes. "She's some looker, huh?" he said to Joshua, and his eyes smiled knowingly.

Joshua nodded. "That she is," he said.

Adam walked up to his father. "What do we feed him, Dad?"

"Hay," Joshua said.

"Well I know *that*, Dad," he said, a little insulted, "but we don't have any."

"Oh, yeah, right." Joshua turned to Alfredo. "Is there a feed store around here?"

"Sure. Go up to Valencia Road and turn left. It's about a mile down."

▼▲▼

Adam would now be Jimmy Hendly's equal. When Jimmy had had Charger and Adam had no horse, it had been different. Jimmy was the big shot then. But now I'm a big shot too, thought Adam. Wow, things are sure looking up. And now I'm going to get a saddle and a bridle, if Dad will let me. Jimmy doesn't have either, just that old rope hackamore. But after I get one of those saddles like the cowboys use, with braided leather thongs all over and silver conchos, I bet Jimmy's going to be jealous. Now he'll have to ask *me* to borrow them, and I'll let him, so long as I don't want to use them. Boy, the kids at school are really going to be jealous. A bunch of them have horses, but none of them has a real cowboy saddle and bridle like I'm going to get.

▼▲▼

When Joshua looked in on Adam at ten-thirty that night, Adam was sleeping on the edge of the bed, crowded there by the new cowboy saddle. The bridle was beside his face on the pillow.

CHAPTER SIX

On Thursday morning, the approved contract came back from the Office of Land Management in Washington. Avra Valley Concrete Company had won it for $18,420,000. Now the hard part, thought Joshua, getting the Mexican government to go for it and agree to supply labor at a dollar a day per man. Joshua called Ferdie Molina and asked him to come down to Tucson in the morning and go with him to Nogales to interpret if necessary.

▼▲▼

They walked into the Nogales mayor's office at ten o'clock Friday morning. Mayor Don Carlos Menendez was a short slender man of fifty or so, very handsome, with long wavy white hair and black eyes and shiny manicured and polished fingernails. He spoke very little English and had an interpreter with him. Ferdie explained to him at length what the United States government proposed doing for Nogales, and the Mexican interpreter translated long portions of the contract for the mayor. The mayor was all smiles and fawning enthusiasm. Sure, he could supply as many as two hundred laborers

at a dollar a day. It was a handsome wage in Nogales. He would need the governor of Sonora's signature on the contract, of course, and the governor
would also have to sign entry permits for American
vehicles bringing construction materials into Mexico. But that should be no problem at all. The mayor
ushered them to the door and told them to have
lunch and buy some souvenirs for their families.
Come back at two o'clock, he said, and he was sure
he'd have the documents in order. Governor Alfonso
Calderon had an official airplane, a twin-engine
Cessna, and he could fly the documents to Hermosillo
and back for such an important matter as this.

Joshua was surprised but delighted. He had been
prepared for an arduous negotiation with a bunch
of crooks, as both Edgar Hendly and Harry Morland
had assured him would be the case. But this mayor
had been just the opposite: businesslike, professional, polite, and straight as an arrow. But if it
were really just the opening number in a long song
and dance, Joshua would know in three hours. If
the mayor wrung his hands and apologized effusively and told them how sorry he was, that the
governor's office had to study the matter and needed
more time, et cetera, et cetera, then the price of
the contract would be going up. How high? As high
as some corrupt politician's imagination allowed it
to soar.

But nothing like that happened. Joshua and Ferdie were ushered ceremoniously into the mayor's
office at two o'clock and handed a sheaf of papers.
Ferdie examined them, and his eyes fairly bulged
out of his head. Everything was there, the contract
for Mexican laborers to be supplied through the

mayor's office at a dollar per day paid directly to the men in cash each seventh workday. There was an "Attestation" sheet bearing the signature of the governor of Sonora and a gold seal attesting to the authority of Governor Alfonso Calderon to execute all contracts related to the sewage project on behalf of the President of the United States of Mexico, and approving the principal contract, the contract for labor, and all port of entry permits for importing American construction supplies for the project into Mexico on the approval of the mayor of Nogales, and directing the mayor to expedite all necessary permits. There were four copies of everything, and Joshua countersigned the documents as the authorized agent of the Federal Office of Land Management.

By three o'clock, everyone had shaken hands and exchanged effusive pleasantries, and Joshua and Ferdie left for Tucson. On the Mexican side of the border, the Corps of Engineers car was searched by a Mexican customs inspector. He opened the trunk, pounded the spare tire, looked in the tool box, closed the trunk, looked under the seat, and searched the glove compartment. Then he waved them through. They went through the same search by a Customs inspector on the American side. Then they rode in silence for almost a half hour, filled with the pleasure of their overwhelming success. Ferdie broke the silence.

"I don't believe it happened," he said.

Joshua cocked his head toward him. "I know what you mean. But it did happen. I've got a briefcase full of signed and sealed documents to prove it."

Ferdie breathed deeply and shook his head resolutely. "It just ain't the Mexican way. The normal negotiation is like what we did when we walked through the market after lunch and bought the serapes. They start with a huge price. You offer them a few cents. You haggle and argue for ten minutes and then finally agree on a price. But this scene with the mayor? It just ain't Mexico."

Joshua was listening intently. He thought about it for a moment. "Well, maybe it's just economic reality. Their economy down here is bankrupt, they've got huge unemployment, no medical care for most of the people, no chance of improving things without the help of the U.S., especially in a border state like Sonora. Maybe they just jumped at the chance to improve Nogales."

Ferdie snorted. "It just ain't Mexico, I'm *telling* you. If the mayor and the governor can't line their pockets, it just ain't Mexico." He shook his head grimly.

Joshua didn't share such extreme skepticism. He shrugged and went back to staring languidly out the window at the passing sights of the Santa Cruz Valley.

It was four o'clock when he got home. Hanna and Adam hadn't gotten back from school yet. He told Magdalena that he might be late and not to hold supper for him, and he took his briefcase and drove to George Callan's Lazy G Ranch. It was very quiet. The hands had apparently wound up their work for the day. Joshua parked next to the house beside several pickups and a fire-engine-red Cadillac convertible with its white top down.

He walked through the gate in the picket fence, and the front door opened. Diana Thurber came

toward him wiping her hands on a dish towel. She
wore a cowboy shirt and Levis.

"I saw the dust from your car on the road, even
before you topped the rise," she said. "I was peeling
potatoes at the kitchen window." She smiled at him.
"It's very nice to see you again. Do you have business with Uncle George?" She glanced at his
briefcase.

"Yes, I have some documents to show him."

"Come on in. He'll be up from his nap soon. You
can help me peel potatoes—" She caught herself as
soon as she said it and looked at him apologetically.
"Oh, I'm sorry, I guess you'll just watch, huh?"

He smiled at her. "You don't have to be sensitive
about my arm. I'm not. Really."

"Okay," she said and linked her arm through his
mechanical arm.

They went into the kitchen. "Why don't you take
off your jacket and tie and make yourself comfortable," she said.

Joshua struggled out of his beige cavalry twill suit
jacket and wrapped it around a chair at a small
dinette table. He took off his tie and laid it on the
jacket. He sat down on another chair at the table.

"Would you like a drink?" Diana asked.

"Sure, if you will."

"I will. Uncle George and I always drink a couple
of margaritas before dinner. Constancia," she called
out in a louder voice, *"dos margaritas, por favor."*

A moment later a plump middle-aged woman appeared with two drinks on a tray. She placed one
for Joshua on the dinette table and the other on the
sink counter next to Diana.

"Salud!" Diana said, holding up the glass.

"*L'chaim!*" Joshua said.

She smiled at him. "Don't you feel a little out of place in Tucson?"

He shook his head. "Not now. I did at first, in June and July. But now I really like it here."

"What brought you here?"

"I was in a veteran's hospital in Brooklyn recuperating from this—" he held up his steel hand "—and a bullet wound to my lung, and the doctors told me the climate in Arizona would be ideal for me." He shrugged. "They were a hundred percent right."

She nodded. "Yes, it really is wonderful here. Hot as hell during the summer, but it's dry heat, not muggy like Kansas City." She wrinkled up her brow. "I hate the summers there."

"Constancia told me we had a guest," said George Callan, walking into the kitchen and holding out his hand to Joshua. "What a nice surprise. You'll stay for dinner, of course." They shook hands.

"If I'm not intruding," Joshua said.

"Nonsense," Callan said. "We'd be delighted, wouldn't we, Diana?"

"I'll just peel one more potato," she said, smiling at Joshua.

"You got something for me?" Callan asked, nodding at Joshua's briefcase. He sat down at the dinette table and stretched out his long legs and arms like a dog just aroused from sleep. He was wearing Levis, a faded yellow polo shirt, and tan leather slippers.

"If you're the Avra Valley Concrete Company, I certainly do."

"That I am, son, that I am. It was one of my first ventures after my dad died. He left me the land and the livestock. I built the plant a year later. It's been real good to me."

"Well, it's about to be even better to you," Joshua said. He opened the briefcase, pulled out the documents, and handed them to Callan. "The OLM accepted your bid, and the Mexicans went for the project. They'll supply the labor in Mexico, and you've got the rest of it."

"Now that's damn good news," Callan said. "Yessir, I'm mighty pleased." He thumbed through the papers, examining them closely. "Anything else that has to be done?"

"No, not a thing. Start as soon as you can and complete it by April 10."

"Well, that's a cinch!" George said, slapping his thigh. "Constancia," he called out excitedly, "bring in that pitcher of margaritas." He smiled broadly at Joshua. "This calls for a celebration."

"I'm curious how you could bid the concrete so low," Joshua said. "You came in a half million less than the next bid, and that was precisely at the wholesale price for concrete."

"Well, I got a different setup here. I own the Rillito River bed for over twenty miles, so I don't have to pay any licensing fee for the sand and aggregate. You know, like old Jake Lukis does over at Mission Sand and Gravel. He has to pay a licensing fee and a raw materials fee to the Papago tribe because he's over there in the Santa Cruz River bed by San Xavier Mission. But not me. I got my own raw materials. So I can undercut most everybody's bid by a mile and still make a half million profit on the deal."

Joshua well knew what Mission Sand and Gravel

paid for its materials, since he had negotiated the
contract himself just last month. The license with
the Papago Tribe cost $225,000 per year, and Sena-
tor Lukis paid a dollar a yard for sand and pea gravel
and two dollars and nineteen cents for larger rock.
This would obviously make Mission's cost for a yard
of concrete much higher than Avra Valley's.

Three margaritas later, they ate supper. Delicious
roast beef and potatoes and boiled carrots. After-
wards they sat on the back porch and drank Cour-
voisier. The alcohol made Diana talkative, and she
told Joshua that she had been married when she
was seventeen. He was a beautiful man, a thirty-
two-year-old oil field roustabout from Oklahoma.
They were both pretty wild. The marriage had lasted
just ten months. She was now twenty-four years old
and didn't feel pressed to get married again. There
were other things for a girl to do in life rather than
shackling herself at her age to house chores and
children.

"Well, I'm a tired old man," George said, standing
up and yawning. "An old geezer like me needs his
sleep." He shook hands with Joshua and went into
the house.

Joshua was sitting on a thickly padded rattan sofa.
After a few minutes, Diana got up from her chair
and sat down next to him. She nestled her face to
his and pulled up her legs on the sofa. They were
both lazy from the alcohol, but Joshua's fatigue left
him when she kissed him softly on the cheek. He
turned to her and kissed her, and she slowly ran
her tongue around his lips. Her hand touched his
thigh lightly, and he put his hand on hers and drew
it up to the zipper of his trousers. She worked the

zipper down and reached in and touched him. Joshua unbuckled his belt and unfastened the snap of his pants and pushed down his underwear. She lowered her head and he felt her lips on him, and then her tongue, and she moved her mouth around him hungrily and he came with a groan. He was enervated for a long moment. Then he smoothed her rich long hair away from her face. She lifted her head and kissed him deeply.

"Let's take a walk," she whispered.

She stood up quietly from the sofa. He was still hard, and he stuffed himself back into his underwear and pants and awkwardly zipped them up. They walked slowly, hand in hand, to the small barn behind the corral. The door was open. A square opening in the roof let in the moonlight, and she led him to a low heap of hay. She took off her cowboy shirt and laid it on the hay. Then she took off her brassiere. She stepped to him and kissed him, and he cupped her left breast in his hand. She unbuttoned her Levis and pushed them and her panties down. She was wearing moccasins, and she stepped out of them and her Levis and panties. She laid the pants on the hay. She unbuckled his belt and unzipped his trousers. He kicked off his loafers and pushed down his pants and underwear and kicked them off in a pile. She lay back slowly and he lay down on her. She guided him into herself with long slender fingers wrapped around him, and she gasped and wrapped her legs tightly around him. He went for a long time this second time, and then they both lay exhausted and a little drunk from the alcohol and even more drunk from each other.

They made love again after a half hour, and after

another hour they walked hand in hand to his car
and kissed, and she said that she hoped he would
come to dinner again. Joshua said that he'd never
had a better offer. He drove home at one in the
morning with a marvelously cool breeze blowing his
hair wildly under a dazzling citron moon.

▼▲▼

A knock on his bedroom door awoke him early
the next morning.

"Daddy, you awake?" Hanna said.

He rubbed his eyes and glanced at his wristwatch.
Six-twenty. "I am now." He yawned.

She opened the door a crack and peeked in. "Can
I come in?"

"Of course," Joshua said.

She was dressed in a pair of wide-legged celery
green cotton shorts and an off-white halter tied
around her midriff. She had the fresh glow in her
cheeks that only a kid could possibly have at six-
twenty on a Saturday morning. But her eyes seemed
very sad.

"What's wrong, honey?"

"It's Magdalena."

"Yes?"

"She's in trouble."

"What's the problem?"

Hanna stared at him as though he didn't want to
understand. "*Daa-aad,* don't you get it? In *trouble,*"
she whispered.

Joshua knitted his brow. Then he nodded. "Oh.
Oh yes." He sat up stiffly in bed. "That's terrible."
He thought for a moment. "Sam?"

She nodded.

"God, that's just awful," he murmured. He grimaced with the pain of it.

"What are we going to do, Dad?" she whispered.

Joshua just sat up thinking, with no ready answers. "I guess that's up to her, isn't it, honey?" he said finally.

"She says she's going to have an abortion." Hanna looked away embarrassed that she had spoken a dirty word.

"How would she get one? It's illegal."

Hanna shrugged and shook her head. "Please come talk to her, Dad," she whispered. Her eyes were pleading.

"Well, wait a minute, Hanna," he said somberly. "This is not something I can do anything about. She's our acculturation girl, remember, and she'll probably be leaving us in a few months anyway."

Hanna recoiled. She gave him a sour shocked scowl as though she'd just bitten into an unripe persimmon. "Dad, that's a terrible thing to say," she scolded him. "She's like my own sister and Adam's mother, and she loves us all. You can't just throw her out or ignore her, like, like—" she grabbed for an appropriate allusion "—like she was a *scarlet woman*—" Hanna suddenly thought of a better simile. Her eyes flashed with her discovery "—like Abraham casting out Hagar and Ishmael."

Joshua looked down his nose at her and frowned. She appeared triumphant. Damn it all, he thought, she's right. Magdalena *is* family. I just can't treat her like a stranger and wash my hands of her. But Hanna's only fifteen, and I hate to have her exposed to a mess like this. Oh hell, what am I saying? Hanna's a full-grown woman. In fact, the way kids are growing up so fast these days, she could probably teach me a thing or two. Joshua felt uncomfortable.

He pursed his lips and nodded. "Okay, honey. Give me a while to shower and shave and we'll talk."

Hanna left her father's room looking very relieved.

A half hour later, they sat close together on the front-porch steps of the little house. The morning was a cool fifty-five degrees, and the sun was just breaking over Martinez Hill about three miles east. Shafts of roseate light probed at the last shreds of darkness.

"Have you thought about the alternatives?" Joshua asked.

Magdalena looked deeply unhappy. "I'm so ashamed." Her voice was guttural and low.

Joshua leaned over and kissed her on the cheek. "We're your family. Don't be ashamed. You were going to marry Sam. It's just a terrible tragedy no one could have predicted that changed everything. We understand that."

She breathed deeply and sat silently for a couple of minutes. "If I have the baby, my grandparents will be humiliated. The former chief of the tribe can't suffer such a thing."

"Stay off the Reservation. Just stay here with us," Hanna said.

Magdalena shook her head. "I can't do that. They're my people, I can't run away from them." Tears rolled down her cheeks. "If I keep the baby, Chuy Leyva will never go out with me again. There's a dirty Papago word for a man who goes out with a woman carrying another man's child."

They sat still for minutes, letting Magdalena cry

herself out. Hanna's eyes filled with tears and her chin quivered.

"I have to get an abortion. It's the only thing I can do," Magdalena said.

Joshua looked at her gravely. "How are you going to do that? It's illegal, and the people who do it with coat hangers may kill you. It's too dangerous."

"I can go to Mexico. Mexican doctors will do it. They're real doctors. There's one in Nogales, I got his name." She reached into the back pocket of her Levis and pulled out a piece of an envelope. "Humberto Fulgencio, *Clinica de las Mujeres*. It's on Canal Street."

"You mean where the open sewer goes under the bridge?"

She nodded. "About a mile west of the bridge is where all of the houses of prostitution are. Mostly Americans go to those places. I heard the doctor has a 'women's clinic' somewhere near there, where he can do the most business." She wrinkled her brow and looked away from Joshua and Hanna.

"How is this all going to go over with Father Boniface?" Joshua asked. "As religious as you are, are you going to be able to live with an abortion?"

She stared at him, her eyes twitching. "Do you think it's against God's law?" she whispered.

He shook his head slowly. "No. I think it's against God's law to force a woman to bear an unwanted child. The passion of a single moment shouldn't be punishable by a lifetime of suffering for both the mother and the child. And in a situation like yours, there's simply no question about it."

She gave him a grateful look, and then her shoulders seemed to sag with the weight of her problem.

"I asked Friar Boniface to marry Samuel and me. He said he couldn't because it would be against canon law since Sam was in a coma. And Friar Boniface knew that I loved Sam and that I was pregnant with his child. So what am I supposed to do? Canon law says I can't marry the father and make my child legitimate, and it also says I can't have an abortion. Am I supposed to have the baby and get thrown out of my grandparents' home and shunned from the Reservation and avoided like a whore with syphilis by every man I would ever want to marry?" Her voice was bitter and hoarse. She began sobbing.

Joshua put his arm around her and hugged her, and he closed his eyes hard to press back the tears welling up against his eyelids. Hanna wept silently.

"So what do we do?" Joshua asked gently.

Magdalena sniffed and wiped her tears with the back of her hand. "It's fifty dollars," she said, looking at Joshua fearfully.

"Don't worry about that. I'll take care of it. But how are you going to set it up?"

"I'll call on Monday, see what I have to do."

CHAPTER
SEVEN

"Couple of men in the lobby are wanting to see you," Frances Hendly said, standing in the doorway to Joshua's small office in the BIA.

He looked up from writing on his legal pad. "What do they want?"

She shook her severe, pinched face. "They wouldn't say. But they don't look friendly."

Joshua shrugged. "Well, it's Halloween. Maybe they're witches in disguise, or male witches. What are they called?"

"Warlocks," Frances said.

Joshua winked at her, showing her demonstrably how impressed he was that she had come up with a word that he'd forgotten. "Send in the warlocks."

Frances walked down the hallway, and a minute later two men walked into Joshua's office. Joshua stood and shook hands with them. The shorter, older man stared at Joshua's steel hand.

"Have a seat, gentlemen. What can I do for you?"

They sat down in the straight-backed oak chairs. Joshua sat in his creaking swivel chair. It had held his two hundred pounds for almost five months now, but it always seemed on the verge of collapse.

"I'm Henry Jessup, president of Transcon Contracting." He was tall and heavy, in his mid-forties. He was dressed in what appeared to Joshua to be a very expensive gray sharkskin suit. He had bushy dark brown hair and brittle flat brown eyes, small and deep-set. "This is the vice president for engineering of the company, Dan Swirling."

Joshua nodded. Swirling was a little older, probably fifty, and was bald except for a fringe of short gray-blond hair. He had a much softer look to him than the other man.

"I saw the published contract award to Avra Valley Concrete Company in the *Arizona Daily Star*," Henry Jessup said. "I was very disappointed that Transcon didn't win the bid."

Joshua nodded. "Well, you were a half million off the mark, Mr. Jessup. Avra Valley Concrete won it fair and square."

"Well, that's what we're here about, Mr. Rabb," Jessup said. "We don't think it was fair and square at all."

Joshua stared at him, saying nothing.

"You see, Mr. Rabb, my company has been in competition with old George Callan for years. We finally put him out of business about eighteen months ago." He turned to Swirling. "Isn't that right, Dan? The project over on the Tanque Verde Wash, where we concreted and riprapped a spillway for about two miles?"

Swirling nodded.

"That was also a sealed bid for the government, Mr. Rabb. We bid it right at six ninety-three a cubic yard for the concrete and a dollar more for the rock and we beat Avra Valley Concrete by eight cents. Of course prices were a little higher back then during the war. But our bid of seven sixty-one two weeks ago for this sewage disposal contract was bare-bones wholesale and couldn't possibly have been topped by Avra Valley. Hell, George Callan completely shut down his plant about a year ago. He couldn't compete with us for the big jobs."

Joshua studied the man's sober face. "I'm not sure what you're saying, Mr. Jessup. Are you telling me that it's a phony contract?"

Henry Jessup nodded.

"Well, I hardly think that's possible. Mike O'Leary from the Corps of Engineers is the inspector, and he told me yesterday that Avra Valley already had the forms in place for the concrete pouring for the culvert and had poured over sixty feet by four o'clock yesterday afternoon."

"I'm not telling you there isn't *somebody* down there pouring gray goose crap into a frame and calling it concrete." Jessup's tone was harsh, his narrowed eyes accusatory. "What I'm telling you is that no American concrete outfit could afford to do the job for what Callan bid. They'd go bankrupt."

"I spoke to Mr. Callan about that," Joshua said. "He told me that the reason he could underbid the rest of you is that he owns the Rillito River bed at his plant site, and he doesn't have to pay any fees or royalties for his materials."

Jessup looked at Swirling and shook his head disgustedly. He looked back at Joshua. "Pure nonsense, Mr. Rabb. George doesn't own the riverbed, the Chinks do. Hell, he has to pay them more for materials than Senator Lukis is paying the Papagos over at Mission Sand and Gravel."

Joshua swallowed. "Who are the Chinks?"

"The Hing family in Marana. Old Buck Henry Hing came out here as a coolie for the Southern Pacific Railroad forty years ago. The railroad paid off in worthless land along their right-of-way in those days. Old Buck Henry has sixteen sections checkerboarded on both sides of the tracks through Marana. It covers the Rillito River for several miles."

The man doesn't appear to be lying, Joshua thought. So what the hell is going on here? "Listen," he said to Jessup, "I'm a little new in Tucson, but I've been practicing law for ten years, and I didn't think I was so wet behind the ears that I could get duped as badly as you indicate. And the Corps of Engineers boys from Phoenix are in charge of inspecting and holding Avra Valley to the contract specifications. I know you gentlemen are upset about losing the bid, but I can't believe the whole thing is just a fraud."

Jessup sighed deeply, suppressing a geyser of anger. "Tell him, Danny," he said, not taking his eyes off Joshua.

Dan Swirling opened the attaché case in his lap. He withdrew several photographs and laid them before Joshua on the desk. "I went out to Avra Valley Concrete on Tuesday morning and took these pictures. Here, you can see"—leaning over the desk and pointing at specific things in the photos—"that the main doors are chained and padlocked, windows are all broken out, the plant is empty, and all the equipment has been removed. There are no cement-mixer trucks there at all, and look at this one here. There's no conveyor belt on the conveyor crane that goes from the riverbed into the crusher stack."

Joshua studied the pictures. He clenched his jaw.

"Then what the hell's going on in Nogales?" He threw up his arms in frustration. Swirling stared at the ominous-looking steel-pronged hand like it was a bird of prey, a falcon or a hawk.

"Do you know the O'Leary family?" Jessup asked. Joshua shook his head slowly.

"Well, Mike O'Leary's dad Arthur is in the cattle business out by Benson, about fifty miles east of here, and he's a lifelong friend of George Callan's. When they were kids, they went to boarding school together in Prescott. They also served in the same outfit during the First World War. They're thick as thieves."

Joshua got a sinking feeling, as though he were going to be sick. Mike O'Leary. That's how George Callan knew what the other secret bids were. He could underbid by so much that he was sure to win the contract.

"We've been hearing some talk about you and George's girlfriend." Henry Jessup said it slowly. He looked at Joshua with hatred in his eyes. "What are they giving you, pal? Maybe we ought to be sitting at the FBI office right now instead of with you."

Joshua stood up slowly. He felt like tearing Henry Jessup's throat out with his steel claw. Jessup also stood up. He backed away a few steps.

"Listen, Mr. Rabb," Dan Swirling said, trying to calm the confrontation, "we really needed that contract. Times are rough out here right now, not much building going on, a lot of unemployment. We bid the contract low, real low, giving us only something like ninety thousand dollars profit. But it would keep our crews working—we've got thirty-seven employees. This contract would tide us over for another six months and keep us from going under. We just can't afford to lose the contract to a crooked bid."

Joshua relaxed his shoulders and nodded. "I'll go down there myself and check on it. I'll call you."

"When?" Jessup asked. His chin jutted out, and his voice was harsh. "You going to take the cunt down there with you for a nice long weekend?"

Joshua stared at him. His voice was a growl. "Listen, mister, get off that high horse of yours or I'm going to knock you off." His face grew red. "I'll go down there right now and try to call you this afternoon."

"See that you do," Jessup said, walking quickly out of the office before Joshua could make a move toward him. Dan Swirling waggled his hand in a conciliatory gesture and followed his boss out of the office.

Joshua sat down slowly and slumped into his chair. What now, he thought. He was having trouble concentrating, a flurry of thoughts were fogging his mind. He glanced at his watch. Ten-forty. He had to drive Magdalena down to Nogales for her appointment at noon. That was depressing enough. Now *this*. Life was hard enough without shit like this. Diana, he thought, Diana gorgeous Thurber, with lips like the flesh of a Queen Anne cherry and eyes so soft they couldn't possibly harbor malice. Or could they?

He stood up and checked his wallet to see if he had put the fifty dollars in it for Dr. Humberto or whatever his name was. It was there. He walked out of the Bureau. His left foot began to throb. He never knew whether it was real pain in his foot from the loss of the four toes or phantom pain. Or perhaps a psychosomatic reaction to stress. Anyway, it hurt.

He picked up the cane from against the wall of his bedroom, and he and Magdalena got into the Chevy for the ride to Nogales. Hanna had wanted to go along, but Joshua had refused. So she had tearily parted from Magdalena after breakfast and gone to catch the school bus.

They drove down the Nogales Highway. Magdalena was very quiet and brooding. Joshua couldn't manage any small talk to ease her tension. He dropped her at the *clinica* on Canal Street, a small adobe building nestled between two larger ones. The building on the left had a bright neon sign: WAIKIKI BALLROOM. The one on the right had a name painted on its front wall: B-29 CLUB. Another one across the muddy street was the LAS BAHAMAS BAR.

Joshua drove back down Canal Street to the bridge and under it to the west bank of the Santa Cruz River. Several dozen workmen were laying in the wooden forms for the second hundred-yard stretch of culvert. A mixer truck was turning and pumping the concrete up a long tube that had a twelve-inch-wide rubber hose attached at the top. It hung down twenty feet, and two men were holding hard to the tip of it by handles and directing a steady flow into the wooden form beside the already poured piece of culvert. Joshua walked to the dry part of the culvert and stepped into it. It was firm and hard, and it didn't look or feel or smell different than any other concrete he had ever seen. But he had no technical knowledge of concrete or any other building materials.

He climbed out of the culvert and walked over to the two men working the hose. "Where does this concrete come from?" he asked.

The men looked at each other and shrugged. *"No comprendo inglés,"* said one. The other nodded.

"El jefe, allá," said the first and pointed toward a crew of laborers twenty yards away, digging the trench for the culvert.

Joshua walked over to them. "Any of you men speak English?" he asked.

A thin small man who looked like he was at least seventy years old walked up to Joshua. He had a long white beard and bushy salt-and-pepper brows and hair. His face looked like a walnut with eyes. He was wearing soiled white canvas pants, a long-sleeved loose pullover shirt, and leather sandals.

"I speak a little, Mister," he said.

"You know where these concrete trucks are from?"

The old man shrugged. "Sonora license plates, Mister," he said pointing to the tan plate with black numbers.

"Do you know the company?"

The man shook his head.

"Thanks," Joshua said. He walked back to his car. Well, he thought, whatever bullshit is going on, at least the work looks like it's being done properly. He drove back to the clinic and sat outside for less than an hour. Magdalena came out and walked slowly toward the car. She opened the door and settled gingerly into the front seat.

"You okay?" Joshua asked.

"Yes," she said, averting her eyes.

They drove to the border and went through the

mandatory search on the Mexican side and then again on the American side. They drove the fifty miles home in silence. Magdalena had a pill to take, a big fat white sulfa tablet, and Joshua watched her swallow it down in the kitchen. Her usually clear eyes were heavily bloodshot and her cheeks were drawn.

"You look exhausted," he said to her gently. "Why don't you lie down."

She looked at him and smiled for the first time in weeks. "I'm okay. It's just that I feel a little shaky from the anesthetic. I'm going to be fine." She stepped to him and he put his arm around her and they hugged. She wept softly. "I'm so ashamed, having to put you and Hanna through this," she said, looking tearfully at him.

"I told you before, and I meant it, that I don't think you did anything wrong. Neither does Hanna. We'll never mention this again, deal?"

She nodded and a smile slowly replaced her furrowed frown.

"I've got to go to Marana for a few hours. I may be back late."

"We'll be fine. Don't you worry."

He drove to the Lazy G Ranch and found it almost deserted. An old Mexican gardener who spoke no English was trimming rosebushes by the front door. Constancia, the housekeeper, told him that Señor Callan and Señorita Thurber had left for Hermosillo at two o'clock. They drove down in Diana's red Cadillac. She didn't think it was a planned trip. Mr. Callan had gotten a call from *Gobernador* Calderon's office a little after noon, and he said that something had come up and he had to go see the

Gobernador on business. He would be gone a week, he said. Diana went along to drive. Mr. Callan was too old to drive five or six hours all by himself.

Joshua got back into the yellow convertible feeling extremely frustrated. He had to have some answers *now*. He drove to the Avra Valley Concrete Company. It was obvious that the plant hadn't been in operation for a long time. Most of the windows were broken, the doors were chained and padlocked, beargrass and tall lavender penstemon were growing in untroubled clumps in the driveway and parking lot, and there was no equipment of any kind inside or around the building. The place was stripped bare.

Joshua remembered the name of the Chinese family whom Jessup claimed owned the riverbed. He drove five miles north on Highway 87 and stopped at its junction with Marana Road, at a Texas Oil Company gas station, a single rusty once-red pump next to a shack that looked like an outhouse. The attendant pumped a dollar's worth of gas into the Chevy and studied the car with evident admiration. He spat a gob of tobacco juice into the thin dust and wiped some drizzle off his bearded chin with the back of his hand. He pointed west down the road when Joshua asked him where the Hings lived.

Picked cotton fields stretched as far as the eye could see on both sides of the narrow dirt road. Joshua came to a sign that said MARANA GIN, and the road dead ended a hundred yards further at a tin shed as large as a football field with a cotton gin beside it. The gin looked like a huge steel water tower with an open top. Thousands of bales of cotton wrapped in bright yellow canvas were neatly stacked in a field adjoining the gin. Joshua drove through the narrow opening between the bales and the gin.

Behind the shed was a ramshackle house built of adobe with a red tiled roof. The sun had bleached the red to a pale tomato color, and rain and wind had etched the adobe so that straw stuck out of it everywhere. A boy of four or five wearing a big brown felt sombrero with fancy turquoise-colored leather trim around the edge of the brim and a silver concho hatband was playing in the dirt by the front door with several toy figures of cowboys and Indians.

"Is your mother or father home?" Joshua asked.

The little boy nodded. He pulled open the screen door and ran inside. A moment later a young Chinese woman came to the door. She was wearing a sleeveless Kelly green straight silk dress that reached down to the tops of her black fabric slippers.

"You want?" she said, looking at Joshua through the screen door.

"I'm Joshua Rabb, the lawyer in Tucson for the Federal Office of Land Management. I'd like to talk to you or your husband about the Avra Valley Concrete Company."

She turned abruptly and disappeared into the house. A few minutes later she returned and held open the screen door. "You come," she said.

Joshua walked into the house and was stunned by the contrast. The entryway was a small vestibule with a dusty mud tile floor. But through the door into the living room he entered an entirely different world. The floor was tiled in gleaming squares of veiny beige and green and rust Mexican onyx. The furniture was the sort of thing you'd see in China-town in New York City, a delicate dark bentwood sofa and chairs with thick pads upholstered in white satin. The entire spacious room was paneled in rich black walnut. The lady pointed Joshua to a chair and he sat down.

A side door opened and a middle-aged Chinese man came in. He had shaggy thick black hair with-out a hint of gray and tiny black eyes. He was no more than five feet tall but very stocky, with a barrel chest and heavily muscled arms. He wore a dirty olive-drab army undershirt, grease-spotted fatigue pants, and dirty tan suede cowboy boots. He wiped his hands energetically with a shop rag and sat down on the edge of a flagstone seat that extended out from the tall stone fireplace. He nodded at Joshua. His face was expressionless.

"I'd like to ask you about the Avra Valley Con-crete Company," Joshua said.

The woman spoke to the man in Chinese, he said a few words, and she said, "My husband no have knowing."

Joshua knew that he was getting the "drop dead" treatment. The man had been here for forty years, probably since he was ten or twelve, and undoubt-edly could handle English. The attractive woman looked to be about thirty, and she could probably speak a good deal better than this illiterate patois. But there wasn't anything that Joshua could do to break through the armor.

"Are you Buck Henry Hing?"

The man nodded without translation.

"I was told by a man named Henry Jessup that

you own the bed of the river down where the Avra Valley Concrete Company's plant is located."

The woman spoke rapid Chinese. Buck Henry didn't say a word.

"I need to verify that information for official purposes, Mr. Hing."

Chinese translation. Buck Henry shrugged his shoulders and stood up.

"He no know, Misser Rabb," the woman said. "You leave now."

Joshua had no choice but to leave the house. The door locked behind him. He got into his car and sat tightly clutching the one-arm steering device on the steering wheel, smarting from the "treatment." It was a few minutes after four o'clock. If he hurried, he could reach the Recorder's Office in the Pima County Building before it closed.

He sped down the highway to downtown Tucson and got to the Recorder's Office at four thirty-five. It took only a few minutes for the clerk to find the plat map for Avra Valley Road at the Rillito River. The specific parcel was owned by "Southland Title Company, a Division of First Western Financial Associates, a Delaware Corporation, as Trustee for Trust Number 546-T, a Massachusetts Trust." Joshua knew that he had reached a dead end. "Massachusetts Trust" was the legal term of art for a blind trust, one that was legally entitled to keep its beneficiaries anonymous. There was no way that Joshua could find out who actually owned the land.

He breathed deeply and swallowed his frustration. Well, he thought, might as well try to get it from the horse's mouth. I guess I'd better go to Hermosillo tomorrow and have a chat with George Callan.

▼▲▼

It was almost five-thirty when Joshua pulled up in front of his house, angry and frustrated. The Ford roadster was there with the elderly woman in the same horrible flowery bonnet sitting behind the wheel. She nodded at Joshua and resumed reading the *Saturday Evening Post*.

God help me, he groaned inwardly. This is all I need to top off a real nice day.

He went inside. Magdalena and Hanna and Adam got up from the floor in front of the radio and went into the kitchen. Adam looked back and rolled his eyes at his father. Erma was sitting perched like a crippled woodpecker on the edge of the sofa.

"So nice to see you, Mrs. Carillo," he said.

"I tried calling you at your office all afternoon, Mr. Rabb." Her voice was querulous.

"Well, I was busy."

"Franklin needs you, Mr. Rabb." Tears began to drip from her eyes.

"What's the problem, Mrs. Carillo?" He was having a little difficulty remaining patient. It was too late, and the day had been a hard one.

"Franklin can prove he wasn't anywhere near the duplex where the mother and the baby were kidnapped and murdered."

"How can he do that?"

"There were eyewitnesses where he was."

Joshua pursed his lips and raised his brows. How could there be eyewitnesses that he wasn't there when he confessed to Joshua that he was?

"I visited him this morning, Mr. Rabb. He remembered that it must have been that night that he wasn't able to sleep so he went to the Mexican market down on Valencia to buy some beer. An old woman was parked there and had a flat tire, and Franklin changed the tire for her."

Well, here we go with the phony alibi, thought Joshua. "That's fine news, Mrs. Carillo. But how do we find her?"

"You can advertise in the paper." She said it belligerently, as though she were accusing him of being too cheap to spend a few dollars to provide an alibi witness for her innocent husband. "I gave you plenty enough money, Mr. Rabb, and my Franklin is still rotting away in jail."

Joshua wanted to tell her to quit deluding herself and stop running after imaginary witnesses. But attorney/client privilege prevented him from revealing that her husband had confessed to him. So what am I supposed to do now, he thought? Advertise for someone I know doesn't exist? That would be unethical. But if I don't advertise, then good old Erma will be screaming to the judge that I'm incompetent or dishonest and Franklin was railroaded. And just to keep up his end, Franklin will fire me, and I'll have to give back the money. I really love this. Yessir, yessir, yessir. This is the perfect end to a lovely lovely day.

"Well, Mrs. Carillo," he said, his voice saccharine with earnest concern, "let me think on this over the weekend. I want to pursue the best way to find this witness. I'll start something rolling first thing Monday."

She nodded and sniffed and looked at him as though she didn't quite believe him. She grimaced and stood up slowly with the help of her canes.

"I'll be waiting to hear from you Monday, Mr. Rabb," she said and clacked out of the house. Joshua closed the door behind her.

Hanna and Adam came into the living room.

"What's going to happen now, Daddy?" Hanna asked.

"Magdalena's making chile relleños for supper," Adam said, his eyes cheerful. He sat down in front of the radio.

"That's good," Joshua said, smiling at his son. He turned to Hanna, who sat down on the sofa.

"Well, I suppose some elderly woman is going to pop into my office next week and tell me that she was at the Mexican market at exactly midnight to one in the morning on September 19, 1946, and Franklin Carillo bought a couple of beers and changed her flat tire."

"Well, she'll be lying, Daddy."

Joshua nodded. "Yes, she'll be lying."

"So what are you going to do?"

"I don't know. I'll just have to deal with it when it happens." He shrugged his shoulders.

"That sucks," she said.

He fixed her with a frown. "Where do you get expressions like that?"

"Well, Daddy, I'm in *high school* now, remember? I can't walk around all day with bags over my ears."

"Well, don't speak that way in front of your brother."

"I'm no kid," Adam said sulkily. "I'm eleven, and if *she* can say it, I can say it."

Joshua breathed deeply and shook his head. "I've got a real pair of characters," he said and walked into his bedroom.

"Daddy," Hanna called out. "Can I go out with Mark tonight? There's a Halloween sock hop at Tucson High."

Joshua looked back at her from his bedroom doorway. "Tonight's a school night."

"But *Daa-aad, everyone's* going to be there. I can't be the only one that can't go."

"Okay, but be back by ten."

"Te-en?"

"Yes, ten. Do you see how I form the word with my tongue and teeth," he said sarcastically and pointed at his mouth.

"But *Daa-aad, nobody* has to be in by ten."

"That's not true," Joshua said. "*You* have to be in by ten."

He slammed the bedroom door and sat down heavily on the bed and began undressing. Next thing I'll be doing is beating them up with my razor strop, he thought. Headlines in the *Arizona Daily Star*: CRAZED SELF-RIGHTEOUS BIA/OLM LAWYER BEATS KIDS. And then the body of the story by J. T. Sellner, his favorite journalist, who had slandered him in every article that she had written about him:

DATELINE TUCSON. Avowed lunatic jackass lawyer J. Rabb stropped his kids today and managed to get his innocent client Franklin Carillo convicted of first-degree murder. The kids will survive, but Mr. Carillo will be hanged at Arizona State Prison next Tuesday. Franklin's wife, Erma, suffering terribly from muscular dystrophy, told this reporter that Rabb refused to let the star alibi witness testify. "I just can't understand it," said the devastated Mrs. Carillo between bouts of uncontrollable sobbing. "I'm going to complain to the Bar Association about Joshua Rabb and get Franklin a new trial. There ought to be a law about lawyers like him!"

He lay back on the bed exhausted and closed his eyes.

▼▲▼

Mark picked Hanna up at seven. He was almost as big as Joshua, hazel-eyed and handsome. His handshake was strong and sincere.

"Ten o'clock," Joshua said.

"Oh sure, Mr. Rabb," Mark said. "I'll have her back. Don't worry. We'll be at the Halloween dance at school."

Joshua watched them drive away. Don't worry? My little lamb is in the clutches of a big bad wolf, and I shouldn't worry? Halloween? I forgot all about it. Plenty of witches out today.

Voices outside surprised him. He opened the front door. It was almost dark, and Adam and Jimmy were sitting on their horses in front of the house.

"We're going trick or treating, Dad, okay?" Adam asked.

"Sure, but stay close. Be back by nine. And don't you think you ought to have a shirt on?"

"Aw, Dad. It isn't cold, and it'll ruin my costume."

Joshua shook his head. "Okay, but no later than nine."

"Okay."

The boys rode away from the house toward the Nogales highway. They reached it ten minutes later and rode on to the next road.

"It sure don't seem like Halloween," Adam said.

"Why not?" Jimmy asked.

"Well, back in Brooklyn it's always real cold and we get to go to Prospect Park and buy cotton candy and Cokes and then we go into the apartment buildings. Just a couple of buildings and our bags are full. Not like here. If we have to do all of them, it'll take a year!" He pointed down the dirt road. "There's only maybe ten houses this whole couple of mile stretch."

Jimmy shrugged. "That's why we got the horses. Quit bellyachin'. There's plenny a candy in them there farmhouses."

Jimmy was dressed up like the Lone Ranger. He wore a black bandanna over his face. His mother had sewn some shiny sequins on his gray shirt front and around his pockets. His father had bought him a new hat, silver felt with conchos on a black snakeskin hatband. He wore shiny Mexican silver cap pistols in a fancy two-gun holster with his name engraved on the back and dyed red against the black leather.

Adam was Tonto. He wore a loincloth and deerskin leggings, which Magdalena had made for him from a buck that Macario had killed in the Rincon Mountains just two weeks ago. She had tanned the hide herself and sewed it into leggings with leather thongs laboriously dyed dark red by the juice of pyracantha berries. Adam was barechested because he didn't want to detract from the authenticity of his outfit, even though it wasn't much more than fifty-five degrees.

The headlights of a car were behind them on the road, creeping slowly along. Adam thought that he had seen the same car lights following them all the way back on Valencia, near Indian Agency Road. But he wasn't sure, and Jimmy apparently hadn't noticed. So Adam didn't say anything. Why would anyone be following them anyway?

But it was. Adam started to feel sure of it. Other cars whizzed past them on the highway, but not this one. It just crept along on the shoulder fifty yards away.

The first house they stopped at was a tumbledown wooden ranch house. "This is old man Hoskins' place," Jimmy said. "He's got a son Hubie who's retarded. Dad says to stay away from him, but he's okay, just dumb."

The boys dismounted and dropped the reins and walked to the door. Jimmy knocked. A moment later an old man came to the door, tall and skinny and hunchbacked. He was wearing a filthy wrinkled light blue work shirt and dirt-stiff denim overalls.

"Hello, Mr. Hoskins," Jimmy said.

The old man squinted into the darkness. The only light was from a low-watt bare bulb hanging inside the door.

"That you, Jimmy?"

"Yes, sir."

"Mighty fine outfit, boy. You look plum like the Lone Ranger. Your mama sew alla them shiny things on your shirt?"

"Yes, sir."

"Mighty fine, Jimmy. You tell yer mama fer me."

"Yes, sir. Is Hubie around?"

The old man hesitated, and his voice was tinged with hurt. "No, not right now. He done got hisself in a little scrape agin, and they got him down at the jailhouse."

"Oh. Sorry, Mr. Hoskins."

"Just the way of it all, Jimmy. Here, lemme give you boys a couple sweet corn. I just harvested the back sixty."

He reached down into a burlap sack and pulled out four corns, still wrapped in their green shucks. He dropped two in Jimmy's bag and two in Adam's.

"What's yer friend's name?"

"Adam," Jimmy said. "His dad is the new lawyer over t' the BIA with my dad."

"Nice to meet ya, sonny," said the old man.

"Pleased to meet you, sir."

"Well, you boys be careful, hear?"

"Yes, sir," Jimmy said.

The old man closed the door. Jimmy and Adam remounted their horses, using the bottom rung of the hitching post as a step. They walked the hundred yards out to the road and down to the entrance to the next farm.

"I thought you said there was a lot of candy here," Adam said. "I don't even like corn."

"Well, that's just old man Hoskins. He's real poor. Most a these other folks ain't so bad off."

"What do you suppose his son Hubie did?"

Jimmy shrugged. "Dunno. Must've been awful if they throwed him in jail."

Again the headlights were on behind them, about fifty yards back.

"You see that car?" Adam asked.

Jimmy reined in Geronimo and turned around to look. The headlights were dim in the distance. Then they went off.

"I dunno," Jimmy said.

"I think someone's following us."

"What for?"

Adam had no answer.

"Come on. Quit bein a scaredy-cat."

"But somebody's back there."

"Yeah, a witch and some goblins," Jimmy mocked him.

"I'm not scared." Adam was indignant.

They walked down the driveway to the farmhouse, a much prettier and better cared for place than old man Hoskins'. A Mexican girl answered their knock. She looked admiringly at Jimmy's costume and especially Adam's. She handed them each a small bag tied with string. They remounted, opened the bags, and ate the chocolate quickly.

"I told ya," Jimmy said.

Adam nodded. Stars had begun to shine brightly, washing away the inky darkness. They rode out to the road. Suddenly the headlights of a car went on directly in front of them. Someone in a witch's mask leapt out of the car and ran toward the boys flailing his arms. Golden Boy shied and stumbled and bucked. Adam fell off. Geronimo took off down the highway at a gallop. Jimmy held on as tightly as he could, but his short legs didn't reach down far enough around Geronimo's barrel to get a good grip. He was thrown off about twenty yards from Adam.

The car crawled toward him and Adam on the shoulder of the road. Then it drove onto the roadway and gathered speed. Its dull red taillight was soon lost in the darkness.

"You okay?" Adam asked, walking up to his friend.

"Yeah, sure," Jimmy said. He rubbed his left shoulder.

Golden Boy was grazing nearby in a clump of flowers. Adam took the reins slowly, careful not to spook the horse again, and led him to a rock. He stood on the rock and jumped onto the saddle. He rode to Jimmy and they both went slowly toward

Geronimo, who had stopped running about fifty yards away on the shoulder of the road. As they neared him he nickered, snorted, ran another ten yards away, then stopped abruptly. Adam halted. Jimmy continued on toward Geronimo, stopped cautiously in front of him, and groped in the dark for the hackamore rein. He caught it and held it tightly. The horse whinnied and reared his head but didn't run off. Jimmy led him back toward Adam. He stepped onto a large boulder and jumped on Geronimo's back. The horse settled down.

"Let's get home," Jimmy said. "I gotta tell Dad."

"I don't think we ought to tell."

"How come?"

The horses walked complacently down Valencia Road toward the BIA. "If we tell, then they'll never let us go out riding at night again."

Jimmy considered that for a moment. "Yeah, I guess yer right."

They rode home in glum silence, looking carefully about to make sure they weren't being followed.

"Who d'ya think they were?" Jimmy asked.

"I don't know," Adam answered. "Maybe friends of my sister's playing a trick on us. Or just some jerks trying to scare us."

They turned down Indian Agency Road.

"I wasn't scared," Adam said.

"Me neither," said Jimmy.

▼▲▼

A few minutes after Adam and Jimmy rode off, Joshua ambled down Indian Agency Road to Edgar

Hendly's house and knocked on the door. Frances opened it.

"No rest for the weary, huh, Mr. Rabb?" she said pleasantly.

"Reckon not, Miz Hendly," Joshua answered in his best rendition of a western drawl. "Can Edgar come out and play?"

"Huh!" Frances snorted. "The only thing that old hoss has played in the last ten years is the radio. Wait a second. I'll see if I can haul him out of the chair he's wedged into."

Edgar came to the door in his baggy gray wool suit pants, suspenders hanging down by his hips, and an undershirt. He studied Joshua. "You look like a rattlesnake done bit ya on the dick."

"Come take a walk with me, Edgar. We may have a little problem with the Nogales project."

"Back in a jiff," Edgar called to his wife and closed the door behind him.

They walked slowly down Indian Agency Road. Edgar looked at Joshua and shook his head. "Trouble seems to stick to you like buzzard shit on a mesquite branch. So what's goin on this time?"

" 'Judge not that ye be not judged,' " Joshua said, shaking his finger solemnly at Edgar.

"Right," Edgar said. "And 'A stitch in time saves nine' and all that malarkey." He chuckled. "Now what's yer problem?"

"Well, it seems that George Callan may have made an illegal bid."

"How's 'at?"

"First of all, Mike O'Leary from the Corps of Engineers probably leaked the other companies' bids to him so he'd be sure to be low."

Edgar shrugged. "Normal government contract. Cain't do much about shit like that. Cain't hardly prove it, anyhow."

"Callan told me he owned the Rillito River bed so he got his materials free, that's why he could bid so low. That's probably not true either. It appears that the Hing family owns it. But even so, the Avra Valley plant isn't operational. I have no idea where Callan's concrete is coming from."

"Who gotcha all riled up about this?" Edgar asked.

"Man named Henry Jessup."

Edgar looked at Joshua and nodded knowingly. "Well, that fuckin Jessup ain't exactly a guy I'd put much stock in. Him and that company a his are just a bunch a crooks. They profiteered during the Second World War like Blackbeard's pirates. They got most a the 'cost plus' contracts the government put out for the All American Canal over in Yuma and the flood control on the Colorado River." He shook his head. "George Callan's a wily old fart and a helluva businessman, but he sure ain't any crookeder 'n Henry Jessup. Between the two of em I'd go for George. He may not tell ya every thought that crosses his mind, but when he tells ya somethin, ya can generally take it to the bank."

"Well, I still have to check it out. If he's supplying concrete from Mexico, the contract may be illegal."

"Well, I dunno nothin 'bout legal or illegal, but I do know somethin about George 'n Henry. Ya gotta be careful with old George, but ya cain't believe a solitary word that Henry says. I can guaran-fuckintee ya that."

"Okay, I hear you. I'm going down to Hermosillo

tomorrow. Callan's there on business. I think I'd
better get a handle on this thing right away before
it turns into a bigger mess than it already is. I may
be gone all weekend."

"I reckon little Miz Thurber is down there with
her sugar daddy?" Edgar smiled wryly at Joshua.

"Now, now, Edgar," Joshua chided. "This is
strictly business."

Edgar winked conspiratorially. "I think yer pissin
on my feet 'n telling me it's rainin." He laughed.
"You are one crazy som bitch, I'll tell ya that. One
a these days a hoppin-mad rooster's gonna peck yer
eyes out."

CHAPTER EIGHT

The great Sonora Desert is some eight hundred miles long and as wide as four hundred miles in some places. It extends south from Central Arizona deep into the State of Sonora, Mexico, and includes the Baja Peninsula all the way to its tip. On the east side are the Santa Rita and Chiracahua mountains in Arizona, which become the eastern Sierra Madres in Mexico. In its center, splitting mainland Mexico from the Baja, is the rift of the Gulf of California, the Sea of Cortez, as it is called by the Mexicans. The Pacific Ocean and the western Sierra Madres are its western boundary. The variety of terrain in the Sonora Desert is stunning, from an elevation of nine and a half thousand feet with pine and fir and spruce forests in the Santa Catalina mountains north of Tucson to hundreds of miles of white sand beaches that line the Sea of Cortez and the coast of Baja.

The five-hour drive to Hermosillo was on a narrow two-lane asphalt highway that was deserted but for an occasional slow-moving diesel truck overladen with tomatoes or carrots or onions or squash. The first sixty miles into Mexico past Nogales followed the Magdalena River through the Pinito

Mountain range, five and a half thousand feet high, so wet with recent rain and so green and thick with oaks and cedar trees and natural pastures of calf-high grass that Joshua felt as though he were back in the Catskills. The little towns along the highway here were just a few crumbling adobe houses with tarpaper roofs surrounding a grassy square with a tall church in the middle.

After the mountains Joshua followed the lush Magdalena River Valley, studded with vegetable farms for mile after mile. But past the picturesque town of Magdalena the elevation began to decrease and so did the lushness of the countryside. The land became rocky and parched as he neared Hermosillo. Yet it was still not barren. It was dotted with palo verde trees covered with tiny heliotrope blossoms and queen's wreath bushes with long vines crowded with hot pink flowers and mesquite trees loaded down with long yellow bean pods.

Hermosillo was a real city, several times larger than Nogales. It was a hodgepodge of contrasts, sprawling neighborhoods of desiccated wood-slat hovels with cardboard roofs and then suddenly a mansion—at least by contrast—with a red brick wall surrounding a two-story house covered densely in English ivy and bougainvillea, with its own water tower and electric generator shack behind it. There was no separate neighborhood where the rich lived.

Joshua passed several hotels that were clearly too modest for George Callan. But in the city square there were two large and attractive hotels. They were on opposite sides of a quarter-mile-square field of grass and carefully tended flowers, leading up to a huge cement building with tall cement Doric pillars along the front. It must be the State Building, thought Joshua. He turned behind the first hotel he came to and drove slowly through the parking lot. No red Cadillac convertible. He drove to the hotel across the square and still found no red Cadillac. He drove to the parking lot of the State Building and went inside. The huge lobby was tiled in glossy red ceramic tiles. There was a stairway on each side. In the center sat a man at an elegant maple dropfront desk. Joshua walked up to him.

"Do you speak English?"

"Yes, of course," the young man said. He wore a light blue cotton suit and a white cotton shirt with frayed collar and cuffs.

"I'm looking for a man named George Callan, tall, gray hair. He has a young woman with him, very pretty. They were supposed to be visiting here in Hermosillo."

"Yes, they come here often," the man said in fluent English. "They are friends of Governor Calderon. They all went down to the Posada Hotel at Bacochibampo Bay yesterday afternoon."

Joshua felt frustration rising in him again, and he wondered why he had even embarked on this wild-goose chase. "How far is that from here?" he asked.

"Only a hundred forty kilometers," said the man, "an hour and a half. Just this side of Guaymas."

"Thanks." Joshua walked down the broad cement steps of the State Building and got into his car. In for a dime, in for a dollar, he thought.

As he descended toward Guaymas on the Sea of Cortez, the land became increasingly brown and dry and rocky. The vegetation became smaller and sparser, and the dry air became humid. At the outskirts of Guaymas was a huge billboard with an arrow pointing to the right: LA POSADA DE GUAYMAS, 5 KM. Joshua followed the narrow dirt road for three miles around a hill and suddenly Bacochibampo Bay was spread out in front of him. It was one of the most beautiful places he had ever seen. There were twenty-five or thirty villas lining the bay on the right, nestled among banana and kumquat and bird of paradise trees. To the left were several dozen red-tile-roofed bungalows around a central two-story building surrounded by huge palm trees. The backdrop for it all was a radiant cerulean bay with a little island in the middle of it and several yachts tugging softly on their anchors in a seemingly endless blue sea.

Joshua drove through a portal made of two tall cement statues in the shape of St. Francis of Assisi holding a fawn in his arms with a cement macaw standing perennially on his shoulder, staring out to sea. The grounds of the hotel were fabulous. There were high privet hedges trimmed in the shape of elephants and lions and deer and dogs; stately bird of paradise trees lined the cobblestone road, with long black pods hanging under their orange and yellow and red flowers so that the trees appeared to have hundreds of baby peacocks hanging from them.

He parked in a lot across from the main entrance to the hotel. The red Cadillac convertible was not there. Not more of the goddamn wild-goose chase, he thought. A hell of a long drive for nothing.

The desk clerk said that the Callans were in the large bungalow with the private beach. It was across the bay on the south side and could only be reached by boat. He pointed to the small pier, visible through the rear glass doors of the hotel lobby.

Joshua walked down the plank pier to the end. There was a twenty-foot motorboat moored there with a Mexican boy sitting in it fishing. The boy stood up, bowed deferentially, and wound up his fishing rod, a rusty tin can and a hundred feet of cord with a glistening steel hook on the end. Joshua pointed to the bungalow at the south end of the bay, maybe two miles away. He stepped carefully into the boat, anxious not to lose his balance and topple over the side. He sat down slowly. The boy cranked the motor with a rope pulley and untied the mooring line. The old wooden speedboat moved powerfully through the water and the boy beached it in the sand fifty feet in front of the bungalow.

Joshua got out and walked toward the bungalow. Suddenly a jeep pulled out from behind it and sped toward him. Two soldiers were in the front seat. It skidded to a stop ten feet from him. Another soldier came out of the bungalow carrying a Thompson submachine gun and ran up to him. All three men were wearing clean, crisply starched and pressed black combat fatigues and highly polished black painted helmet liners. Joshua was startled and reflexively raised his good arm in a gesture of surrender. The mechanical arm hung by his side. He was wearing a long-sleeved polo shirt that covered all but the prongs.

"*Levante las manos!*" yelled the man with the submachine gun.

"I don't speak Spanish," Joshua blurted out.

Diana Thurber stepped out of the front door and called out, "It's okay, *está bien, el es nuestro amigo.*"

The soldiers relaxed. The two in the jeep drove away and turned behind the bungalow. The one with the Thompson lowered it reluctantly, as though he were annoyed that there was no opportunity to shoot.

"You should have called first," Diana said. "These are a few of Governor Calderon's personal body-guards, and they're a little touchy."

Joshua managed a thin smile. "A *little* touchy?"

"Hey, *macho*," Diana said to the soldier, who appeared reluctant to leave. He was still holding his machine gun pointed at Joshua's knees. *"Mejor suerte próximo tiempo,* huh?" She grinned at him.

He was obviously pleased by the attention from this beauty, and a great wolfish smile spread over his face. *"Que lastima!"* he said and walked back to the house.

"I told him better luck next time, and he said it was too bad he couldn't shoot you this time." She laughed.

Joshua laughed less exuberantly. She took his right hand and they walked into the bungalow. It had a thirty-foot-square living room with three doors in the rear. The kitchen was to the right. The three soldiers were sitting around the kitchen table playing some kind of board game.

"My bedroom's through the middle door," she said. "Didn't you bring any luggage?"

"I just kind of came on the spur of the moment. I never even thought of luggage." He shrugged.

She looked at him thoughtfully. "I'm delighted you came." She paused. "But why did you come?"

"I have to talk to your uncle about the Nogales construction job."

"Oh, *official* business." She mouthed the word importantly. "Well, Uncle George is over at the governor's villa for the afternoon. It's on the other side of the bay. You'll just have to make do with me for the time being. There's a big banquet over there at four o'clock." She glanced at her watch. "That gives us a couple of hours to swim." She looked at his Levis. "But I guess you didn't bring a bathing suit either, huh?"

He shook his head.

"Well, Uncle George is a lot thinner than you, but he wears these big baggy bathing suits. Maybe one will fit."

She left him and went through the door on the left. She returned a moment later and held up a large pair of black boxer trunks.

He shrugged and nodded. "They look big enough."

"Come on and change in here." She walked into the middle bedroom. He followed her and she closed the door. She walked to a dresser, opened a drawer, and pulled out a skimpy bra top and separate bottom that looked like panties. They were shiny red.

"What's that?" he asked.

"A bikini. It's the newest thing from Europe."

"You'll look like you're out there in your underwear."

"Neat, huh?" She smiled alluringly. She unbuttoned her short-sleeve white cotton blouse and took it off. She stepped to him and turned around. "You can help," she said.

He threw the trunks on the bed and unsnapped

the lacy pink brassiere. She pulled it off and turned slowly around. "I'll help you."

He held up his arms and she lifted his polo shirt up and pulled it off.

"That's a mean-looking contraption," she said, staring at the leather shoulder harness and the strap that went under his right arm.

"Wait'll you see what's underneath."

"I'll live." She unbuckled the strap at the front of the harness and the mechanical arm came off in her hands. She laid it on the floor.

What was left of his arm was a puckered stump several inches long below the shoulder. She kissed the shoulder. "That must've hurt, huh?" she said quietly.

He shrugged. "I don't think about it anymore."

"Come on, let's go swimming," she said, changing her mood quickly.

She pulled off her cotton shorts and lacy panties and put on the bikini.

Joshua swallowed and tried to will away the excitement between his legs. But he couldn't. He unbuckled his belt and pushed down his pants and underwear and stepped out of them. He bent over and untied his black Keds sneakers and kicked them off. He lifted one leg at a time and pulled off his socks. She busied herself folding his clothes and laying them on the bed. He turned away from her self-consciously and struggled into the bathing suit. It was almost the correct size, just a bit snug, and the front of it bulged out. She looked at him and smiled the same sultry smile that had attracted him to her the first time.

She pulled off her bikini bottom and pushed him

gently back onto the bed. She pulled down his trunks. She sat on top of him, and they made love hungrily.

Then they dressed in their bathing suits and walked out onto the beach. They spread towels on the sand and lay lazily looking at the sea, enjoying each other wordlessly, excited by the newness and freshness of their love.

▼▲▼

Two soldiers drove them in the jeep to the governor's villa. It was a ten-minute ride around the bay on a bumpy cobblestone road. A high spiked wrought-iron gate was opened for the jeep, and it drove slowly into the circular driveway filled with expensive-looking cars parked in front of a Spanish colonial mansion, two stories, square, with a colonnade of marble pillars along the front leading to tall double wooden doors surrounded by a ten-foot-wide rococo frame of hand-carved rosewood. Joshua and Diana walked through the doors into a huge pink-marble-floored atrium filled with lavish tropical plants in large ceramic pots and furnished in various spots with metal lawn chairs and chaises and tables with pastel canvas umbrellas. On the left side of the courtyard was a long room walled entirely in glass with several sliding-glass doors. On the right side was a long row of enclosed rooms. The courtyard opened at the back to a hundred-yard stretch of beach and Bacochibampo Bay. Anchored in the rippling glinting water about a hundred feet from the shore was a forty-foot motor yacht.

Diana led Joshua through a sliding-glass door on

the left into a long room with a buffet table in the center covered with platters of cheeses and fruit and pickled and smoked fish and cold meats. A roast pig was in the middle of the table with a red apple in its mouth. Joshua had only seen this kind of feast in the movies.

A dozen or so people grazed at the table, mostly elderly men in various-colored Bermuda shorts and sandals and Acapulco shirts of white cotton lace. Their ladies were all in silk sundresses, even the fat ones, and they wore spike heels in gaudy bright colors. Diana was also wearing a silk sundress, pale rose, simple and low on her large bosom, with a tight sheath skirt.

A short man in white Bermudas, white suede bucks, white silk knee socks, and a white silk Acapulco shirt came up to Diana, his hands outstretched, and hugged her warmly. He had wavy hair plastered to his skull and obviously dyed dark blond. He was heavy but compact, like a man who is vain about his figure and runs every day on the beach to slim his bulging hips. But his deeply lined face and washed-out blue eyes displayed his age. He must be at least seventy, thought Joshua, maybe even seventy-five.

"This is Joshua Rabb," Diana introduced him, "the lawyer I told you about last night at dinner. He dropped in for a surprise visit this afternoon. Joshua, this is the Honorable Alfonso Calderon, Governor of Sonora."

"I'm very pleased to meet you, my boy," the governor said in perfect unaccented English. "If my Diana is taken with you, you must be one hell of a man." He smiled and shook Joshua's hand gustily.

George Callan was dressed almost identically to the governor, except his shirt was pale turquoise. "What a nice surprise," he said, shaking hands with Joshua. "Here just for a visit?"

His smile was just a little too fixed, and his baby blue eyes were too flat, to really be pleased, Joshua thought. He shook hands with Callan. "I just came down to talk with you about the Nogales contract."

Callan's smile turned brittle. He blanched slightly, but quickly regained his composure. "We can do that later. No need to interrupt this magnificent banquet for my old friend's seventy-second birthday." He turned toward Calderon. "How have you managed to stay so young, my friend?" he said warmly. "You don't look a day over seventy." The old men laughed.

"I remember him the first day I met him at school," George said to Joshua, feigning confidentiality. "We were sent to boarding school in Prescott, eighth through twelfth grades, and we hated it there. We had to sneak out the window on Saturday nights just to go to a show. Remember, Alfonso? Where has the time flown, huh, my friend? What have we to show for all the years?"

The governor shrugged and wrinkled his brow. He lifted up his arm and swept it around in a slow arc. Both old men burst out laughing.

"Yeah, yeah, you're right, Alfonso. The years have been good to us, there's no complaining." George turned to Joshua again. "His father owned the biggest cattle ranch in Sonora, a hundred square miles just east of Guaymas. It was one of the old Spanish land grants from colonial times, when the Calderons first came here from Spain. My father bought most of his stock from the Calderon Ranch." He turned back to the governor. "Now there was a man, huh, Alfonso? Don Alberto Calderon was a real *patron* in the old days, when Calles was president of Mexico. Those were the days, huh, Alfonso? Your father could snap his fingers and have ten senators from Mexico City licking his toenails." George turned back to Joshua. "Plutarco Calles was from Sonora and the Calderon family helped him become president. There wasn't enough that Calles could do to show his gratitude." He shook his head wistfully. "Those were some days."

Joshua had the ominous feeling that he was being warned not to make any trouble. George Callan's power stretched all the way into Mexico, and his network of friends was rich and influential. Joshua fully expected that the next thing George would do would be to plant his chin close to Joshua's and breathe anchovy breath in his face and say, "You really think I'm going to let some pissant slimebag like you fuck me out of millions of dollars? Keep your mouth shut or you'll end up with cement boots at the bottom of that pretty little bay." But George said nothing of the kind.

He turned to Joshua and said, "You'll be our guest, of course. We have an extra bedroom, and I won't take no for an answer." He patted Joshua on the shoulder.

"Well, that's very nice of you. I'll stay tonight, anyway. It'll be too late to drive all the way back to Tucson."

"Splendid, splendid! We'll talk later." Callan winked at Joshua and walked off with the governor.

▼▲▼

"Now what was it that was so important for you to come all this way?" George Callan asked pleasantly. They were in the living room of the bungalow. It was almost eight o'clock. Both he and Joshua were sipping Presidente brandy out of snifters. George sat slumped in an overstuffed armchair. Joshua and Diana sat close together on a sofa.

"Maybe we ought to talk about this privately," Joshua said.

"No, no, don't be silly. Diana is all I have. I have no secrets from her."

"Okay," Joshua said. "I had a visit yesterday morning from a couple of guys from Transcon Contracting. They said your bid for the Nogales job was phony."

Callan's face turned sour. The pleasantness left his voice and his body stiffened noticeably. "You mean Henry Jessup, I guess, and that mousey prick that does his dirty work. Swirling, I think his name is."

Joshua nodded.

"Listen, son, those guys would sell their mothers to a nigger whorehouse if it meant ten cents in their pockets." He clenched his jaw and shook his head disgustedly.

"Well, I don't know about all of that," Joshua said. "But the information they gave me appears to be true. The Avra Valley plant isn't operational. You apparently don't own the riverbed—some Chinese people do—and therefore you can't underbid Transcon's price for concrete. And Mike O'Leary illegally revealed to you the other secret bids so you'd be sure to get the contract."

Callan stared hard at Joshua, then snorted and sipped some brandy. "It sounds awful suspicious when you say it that way, but it just isn't anywhere near that sinister. Sure, I played a little hanky-panky with Arthur O'Leary's son, but hell, what are friends for? And I do own the riverbed, at least an interest in it. I bought it from Buck Henry Hing six or seven years ago when he needed a few dollars, but you'd never be able to prove the ownership because I've got it buried deep in a blind trust." He stopped talking and studied Joshua. "But I suppose you know that already."

Joshua nodded.

"Well, good, I respect a man who does his homework. But the bottom line is that the contract is four-square one-hundred-proof valid. I didn't guarantee in that contract to *produce* the concrete at the Avra Valley plant. All I guaranteed was that the Avra Valley Concrete Company, which I own, would *supply* the concrete at the bid price. And by God, I'm doing it. I'm sure you stopped in Nogales and checked, and you found out that the job has started already and the concrete is first-quality Type 5, the exact product specified in the contract."

Joshua carefully considered what Callan was telling him. "But that contract was intended for an *American* company. You can't possibly be supplying concrete that cheap from an American supplier."

"Listen, Joshua," George said earnestly, "the Office of Land Management specs didn't require an American supplier. That'd probably even be illegal for all I know, restraint of trade and unlawful protectionism and all of that horseshit. I'm an Arizona corporation that has a valid contract with the Federal Office of Land Management, and I supply my product through a legitimate Mexican subsidiary in Guaymas. Perfectly legal."

"Let me guess," Joshua said. "You have a friend named Governor Alfonso Calderon who owns a concrete company, and that's where you've taken all your equipment from the Avra Valley plant."

Callan nodded, his face bland. "I moved the equipment down here a year ago. I've been doing a lot of business with Alfonso."

"That's why I didn't have to bribe anybody."

Callan nodded again. "I probably saved the U.S. taxpayers five million dollars."

"What's the price for concrete down here?"

"Well, son, not that it's really any of your business, but I like you. And what's more important, Diana likes you." He smiled at her. "I buy it from Alfonso for four fifty-eight a yard and it costs me right at ninety-three cents to truck it up to Nogales."

Joshua calculated quickly in his head. "That's $2.20 profit per yard times 2,250,000 yards, about five million dollars profit."

Callan nodded. "Of course, Alfonso needs part of that, and I have to spread a few bucks around to grease the rest of the greasers, so to speak," he chuckled, "but I still come out with a little profit at the end, and the Papago Indians get a clean supply of water for a hell of a lot lower price than anyone else bid for the project. Nothing wrong with that, is there, son?"

Joshua sat staring at the old man. He shook his

head and shrugged his shoulders. "I don't really know," he said. "Probably not."

Callan smiled. "Thataboy." He got up stiffly from the chair. "I reckon I've had enough talk for one day. Time to rest these bones. You kids have a nice evening." He walked into his bedroom and closed the door.

"Let's go for a walk on the beach," Diana said.

They got up and left the house. An almost full moon spilled fuzzy fluorescent light into the aubergine sky. It was sixty degrees and windless. They sat down on the sand next to the susurrating lip of the docile water and watched pelicans dive for dinner into the tenebrous beryl green sea.

"He's a good man, Joshua, he really is," Diana said reassuringly.

She lay back on the sand, and he lay next to her. A formation of cormorants soared overhead, cawing, and disappeared into the sable darkness.

▼▲▼

The next morning, Joshua awoke comfortably with the sun just beginning to crest over the low hill beyond the bedroom window. Diana stirred beside him and snuggled her head on his chest.

"I'd better go," she whispered. "I don't want to be sneaking out of your room in front of Uncle George. I'd be so embarrassed."

She got up and put on her rose-colored silk nightgown. She opened the door a crack, peeked out, and then tiptoed out of the bedroom and closed the door softly. Joshua lay there another few minutes gathering the energy to get up.

He went into the bathroom and showered. He hadn't brought along his Dopp kit, so he had nothing to shave with. In the medicine cabinet were a half dozen toothbrushes in sealed cardboard boxes with LA POSADA printed on them. There was also a can of tooth powder. He brushed his teeth. He ran his fingers through his thick brown hair and combed it back from his widow's peak. When he came out of the bathroom, George was sitting on the beach outside the front door, drinking coffee.

Joshua poured a mug of coffee from the pot on the kitchen stove. He went outside and sat down beside the old man.

"Isn't this something," George said, looking around the Bay. "You can't find anything better than this on the French Riviera or Spain or Greece. What a place to live, huh?"

Joshua nodded. "All you need is a hell of a lot of money. Then you can buy one of those villas over there."

"Hell, money's no problem!" George said. "It's this goddamn *country*! The electricity goes off for days on end, the roads are impossible, except for Highway 15 which you came down on. But it doesn't matter much anyway, 'cause most of the damn time there's fuel shortages and you couldn't buy a gallon of gas to save your soul. No, you can keep Mexico. I'd just like to pick this bay up and move it to Tucson!"

Joshua laughed. "With the profit you're making on the Nogales project, you can probably afford to do it!"

George chose to take it as a joke and laughed happily. "By the way," he said, "you can get some shaving gear and toilet articles at the hotel gift shop this morning. You don't want to be sandpapering poor Diana's chin." He winked at Joshua.

Diana came out to join them. "What's got you two so happy?" she asked, sitting down beside Joshua. She was wearing flimsy pink gauze harem pants buttoned tightly around her ankles and a matching halter that left her midriff bare. She had her hair in a ponytail, and Joshua couldn't take his eyes off her. Her hair glinted deep red in the sun, and her brown eyes looked to Joshua like they were flecked with gold.

"You look very pretty this morning," he said.

She smiled happily at him and turned to her uncle. "Sleep well?"

"Oh, not so hot," he said. "The humidity down here kind of stuffs me up."

They sat for a while making small talk. Then Diana asked Joshua, "What are your plans?"

He was thoughtful for a moment. "Well, I'm going to go back to Nogales and get the concrete tested. I'll have Harry Morland come down from Phoenix to do it. I've got to be able to assure the Transcon Company people that Avra Valley's contract is on the up and up."

"You won't be able to do that until tomorrow," Diana said. "The man from Phoenix isn't going to want to come all the way to Nogales on Sunday."

Joshua nodded.

"Good!" she said. "You stay here with us today and tonight, and I'll drive up with you tomorrow morning. We left my Cadillac at the federal police compound in Nogales. Governor Calderon sent his plane to pick us up at the airstrip there." She turned to her uncle. "Can Alfonso give you a flight up to Nogales tomorrow?"

"Yes, I'm sure he can. I'll meet you at the construction site at about two o'clock. Okay?"

"Fine," Joshua said.

"Come on, let's go for a walk and find some seashells," Diana said to Joshua and stood up. She held her hand out to him and pulled him up. He brushed the sand off his Levis, and they strolled slowly down to the placid water's edge.

CHAPTER NINE

Joshua and Diana drove up Highway 15 on Monday and reached Nogales at one o'clock. At the project site, at least a hundred men were working. A concrete truck was pumping product into the wooden frames, and pick-and-shovel crews were on both sides of the river digging trenches for the culverts.

They ate at the restaurant in the Fray Marcos de Niza Hotel, and afterward Joshua bought a new shirt in the hotel gift shop. It was a very cheap Mexican cowboy shirt, dark green with white trim around the yoke and collar and down the buttons in front. At a little before two, they drove back to the work site. The place was almost deserted. It was siesta time and most of the men had left. Work would resume at five o'clock.

Harry Morland arrived just minutes after Joshua and Diana. Joshua got out of the car and walked up to Harry, who was getting something out of his trunk. It was a three-foot cone, several inches across the top and truncated on the bottom to a one-inch opening.

"What's that for?" asked Joshua.

"This is the instrument for the slump test. I'm going to load the top of the cone to this line"—he pointed—"with fresh mixed concrete. Over a period of five minutes, the concrete will roll down the cone. If it slumps more than four inches, it means that there's too high a content of water in it, more than a ratio of .45 water to dry solids, and that means the concrete won't hold proper compression and it'll soon begin to decompose."

They walked over to the concrete truck. Harry banged on the driver's door. A man straightened up on the seat and looked annoyedly out the window.

"I need you to pump some concrete out so I can fill this thing," Harry said, holding up the cone.

The man shrugged. Harry pantomimed what he thought looked like pumping motions, and the driver got the idea. He turned on the engine, and the mixer turned for a minute and dropped a small pile of concrete on the ground through its rubber tube. Harry walked over to the concrete and packed the truncated cone. Then he stood the cone up, took a small stopwatch out of his vest pocket, and started it. He and Joshua watched the concrete slowly slump down the tube. After five minutes, Harry knelt beside it and pointed at the gradation mark that the cement had reached.

"It's just under three inches," Harry said. "No problem. The product meets our specs. I'm going to take a cylinder of it back to Phoenix with me and dry it and give it a compression test tomorrow afternoon, but I can tell you right now that it'll pass the test."

"Good," Joshua said.

Harry shook the cement out of the cone and brought it back to the trunk of his car. He wiped out the residue with a shop rag and laid the cone down. He picked up a stainless steel cylinder about two feet long and a foot in diameter and filled it with concrete. He screwed a steel cap over it and put it into the trunk. As Morland closed the trunk, George Callan drove up in the red Cadillac convertible with the top down.

"Well, you boys get your testing started yet?" he asked, getting out of his car and walking over to Harry and Joshua.

Joshua introduced the two men, and they shook hands.

"I've already finished," Harry said. "The slump test was fine. I don't think there'll be any problem with compression. It looks like your product is okay."

"Well, I knew it," George said. "I've never had a problem before."

A car came onto the bank of the river and came slowly toward them and parked. Henry Jessup and Dan Swirling got out. Both of them were dressed in gray workshirts and pants and gum-soled work boots.

Callan turned to Joshua. "What are these assholes doing here?" His face was ugly.

Joshua shrugged. "I didn't invite them."

Jessup stood ten feet away from the other men. Swirling got a small black briefcase out of the trunk of his car and walked over to the fresh pile of cement under the concrete truck pump tube.

"What are you doing here?" Callan said to Jessup.

"Your pal Rabb said he'd call me Friday afternoon. I waited. And I waited again all this morning. I figured I better get down here and find out what's going on."

"You fuckin asshole," Callan said through clenched teeth. "Where the fuck you get off checking up on me? I'll have your balls delivered to you in a bag."

Jessup backed away cautiously and then turned and went to the trunk of his car. He pulled out a three-foot-long steel jack handle and stood still, staring malevolently at Callan.

Swirling walked up to Jessup holding a small glass cruet. "It's not Type 5," he said.

"What in hell does that mean?" Joshua asked, looking from Callan to Morland.

"Well, it's kind of complicated," Morland said, "but our specs called for Type 5 cement. That's the chemical composition that we use for any concrete that's going to be heavily exposed to sulfates. Sulfates are what you get in sewage, and they also develop naturally in soil that gets a lot of rain. Down here in Nogales there's a lot more rain than in Tucson or Phoenix."

Joshua shook his head. "I'm still not following you."

"Type 5 cement contains no more than five percent of tricalcium aluminate," Morland said. "When sulfates interact with tricalcium aluminate, they create a new compound in the concrete called calcium sulfoaluminate. This particular compound expands into larger granules than the original tricalcium aluminate, and this expansion simply starts breaking up the concrete. A concrete with less than five percent of this stuff will not suffer significant decomposition, but the higher you go up from there, the higher the probability that your concrete will start cracking up."

"That's how I knew his bid was phony," Jessup said, pointing the jack handle toward Callan. "To be priced that low, his concrete has to be coming out of Mexico, and none of the outfits down here have the technology to turn out Type 5. Have you ever seen their plants? They look like Arkansas moonshine stills."

"I got all my equipment down in that plant," Callan said angrily.

Swirling held up the cruet and walked toward Morland. "I titrated it," he said. "I'd estimate the tricalcium aluminate is in the ten to twelve percent range, way over Type 5."

"Well now, mister," Morland said to Swirling, shaking his head, "I don't know you, but I know a little something about concrete. And I know you can't come close to analyzing it with that old reagent test. We stopped using it before the war. You've got to crush up a hunk of concrete and check the crystals microscopically."

Dan Swirling's face took on fierceness, the first time that Joshua had seen him lose his composure. "Well, I don't know who the hell you are," he said, "but I've been a chemical engineer for thirty-one years and in the concrete business for twenty. This color doesn't lie." He pointed to the cruet.

Callan's face was red with anger. He turned toward Joshua. "You going to listen to this shit?"

Joshua shook his head slowly and shrugged. "I don't know what to listen to."

"Well, I'll tell you what you do, you fucking corrupt kike," Jessup growled, still standing at the trunk of his car, slapping the jack handle into his open palm. "You fuckin people gotta be watched all the time. Throw ten bucks and a nice piece of ass your way and anything goes. What you damn well *will* do is terminate the contract with this cocksucker and by law award it to the next lowest bidder, which is me."

Joshua walked slowly toward him. This time Jessup didn't back away. He swung the jack handle, and Joshua parried it with his mechanical arm. The steel jack handle shattered the wooden arm. The stainless-steel-pronged hand hung loosely, suspended by the two thin steel cables that attached to the shoulder harness. Joshua hit Jessup full in the face with a hard right cross. Jessup fell back against the car, steadied himself, and shook his head groggily. Joshua smashed him in the solar plexus. Jessup fell to his hands and knees, gagging and heaving for breath. Blood dripped from his nose.

Diana watched open-mouthed from the Chevy convertible. She put her hand over her mouth to stifle her shocked gasps.

Callan's face was all smiles as Joshua walked back to rejoin him and Morland. "I like to see a man who knows how to deal with assholes," Callan said.

Joshua gritted his teeth and spoke low. "Let me tell you something, Mr. Callan. You better be putting Type 5 cement in that culvert or I'll terminate your contract so fast your eyes will spin."

Callan caught his breath and clenched his jaw and his fists. He stared defiantly at Joshua.

Joshua turned to Harry Morland. "How do we get this stuff tested so the results will stand up if we have to go to court?"

"I can test it," Harry said. "I'll bring a sample up

to the Engineering Department at the University of Arizona in Tucson, use their microscope. I did it there once before."

"No, no, no!" said Dan Swirling, joining them. Jessup was leaning against his car now, his head back, pressing a handkerchief against his nose to stop the bleeding. "We have to get Chester Milliken from the Portland Cement plant up in Phoenix. He's the best concrete chemist in Arizona. I'll call him and ask him if he can come down tomorrow morning, pick up as much as he needs, and bring it back for testing. Or he can test it down here, for that matter, if he can bring the equipment with him."

Morland shrugged, looking a little insulted. "Okay, I know Chester pretty well. I'll call him."

"Let's do it," said Joshua. "We can get a couple of rooms at the Fray Marcos and stay over."

Swirling nodded. Joshua walked to his car and got in. Diana fixed him with a hostile look. "How dare you say those things to my uncle," she whispered. "He wouldn't knowingly do anything wrong."

"Listen, Diana," Joshua said soothingly, "I'm sorry I lost my temper. I guess I'm just not the perfect gentleman I always thought I was. But I've got to get an answer to this. I can't let a twenty-million-dollar project be built which will last two or three years and then wash away into the Santa Cruz River. The FBI will be looking to put *me* in prison." He looked at her grimly and shook his head. "It's a goddam rotten situation," he muttered.

She breathed deeply. "Well, I better go with Uncle George. He looks like he's about to have a stroke. We'll get a room at the Fray Marcos. Maybe I can cool him off and we can all have dinner together. I'm sure that whatever happened, it isn't his doing."

Joshua nodded. "Okay."

She got out and walked over to her uncle and put her arm protectively around his slumped shoulders. Joshua struggled out of his shirt. He unbuckled the shoulder harness and pulled it off and laid it on the passenger seat. The steel hand hung over the seat on the two cables. Edgar Bergen could have a great routine about this, he thought. Charlie McCarthy's arm falls off right in the middle of the act, and Edgar picks it up and looks at Charlie in horror, and then Charlie says something incredibly idiotic, like, "Hey, Bergen, give me a hand, willya?"

He struggled back into the cowboy shirt and drove away.

▼▲▼

Joshua went to the Fray Marcos restaurant for supper at a little after six. He had spent the last three hours in his room trying to stay calm and read and relax. He had been carrying around the novel *Siddhartha* in the glove compartment since he had bought it in New York City last May. Hermann Hesse had won the 1946 Nobel Prize for Literature, and all of his books had been reprinted in German. Joshua's father was a high school German teacher in Brooklyn, and Joshua had been reared with it as his second language. He had read Hesse's novel *Knulp* a couple of years ago, and it was literally enchanting.

He had been reading a couple of pages of *Siddhartha* now and then for the past few months, but he never seemed to have the patience to devote several hours to it. But today he had forced himself to read, and he had managed to lose himself in Hesse's magnificent style and marvelous story about the Buddha's voyage of discovery of life and the meaning of man's existence. A literary review that Joshua had once read said that Hesse was under the spell of Schopenhauer's philosophy when he wrote *Siddhartha*. Well, Joshua didn't know a thing about Schopenhauer, but he knew a lot about novels and even German novels, and there was no doubt that Hesse had earned the Nobel Prize.

It was hard for Joshua to think good thoughts about Germans, even now that his searing memories of the Battle of the Bulge and the concentration camp near Medzibiez were beginning to dissipate and grow cooler, even now that he didn't think of his missing toes or missing arm every minute of the day. But anyway, Hesse wasn't exactly German. He had left Germany in the mid-twenties and adopted Switzerland as his home. So that separated him from the evil that had swept over Germany, and you didn't have to hate him for being a kraut.

This asshole Jessup was a different story. He would have fit right in with Hitler's crowd, probably have risen in the SS and become the commander of Mauthausen or Dachau, or if he was really good at his job, Auschwitz.

Stop it, Joshua chided himself. Just because the guy calls me a kike doesn't make him a concentration camp commander. He sat musing to himself, his mind gliding ponderously from his war memories to today's events. The waiter brought him a large fillet of cabrilla and roasted potatoes, which he ate without much appetite. Diana and George didn't come down for supper—at least not to this restaurant. At eight o'clock, Harry Morland sat down across the table from him.

"Well, I got hold of Chester Milliken. He'll leave at six tomorrow morning. Should be here by ten. He said he can bring along everything he needs, and he'll be able to test the concrete right here. I'll give him my cylinder for the compression test."

Joshua nodded. He was on his fourth margarita, and the edge was off his anxiety. "If I just stay a little drunk all the time," he said to Harry, "none of this crap will bother me."

"Yep," Harry said. "Pickle your liver and anesthetize your brain, and I'll be in Scotland afore ye."

Joshua laughed. "You been taking poetry lessons from Edgar Hendly?"

"I don't know the man."

"Well, you two ought to get together. Birds of a feather." Joshua smiled. "See, I'm learning from you guys." His words ran together a little.

"You'd best lay off that firewater, or you're going to wake up with one hell of a headache."

Joshua nodded. "I'm just drinking enough to keep me asleep all night."

After another drink, he went upstairs. His shoulder ached from the blow that had shattered his arm. He lay back on the bed and willed Diana to come to his room. But she didn't. He woke up at two in the morning with a small headache, and there was no one else in the room. He undressed clumsily and went back to sleep.

▼▲▼

He went downstairs to the restaurant at eight o'clock in the morning. Diana and her uncle were already there. They were sitting with Harry Morland, who for the first time was dressed in something other than a shapeless business suit. He was wearing a short-sleeved white shirt and tan cotton pants and cowboy boots that were shiny new.

Diana waved to Joshua, and he walked over to the table. Her long auburn hair was tied at the nape of her neck and fell loosely below her shoulders. She wore a red silk blouse with big yellow flowers with black centers. The gay short-sleeved blouse seemed to match her mood this morning. Joshua felt very relieved. If she was happy, her uncle must be happy.

"Good morning, Joshua," Callan said pleasantly, holding out his hand across the table.

Joshua shook hands with him. "May I join you?"

"Of course, of course," said Callan, flashing a friendly smile.

"Mr. Morland was telling us about Paris," Diana said. "He was there just after the liberation and helped rebuild several buildings and a bridge over the Seine."

Joshua nodded, feigning interest. All he wanted to do right now was eat breakfast quickly and get Diana to go back upstairs to his room and jump in bed with her. Her sensual look said the same thing to him.

"Well, I'm sure it was a lot different than when I saw it," George said. "I was in the hospital there in 1918, got shot in the leg in the Argonne Forest, October third it was. Damn, I remember it like it was yesterday." He rubbed his right thigh. His lachrymose soft blue eyes had a wistful, distant look. "Funny how your memory goes when you're seventy-two years old. I remember October 3, 1918, better than I remember last week. Huh!" He snorted and wrinkled his brow. "Of course, I wasn't a kid back in the Big War either, I was almost forty-five years old, a colonel in the Arizona National Guard. President Wilson mobilized us and bang"— he snapped his fingers—"a week later I'm slogging through a foot of mud trying to keep up with the eighteen-year-olds." He laughed. "Man, that was a time, I'll tell you that." He looked around the table at the others and nodded resolutely.

They ate breakfast with scant conversation. Callan turned to Diana and patted her on the arm. "You go along with Joshua, now. No need boring you while I talk concrete with Mr. Morland."

"We'll meet you over at the culvert at ten o'clock," Joshua said.

Diana got up and kissed her uncle on the cheek. Joshua followed her out of the restaurant.

She took Joshua's arm and they walked up the stairs.

"I missed you last night," he said softly.

"Me too," she said and squeezed his arm. "But Uncle George was feeling terrible, coughing and wheezing, and I sat up with him practically all night. He must have something wrong with his lungs from all the smoking he used to do."

They went into Joshua's room, and she turned to him and kissed him. She unbuttoned his Mexican cowboy shirt and threw it on the chair. He kicked off his sneakers, and she unbuckled and unzipped his pants and pulled them down, kneeling in front of him. He put his hand on her shoulder, and she nuzzled him and licked the tip and slid her mouth around it.

"You cute little devil," she said.

"Ooh," he groaned.

She stood up and took off her blouse and yellow linen skirt. He watched her undress, her eyes on his, and they stood and held each other tightly, feeling each other, loving each other. And then they lay down on the bed together, and they became one body.

▼▲▼

When Diana and Joshua reached the culvert, it was a few minutes after ten. The site was bustling with workmen, and three trucks were in a line by the wooden forms pumping concrete. Joshua parked his yellow convertible next to George's red convertible. George was sitting in the front seat chatting idly with Harry Morland. They all waved at each other and remained in their cars, waiting for Chester Milliken.

Henry Jessup drove up about a half hour later. He parked forty feet away from the two convertibles. Dan Swirling wasn't with him.

At eleven o'clock, Jessup got out of his car and walked toward Callan's. He stopped twenty feet away. "What the hell's going on?" He pointed to his wristwatch. His left jaw was black and blue.

"Have no idea," Harry called out. "Maybe he tied one on last night and got a late start."

Jessup growled something angrily and walked

back toward his car. He paced up and back on the riverbank, over and over.

At noon he walked up to the red convertible. "You sure you gave him the right directions and time?" he called out to Morland.

"I'm damn sure," Morland said. "We're all in the same boat, pal. Just take it easy. If it don't happen today, it'll happen tomorrow. Let's give him another little bit, and if he don't show up I'll go back to the hotel and call him, see what happened."

Jessup walked away and continued his agitated pacing. At one o'clock, Jessup again started walking toward Callan's car. Callan waved him off. "We're going to the Fray Marcos," he called out.

All three cars pulled away from the riverbank.

Joshua had spent the last two hours translating bits of *Siddhartha* for Diana, telling her the story, sharing with her some of Hesse's lofty poetic phrases. The time had passed swiftly for them both, absorbed deeply in each other like all new lovers.

There was an enclosed wooden phone booth in the lobby of the hotel. Morland went into it to make his calls.

"This is going to take at least an hour," said George. "Let's have some lunch."

Joshua and Diana and George sat down at a table in the restaurant. Jessup sat at a table across the room. They all ate and waited in agitation for Harry to return. Almost two hours later, he came into the restaurant.

"I couldn't even get through to Arizona Portland Cement. A telephone line problem. Operator said it may be okay at four or five o'clock." He shrugged, his thin face haggard.

"Damn!" Joshua said, slapping the table in frustration. "I've got to get back to Tucson and see my kids. I can't leave them like this for days on end."

Jessup came toward the table. "What the hell's going on now?" he growled. The bruise on his left jaw and cheek was deep purple.

There were ten or twelve other people in the restaurant, and they all stared at the Americans.

"Take it easy," said Morland. "I couldn't get through to the company, phone line's down somewhere. I'll keep trying. We'll get it done."

"You fuckin' bunch of thieves," Jessup muttered. "What'd you do, bribe the bastard?"

Joshua stood up, his face flushed red with anger. "I've had you up to here," he said hoarsely, drawing a line across his forehead. "You got a real bad mouth. I'm a crook and a kike and a thief. You have a very limited vocabulary."

He walked slowly toward Jessup. Jessup backed up quickly. At the doorway to the restaurant, he turned and shouted, "That bastard better make it here by tomorrow at ten or I'm going straight to the FBI."

Joshua returned to the table. "This is great. I can't even call Tucson and tell Edgar I'll be down here another day and ask him to have Frances look in on Magdalena and the kids." He turned a sour look toward Diana.

She patted his hand. "Why don't we drive up there, and you can see them. It'll only take two and a half, three hours up and back. And I'll drive. We'll take the Cadillac."

Joshua's face relaxed. "Okay, great idea. You're

on." He stood up. "We'll be back by dark. I hope we have some answers by then."

Harry nodded. George shrugged his shoulders, frowning.

▼▲▼

Joshua and Diana reached Joshua's house at four-thirty. Magdalena was in the kitchen making green chili and Papago fry bread. She looked comfortable. Her face had lost the sorrow that had disfigured it last week. She told Joshua that everything was fine, and the kids were under control. The sixty-five White Rock chickens in the coop outside were content, and Adam's horse Golden Boy was getting fat and lazy.

"All's well in Shangri-La," Joshua said to Diana. He smiled wryly.

Diana laughed. She sat comfortably on the over-stuffed couch and listened to the radio. Joshua went into his room to pack a small overnight bag with a change of clothing and his Dopp kit. He packed an extra shirt just in case.

Hanna walked into the house and looked warily at Diana. She walked past Diana nodding her head and smiling pleasantly. She knocked on her father's bedroom door.

"Yes," he called out.

She walked inside and closed the door behind her. "You get another paying client?" she whispered.

"No, honey, she's just a friend."

Hanna's eyes narrowed a bit. Then she relaxed. "Well, she's sure pretty."

"Not any prettier than you."

She smiled, "Do you really think so?"

"Yes."

"Thanks, Daddy." She kissed him on the cheek. "You leaving again?"

"Yes, I'm sorry. I've got to spend one more night down there. I'll be back by the time you get home tomorrow. Everything okay?"

"Yeah, sure. But Adam's been acting real crazy with Golden Boy. He and Jimmy went over to the pasture on the Reservation and chased Mrs. Antone's cows yesterday afternoon. I told him not to, but he wouldn't listen."

"Okay, honey. I'll talk to him."

They walked into the living room. Adam came through the front door, and Joshua said, "Hold on, Buffalo Bill, I want to talk to you." He went outside with his son, who had a scared look on his face.

Hanna flopped down on the sofa next to Diana. "Adam's about to get killed," Hanna confided. "He's not supposed to chase Mrs. Antone's cows. Jimmy Hendly and him shoot at them with BB guns."

"Oh," Diana said and smiled. "That sounds painful."

Hanna shrugged. "I really don't know, but all the running around isn't good for them. They're real skinny old cows."

"Oh," said Diana.

Joshua came back inside. "You've already met Hanna, I see," he said. "This is Adam. Diana Thurber."

The boy smiled shyly at her. "Hello, Miss Thurber. Nice to meet you," he said. His chin quivered a little and he walked into his bedroom and shut the door.

"Well, we've got to get going, Hanna. I told Adam he was grounded tonight. You take care of him and Magdalena, okay?"

"Don't worry, I will," she said seriously. "Nice meeting you, Mrs. Thurber."

"Miss," said Diana.

"Oh, sorry," Hanna said sweetly. "We never know around here."

Joshua looked sternly down his nose at her and frowned. Then he and Diana left the house.

▼▲▼

When they returned to Nogales, George and Harry weren't at the hotel.

"They're probably over at the Caverns having dinner," said Diana. "Uncle George loves it over there."

They walked hand in hand to the restaurant. It was after six and a thick overcast had enveloped Nogales. Joshua had changed clothes in Tucson and was wearing tan loafers, Levis, and a navy blue crew-neck sweater over a light blue polo shirt. The left sleeve of the sweater was safety-pinned to the shoulder. The weather had begun to turn in Tucson, and it looked like winter was about to arrive.

It began to sprinkle lightly. Diana pulled her black calfskin gaucho closely around her. "Brrr," she said.

They walked into the Caverns and through the bar. Harry and George weren't among the maidens. They walked into the restaurant. There were only about twenty people at several tables. George waved to them from a rear table for four.

They walked through the restaurant toward the table.

"Hey, *amigo*," someone called out.

Joshua looked toward the sound. Far to his left was a long table. A youngish fat woman sat at it in a frilly tulle pinafore, and beside her sat four little girls in puff-sleeved dresses of matching fabric. At the head of the table was Agostino Diaz. Opposite him, at the other head, was Juan Iturbe wearing a neck brace. Two elderly women sitting with their backs toward Joshua turned to look at him.

"Come on over here, *amigo*," Diaz called out, standing up at the table.

"Go on," Joshua said to Diana. "I'll be there in a minute."

Diana went to her uncle's table and sat down. Joshua walked slowly up to Diaz. The Federal police chief stretched out his hand and pumped Joshua's. He smiled a broad false smile and said something in Spanish to the others at the table. They all looked at him warily. Iturbe sat stiffly in his chair, his neck bunched up under his chin from the pressure of the long neck brace. He gritted his teeth.

"I just told them who you are, *amigo*," Diaz said. "They are very impressed with you." He chuckled maliciously. "Especially Juan's wife Josefina and her mother, my sister Maria Angelica. They just love what you did to Juan."

Joshua glanced at them, and they looked at him with hatred. "Real nice to see you again, Chief," he said. "And nice to meet alla you folks." He drawled like a good old boy, waved at them and smiled, and walked across the restaurant and sat down next to Diana.

"You know Augie?" George Callan asked.

"Oh, yeah," Joshua said. "We're old friends."

Callan studied his sour look. "Did you have something to do with the other guy's neck brace?"

Joshua nodded.

"Yeah, I heard a little talk about that from the mayor, Don Carlos Menendez. I didn't realize it was *you*." Callan's face was serious. "Augie's the mayor's cousin. They're real unhappy Juan got a broken neck. It's not a real good idea to make the mayor and the head *Federale* unhappy."

"The guy came at me with a switchblade. What was I supposed to do?"

Callan shook his head gravely. "Better watch your step down here," he said. "Those scumbags are pure shit. They'll do a job on you that an American scumbag couldn't even contemplate. And that piece of garbage is the *law* here." He gestured toward Diaz.

Joshua frowned. "After tomorrow, I don't ever intend to come back to this muckhole."

A waiter passed out menus. They ordered dinner and the waiter picked up the menus.

"So what's going on with our concrete man?" Joshua asked.

"Still don't know." Morland shrugged. "With this storm, the lines may not be up till tomorrow morning."

"Well, try again early," Joshua said. "There's no sense wasting another whole day down here."

Morland nodded.

They ate slowly and drank several whiskey sours. The band began to play, and Joshua and Diana danced. The band appeared to have learned the entire score of Jerome Kern's *Show Boat*. They played

"Why Do I Love You?" and "Make Believe," and "Can't Help Lovin Dat Man," and "You Are Love," and "After the Ball Is Over," and "Bill."

They danced closely together, and Diana sang in his ear, *"And yet to be / upon his knee, / so comfy and roomy, / feels natural to me."* Her voice was throaty and sexy. *"Oh, I can't explain, / It's surely not his brain / That makes me thrill— / I love him because he's—I don't know . . . / Because he's just my Josh."*

Joshua danced with her like a fourteen-year-old boy on his first date, with a perpetual hard-on and a hotly beating heart. Then they walked jauntily through a downpour back to the Fray Marcos de Niza Hotel.

CHAPTER TEN

Diana and Joshua and George sat in the hotel restaurant at seven-thirty the next morning eating breakfast. Harry Morland rushed up to them.

"He's dead! The poor guy is dead!" he blurted out.

"What?" Joshua said, rising from the table. "Who's dead?"

"Chester Milliken. Goddamn Chester Milliken is dead." Morland shook his head in disbelief.

"How the hell did *that* happen?" Callan asked.

"He apparently was fixing a flat tire a few miles south of Tucson. Somebody put a tire iron through his skull. But he wasn't robbed. Just left for dead." He looked around at the shocked stares on Joshua's and Diana's faces.

"Goddamnit!" George Callan slapped the table. "That fuckin Dan Swirling must have killed him to keep him from testing the concrete. I knew they were up to something when Swirling didn't show up with Jessup yesterday morning."

Joshua sat down slowly, shaking his head. "What the hell reason would they have to do that? There are plenty of other men who can test the concrete."

"I don't know," Callan said. "But with those assholes, it doesn't have to be any real reason. Maybe just to keep someone from coming down *here* to do the testing. After Milliken's murder, nobody else is going to be willing to come *here*. A sample will have to be sent to wherever the expert is, and who knows what'll happen, maybe they'll bribe him or shoot him or taint the sample." He shook his head and breathed deeply. "Who knows *what* those assholes got up their sleeves."

It sounded like hollow nonsense to Joshua.

"Harry," Joshua said, "if you have the proper equipment, you can test the concrete, right?"

"Right."

"Chester Milliken must have had the equipment in his car with him," Joshua said. "Do you know where the car is?"

"They said it was impounded by the Highway Patrol up at Sahuarita, hauled back to Tucson."

"Can you call the cement company and see if anyone has gone down there yet to pick up the car? If not, ask them if they'll call the Highway Patrol and have the equipment released to the Corps of Engineers."

"Sure," Morland said. "But how do I keep from getting killed?"

"The only ones who'll know about it are us." Joshua turned to Callan. "We'll keep our mouths shut, right, George?"

Callan nodded. His face was grim.

"I'll send an Indian policeman from San Xavier Reservation along with you when you pick up the stuff," Joshua said. "He'll come down here with you and then ride all the way back to Phoenix with you."

Morland nodded. He left the restaurant to use the phone in the lobby. They sat tensely, waiting for him to return. Finally, ten minutes later, he came back into the restaurant and sat down.

"Okay," Harry said. "They'll release it to me."

"Good. I'll go back to Tucson and talk to Jesus Leyva. He's the Papago policeman. Can you meet me tomorrow morning at my office at, say, ten o'clock?"

Morland nodded.

Joshua stood up from the table. "You going to drive your uncle back?" he said to Diana.

She nodded, looking grim.

"I'll call you later," he said to her gently and touched her shoulder.

He walked into the lobby, and Dan Swirling rushed through the front door of the hotel and ran up to him, his face furrowed with shock. "I just heard. I can't believe it." He was breathing heavily, almost out of breath.

"Where were you yesterday?" Joshua asked.

Swirling stepped back a couple of feet. "What the hell does that mean? I was at the plant in Tucson. Either Henry or I have to be there. Yesterday was my day. Today is Henry's."

Joshua stared hard at him.

"Listen, Mr. Rabb," Swirling said urgently, "there's no damn reason in the world for me to harm Chester Milliken. We want that concrete tested by an independent expert because we want the contract. The only motive is in *that* room." He pointed to the restaurant. They could see George and Diana still sitting at the table.

Joshua shook his head in frustration. Unfortunately, Swirling made a lot more sense than Callan. "I don't know what the hell is going on. I'm going back to my office to figure out what to do next." He pointed his forefinger at Swirling. "Don't you or Henry Jessup come see me unless I call you." He walked upstairs to get the small overnight bag he had brought with him from Tucson. He sat down on the bed, and then he lay back to rest for a moment. This whole mess was getting worse.

There was a quick faint knock on the door, Diana's kind of knock. Joshua got up and opened the door.

"Can I come in?" she said quietly.

"Of course."

She came in and sat down on the bed. Her slender shoulders in the soft white cotton blouse slumped dejectedly. She looked at him with melancholy eyes. "It sure makes Uncle George look bad, doesn't it?"

Joshua sat down beside her and put his hand on her hands in her lap. He nodded. "First there was just a problem with the quality of the concrete," he said gently. "But now we're talking about murder. That's a radically different thing. Concrete can be fixed up and corrected. Murder can't."

She sighed deeply. "I just can't believe that he had anything to do with any of it," she said hoarsely. "He's an honest man, and a *gentle* man, too. He wouldn't have any part in a fraud like this, and he certainly wouldn't commit murder." She shook her head. "It's out of the question." She looked at Joshua for reassurance. He said nothing.

They sat silently for several minutes. She cried softly. He dried her cheeks with the sleeve of his long-sleeved polo shirt.

She kissed him softly on the cheek. "I love you,

Joshua," she whispered. "Please don't hurt him." She stood up and left the room.

Joshua sat on the bed for another few minutes, very gloomy. Then he put his Dopp kit in his overnight bag and left the room. He walked to his car in the lot behind the hotel. It was practically deserted. The red convertible and Harry Morland's drab gray Corps of Engineers car and the car with TRANSCON CONTRACTING painted on its door were still there. It began to sprinkle lightly from a high thin overcast. The white top was up on the car, and Joshua got in.

He drove to the Mexican border inspection station. The same slovenly inspector whom he had seen several times before came out of his guard shack and approached the car window. Joshua cranked it down.

"Anything to declare, *señor*?" He smiled through rotted brown teeth. He smelled like a cheap cigar.

"Just the *touristas*."

It was a common joke at the border crossings. The Mexican customs inspector laughed appreciatively. "*Sí, amigo*, too many *frijoles*, huh? Please step out, *señor*."

Joshua got out, walked over to the guard shack, and stood under the extended roof to avoid the increasingly hard rainfall. The inspector turned the handle on the trunk, opened it, pulled the spare tire out of the trunk, and bounced it on the ground. Then he laid it flat on the muddy ground, took a small tool out of his pocket, and unscrewed the valve stem. The tire whistled out its air.

Joshua walked up to the inspector. "What the hell are you doing letting the air out of my tire?"

The inspector said nothing. He knelt over the tire and pressed his knees down on it, separating it from the rim. He reached inside and worked the deflated tube out. The tube had a foot-long slit in it covered by several layers of rubberized canvas electrical tape. He pulled off the tape, reached inside, and pulled out a small package. He dropped the tube, pulled a hunting knife out of the sheath on his gun belt, and plunged the tip of the knife into the oilcloth-wrapped package. The tip of the knife came out with a brown powdery residue. The inspector sniffed it and then touched the tip of his tongue to it. He held the package up triumphantly toward Joshua.

"*Caballo, señor. Caballo puro, uno kilo, yo creo.*"

"What the hell is that?" Joshua said, his throat tightly constricted.

The inspector pulled the Colt single-action revolver out of his belt and pointed it at Joshua. "Lay down on your belly, *señor.*"

"Listen, goddamnit, I don't know what the hell—"

"Lay down on your belly," growled the Mexican.

Joshua knelt in the mud and then lay facedown in it. Out of the side of his eye he saw the inspector's leg swing toward his head and saw the tire-tread sole of the huarache and then felt the severe pain of the kick in his left temple and ear. He passed out, he didn't know for how long, and came back into partial consciousness. There was a belly chain around his stomach and his right hand was cuffed to it behind his back.

Two men lifted him roughly by the chain and his shoulders. He stood up swaying, his head pounding painfully. Blood from his ear and temple poured down his cheek to his shirt. The heavy rain washed the blood and mud off his face and neck. It discolored the front of his once cream-colored polo shirt.

The two men walked him to the Mexican Federal Building less than a block away. Joshua was only barely aware of what was going on around him. He was in too much pain to focus his mind. His vision was blurry. They went into the building and down a stone stairway to the basement, which consisted of a line of steel-barred cells. There were several dozen inmates. Joshua was thrown into an eight-foot-square cell with three men in it, all sitting on the bare ground against the rear earthen wall. Joshua passed out.

He awoke slowly and shook his head to check the injury. A lancing pain shot through his ear and then turned to a throb that subsided slowly. He could hear voices all around, so he knew he wasn't deaf. His vision had cleared. He hunched into a kneeling position and looked around. The other three men were disinterested, sitting back against the wall and dozing. The cell was completely bare. The only things on the hard-packed dirt floor were stinking piles of feces and vomit and wet patches of urine. There were no buckets for toilets.

Joshua gagged and almost threw up, and then he did, spilling vomit onto the floor in front of him. He coughed the last of the puke out of his mouth and spat it on the ground. He walked on his knees backward and sat down against the cell door. He tried to relax and stay calm and stretched out his legs. The blood had stopped flowing from his ear. His clothes were soaking wet, his shirt heavy with a blackish mixture of blood and dirt. His Levis and loafers were covered with mud.

He closed his eyes and tried to sort out what had happened, but his thoughts were a jumble. His ear and temple throbbed dully. He receded again into unconsciousness.

Suddenly he fell backward onto the ground. The cell door had been opened. Two men lifted him up and walked him up the stairs. They went down a corridor and knocked on a door with a stenciled name: COL. DIAZ—EL JEFE DE LAS POLICÍAS FEDERALISTAS.

"Entre," called a voice from inside the room.

They pushed the door open and walked Joshua into the room. It had moldy gray stucco walls and two metal chairs in front of a small metal table. Behind it sat Agostino Diaz, his hands folded on the table. Behind him was a window looking out at the drizzle on the central square of Nogales, now a great mud puddle with a bronze statue in the center of someone holding his sombrero in his hand and rearing back on a horse.

"I can't tell you how much I have looked forward to this," Diaz said, smiling at Joshua. A guard handcuffed Joshua's belly chain to the steel arm of the chair.

"I already found someone who fell in love with you," Diaz said pleasantly, nodding his head and smiling broadly, displaying perfect bright white teeth.

"Juan Pablo, he's one of my regulars, gets drunk all the time, gets mean, I gotta lock him up to keep him from killing somebody. You gonna love him. He got a cock on him like a burro. He gonna *chinga* you so hard in the ass, you gonna have his baby." He erupted in peals of laughter.

A knock on the door.

"*Sí,*" Diaz called out.

The door opened, and a guard pushed a man inside and closed the door. The man was a few inches shorter than Joshua but at least fifty pounds heavier. He had filthy matted black hair and beard and wore the tattered canvas work clothes of a farm worker. His stench was almost unbearable to Joshua. His eyes were weird, tiny pinholes of glistening ebony.

"You know I was set up," Joshua said lamely to Diaz, his voice shaky and weak.

Diaz just stared at him with frigid eyes. He looked at the huge man and nodded. The man unknotted the rope belt holding up his pants and they fell down around his legs. He stepped close to Joshua. He held his penis and began rubbing it, holding it close to Joshua's mouth. Joshua pulled his head back and twisted it away, but the man grabbed his hair and pulled his face toward the now-erect penis.

There was a knock on the door, and this time the guard outside opened it without waiting for Diaz to say anything. The chief of the *Federales* stood up slowly at his desk. His mouth fell open, and his eyes bulged. Alfonso Calderon and George Callan walked up beside Joshua. Callan touched Joshua's ear and cheek tenderly and then patted him on the shoulder.

The governor was in an impeccable blue wool business suit, crisply starched white shirt, and black patent-leather shoes. He spoke rapidly and harshly to Diaz, gesturing demonstratively with his hands. Diaz came quickly around the desk and pushed Juan Pablo out of the office and closed the door. He went to Joshua and unlocked the cuff holding him to the chair.

Callan helped Joshua stand up. Diaz unlocked the belly chain and the cuff holding Joshua's hand behind him. Joshua stretched his arm out and worked it back and forth.

"Who did this to you?" the governor asked, pointing at Joshua's ear.

"The inspector at the border," Joshua said hoarsely.

Alfonso turned toward Diaz and sputtered angrily at him for a minute. The only word Joshua understood and caught was *"muerto"* over and over. "Dead." Diaz gulped and swallowed and looked fearfully at the governor.

Alfonso took Joshua by the arm and walked him out of the office. George followed. They walked down the steps of the Federal building in a fine drizzle. A black-uniformed soldier ran up to the governor and held an umbrella over his head.

"I can see that you are in no condition to drive," Alfonso said, businesslike and fully in command. "I will send Alfredo Vega up here tomorrow to pick up your car. He will deliver it to your home in Tucson. If you would just be so kind as to bring him to the airport, my airplane will bring him back."

Joshua stared at him, almost dumbstruck from the dizzying turn of events. "I, I, I, I just don't know, uh, I can't, uh—" he stuttered.

"Don't think a thing about it, my boy. You are not a heroin smuggler, I know that. And when my dear friend George Callan asks me for a favor, there is nothing that is too much for me to do to help him. *Adios.*" He bowed slightly, shook hands with

Joshua, and got into the back seat of a Mexican Army staff car.

Joshua turned to George. "What can I say? I owe you my life."

George put his arm around Joshua's shoulders. "We saw what happened at the border. We drove up while you were unconscious on the ground. I couldn't let that happen. Diana is in love with you." He smiled at Joshua. "Come on, she's waiting for us at the hotel. She'll be terrified if we don't get back right away." He patted Joshua on the shoulder, and they walked through the mud toward the Fray Marcos de Niza Hotel.

"What was the governor shouting at Diaz about *'muerto, muerto'*?"

George looked over at him and raised his eyebrows. "He ordered Diaz to execute the customs inspector who hurt you."

Joshua stopped abruptly. "Are you serious?"

George nodded.

"Can he really do that?"

"In Mexico, he can do anything."

"But the death penalty, just for the kick in the head?"

"He's showing you his affection."

Joshua shook his head gravely. "This is one hell of an affectionate guy. Let's get out of here."

They walked quickly to the hotel.

Diana jumped up from a sofa in the lobby and rushed to Joshua. He held her away gently. "Careful, you'll get this stuff all over that white shirt."

"Are you all right?" she gasped.

"Yes, I'm okay."

"Thank God."

"This time it wasn't God," Joshua said. "It was your uncle and Governor Calderon." He looked at George Callan. "Again, I just don't know what to say. You've done more for me in one day than anyone has done for me in my entire life."

Callan nodded. "Loyalty is the only virtue that counts for anything," he said, his face sober. "If a man has a problem, even if it may be one of his own making, he can only count on a true friend for help. Many who claim to be friends will fade into the woodwork or even betray him. But his true friends will stay at his side. The story of our Lord's last supper and His abandonment by His disciples is not an idle lesson. When Judas betrayed Jesus and He was arrested, all of His disciples fled and hid. Only Peter went to the high priest's palace to give aid to his Lord. And when he was asked if he was one of the followers of Jesus of Nazareth, even Peter denied it. Three times." George held up three fingers. "Three." He nodded intently at Joshua, letting the lesson sink in. "Alfonso and I are your friends." He paused, waiting for his words to sink in. "Take him upstairs and help clean him up," he said to Diana. "We can't take him back to his children like this." He smiled at Joshua.

She linked her arm in his and they walked upstairs. In the room, his overnight bag was on the bed. A fresh white short-sleeved polo shirt was spread out on the bed, along with a clean pair of Levis. Diana helped him undress, and he stood in the shower for fifteen minutes, letting the hot water pelt his body. He drew back the curtain and she was waiting, holding a bath towel stretched open. She dried him tenderly.

He brushed his teeth and combed his hair and studied the bruise on his ear and temple. The ear was badly swollen, like a fighter's cauliflower ear. The eardrum must be okay, he thought, because there was no lingering pain deep inside. He was still slightly disoriented, both by the physical injuries and the dizzying turn of events in just a few short hours.

Diana was behind him, hidden from the mirror, but he could see in the mirror one arm encircling his waist and the other reaching down and rubbing him. He became stimulated, and it felt very good. He turned around and kissed her. She took his hand, led him to the bed, and pushed him back on it. She undressed and lay down beside him and kissed his lips. He rolled on her gently and they made love.

▼▲▼

They walked down to the lobby hand in hand, Diana carrying his small bag, and George got up from a big armchair. "Well," he said, scrutinizing Joshua, "you look human again." He chuckled. "Another week and your swelling will be gone."

The Cadillac convertible was parked on the street in front of the hotel. It had stopped raining, but the air was chilly. The overcast was even heavier than before, great blackish balloons of water on the verge of bursting. Joshua looked at his watch, but he had no watch. He studied his wrist for a moment and realized that his one-hundred-thirty-dollar Benrus was now somebody's prized possession. Thank God that's all I lost, he thought grimly.

"What time is it?" he asked. He was in the back seat. Diana was driving.

"Little after one," George said. "Just lay back and relax. We'll have you home in no time."

They were waved through the Mexican border station but searched as usual on the American side. They all were quiet on the ride back, pensive and a little grave. The water on the highway splashed loudly under the wheels of the car, and the convertible top seemed to have an endless variety of noises, so conversation would have been difficult anyway. They rode in silence.

Suddenly Joshua knew that he'd been had. There was no question in his mind. It overwhelmed him like a religious revelation, instantaneous, absolute. Like Saul being struck by a great light on the way to Tarsus. George Callan and Alfonso Calderon had set him up. One of their minions had hidden the heroin in his spare tire, a place they knew that every border inspector always checked, and he had been arrested and mistreated and jailed, but then rescued in the nick of time. George and Alfonso had burst into Diaz's office and saved Joshua two seconds before the really bad shit happened. Just like Errol Flynn in *Robin Hood*, rescued from the brink of death by his band of merry men. Or was that in *The Scarlet Pimpernel*? Saving some royal family from the guillotine tumbrel and escaping from Paris by a ruse, putting the family in coffins as though they had died of the plague, so the guards at the gates wouldn't search them.

Joshua stared morosely out the window. Did Diana help them? he wondered. Was she the decoy? Was she really Callan's niece, or a fantastic whore from Kansas City who did her job well? It's not out of the question, he thought. It would be ridiculous to fall for the same shit again. What would George Callan pull next? Photographs of me being sodomized by that cretin in the jail? Come on now, quit thinking bullshit. Diana had nothing to do with this. She fell in love with me at first sight, and the first chance she got, she jumped on my dick like a kid lapping at a snow cone at the county fair.

It's only natural because I'm so irresistible. I'm rich. I'm tall, dark, and handsome. Well, actually I'm tall and dark. I was reasonably good looking before the war. But now I have a hound-dog face and a shriveled stump for a left arm and no toes on my left foot and an eight-inch scar on my chest where they took a bullet out of my lung. So why wouldn't a smashing beauty with a fabulously rich uncle fall for me in a big way? Bingo!

He gritted his teeth and sighed deeply and stared morosely out the window, seeing a kaleidoscope of images in his mind's eye. What will I do when Harry Morland walks into my office and tells me that George's concrete has double the percentage of tricalcium aluminate called for in the specs and that the culvert and the treatment plant are going to crumble up and wash away into the river in two to four years? Will I call George and tell him that I've just voided his contract and awarded it to that vaudeville team of Jessup and Swirling? And where will I end up? Alfonso will send two average-looking guys to visit me and I'll be hanging by my *cojones* from a mesquite branch with my heart cut out and stuffed in my mouth. Then they'll send up that Mexican band from the Caverns to play Jerome Kern love songs from *Show Boat* at my funeral. Diana will weep softly and sing in a torchy, tragic voice, *"After the ball is over . . ."*

Martinez Hill loomed up on the left, fuzzy in the rainfall, which began heavily again. Joshua gave Diana directions to Valencia Road and then left on Indian Agency Road, and she pulled up in front of the little adobe house across from the irrigation ditch with the Padre Kino Mission of San Xavier Del Bac looming up from a barren weedy field a half mile deep into the Reservation. He got out of the car and waved at them as they drove away.

He stood in the rain, hoping to wash the filth from his body.

CHAPTER
ELEVEN

Edgar Hendly walked into Joshua's office early the next morning. He stared at Joshua's ear and sat down on the straight oak chair in front of the desk.

"What in hell happened to you?"

Joshua told him about the heroin, the arrest, and the rescue.

"Holy shit, man! You are the luckiest som bitch in the whole damn world," Edgar said.

"I don't think it's luck. I think it was cooked up by George Callan. He's running gray mud up to Nogales and calling it Type 5 concrete and probably making ten million dollars in profit. I was about to terminate his contract. I think he got somebody to plant the heroin in the spare tire. Even the dumbest Mexican border inspector would find it—that's where they look first—and I'd end up staring at the acne scars on the chief of the *Federales'* face. Hell, Diaz didn't even have to be in on it. Because of what I did to him and his pimp nephew, I'd end up hanging like butchered meat in one of his jail cells. And then in the nick of time George Callan rescues me." Joshua shook his head. "And now I owe him my life. He now figures his contract isn't in danger, and he calculates that I can find a way to get Henry

Jessup off his ass." He looked hard at Edgar. "Hell of a deal, huh?"

"But you're not *certain* that's how it is?"

Joshua shook his head. "I just have a real strong gut feeling about it."

Edgar shrugged and snorted. "Joshua, you always look at everything in black or white. It's either absolutely right or it's plumb wrong. But *gott damn* it, boy, that ain't how life is! Life is just plain shades a gray. That's all it is, shades a gray. There ain't no perfect right and there ain't no perfect wrong. There's just ordinary people pokin along, trying to make it from here t' tomorrow the best they can and get somethin outta life. And then here comes Joshua Rabb, righteous old Rabbi fuckin Rabb, and you're tryin to be more *just* than *God*. What the hell you think yer doin? If God had wanted a world full a perfect people, he sure could've made it thataway. So that cain't be what he was after, huh? He must've been after a world where us plain folks do the best we can do and just get along the best we can."

Joshua shook his head and couldn't suppress a small smile. "I think they need you to lecture at Union Theological Seminary, Edgar. You'd have them bug-eyed and open-mouthed with that religion of yours."

"Well, shit, I dunno. I reckon I just see life a little different than you do. I see a plumb gorgeous lady who's ready to stick with you like a hen on a pump handle, and she's gonna inherit a movie dream ranch and twenty million dollars to boot, and you're fuckin yer life up worryin which crook set you up, Jessup or Callan! Hell, man, quit bein such a self-righteous asshole and feather yer nest a little.

You stick with George Callan and forget all the other bullshit. I mean is it really gonna change the history a the world one tick bite's worth if there's Type 2 cement in that culvert instead of Type 5? Hell, I talked to Harry Morland myself just a hour ago, and he says that if there really is ten percent tricalcium, whatever the hell it is, it ain't probably gonna make no difference for twenty-five years. It may crack up some in three to five years, but it ain't gonna turn t' dust and wash away. It's just gonna need a little resuscitatin, and then maybe in twenty years some of it will have to be replaced. Well, that's the way a the world, ain't it? So some other contractor makes a few bucks, and another after him. What the hell's so wrong with that? Harry Morland says he's willin' to recertify the specs on the contract down to Type 2 and require Avra Valley Concrete to post a one-million-dollar performance bond for five years to guarantee all repairs and maintenance. Hell, that's fair! I betcha my left dick George goes for it just like that." He snapped his fingers. "Just take it easy. The whole thing'll work out, and nobody has to get murdered over it."

"And how about the Papagos, Edgar? When the culvert starts breaking up and the sewage leaks through into the Santa Cruz River and pollutes the water supply and they start dying again in another cholera epidemic, do we just tell them not to worry, we'll throw a few patches in it and it'll be all right for a few more months until the culvert starts dissolving again?"

Edgar wagged his finger sternly at Joshua and left the office.

Joshua sat in his creaking chair and slowly swiveled right and left, then rocked it slightly on its ill-fitting central post. Morland called and said that he had spoken to Edgar just a few minutes ago and there was a way out. They could rewrite the specifications for the contract and force the contractor to post a bond for performance. But, of course, they'd still need to get a sample of the concrete to test.

Jesus Leyva came into Joshua's office at a quarter of ten as he had been instructed to do, and Joshua asked him to have a seat. Chuy was very big for a Papago, almost Joshua's height, and strongly built. His biceps bulged tightly and filled the short sleeves of his tan cotton uniform shirt. His forearms were veiny like a weightlifter's. He had straight black hair and wore it in the traditional style, shaggy to the shoulders with a plain headband of a hank of twisted coarse red muslin. He had the obsidian eyes of the pure Papago and he stared at Joshua, studying him.

"I asked you to come because I was going to send you down to Nogales to guard a guy from the Corps of Engineers while he picked up a sample of concrete, but our plans have changed."

"Yeah, I heard." His voice was deep and strong.

"Word travels fast on the Reservation."

"Especially when it's you who's in trouble," Leyva said.

"Well, I'm glad somebody cares about me." Joshua chuckled lightly and smiled.

"My people care about you. Because of Chief Macario's son. We went to school together. He was my friend." He stared unsmiling at Joshua.

Joshua was sobered by the Indian's intensity. "Thanks, I really appreciate it." He nodded at Leyva.

"You still thinking about getting a sample of concrete up here for testing?" Chuy asked.

Joshua nodded.

"Why not just ask Avra Valley to drive one of its trucks up here fully loaded?"

"Because he can taint the load, doctor it up. We have to pull a random sample from a truck pumping at the culvert."

"I'll go get one," Chuy said.

Joshua shook his head. "You'd probably be dead before you reached the work site. You can't take a gun across the border, and without it you're dead meat. These are very determined people."

Jesus shrugged. "I'm a very determined man, Mr. Rabb."

"Call me Joshua."

The Indian nodded. "I will get your sample."

"How?"

"I don't know." He shrugged. "I'll have to go down and see. Mexicans are frightened of people in uniform. The drivers will think I'm a Yaqui policeman from down in Sonora where most of them live, between Hermosillo and Guaymas. And I speak Spanish. I have a lot of relatives down in Imuris and San Ignacio and Magdalena." He stopped and creased his brow and thought for a moment. "Maybe I'll take Magdalena with me. We'll dress up like poor Indians. Once we're in Nogales, I'll put on my uniform, get some concrete in a big bucket or something, then we can come back across the border. It'll still be wet, and if the inspector wants to, he can poke a stick in it to search it. We'll tell him it's for a porch step or something. He won't care." He looked inquisitively at Joshua.

"I'm afraid to let Magdalena go down there."

There was a sly twinkle in Leyva's eyes. "You afraid because of me?"

Joshua smiled. "I wish that's all it was."

The Indian became serious again. "Actually it sounds like fun, like we're sleuths from a Charlie Chan movie."

Joshua nodded. "But in the movies you know that everything's going to turn out okay." He thought about it for a moment and shook his head. "I just can't let you do it. It's too dangerous. I'm going to have to find a safer way." An idea had been growing on him. "Maybe I'll just freeze the progress payments," he said, thinking aloud. "The contract price is divided into twenty equal parts for the twenty weeks until completion. Avra Valley draws a check from the Bank of Douglas every week by presenting a government form called a 'Proof of Progress,' which has to be countersigned by a Corps of Engineers inspector."

Joshua's face brightened as he thought about it more, and it became increasingly appealing. "I like it," he said. "I'm going to call the bank and stop the payments. I can do that. I'm the Project Administrator. On Friday when he can't get his check, George Callan will be sitting right there in front of my desk. I guess that he and I will just have to come to an understanding."

"How are you going to keep from getting shot?"

"I'm going to set you up with an office right next door." Joshua gestured with his thumb. "We've been using it for storage because we didn't need it for anybody. Now we do."

Leyva nodded. "Okay. Fine by me."

"Why don't we move the stuff in the room out to the shed behind the building." Joshua took off his gray suit coat and draped it on the chair. He slowly rolled up the empty sleeve of his dress shirt.

"I can move the stuff," Leyva said.

Joshua looked up from his intent concentration on his sleeve. "So can I," he said, and returned his attention to his sleeve.

There was very little inside the small office. Several cartons of old files, a big metal bookshelf, two army surplus metal desks, six straight-backed oak desk chairs. They put everything but one desk and two chairs in the tin shed behind the Bureau. Then Chuy got steel wool and bleach and a bucket and mop and scrubbed the terra-cotta-tiled floor and the furniture. The window was so dirty that its layer of dust smeared into mud circles when he tried to wash it. He got some ammonia and old newspaper and had it sparkling, inside and out, in ten minutes.

Joshua looked in a few minutes later. "Very nice," he said, "a lot cleaner than mine."

"I learned it in the marines," Chuy said. "Three years as a gunner on the U.S.S. *New Jersey*. I had a hell of a lot of practice scrubbing floors." He grimaced.

Joshua heard the ominous clack of metal canes in the corridor. He knew without having to turn around who was behind him.

"Mr. Rabb, I need to see you." Her voice was hard.

"Nice to see you, Mrs. Carillo. Come on into my office."

She sat down slowly on the chair and held her canes in both hands, planted on the floor, like a centurion with two lances guarding the gates to Pontius Pilate's palace.

"I looked for the ad. You didn't do what I said."

"I'm really sorry about that. I had to go to Nogales on business for a few days. I just got back last night. I'm sorry, but it couldn't be helped."

"Franklin's trial is coming up fast." Her voice was harsh. She gritted her teeth and her chin quivered.

He'd better tell her something to mollify her, before she drove one of the lances through his heart. "I'm going out to see Franklin at the jail early this afternoon, Mrs. Carillo. I've got to get a close description of the woman. Then I'll stop at the newspaper offices and put the ad in."

Her eyes became shinier. "You're not just saying that so I'll leave you alone?"

"No, Mrs. Carillo. That would only work till tomorrow when you discovered there wasn't any ad in the paper. No, don't worry, I'll try to find our witness."

She smiled and nodded, and the accusation left her eyes. "Will you call me as soon as someone shows up?"

Joshua kept his face pleasant and his eyes friendly. Notice she didn't say "if someone shows up." She probably has the "witness" living with her at home, waiting for the day after the ad comes out to miraculously appear. What would I do if she fires me, go over to the Chevrolet dealer and beg him to take the car back? He's probably sold the DeSoto by now. And I've spent most of what was left of the $2,732 she gave me. Shit!

"I'll call you just as soon as anyone answers the

ad, Mrs. Carillo." He kept his voice eager and reassuring.

She got up slowly and gave him a sad smile. "I want my Franklin back, Mr. Rabb. I need him. Get him back home for me." She hobbled out of the office.

It was eleven-thirty. He decided to go to the jail first, so he could get there before lockdown for lunch. Once they locked down, he couldn't see Franklin Carillo until two or two-thirty or even three, depending on the whim of the particular commander on duty. So he drove to the jail and sat uneasily on the uncomfortable metal chair in the interview cell. Carillo shuffled into the cell in belly chain and ankle cuffs. He sat down across from Joshua but didn't look at him.

"The story I heard in court wasn't exactly what you told *me*, Frank."

Carillo sniffed and glanced quickly at Joshua like a frightened raccoon with timid eyes. He must have been in a jailhouse brawl, because he had black rings around both eyes and a bruise on his left cheekbone.

"I was afraid to tell you, Mr. Rabb," he stammered. He stared at his hands, cuffed in front of him. "I was afraid you'd refuse to defend me."

"I'm a lawyer, Frank. I don't care whether you're guilty or innocent. You have a right to be defended, and that's what I do, defend people. But I don't like to be lied to."

Carillo swallowed. "I'm sorry," he murmured.

"Now, what's this bullshit about an alibi witness, changing an old lady's tire, all of that crap?"

He looked up quickly, his eyes wide with anxiety. "You didn't tell Erma I was lyin, didja?"

"No, Frank. What you tell me is privileged. I can't tell anyone else, not even your wife. But I can't ethically be a party to a fraud on the court. I can't bring a witness in to testify knowing that she's lying. That's suborning perjury."

"Listen, Mr. Rabb." His voice was pleading. "It ain't perjury to tell your wife whatever she's gotta hear to stick by you. If I lose her, I lose everything. I don't give a shit what you do when this witness of Erma's shows up. But you gotta put an ad in the paper and make Erma believe that you believe me."

Joshua frowned at Carillo and shook his head.

"Look, Mr. Rabb." His demeanor was decidedly more combative. "Them are the only white people ever gave me the time of day, Erma and her mother. Ya know I got a prior?"

Joshua shook his head.

"Yeah, when I was nineteen. I done a burglary at some old broad's house out on the east side by the University. Some neighbor heard her scream, and I got busted for it. But she didn't want to testify about me fuckin her, you know, so I just went down on burg. Did two years at Arizona State Prison. When I got out, I got a job as handyman with Erma's mother, you know, workin for her real estate business. And I told em about my burg and the time I done—I left out the part about the old bitch—and they still stuck by me, didn't fire me. And I ended up marryin Erma. She was real pretty back then, before she got sick. And now I gotta protect her, Mr. Rabb. She don't think I done none of this, and I gotta keep it that way."

Joshua stood up, a sour look on his face. "I'll do what I can for you, Frank." He left quickly.

At the newspaper office downtown, he wrote out the ad that was to run for the next seven days, through the first day of the trial: "Would the woman who had her tire changed by a Papago Indian at midnight on September 19, 1946, at the Ochoa Mercado on Valencia Road, please contact attorney Joshua Rabb at the Bureau of Indian Affairs, telephone 29548."

He drove over to Georgette's Diner and had an open-faced hot beef sandwich and a Lucky Lager beer. Then he walked across the street to the Bank of Douglas. He came up in front of the big plate-glass window with the bank name in gold leaf outlined in black, and he was arrested suddenly by his reflection. A tall and strongly built man in a gray wool suit, double-breasted coat, tailored with a little nip at the waist and fitted around the hips, brown hair with a smattering of gray on the temples and around the ears, a scholarly face, a serious face, honorable and trustworthy and sincere-looking. He stared at himself in the mirror of the window, and he knew that the image was false. This was not the Prince of Nobility staring back at him. This was just one of Edgar Hendly's ordinary guys who was getting along the best he could, neither a perfect specimen nor a gravely flawed one, just an ordinary man. He had placed a fraudulent ad in the newspaper for a nonexistent witness who would show up and lie on the witness stand and set a dangerous criminal free. What for? For a yellow Chevy convertible and a few extra bucks.

What the hell am I doing here at the Bank of

Douglas? I'm taking it upon myself to pass moral
and ethical and legal judgment on George Callan
without even knowing for sure that I'm right? What
a prince of a guy I am. A little hanky-panky is okay
for me. After all, who wouldn't suborn perjury for a
yellow Chevy? But George isn't entitled to any
hanky-panky. Why, you ask? Because I just made
the rules. I've got one rule for me and another rule
for the rest of you assholes. Oh, okay, now I
understand.

But now Joshua didn't understand. His sense of
moral certainty had suddenly evaporated, leaving
only a puzzling void where everything was shades of
gray, fuzzy around the edges.

The two men stared at each other for another
moment, and then Joshua walked to his car. He
drove slowly out of town, uncertain whether he
should do this, and then with increasing resolve that
he had to bring the matter to a head, he headed up
the Highway, got off at the Tangerine Road exit,
and drove to the Lazy G Ranch. As soon as he
topped the rise he saw Diana on a gray horse in a
rectangle next to the corral. The rectangle was
about sixty yards long and half that wide, delineated
by a single line around it of small-diameter white
painted poles laid on the ground. George Callan and
a couple of the hands sat on the top rail of the
corral watching her.

As Joshua got closer, he could see that Diana
was dressed in English riding clothes, tan breeches
tucked into high black boots all the way to the knee.
She had exchanged her usual cowboy shirt for a
sleeveless white cotton blouse with a ruffle down
the front. Her hair was pulled up under a black

derby hat. Joshua parked and walked toward the corral. George waved. Diana was leaping the horse, looking like a carousel horse and rider.

"How ya doin today, son?" George asked. "That ear healing up?" He scrutinized Joshua's ear as they shook hands. "Yeah, well, I reckon you'll live. Swelling's gone down pretty good."

"Yeah, I don't feel it anymore," Joshua said. "It'll be okay in a few days." He climbed up to the top rail and sat next to Callan.

"You ever see *haut école* dressage?" George asked. "No."

Diana was forty yards away across the rectangle, finishing another one of the carousel leaps.

"That's a *ballotade* and *capriole*," George said. "She's really got a good animal there. I picked up two of them in Vienna at the Spanish Riding Academy last year, four months after the war ended. The Academy needed money, and my wife and Diana just loved those Lippizaners. They're bred perfectly for dressage." He pointed at the horse, which was now hopping toward them across the rectangle like a kangaroo on its hind legs. "That's a *courbette*," he said. "Diana's some terrific rider, huh? We had a thoroughbred named Fred Astaire that she rode for five years, but it couldn't compare with the Lippizaners. And Diana took lessons in Vienna for two months from Szegedy himself, one of the *reitmeisters*. Look at that *piaffe*. That's a horse and rider who are perfectly in harmony."

Joshua watched the horse trot in place and knew that no Kansas City whore could be the rider. No one could learn to ride like this in just a few months. At least Diana was real.

She waved at Joshua as she rode by him, and he watched her and the big white stallion do various complex maneuvers for another fifteen minutes. Then she rode to the edge of the ring and dismounted, and the men climbed down from the corral railing. The two hands led the horse away.

"That was wonderful riding," Joshua said.

"Thanks," she said. "We're having a little trouble on the *croupade* and the flying changes, but we'll get there."

"Come on in the house," George said. "I don't suppose you came all the way out here just to sit on a fence and chew grass straws."

They went into the house and sat down in the living room. Constancia brought a pitcher of lemonade. The sliding-glass doors and picture window looked out on an enclosed porch and then to hundreds of yards of thick ryegrass surrounded by a tall chain-link fence. At least two dozen horses grazed in the pasture.

"I'd better go change," Diana said. "I smell a little horsey." She wrinkled up her nose and smiled at Joshua. She left the living room.

"Okay," George said, "what's on your mind?"

"The contract."

"You got a fuckin one-track mind, son."

"I just can't make it all go away with a touch of my magic wand. We both know that. Dan Swirling's reagent test on that concrete was legitimate. Now we've got to deal with it."

George Callan's face became harsh, the tip of his nose appeared to blanch. "I'm damn tired of this shit, boy. Them fuckin thieves from Transcon do a little dog-and-pony act for you and you jump right on their bandwagon and go looking for my ass. That's not a very loyal way to act toward me, considering all I've done for you."

"Come on, George, that's wrong and you know it. If I was out to get you, I'd be sitting in the FBI office, not in your living room."

Callan stared acidulously at him. He started coughing and hacked for a full minute. He pulled a handkerchief out of his back pocket and wiped his mouth and rested for a moment.

"So what do you want from me?" he asked.

"Harry Morland talked to Edgar Hendly about it. They're willing to reissue the contract specifying Type 2 concrete on one condition." He paused.

George's face was bland. He stared out at the pasture.

"We want you to post one million dollars as a performance bond for five years. It'll cover any repairs that have to be made for that time. You'll get back the unused portion."

George turned his face slowly toward Joshua. His eyes were bloodshot and his voice mordant. "Let me just clue you in on something, boy. I bid that contract fair and square. I had a little inside information on the other bids, I admit that, but I didn't do it to be sure I'd be the low bid, I did it to be sure my bid wasn't *too* low. Shit! I could've bid fifteen, sixteen million and still made a profit. But I'm not about to put my tail between my legs and run off like a coyote in a chicken coop. You can take that performance bond and shove it up your ass."

Joshua swallowed hard and shook his head in frustration. "Damn it, George! Every Indian on the Reservation will be in constant danger of dying of cholera if that culvert starts breaking down. The least we can do is to have a guaranteed source of funds to repair it with. Otherwise, the only alternative I have is to terminate the contract and award it to the next bid, which is Jessup's."

"Don't even think it, boy," George growled. "Don't even be thinkin' such bullshit."

"Well, what the hell do you think is going to happen if I do nothing? Jessup is going to file a fraud action in federal court against both of us and have an order-to-show-cause hearing a day later to have the judge cancel your contract and award it to Transcon. Now damn it, George, you can't just stick your chin out like a bulldog and ignore it."

"What the hell do you think I got lawyers for? Harry Chandler will blow Jessup away in front of old Judge Buchanan. Buck Buchanan was my lawyer for twenty-five years till President Truman appointed him to the federal bench last year. And Harry Chandler was Buck's partner for thirty years. I got my bases covered."

"Not if your concrete doesn't test Type 5, you don't. I'll guarantee you that Judge Buchanan won't pervert the law and jeopardize the health of the entire San Xavier Reservation just to save your ass if you're pumping subgrade product out of your trucks."

"No problem there. I'll bring a whole damn truckload of cement up to the courthouse and the whole damn chemistry department at the U of A can test it till hell freezes over. It's Type 5, just like the contract calls for."

"Well, that's not good enough. The judge is going

to want to have a sample drawn from the culvert itself."

Diana came in quietly and sat down on an armchair, watching the two angry men. She had changed into a Mexican sundress of white cotton with parrots embroidered on the strapless bodice.

George's tight face relaxed slowly. His pale blue eyes softened, and a smile spread slowly over his face.

"Well, now, it's a little dangerous down in Nogales. I guess you can vouch for that." He let out a long trenchant laugh. "But if Old Buck wants to dig up a bucket of cement or sledgehammer a hunk off the side of the culvert, why, hell, more power to him!"

Joshua nodded at George and frowned. "I'm going to recommend that we send the FBI agent, Roy Collins, down there with my Papago policeman, Jesus Leyva, and that Governor Calderon meet them in Nogales and make sure everything goes all right."

George's face went from mirth to melancholy. His speech became a thick western drawl, like Edgar Hendly's. "Now ain't that somethin. Old Alfonso gonna be drug up t' Nogales t' guard Jesus and his apostle Roy Collins. Be damn lucky if both a them boys don't end up floatin like big turds in the Santa Cruz River with nail holes in their hands 'n feet."

Joshua breathed deeply and clenched his jaw. He looked at Diana, and she stared at him with wide, shocked eyes. George's face was blank. He took a long drink of lemonade and smacked his lips appreciatively. Joshua left the house, got into his car, and drove quickly back to Tucson.

CHAPTER
TWELVE

She showed up at the BIA like clockwork at ten o'clock the next morning. She was at least seventy years old, dark-skinned, with long well-groomed gray hair and black eyes, either a Papago or Mexican, tall and a little overweight, wearing a clean cotton muumuu with Gauguin-like figures on it, yellow people and beige animals reposing under emerald green trees in a purple tropical jungle.

"I came as soon as I saw the news*paper*," she said in a heavy Mexican accent, putting stresses on words in strange places. "That nice boy, he change my tire. I am too old, I got arthritis, I can't change no tire. He change my tire."

Joshua looked at her and nodded sourly.

"It *was* at mid*night*, I am *pos*itive. I look at the clock at the market, I look at my own *watch*." She held up her left arm and rotated her wrist, displaying the watch to Joshua. "It take him maybe half *hour*."

"Had you ever seen the man before?"

"No, uh-uh. First time."

"How do you know it was Franklin Carillo?"

"I seen the picture in the papers, two times now.

I thought I reco*gnize* him, and then I see the ad, and I know he's the same *guy*."

"How long have you known Martha Joslin and her daughter Erma?"

She stared at him, thinking. Then she shook her head. "What do you mean, mister?"

"I mean just that. Do you know Erma Carillo or her mother?" Joshua asked.

"I dunno dem." She shook her head.

"Where do you live?"

"Tubac."

"That's thirty-five miles from here. Why were you here that night?"

"Visiting my daughter. She marry to a Papago, live near San Xavier Mission on the Reservation. Not far from Franklin Carillo. He told me when he change tire he was live on Reservation right off Valencia, near Ochoa Market. My daughter, she just have her eighth baby. Antonio we bap*tize* him two weeks a*go*." She smiled sweetly at Joshua.

Joshua studied her thoughtfully. He walked to the doorway, looked back at the old woman, and waited. She shifted uneasily in her chair, then stood up and followed him out of the BIA.

"This yours?" He pointed to a battered fifteen-year-old Ford Model T pickup truck.

She nodded.

"Which tire was changed?"

She hesitated, then pointed to the front passenger side. Joshua stooped next to it. The nuts were rusted hard and years of road tar and dirt were caked around them.

Joshua took a pen and pad out of his shirt pocket. "Okay, give me your name and address."

"Esmeralda Bojorquez," she said. "Rural Route 3, Tubac."

Joshua wrote it down. "I'll need you to testify at the trial. It's on the eighteenth. Will you come to the courthouse at ten in the morning?" He wrote the date and time on a sheet of paper and handed it to her.

"Sure, sure, Mr. Rabb. I come." She walked away to her car.

Joshua went back into his office and telephoned Erma Carillo. He said that he wanted to talk to her in person about the witness and would like to come over right now. She was pleased at finally having so much attention from him and gave him directions to her house. He took a roll of maps off the lower shelf of the bookcase, found the one of San Xavier Reservation, and spread it on the desk. He hadn't realized before that there was a two-mile-long and a half-mile-wide finger of the Reservation that jutted north of the irrigation ditch past Valencia Road for another mile. The Carillo house must be in there. The finger of land was bounded on the east by an unnamed dirt path and on the west by Mission Road, which ran south out of downtown Tucson for six miles, then crossed Drexel Road, became the western boundary of the peninsula of Reservation land for two miles, then entered the Reservation just past where the irrigation ditch ended in a reservoir.

Joshua drove west down the road in front of his house along the irrigation ditch and reached the unnamed dirt path. He turned right and followed it for about three quarters of a mile, then turned left onto a rutted trail through a thicket of mesquite to the Carillo house. To the north less than a hundred yards was Valencia Road. The house was much larger than most of the others on the Reservation. It was about eighty feet long, constructed of masonry block painted bright yellow with an asbestos tile roof, a two-car carport with a late-model Dodge sedan parked in it, and a large garden in front with lavender trailing lantanas and orange-flowered honeysuckle bushes and late-blooming moss roses. Trumpet vines climbed the wall around the front door and picture window.

A Papago Indian maid answered Joshua's knock and showed him into the living room. It was simply furnished with Mexican leather and wood furniture on a bare Mexican ceramic tiled floor in a geometric pattern of yellow and red and blue. Joshua looked at it, tilted his head, and studied the pattern. It looked like it was supposed to depict a streaming sun rising over a hill, the semicircular sun being the center of the room.

Erma Carillo rolled into the living room in a wheelchair. "How nice of you to finally take interest, Mr. Rabb." She smiled at him, meaning for her caustic remark to be taken in good humor.

"I've been very interested from the start, Mrs. Carillo," Joshua said lightly. He looked around the room. "This is a lovely house, one of the nicest I've seen on the Reservation."

"Thank you." She smiled pleasantly. "Franklin inherited one hundred and sixty acres from his grandfather five years ago. We have some money from the real estate business, so we put a little extra into this house." Her face turned eager. "So what about the witness?"

"Well, she's a nice lady. She says she was visiting

her daughter here that night, and Franklin changed her tire."

"That's wonderful. Then you'll get Franklin off?"

"That's not a certainty at all. The jury has to believe the witness and has to be convinced that it happened the night of the murders. We're a little thin on proof of that, but at least we have something to go on. I'll certainly give it my best."

She nodded. "Good, good. I got faith in you, Mr. Rabb. Everybody says how good you did for Ignacio. I got faith." She crossed herself.

"Okay," he said, rising. "It's nice to see you again, Mrs. Carillo. See you Tuesday."

He drove back to the BIA, drumming a tune on the steering wheel with his thumb and humming, "I can't explain, it's really not his brain, that makes me thrill. I love him, because he's, I don't know, because he's just my Josh."

▼▲▼

Roy Collins knocked on the doorjamb and came into Joshua's office late in the afternoon. Joshua had just gotten back from the Pima County Law Library at the courthouse, where he'd spent the last three hours.

"To what do I owe the honor of a visit from the FBI?"

Collins settled into the straight wooden chair. "Well, I've been hearing rumors about the problems you have on the sewage project down in Nogales. And then a cement expert gets murdered on his way down there. And then you come back with a cauliflower ear and a purple cheek—"

"I thought it was going away," Joshua said, touching his ear gingerly.

"Well, it's going, but it ain't gone," Collins said, "and I hear that George Callan would kill for a nickel, let alone eighteen million dollars, and that all adds up to a ration of shit in my expert opinion." He eyed Joshua closely.

Joshua shrugged. "That would about describe it."

Collins nodded. "Is this a matter that's in my jurisdiction?"

"I honestly don't know. That's the truth. I'm not certain that there's been any contract fraud by Mr. Callan. Nobody is certain that Chester Milliken's death had anything to do with any of this at all. Maybe some asshole just conked him on the head, and that's all there is to it."

"And left his wallet and car and equipment?"

Joshua nodded. "Yes. I've been in the law business long enough to have seen purposeless crimes. You have, too."

Collins rolled his eyes and shrugged.

"I guess," Joshua said thoughtfully, "that I just don't jump to the conclusion that there's a major conspiracy going on unless I see pretty convincing evidence of it. And I haven't seen it yet. There are plenty of loose ends and a lot of questions, but the answers are pretty elusive right now."

"So what are you going to do?"

"Just wait. I think that's the only thing I can do. There's no legal justification for me to screw around with Callan's contract unless Transcon files an action in court. If they don't, the whole problem is going to die away. If I take some independent action on behalf of the Office of Land Management, then the burden is on me to prove that the concrete is not up to specs and Callan committed fraud. That's damn hard to do. So I'm going to wait and see what Henry Jessup does. If he files a lawsuit, *he* has the burden of proving that the concrete is substandard."

"Okay, sounds pretty damn reasonable," Collins said, rising from his chair. "Watch your ass."

"I always carry a little mirror with me."

"Better to carry a .38," Collins said, patting the right side of his gray suit jacket. He chuckled.

They shook hands sincerely and Collins left.

Joshua felt a little soreness in his left hip. He hadn't been getting enough exercise lately, and he had been favoring his left leg because of real or imagined pain in his injured foot. The result was always the same: he would have to walk out the soreness in his hip and concentrate on not limping. He walked briskly down Indian Agency Road to the irrigation ditch in front of his little adobe house, waved at Magdalena, who was throwing corn kernels to the squawking, fluttering chickens, saw Adam and Jimmy riding their horses in the mesquite field across the road, and suddenly remembered that he hadn't taken his shattered arm over to the prosthetician at the veterans hospital. Better get that done. It was a pain in the ass not to have his stainless-steel hand. It was useful for a whole range of things: cracking walnuts, scaring the hell out of strangers, rolling up his right sleeve. And what was the newest idea, that George Callan had? Turning bulls into steers at roundup time. Yessir, yessir. Ripping the nuts off a bull sounded real nice. He wrinkled his face, walked into the house and got what was left of his mechanical arm, walked back to the

BIA, and drove his yellow convertible to the VA hospital.

▼▲▼

Joshua got to the office at a few minutes past eight the next morning. Frances Hendly slid open the reception cubicle window. "George Callan called twice already. He doesn't sound happy."

"My day is shattered," Joshua said, clutching his suit jacket over his heart and feigning trembling knees.

Frances smiled wryly at him. He walked down the corridor to his office. The phone rang as he sat down on his swivel chair. He picked it up, and George Callan's angry voice clawed at him.

"What the hell are you doing with that FBI agent in your office for a half hour?" he asked.

"Who told you that?"

Callan hesitated. "Edgar."

"Edgar has no right to be talking about my business."

"T' hell with that bullshit. This is *my* business. Now what the hell's going on?"

Joshua sucked in his breath and suppressed his rising anger. "Nothing is going on," he said slowly, his jaw tight. "Roy Collins just got a little curious because of all the rumors about poor-quality concrete in a federal project and a dead guy named Milliken. Little things like that. Nothing for *you* to worry about, huh, George?"

"You didn't call him?"

"No."

Callan was silent for a moment. His voice relaxed. "You know, I'm really sorry things got out of hand.

You must have the impression that this is the way I always operate. Well, that's dead wrong. What's going on here is not of my doing, despite everything you think."

George paused. Joshua didn't fill the gap with words.

"Look, Diana insisted that I call you and invite you to dinner tonight at six. How about it?"

Despite an intense desire to tell him to drop dead and then slam down the telephone receiver triumphantly, Joshua knew it would be no triumph. He would be the loser. He wanted to see Diana, to touch her.

"All right, I'll be there," he said.

▼▲▼

When Joshua picked up his new arm at the VA hospital late that afternoon, he got a pleasant surprise. Instead of a ten-pound wooden thing that resembled a bent axe handle, it was made this time of tubular aluminum, a newfangled metal developed during the war that didn't rust and was much lighter than steel and stronger than wood. Because it was eight pounds lighter than his first arm, he could manipulate it far faster and more finely. And this one had a hinge at the elbow that allowed him to bend and straighten the arm. He practiced with it in the prosthetician's office for almost an hour and it didn't even make his shoulder sore.

He had lost track of the time. It was a little after five-thirty, and he hurried to his car and drove quickly through downtown Tucson to Highway 87. He would be twenty or thirty minutes late, but that wouldn't matter. A few miles out of town, near Cordes Junction, was a series of Burma Shave signs that he hadn't noticed before. Maybe they were new. The eight signs added up to a jingle: "Don't drive crummy/Don't be a dummy/Bad things can happen/If you go too hasty/Your mangled body/To a coyote/Would be so yummy/Would be so tasty."

Joshua pulled off onto the shoulder of the highway and parked next to a huge saguaro cactus. A tiny Elfin owl peeked out at him curiously from a hole in the trunk, then hunkered backward into the darkness. Several quail fluttered around a creosote bush and darted out of sight into a wash.

"Bad things can happen if you go too hasty," Joshua murmured. What the hell am I doing here, he thought, speeding out to Callan's ranch like a homing pigeon, trained dumbly to respond to the specific stimulus that sends me straight to my destination. And Diana is the stimulus. She smiles, she crooks her finger at me and runs the tip of her tongue around her lips, and I get a hard-on and obey like a horny kid. Well, not this time. If I keep going out there with all that's happened, Collins will be investigating *me*. And if I have to go to court on this contract mess, Judge Buchanan is going to wonder why in hell I got so cozy with the coyote, if I'm such an innocent lamb.

He shook his head with the frustration of the situation and grimaced. He started the car, made a U-turn on the highway, and drove home. He had no phone at home, so nobody could call him to find out why he hadn't come. And the next Monday in the office, there was no call from George Callan or Diana Thurber. And not Tuesday. And not Wednesday.

CHAPTER
THIRTEEN

Hanna's cheerleading outfit consisted of a red sweater with a big white felt T stitched on the front and a white pleated skirt reaching almost to her knees. Tonight for the first time she was wearing the winter uniform, the wool one. It was too cold for cotton. Just this afternoon a storm had billowed up and it had rained, and there was now an ominous purplish overcast and it was only about forty-five degrees.

Chuy Leyva came by the house at four-thirty to pick up Magdalena. He had asked Edgar Hendly if he could use the Indian Police pickup for the evening—after all, what's a Friday night date without a car—and Edgar had responded, in his inimitable fashion, that Chuy could use it as long as he and Magdalena "didn't go jumpin into the bed a the truck like a coupla jackrabbits in heat." He chortled knowingly, and Chuy smiled and took the ribbing because he wanted to use the pickup.

Tucson High School home football games attracted as many fans as the games at the University of Arizona stadium just six blocks away. In fact, the high school games were held on Friday nights and the U of A games were on Saturday nights so that they wouldn't have to compete for spectators. The high school stadium ran a hundred yards along the west side of the football field. It was built of dark yellow brick, had two huge dressing rooms for the teams, and forty rows of wooden bleachers. Tonight, because of the rainstorm and the cold, only two thousand of Tucson's forty thousand residents had come to see the game. Tucson High was playing St. Mary's, a Phoenix parochial school. St. Mary's had expensive, flashy uniforms, green and white with shiny gold painted leather helmets, in contrast with the pedestrian red and white of Tucson High with its dull brown helmets.

Very few St. Mary's fans had braved the storm, so their purple-clad pom-pom girls and golden cheerleaders were down at the south end of the stadium jumping around and doing their cheers in front of about thirty shivering Phoenicians. The six Tucson High cheerleaders and eight pom-pom girls were in front of the band, their cheers drowned out by the sixty-piece band playing, "On you Badgers, on you Badgers, fight, fight, fight, fight, fight . . ."

Joshua and Adam still had Brooklyn in their blood, so forty-five degrees was hardly intimidating. Two of the cheerleaders were boys, and one of them lifted Hanna and balanced her in the air, flat and outstretched, with his hand on her pubic bone, and Joshua felt like running down there and telling the kid to take his goddamn hands off his daughter's crotch before he smacked him silly. But then Hanna twirled around and landed agilely on the ground, beaming with pleasure, and Joshua chided himself with the assurance that there was less sex involved in the maneuver than physics, levers and fulcrums and all of that, and his daughter's center of gravity appeared to be her *mons veneris*. Not a particularly soothing thought, at that.

By halftime, Mark Goldberg had scored a touchdown with a thirty-seven-yard run around right end. Near the end of the fourth quarter, he scored again on a short pass, and that touchdown was Tucson's margin of victory. After the game, there was a short fight. The St. Mary's boys had to show the Tucson boys that they were tough despite losing the game, and a few fists flew and there was some grappling on the ground until the referee and the umpire and the two coaches pulled the boys apart.

Mark came off the field, his nose bleeding slightly, and Hanna ran up to him and hugged him as though he were her victorious gladiator. Joshua walked down from the stands followed by Adam, jumping down the benches, and Joshua saw the look that passed between his daughter and Mark. It made him feel good. She'd had her first love last year, a sad-looking boy in her homeroom class. But she had been more like a sister to him, and there had never been the electricity of real passion between them. But not this time. Joshua could feel the heat radiating from them. This wasn't puppy love, and Hanna didn't look sisterly at all. The one good thing about Brooklyn was that none of the kids had cars. But here in Tucson everybody seemed to have a car, because there were no subways and only a few buses downtown. And cars were dangerous for teenagers. They could get away from everybody and park off the road in pitch blackness and do things that a Brooklyn kid couldn't do hanging around the corner soda shop.

"Hi, Mr. Rabb," Mark said, smiling bravely despite his bloody nose.

"Somebody belt you?" Joshua asked.

"Yeah, that son of a—that linebacker. He was gunning for me all the game, and I still beat him twice. He punched me when I wasn't looking."

"Why don't we lie in wait for him outside the locker room and blow his brains out?" Joshua said, his face serious.

Mark's eyes widened and he stared at Joshua.

"*Daa-aaad,*" Hanna said, "please cut it out. Mark isn't accustomed to your sense of humor." She looked at her father peevishly.

Joshua smiled. "Okay, sorry, honey."

Mark laughed.

"I'll wait for Mark, Dad," Hanna said. "We're going over to Mama Louisa's for pizza."

"Ten o'clock," Joshua said to her.

She frowned.

"Ten o'clock," he repeated.

She nodded. Mark walked through the stadium arch into the locker room.

It was almost seven and almost dark, made even denser by the overcast. Joshua and Adam drove to McClellan's downtown for ice cream cones and then drove home. Joshua unlocked the front door and switched on the living room light and the porch light. The first thing that assailed him was the stink, like excrement, and then he saw blood splashed everywhere on the floor and the walls and the couch and chair. Billy the Cat's head was on the overstuffed chair, the lower half of his body was on the floor by the couch, and his forelegs were by the wall.

Adam gasped and began weeping. Joshua put his

arms around him to shield his vision and pushed him out the door onto the front porch.

"Who did it?" Adam sobbed.

"I don't know," Joshua muttered. He hugged Adam until the boy's shoulders relaxed and he stopped crying.

"Go over to Jimmy's, okay?" Joshua said.

Adam ran toward the Hendly house.

Joshua turned on the hose spigot by the chicken coops and uncoiled the hose. He walked into the house and began spraying down the walls and the floor. The doorjamb on the rear door into the kitchen was splintered and the door was wide open. Joshua hosed the offal from the living room out the back door. He picked up the parts of Billy and walked into the field next to the house and dropped them on the ground. The coyotes would not have to prowl too far for food tonight.

The stink of the dismembered cat had given way to a moldy smell from the wet plaster walls. The couch and armchair were threadbare and old, and blood had penetrated deep into the kapok. They were beyond redemption. Joshua struggled them through the front door and toppled them down the porch steps to the ground. He shoved them away from the front door toward the chicken coop. The chickens were unnerved by the commotion and the smell of Billy's blood, and they fluttered and squabbled.

Joshua walked into the house and locked the front door. He pushed the kitchen door closed and propped one of the dinette chairs against the knob. He went into his bedroom and took the Smith and Wesson revolver and the box of shells out of the closet. He went into the living room and turned on the radio. "The Shadow" was whistling his signature tune, and then a dark voice narrated something or other, but Joshua didn't even hear it. He sat down against the moist wall and began loading six cartridges into the revolver.

He had bought it three or four months ago, when the troubles with Mission Sand and Gravel Company had gotten bad. But that had passed, and he had taken the shells out of the gun and hidden it away. His knees began shaking, and a tremor passed through him, and the memory of Billy's smell almost made him nauseous.

Adam came home a little after ten, and Joshua made him go to bed. Adam left his bedroom door ajar. A half hour later, Hanna came home. Her hair was tousled and her cheeks were flushed and her lips were kissed clean of lipstick. She looked with large frightened doe eyes at Joshua as he told her what had happened.

"Not again," she whispered. "Is all that stuff going to happen again?"

Joshua breathed deeply and let his breath out slowly. He shook his head grimly. "I don't know," he murmured. "But this time we'll move. I don't want to put us through any of that again."

"Let's move tomorrow."

"We can't, honey, I don't have the money. When I get paid at the end of the month, we'll move. It's only ten days."

She nodded and went into her bedroom and closed the door.

Joshua dozed, slumped against the wall. He jerked awake as the front door creaked open. He reached for the gun. Then he saw Magdalena come into the house followed by Chuy Leyva.

She stared at him, her brow wrinkled. "What happened?"

"Someone killed Billy the Cat. Butchered him and sprayed blood all over the room. The furniture is ruined."

"You okay?" Leyva asked.

"Yeah."

"What are you going to do with the gun?"

Joshua looked at it, then back at Chuy. "Make sure nobody comes back."

Chuy nodded. "I've got a sleeping bag in the truck. I can sleep in here tonight." He didn't wait for an answer. He went outside and came back a moment later with a bedroll under his arm and a small shaving kit in his hand. "Sometimes I've got to camp out on the Reservation. Got to be prepared." He dropped the bedroll on the floor and put the kit on the end table next to the lamp, the only furniture in the room.

Joshua looked at Magdalena, and her face was softer than he had seen it in months. Her eyes glittered in the thin lamplight, and she was beautiful, like she had been back in July, before Sam had been hurt. Joshua edged up the wall and stood up. His legs felt sore and weak.

"I appreciate this, Chuy," he said. He shook hands with the Indian and went into his bedroom. As he closed the door, he glimpsed Magdalena's face for an instant, and he had a fleeting yearning to be Jesus Leyva just for tonight.

▼▲▼

It was a clear day, and the sun dried the upholstery on the sofa and the overstuffed chair. The stench was shocking. Joshua and Chuy loaded the furniture on the pickup, drove to the town dump near the airport, and pushed it off the truck into the landfill pit.

"Where do you think I can get some cheap furniture to replace it?" Joshua asked.

Chuy shrugged. "We can go down to Nogales, Arizona, get some Mexican stuff, you know, ocotillo rib frame and leather sling chairs, steer-hide couches with wood frames, probably some pillows."

"That stuff is great to look at but impossible to sit in," Joshua said.

Chuy laughed. "Yeah, but it's cheap."

"Who sells furniture here?"

Chuy thought for a moment. "I know Goldberg's does downtown. I've also heard ads on the radio for Hal Dubin City. I think it's out east on Speedway."

Goldberg's was the most expensive department store in Tucson, and Joshua could hardly afford any furniture that carried a luxurious price tag. But suddenly he was curious. He'd met Mark and was impressed by the boy. Mark seemed quieter and deeper than the average seventeen-year-old high school hero would ordinarily be. Joshua wanted to meet Mark's father, not formally so that both men were on guard and on their best behavior, but just casually, at his store, when Joshua was simply an anonymous shopper.

They drove to downtown Tucson and parked in the lot next to Goldberg's. Joshua was wearing Levis and a long-sleeved green wool slipover. Work clothes for handling filthy furniture. Chuy had on his uniform and gun belt. They walked into Gold-berg's and strolled slowly through the men's cloth-ing and ladies' apparel to the center of the store. A sign there indicated that appliances and home furnishings were in the basement. They walked down the stairs, past the small restaurant where Joshua and Penny had met for lunch—their first date. Joshua was instantly seized by the memory of her face, smiling seductively at him, and he pushed away the vision with an act of will.

The furniture department was huge, covering al-most a football-field-size carpeted floor. Joshua and Chuy weaved their way through the displays of di-nettes and dining tables and bedroom "suites." Why are they "suites" and not simply "sets," Joshua thought. I wonder how much more a "suite" costs than a "set"? Kind of like pork and pig, mutton and sheep. No one would order pig's ass in a restaurant. Pork shank was rather more appetizing. Or sheep's butt instead of sirloin of mutton. Give it a French name and you converted it from slaughterhouse gar-bage into expensive cuts of meat.

They reached the rows of dozens of sofas and upholstered armchairs. Joshua glanced at the price tags pinned to the arms as he slowly meandered among the furnishings. There were several pieces he would love to load on the truck and take home, but not at these prices. The only thing he could afford was a skinny little oak rocker with a thin pad tied on the seat. He looked down at it, imagining how uncomfortable it would be and lamenting the loss of his big overstuffed chair.

A salesman stared from across the room at the man with one arm and one hook and the big Indian wearing a gun and knife on his belt. He walked to a desk in the corner and used the telephone. A dapperly dressed man came down the stairs a moment later. He was of medium height and build, tanned, with balding brown hair fringed with gray, and soft brown eyes. The salesman had walked over to the bottom of the stairwell to wait for the man. They walked together toward Joshua and Chuy.

"Can I help you?" the dapperly dressed man asked. On the pocket of his gray sharkskin suit coat he wore a brass tag with his name engraved in black: DAVID GOLDBERG.

Bingo! Joshua thought. It worked. They think we're a couple of sofa thieves from the Reservation.

"I was just looking at sofas and side chairs," Joshua said.

David Goldberg's smile was fixed, etched permanently into a rugged, outdoors face that pleasantly bespoke the swimming pool, the tennis court, the links at the country club.

Chuy reached down and rubbed the arm of a beige velveteen armchair. "Nice fabric," he said, feigning a thick Indian accent. The word "fabric" came out sounding something like "fabbareeka."

Joshua gritted his teeth to suppress a smile. David Goldberg looked a little alarmed. Can't have a stinking Indian from the Res fingering the velveteen chair that some little old lady would be coveting to put into her sewing room.

"We have another display of furniture that might be more suitable to your needs," Goldberg said, not losing his diffident smile.

"Oh, yah?" Chuy said. "What be more *sootaybell*?"

Joshua couldn't help it. His face broke into a grin. He looked away from Goldberg to hide it.

"Are you gentlemen playing some kind of game?" Goldberg asked slowly, looking from the Indian to the white man. Then a glimmer of recognition came into his eyes. "Have I been reading about you?" he asked Joshua.

Joshua shrugged.

"Sure I have," Goldberg said. The phony salesman's smile relaxed from his face, and he looked at Joshua seriously. "You're Hanna's father."

"Yes."

"Mark has told me so much about her and you. I'm pleased to meet you." He extended his hand and Joshua shook it.

"This is the chief of the Indian Police for the San Xavier Del Bac Reservation," Joshua said. "Jesus Leyva."

Goldberg snorted and chuckled. He did not extend his hand toward the Indian. "You guys put me on pretty good," he said.

"Sorry," Joshua said. "I'm looking for a sofa and side chair."

"Well, you certainly came to the right place." His voice was effusive, his look once again the eagerly endearing salesman's smile. "What is your decor?"

Joshua considered for a moment. "Moldy gray plaster walls and unvarnished terra-cotta floor."

" 'Contemporary Southwest,' shall we call it?"

Joshua laughed. "Hell, yes, why not. Let's call it 'Contemporary Southwest.' And I guess what I need is a 'living room suite.' "

Goldberg didn't register the sarcasm. "I think I have just the thing. Over here."

He led the way to a lovely sofa and matching side chair, upholstered in cotton, with a pastel desert scene, pale rose and azure wildflowers on a beige desert, lush green barrel cacti, and a backdrop of soft purple hills in a magenta sunset. It was a beautiful scene of muted color. The sofa was long and had soft high piled pillows on the seat. The matching armchair was equally lovely. The ticket on the chair read "$185," and on the sofa, "$300."

"This is hand painted on long staple Pima cotton," Goldberg said.

"I don't really think I can spend that kind of money," Joshua said. "It's fine-looking furniture, but I really think it's a bit much for what I have in mind."

"Don't worry about it, Mr. Rabb. For you, three hundred dollars, nothing down and just twenty dollars a month. They're both yours."

Joshua looked at him, surprised. He had never heard of anybody walking out of a store with merchandise he hadn't paid for. "I couldn't do something like that, Mr. Goldberg."

"It's credit, Mr. Rabb. Don't worry about it. I'm going to charge you four percent on the unpaid balance. You get a living room suite, I make a few bucks."

Joshua looked at the eager-faced man, trying to get behind the stone smile. He couldn't. Suddenly he didn't want David Goldberg doing him a favor. It might compromise him as Hanna's father. What if he had to rip Mark's head off or something? He couldn't do it if he was taking charity from the boy's father.

"It's a good offer, Mr. Goldberg. Let me bring

Hanna and Adam by to look it over, see if they like it."

That appeared to satisfy Goldberg. "Fine idea, fine. Just ask for me when you come back."

He shook hands with Joshua. Chuy said "Ugh," and held his arm out in either a Nazi salute or what the movies always depicted as the redskins' greeting. They left the store and walked to the parking lot.

"Ugh?" Joshua said, looking at Chuy.

"Ugga bugga," Chuy said.

Joshua burst out laughing. "We can make a ton of money with a medicine show. I'll be the doc, you be the patient."

They both laughed. Chuy drove out of the lot and turned left on Stone Avenue. "Hal Dubin City?" he asked.

"Yep," Joshua said. "Let's look their living room *suites* over."

"Ugh," Chuy said.

They erupted in laughter.

Hal Dubin City was a large cinder-block building near the Dixie Diner on East Speedway Boulevard. Inside the store there was none of the opulence of Goldberg's. There were rows of closely placed ice-boxes and several washing machines and cheap-looking dinettes and several dozen couches and chairs.

"How you boys doing today?" said a short fat man gaily. He was wearing a royal blue silk suit, baby blue shirt, a screaming red polka-dotted tie, and black patent leather slip-ons. "My name's Hal. This is my joint. What can I get you?"

"I'd like to look at your living room furniture."

"Well, you boys have come to the right place.

Come on with me, I'll fix you right up." His accent was straight out of the Lower East Side of Manhattan. He sounded like the guy who used to sell pickles out of a barrel on Houston Street, or the one who sold pastrami and corned beef on the corner of Essex.

They walked among the couches, and Hal pointed at one that was actually very attractive, a soft pink cotton, plumply stuffed, embroidered with big white roses.

"This is made of pure *cockamoon*," Hal said.

Joshua stared at him oddly. "What?"

"*Cockamoon, echt cockamoon*, it's the best fabric on the market."

Joshua looked at Chuy. Chuy shrugged.

"He's the Indian," Joshua said, pointing at Chuy. "I'm from Brighton Beach and Eastern Parkway."

Hal Dubin's look slowly became a genuine smile. "You mean you ain't interested in *echt cockamoon*?"

Joshua laughed. "I never heard of 'shit on him' being used for the name of an upholstered fabric."

Hal laughed maliciously. He confided in a low voice, although no one else was in the store, "None of the *goyim* out here know what it is. I tell em *cockamoon*, they think they're getting spun gold. Rapunzel's hair." He laughed. "Aw right, for a *lantsman*, I got a real deal for you. A hundred bucks the two of em, the couch and matching chair over there." He pointed.

Joshua raised his eyebrows and nodded. "Good price. It's not made out of shit, right? It'll hold up?"

Hal laughed. "My lips, God's ear. Ashwood frame, cotton batting, good-quality cotton cover. It's not a fashion statement," he shrugged, "it's just living room furniture. But I stand by it. I got my own upholstery shop here." He pointed to the rear of the store. "You get a tear, one of the tacks comes out, you bring it back. Hal guarantees it." He nodded earnestly at Joshua.

"Okay. Load them up."

"Hidalgo," Hal called out. A middle-aged Mexican came out of a room at the rear of the store. "Gotta load this junk. I just made a hunnerd bucks, and I got to get em outta the store before they change their minds." He roared with laughter. It was infectious, and Joshua and Chuy laughed.

"Abraham, get your ass out here. Gotta work," Hidalgo called out.

An ancient negro, thin as a gnawed dog bone and totally bald, his pate shiny as an onyx mirror, came out of the rear room. He limped slowly toward Hal and Joshua and Chuy. When he was a few feet away from Joshua, the stale odor of whiskey was unmistakable. The whites of the old man's eyes were tanned almost to brown. They appeared to move freely, focusing on nothing, as though they were little fish swimming around in a bowl.

Abraham and Hidalgo loaded the furniture. Hidalgo growled a constant series of commands. Abraham complied slowly, docilely, coughing constantly like a consumptive.

CHAPTER FOURTEEN

When a lawsuit was filed against the United States or one of its agencies, it was served on the United States Attorney, mailed to the agency director in Washington, D.C., and hand-delivered to the local agency representative. Joshua received a copy of Transcon's complaint Monday afternoon at one o'clock. The complaint alleged that Joshua Rabb had conspired with George Callan to rig the bid for the Nogales Sewer and Sewage Disposal Project, U.S./OLM #4732/46, and that inferior-grade concrete was being supplied by an unauthorized foreign subsidiary of George Callan's that was nothing but a sham. The prayer for relief asked for an injunction against Avra Valley Concrete continuing with the project, piercing the corporate veil, disgorgement of fees wrongly paid to Callan, and an award of the project to Transcon Contracting at its next-lowest bid of $18,923,000. An order to show cause hearing on the injunction was scheduled for Wednesday at ten o'clock in the morning.

Joshua chewed his lower lip as he finished reading the complaint. Edgar Hendly came into the office and sat down heavily on one of the straight chairs. His pink jowls seemed to be sagging more today.

"I was over at the M.O. Club havin a nice lunch, babyin my peptic ulcer with a slab a poached sea bass, and whattya s'pose happened?"

Joshua looked at him blandly.

"Old George Callan come up to me shakin his fork and lookin like he was about to rip my nose off with it." Edgar scowled at Joshua. There was no humor in his voice. "Yep, seems like that lowlife crook Henry Jessup done sued George."

Joshua nodded. "He sued me, too. I guess that's life in the big city." He shrugged.

"That's it?" Edgar said, his tone acidulous. "Life in the big city? Just a fuckin joke to you that George is about to lose three, four million dollars profit?"

"Listen, Edgar, I'd have to be an astronomer to understand numbers like that. All I understand is contracts. And if old George screwed old Henry, then that's for old Judge Buchanan to sort out, not me. I'm just a country lawyer."

"Yeah, in a pig's ass. Yer the smartest sombitch I ever met! So why don't ya figure out somethin to make this shit go away?"

Joshua shook his head. "I appreciate your kind words, Edgar, but legerdemain isn't one of my skills."

Hendly looked at him sourly. "There you go again usin them big turd-sized words that don't mean jack shit to me. All I wanna know is why you cain't have Harry Morland rewrite the specs on the concrete and get George to post the performance bond we talked about."

"I tried that. Callan refused."

Edgar's mouth opened wide. "Yer kiddin me."

"No. I went out to the ranch and asked him. He turned me down."

"Whew!" Edgar expelled his breath. "That old fart's takin one helluva risk."

"He says he's got Judge Buchanan under control, and he says the concrete's Type 5 anyway, so he has nothing to worry about."

Edgar rolled his eyes and pursed his lips. "Well, I reckon if he takes that attitude, it's on *his* head." He shrugged.

Joshua nodded. Edgar left the office, and Joshua returned to writing the motion to suppress evidence that he had been working on before he had received the complaint. In New York, Joshua had often worked on forty or fifty cases at any one time. It was a skill that a lawyer had to cultivate, to be able to shift gears from one case to another without a great deal of refresher time. But the skill to do this had dulled over the last four years, and Joshua found it difficult to put the problems with Callan and Transcon completely out of his mind and concentrate intensely on Franklin Carillo. It took him almost an hour to review the notes in his file and to put order to the legal research on the exclusionary rule that he had done at the county law library.

Under the rule in *Weeks* v. *United States,* a U.S. Supreme Court decision from 1914, in a criminal case in a federal court the United States attorney could not introduce evidence against a defendant that had been seized in violation of the Fourth Amendment to the United States Constitution. The Fourth Amendment established safeguards against "unreasonable searches and seizures" and required search warrants, especially to search a person's home. But the exclusionary rule of *Weeks* had never been imposed on state courts, and the states were free to permit the introduction of illegally seized evidence.

Franklin Carillo had a serious problem, a potentially terminal problem. Joshua had received the FBI ballistics report on the bullet found at the scene. It matched the riflings on the test bullets fired from Carillo's Ruger. The .44 magnum revolver had to be excluded from evidence or Carillo would be convicted. The gun had been illegally seized from his home on Federal land, but he was being tried in state court. Arizona didn't follow the exclusionary rule.

Joshua spent the rest of the afternoon drafting a motion to suppress. The trial would begin tomorrow at ten o'clock in the morning.

▼▲▼

The courtroom on the second floor of the Pima County Courthouse was far more elegant than would be expected, given the exterior appearance of the Mexican-style pink stucco building with the green- and yellow- and red-tiled cupola. The first floor was a courtyard surrounded on three sides by a porticoed walkway in front of the Justice Court and various county offices. The yard was a newly planted hundred-foot square of ryegrass with a shrubbery border of orange- and red-blooming bird of paradise bushes. The second floor housed the Superior Court and the law library.

Joshua got there a few minutes before ten, and

the room was full of spectators. He sat down at the defense table and opened his briefcase. He took out the motion to suppress and the two carbon copies he had laboriously made and laid them on the table in front of him. Randy Stevens, the chief deputy county attorney, was seated at the prosecution table looking over some papers. He looked toward Joshua and nodded quickly. It wasn't good public relations for the prosecutor to appear friendly with the defense attorney. In the public's eyes they were supposed to be enemies, devoted to diametrically opposed principles of law and justice.

Joshua walked over to Stevens. He handed a copy of the motion to suppress to him and resumed his seat at the defense table. Stevens began to read the motion.

A murmur arose among the spectators as Franklin Carillo was brought into the courtroom, shuffling in leg cuffs, his hands cuffed behind his back. He was in regular clothes, a plaid cowboy shirt and Levis and shiny black boots. The two sheriff's deputies led him to the defense table and uncuffed his hands, but not his ankles. He sat down next to Joshua.

"You okay?" Joshua asked.

Carillo nodded and clenched his jaw. He chewed his lower lip.

"Shirt fits fine," Joshua said.

Carillo said nothing. He stared straight ahead at the ornately carved walnut judge's bench. The jury box and the walls of the high-ceilinged courtroom were paneled in the same carved walnut. There were enough wooden pews in the spectators' section to seat at least two hundred people.

The courtroom's rear door opened, and a sheriff's deputy came toward the judge's bench and rapped a gavel slowly three times on a wooden block.

"All rise. Pima County Superior Court is now in session, Honorable Bernardo Velasco presiding," the deputy said.

Velasco came into the courtroom in a long black robe and ascended the two steps onto the bench. He sat down in a tall leather swivel chair. He took a pair of rimless "readers" off the bench and opened the file.

"This is the time set for the trial of State versus Franklin Carillo. Announce your appearances."

"William Randolph Stevens for the State, your honor." Randy stood up at the prosecution table.

"Joshua Rabb for Mr. Carillo, your honor," Joshua said, standing.

"Anything before I call the jury panel, gentlemen?" asked the judge.

"No, your honor," Randy said.

"May it please the court," Joshua said, "I have a motion to suppress."

The judge held out his hand. "Let's see it."

Joshua walked forward, handed it to him, and resumed his place next to Carillo.

The judge read absorbedly for ten minutes. He put it down on the bench in front of him and rubbed his chin hard.

"You get a copy?" He looked at Randy Stevens.

"Yes, sir, I just read it."

The judge nodded. "All right, Mr. Rabb. Let's hear your argument on this." He settled back into his deep armchair.

The door to the courtroom banged open, and

Erma Carillo clacked down the aisle on her metal canes, making the sad entrance that she must have timed perfectly. She stood at the end of the first pew, giving the woman sitting there a look of deep pathos. The spectators slid closer together, allowing Erma enough room to lower herself painfully onto the wooden seat. Judge Velasco watched her impatiently, annoyedly tapping his readers on the bench, waiting for the commotion to subside. Joshua stared at her blandly. She smiled sweetly at him.

"Go on, Mr. Rabb," the judge said.

"May it please the court, I have set forth in my motion the citations relevant to this matter. As the court is well aware, *Weeks v. United States* mandates the application of the exclusionary rule where evidence is seized in violation of the Fourth Amendment. In the instant case sheriff's deputies from the Pima County Sheriff's Office searched Franklin Carillo's home without a warrant and found a .44 magnum Ruger. This court should order that the gun cannot be used in evidence."

The judge held up his hand in a halt gesture. "Now hold on, Mr. Rabb. The exclusionary rule doesn't apply in state courts, only in federal courts. I have no authority to exclude the state's evidence."

"With the court's indulgence," Joshua said, pulling a folded sheet of paper out of his briefcase, "I would ask the bailiff to pin this plat map on the cork board."

The judge nodded to the sheriff's deputy. The deputy took the paper to the cork board on the wall to the right of the judge, unfolded it, and thumbtacked it to the board.

"This is a plat map of the San Xavier Papago Reservation, your honor. It's certified in the right hand corner by the Pima County Recorder."

Joshua walked to the map and pointed. "This narrow finger of land outlined in red is on the Reservation. Most people, myself included up to a few days ago, don't realize that the Reservation extends out past the irrigation ditch. But it does, and the Franklin Carillo residence is right here." He pointed to a green dot he had placed in the long strip of land.

The judge came forward slowly and hunched his elbows on the bench.

Joshua continued speaking.

"The .44 magnum was found by sheriff's deputies in a search on federal Indian reservation land. They have no jurisdiction on a Reservation, only the FBI and the Indian Police do. Federal law applies on the Reservation, and therefore the *Weeks* rule applies to this search, and the gun must be suppressed." Joshua sat down.

The judge stared at the map, took his glasses off, and tapped them lightly on the bench several times. "What do you think, Mr. Stevens? Has he got a prayer?"

Randy stood up looking very upset. "Your honor, I'd like a continuance so I can brief this. The motion just got sprung on me, and the issue is much too important to deal with unprepared. I was unaware that the search was on Reservation land."

"Mr. Rabb?" The judge looked at Joshua.

"I oppose a continuance, your honor. The state should have known the situation, and Mr. Stevens should have been prepared to argue the issue."

"Aw, well, Mr. Rabb," the judge drawled, "I think that's being a little rough on the prosecutor. In the interest of justice, I think we better continue the trial. Come ready to try this case two weeks from today." He looked at each attorney. They both nodded at him.

Velasco banged his gavel and left the courtroom. The spectators began to murmur, and their voices grew louder and ill-tempered. They had come to see a show, and instead they had witnessed some incomprehensible legal hocus-pocus.

Erma Carillo stood up unsteadily and propped herself on her canes. "What happened?" she shrieked at Joshua. "We were ready to win. Look, Mrs. Bojorquez came all the way from Tubac to testify." She pointed at the old woman sitting in the rear of the courtroom."

"It has to be done this way, Mrs. Carillo," Joshua said.

J. T. Sellner came up beside Erma Carillo. The journalist held a small steno pad open in her hand and was writing rapidly.

"I'm J. T. Sellner of the *Arizona Daily Star*," she said to Erma. "May I interview you?"

The crippled woman's slumped body straightened, and her look of hatred turned to pathos. She sat down, and the reporter sat next to her. Sellner was small and thin, perhaps fifty years old, and had dark brown dyed hair in a tight wavy thirties hairdo.

Well, that about clinches it, Joshua thought. This skinny old buzzard is about to feed on my liver again. He finished putting his papers in his briefcase and left the courtroom, avoiding the angry looks of several milling spectators.

▼▲▼

Transcon's order to show cause was scheduled for ten o'clock in the morning, and Joshua went to his office at seven o'clock to prepare for it. At a little after eight, Edgar walked into his office, laid the morning newspaper dramatically in front of Joshua, and walked out wordlessly.

The left-hand column on the front page was headed, ACCUSED KILLER'S WIFE DECRIES LAWYER. Joshua read the first couple of lines.

> Erma Carillo, wife of accused rapist/murderer Franklin Carillo, expressed grave dismay yesterday that her husband's attorney, Joshua Rabb, failed to bring the only witness to the stand who could exonerate her husband. "Instead of putting Mrs. Bojorquez on the stand, he raised some legal nonsense about searches on the Reservation, and my Franklin is still in jail instead of being home with me."

The rest of the story was about the crimes and a lot of human interest about Erma and her battle with muscular dystrophy. On balance, the story was neither anti-Rabb nor pro-Carillo. It was simply about Erma's view of it all, and especially her discontent with her husband's lawyer. Thank you, J. T., thought Joshua. I sure do need P.R. like this. Well, at least it isn't nearly as bad as that first story you wrote about me back in July.

He put several documents in his briefcase and left for federal court. It was on the second floor of the main post office downtown, and in contrast to yesterday's horde of angry spectators, today there were only the parties and their attorneys. Harry Chandler sat at the defendant's table with George Callan. Chandler was an old man with a bald head covered with brown splotches. He wore a baggy tan linen suit. Callan had on a dark brown wool western suit. A tall cream-colored cowboy hat sat on the table in front of him. Tim Essert, the assistant United States attorney, sat in the end chair at the long table, leaving a chair between him and Callan.

"What are you doing here?" Joshua asked, walking up to Essert.

The man's dark eyes twitched, and he looked disgustedly at Joshua. "The OLM got sued, I have to represent it."

"I'm representing it," Joshua said.

"Well, I'm your lawyer, too."

Joshua stared at him for a moment, his eyes reddening with anger. He walked close to Essert and leaned over. He spoke just above a whisper, so that no one else would hear. "Listen, Essert, if you don't get away from this table in five seconds, I'm going to rip your fucking face off with these prongs." He raised his mechanical arm and held it a foot away from Essert's face.

The U.S. attorney stood up abruptly and backed away from Joshua. "I'm making a report on this and sending it to the Justice Department."

Joshua ignored him. He put his briefcase on the table and sat down in the end chair.

"Why don't you slit your wrists and write it in blood," Joshua said.

Essert walked stiffly out of the courtroom.

"I guess you're not the forgive and forget type, huh?" Harry Chandler said and chuckled.

Henry Jessup and Dan Swirling came into the courtroom followed by an elderly man in a black wool suit and bright white shirt with an old-time detachable collar, the tips folded over a polka-dotted burgundy bow tie. He walked up to Harry Chandler, and they shook hands vigorously.

"Well, I'll be a son of a bitch, Taft," Harry said effusively, "I haven't seen you in years. Figured you'd have given up the ghost by now, just rolled over like a red-bones hound with your feet stuck up in the air."

"Hell no, Harry. Only reason I raise my legs up anymore is so some nice little broad can get her lips on me."

Both men guffawed loudly and clapped each other on the back.

"You know George Callan?" Harry asked.

"Don't believe I've had the pleasure." He reached his hand toward George. "Taft Greer."

Callan didn't rise from his chair. He reached across his body and shook Greer's hand briefly. Their smiles were thin and brittle and appraising. Taft Greer could have been Callan's brother, tall and thin with a pleasant face, strong blue eyes, and wavy white hair.

An elderly woman with rimless glasses, wearing her gray hair in a tight bun, sat down at the small court reporter's table in front of the bench. She opened a stenographic pad and smiled and nodded at Joshua and Harry Chandler. Greer and his clients sat down at the plaintiff's table. A moment later Judge Robert Buchanan came onto the bench. He settled his slight body into the tall leather swivel chair. He had a full head of hair the same color as the steel rims on his spectacles. He looked out at the men at the tables and nodded at Chandler. He looked at Greer and smiled.

"How are you, Taft? Nice to see you. Missed you at the game last week."

"Good to see you too, Buck," said the elderly lawyer. "First Homecoming game I've missed in thirty years. Janet's dad died in Farmington, and we went back for the funeral. The old bird was eighty-six years old."

"That's what living on a farm will do for you," said the judge. "Clean air, food right out of the ground, clean living." Buchanan's expression changed to serious. "Okay, announce your appearances, and let's get this OSC going."

"Taft Greer for Transcon Contracting, Inc., your honor," Greer said rising at the table. He nodded at the judge and sat down.

"Harry Chandler for George Callan."

"Joshua Rabb for the Office of Land Management and in *propria persona,* your honor."

Buchanan looked down his nose through the spectacles perched there. "Isn't the U.S. attorney going to represent you and the agency?"

"Mr. Essert was here, your honor. I decided that his representation wasn't necessary."

The judge raised his eyebrows and stared at Joshua. Then he shrugged and nodded. "Okay, so noted. Let's go. Mr. Greer, you want to argue first or present evidence?"

"Whatever is the court's pleasure."

"Well, why don't all of you give me a short statement of your position. That'll make it easier on me."

"Very well, your honor," Taft Greer said. "My client bid on a sealed-bid federal contract for a sewage system and treatment plant in Nogales, Sonora. We have evidence that the sealed bids were unlawfully revealed to Mr. Callan so that he could lowball them. We also believe that he is supplying subgrade concrete to the project through a Mexican subsidiary in violation of federal law." He sat down.

Harry Chandler stood up. "It is not true, your honor, that Mr. Callan was aware of the bids prior to the formal unsealing. It is also untrue that Avra Valley Concrete may not legally supply concrete through a Mexican subsidiary. Nothing in the OLM contract or in federal law forbids it. And there is no evidence that the concrete is anything other than Type 5, as specified in the contract."

"All right," Judge Buchanan said. He flipped a few pages in the file in front of him and read for a moment. "Mr. Rabb, Transcon says you conspired with Avra Valley Concrete to pervert the bid process and that you haven't terminated the contract despite the fact that the concrete doesn't meet the specs. What's your position?"

Joshua stood up. "On behalf of myself, your honor, I conspired with no one, and on behalf of the OLM, I simply contracted with the low bidder. As for the concrete quality, the Corps of Engineers inspector on the site has approved it."

The judge nodded. "Okay, we'd best get some evidence on this, Taft."

Greer stood up. "We call Michael O'Leary."

The bailiff left the courtroom and returned a moment later with the witness. O'Leary was sworn and took the stand. He testified about his background and education. His boyish good looks and Irish green eyes were disarming.

"How long has your father known George Callan?" Greer asked.

"Objection, hearsay," Chandler said.

"Well, Harry, I suppose that's right," Judge Buchanan drawled, rubbing his chin thoughtfully. "But it's just family history, and I suppose we can make an exception for that. Go on and answer, Mr. O'Leary."

"I don't know exactly. At least sixty years, since they were kids in boarding school together in Prescott."

"How long have you known Mr. Callan?"

"All of my life."

"You were with Mr. Rabb when the bids were unsealed?"

"Yes."

"The award was not made at that time but later?"

"Yes."

"You spoke to Mr. Callan about the concrete he had agreed to supply?"

"Yes."

"What did you talk about?"

"His bid, as best I can remember, was for over the .45 ratio of water to cement called for in the contract, .52 I think, and Mr. Rabb wanted to see what his bid would be at the .45 required by the contract, so Mr. Callan adjusted his bid upward for the .45 ratio and he still was more than five hundred thousand dollars lower than Transcon."

"Did you tell Mr. Callan what Transcon's bid was?"

O'Leary swallowed and shifted in his chair. Judge Buchanan was rocking slowly in his deep leather swivel chair. He studied the witness.

"No, sir," O'Leary answered.

Taft Greer, a polished cross-examiner, simply

stood at the table saying nothing, staring at the witness, letting O'Leary's body language obviously belie his answer. O'Leary cleared his throat loudly, rubbed his nose, shifted in his chair, and looked around cautiously at the faces in front of him.

Joshua sat stiffly in his chair and stared at the handsome engineer. O'Leary had just committed perjury. George Callan had admitted to Joshua that he had learned the amount of the bids from O'Leary.

O'Leary was excused from the witness stand. He walked to the rear of the courtroom and sat down on the last spectators' bench.

The next witness was Dan Swirling, who testified about the reagent test he had performed on the concrete and his conclusion that it contained 10 to 12 percent tricalcium aluminate and was therefore at best a Type 2 cement instead of Type 5. Harry Chandler cross-examined him about the validity of the reagent test and extracted the admission that only a microscopic analysis of crushed concrete could determine the type with certainty.

Then George Callan took the stand.

"Why don't we just skip all the formalities and get right down to the issue here, all right, Mr. Callan?" Taft Greer asked.

Callan nodded.

"Now, we've all heard young Michael testify about how close your families are for so many years, and we saw how loyal he was to you when he testified here a little while ago. Do you have anything to add to what he said?"

Callan looked hard at Chandler, who sat stone-faced, his hands clasped atop the table. Then he looked at Joshua, studying him, trying to divine what would happen when Joshua took the stand and was asked the same question.

"I wouldn't want to contradict anything that Mike said. It might be considered perjury—by one of us," George said. He looked searchingly at Judge Buchanan.

"Well, if your answer adds something to Mr. O'Leary's testimony," the judge drawled, rocking casually in his armchair, "we'll just assume that his memory is not as good as yours. That's all." He looked at Taft Greer. Greer nodded.

"As I remember it, Mike told me that my bid was lower than the others by over a million dollars. Then he asked me how much more I'd raise the bid if I had to match the Corps of Engineers' specs exactly, and I told him around half a million. Actually, when I checked with my plant manager that afternoon, we arrived at an increase of $520,000. I called Mike, and he said that wouldn't be enough to queer the award of the contract to me."

Joshua studied Callan. The way Callan told the story, there wasn't a trace of wrongdoing in it. Maybe Mike O'Leary shouldn't have been quite so verbose, but after all, he had been sent to Avra Valley Concrete to determine if its bid would still be the winner at the Corps's specs, and that was exactly what he had done. Taft Greer's face was taut, far less than satisfied at Callan's explanation. But twenty minutes of probing, caustic, sarcastic questioning didn't shake George's composure or change his answer.

Then Greer went into the issue of the Mexican subsidiary and the production of Type 5 cement, and George's testimony was exactly what he had told Joshua, except that he didn't answer the questions about his margin of profit. He wasn't quite certain, he said, but he hoped it would be enough to retire on. "These old bones are beginnin to bark at me ever' mornin, and I reckon it's gettin on to begin time to hang up my spurs," he drawled amiably in his best cowboy twang. When Greer asked him about how much he had to bribe the Mexicans, Harry Chandler objected that it was "incompetent, irrelevant, and immaterial," and Judge Buchanan sustained the objection.

Joshua was the last witness to testify.

"Did you tell Mr. O'Leary to inform Mr. Callan that he was the lowest of the sealed bids?"

"Yes, I did."

"Why?"

"Because otherwise he would have had no incentive to rebid the contract at the exact specs. He was originally a million dollars below Transcon, and his rebid was a half million dollars lower."

"Did you tell Mr. Callan how much the other bids were?"

"No."

"Did you tell Mr. O'Leary to do so?"

"No."

Taft Greer cast him a probing, acidic look, and his voice was derisive. "How much money do you make with the BIA and OLM, Mr. Rabb?"

"Two-thirteen an hour for fifteen hours a week."

Greer added up the numbers on his legal pad. "A hundred twenty-five bucks a month, give or take?"

Joshua nodded. "Plus a free house."

Greer pursed his lips thoughtfully. He reached

into his briefcase and pulled out a manila folder. He opened it and held up a sheet of paper victoriously. "Yet you can spend $2,630 cash on a new automobile just a couple of weeks ago?" he bellowed.

"I also get fees from outside clients, Mr. Greer. I received somewhat more than that a few weeks ago to defend Franklin Carillo. It's a high-profile case here in Tucson. I guess you haven't heard about it in Phoenix."

Greer's face went from victory to disbelief to dejection. He retained enough composure to ask, "Can you prove that?"

"Of course. I received a Hartford Insurance Company check from Erma Carillo. Check with her, check with the local Hartford agent. It was drawn on a Boston bank, but I'd guess that she applied for the cash value through the local agency. She's not likely to have had any idea who to contact in Boston."

Greer sat down at the plaintiff's table and had a heated whispered exchange with his sullen clients. "Nothing further," he announced to the judge.

Buchanan looked at Harry Chandler. "You have any evidence to present?"

"No, your honor," Harry said.

"Okay, let's hear your arguments. Taft?"

Greer stood up dramatically and hooked his thumbs in his suspenders. His beautifully tailored black wool double-breasted suit jacket was unbuttoned and casually draped his tall, slender body. He was regal and articulate. He spoke passionately about honesty and clean dealings in contract bidding and the chicanery that O'Leary and Callan and

Rabb had engaged in to sully the bidding process. Then he demanded that the concrete be tested.

"Okay, thank you," said the judge. "You have anything to say, Harry?"

Chandler stood up slowly. He was a complete contrast to the suave lawyer from Phoenix. His tan linen suit was rumpled and baggy and looked lived in. He was overweight, short, and his hair was just a few strands of gray combed over a blotchy, otherwise bald head. He lacked the resonant deep voice and the glib smoothness of his adversary.

"Well, Judge, I suppose the only thing I can say in response to my dapper and learned friend from Phoenix is that for all his bombast and thespian eloquence, he ain't proved that Mr. Callan or Mr. Rabb have done a damn thing improper!" Harry sat down.

Judge Buchanan chuckled good-naturedly. He looked at Greer. "Taft, I do believe Harry's got you on this one. I don't think there was anything criminal or fraudulent about George Callan's bid for the project. Any inside information came after the bidding was closed, and Avra Valley's bid was still $503,000 lower than Transcon's. I can't imagine that saving the American taxpayer that kind of money would be considered an act of impropriety on Mr. Callan's or Mr. Rabb's part. As for the Mexican subsidiary, I just don't know of any statute that prevents such an arrangement or would even prevent a Mexican company from making a direct bid for the project if it had chosen to do so. So that's going to be my ruling on those issues."

The judge turned his attention to Harry Chandler. "But there is this matter of the Type 5 concrete.

Your client is going to have to get that concrete tested."

Chandler rose from his seat. "That's not our burden of proof, your honor. The Corps of Engineers inspector has verified it twice. It's the plaintiffs who have to prove it's substandard."

Buchanan pulled his pocket watch out of his pocket, snapped open the hunting case, and examined the watch face. He wound the stem slowly, then put the watch back in his vest pocket.

"All right, now here's what we're going to do on this," the judge said, looking at Chandler, who had resumed his seat. "I'm ordering that Henry Jessup and Dan Swirling and their agents have free access to the plant in Guaymas, to the trucks, and to the culvert. They will take whatever samples they wish and turn them over to the Chemistry Department at the University of Arizona. I'm continuing this hearing subject to call. Taft will notify me when the testing has been completed, and I'll set the hearing. I want to hear from one of the U of A professors on the concrete tests. Understood?" He looked from Greer to Chandler.

George Callan shifted in his chair. His face was savage, his eyes bloodshot and narrowed. He stood up and stared angrily at the judge. "Why is it that my sworn word and the verification of the inspector from the Corps of Engineers is not sufficient proof for you, Buck? What the hell's going on here?"

Chandler stood up quickly and put his arm around Callan. "Come on, George, sit down. The judge is just doing his job."

"I've known you for thirty years, dammit. My word has always been good as gold. Why not now?"

"Come on, George," Chandler said insistently. "Sit down, this isn't real appropriate."

Buchanan leaned over the bench. His look was sober. He took his glasses off and threw them on the bench. "Take your lawyer's advice and sit down, George. This is a court of law."

Callan slowly descended to his chair.

"I apologize for my client, your honor," Harry Chandler said. "All this impugning of his integrity has him a bit riled up."

"It's understandable, Harry," Buchanan said mildly. He banged the gavel and walked off the bench.

Mike O'Leary joined Callan as the men filed out of the courtroom and walked downstairs to the sidewalk in front of the Post Office. Greer, Jessup, and Swirling continued down the street to their car. Callan stood still, clenching his fists, breathing deeply, trying to quell his anger. He raised his arm and signaled to a man sitting at the wheel of a black Packard parked across the street. The car started up slowly and made a U-turn. Joshua recognized the driver as one of George's ranch hands.

"I was impressed by your testimony, Mike," Joshua said.

O'Leary grimaced.

"Lucky thing your daddy is a good old boy, huh?" Joshua said. "Otherwise the United States attorney might be hauling your ass off to the Federal Detention Center for perjury."

O'Leary clenched his fists and looked savagely at Joshua. "Folks are getting mighty tired of your holier-than-thou attitude, you fucking lowlife. We don't need your kind around here. That contract was fair and square awarded to Mr. Callan, and you'd best be backing off or your dick is going to end up the same place your arm went."

Joshua looked blandly at him. "First time I met you I figured you were a loudmouthed liar. You sure proved me right today, didn't you?"

O'Leary walked toward Joshua. Callan stepped between the two men and put his hand on O'Leary's chest. He pushed the much younger man back. "Take it easy now, Mike. Not here in front of the whole world."

"Why, that's plum neighborly of you, George," Joshua said in a mocking western accent. "Yessir, yer just a shit-kickin cowpoke, ain'tcha, Georgie boy. Butter wouldn't melt in yer mouth when you was up on that witness stand. I reckon yer just chock-full of honesty and good intentions."

Callan turned a fierce look on Joshua. "What did you think I'd do, commit perjury? Not with you sitting there in front of me, you Jew bastard. I saw the look in your eyes. You'd be on that stand spilling your guts about everything I told you in confidence when I thought you were our friend." He swallowed hard. "Mike is a good boy, damn loyal, something you don't know anything about. He was just trying to protect me, because he knew I didn't do anything wrong." He shook his finger at Joshua. "Just stay the fuck away from us, or I'll take care of you good and proper."

The Mexican ranch hand parked the car at the curb. He got out and opened the rear door. Mike O'Leary got in. George followed him and sat staring straight ahead. The car pulled away toward Stone Avenue.

"Hotheaded son-of-a-gun, huh?" Harry Chandler said, shaking his head.

"You think he's got a reason for being so upset about the testing?"

Chandler shrugged and walked toward his office on Scott Street across from the courthouse. Joshua walked across the street to his car, feeling shooting pains in his missing toes. It was a lovely Indian summer day, warm and only a little cloudy. He put the top down on the convertible. A warm breeze on his face would feel good. Next Thursday is Thanksgiving, he thought, and I have so much to be thankful for. Yessir, yessir, yessir, let me list them. He thought for a moment and his mind was blank. Now that's no way to be, he scolded himself. I have Hanna and Adam and Magdalena. I've got a nice little house and a good job. He grimaced. Okay, the house stinks and the job isn't so hot, but things will get better. Hold that thought.

He drove south on 6th Avenue, which became the Nogales Highway about a mile past the Veterans Administration Hospital. Suddenly the steering got harder and the car pulled to the right. He held hard to keep it on the road. Then the car lumbered as though its rear wheels were elliptical. Joshua parked on the shoulder and got out. The right rear tire was flat. He looked around. A car passed by slowly. Another one across the highway sped north. There was nothing around him but desert filled with creosote bushes and mesquite trees and prickly pear cactus. He wasn't about to change the tire and get murdered like Chester Milliken. Back about a mile, just past the VA hospital, he had noticed a hardware store, Pedrano's or something like that. In the window were various garden tools and a couple of white porcelain sinks and a big pegboard with hunting knives.

He walked north on the shoulder of the highway. An occasional automobile or truck went by. He began to run, slowly, feeling his injured leg, and then faster, keeping his stride even. But his mechanical arm flopped on his shoulder and made it sore. He stopped running and kept up a fast walk. A nondescript black sedan across the highway began to slow as it passed him. About fifty yards away, he saw its brake lights glow. It pulled onto the shoulder and stopped. No one got out. The store was about a hundred yards past the car.

Joshua passed the car, and the driver looked out at him. He was young, twenty-three or twenty-five at most, Mexican, and Joshua thought he had seen him on the Lazy G Ranch. Wasn't he one of the men who had taken Diana's Lippizaner off to the stable?

Joshua began jogging again, holding hard to his arm to keep it from flopping. He ran onto the highway and followed the center white stripe. When he reached Pedrano's, he looked back. The black sedan was still there.

Pedrano's was a sprawling gray cinderblock box filled with dusty shelves spilling over with hardware and plumbing supplies and tools of every description. Joshua picked up a miner's pick and hefted it. It had an eighteen-inch-long wooden handle and a nine-inch-long carbon steel head, two inches square and flat on one end, tapering on the other end to a sharp point.

The clerk studied Joshua's stainless steel hand.

"You work down at the copper mines?" he said, a bored man making conversation just for the sake of talking to someone.

"Right," Joshua said.

"Yeah, I worked down there, the Sahuarita side, before I got this bum leg." He patted his right leg. "Ore cart ran over my foot. Practically cut my toes off." He rang up $4.20 on the cash register.

Joshua nodded and handed the man a five-dollar bill. The clerk counted out the change and dropped it in Joshua's outstretched hand.

"Ain't got no bags for the pick," the clerk said. "It's too heavy anyhow, and that point'll just tear right through it."

"That's okay. I'll carry it like this."

He walked outside, and the black sedan was gone. He walked quickly back down the highway toward his car, and as he neared it he saw the same black sedan parked about twenty yards in front of his car on the shoulder. The driver was leaning back against the car door, his arms folded. He was of medium height, broad through the shoulders, dressed in Levis and boots and a blue chambray work shirt.

Joshua walked to the center of the highway again. He passed his car and walked quickly south toward Valencia Road, at least a mile away.

"Hey, *amigo*," the man called out. "I help you change the tire."

Joshua walked faster. A produce truck sped by, and the driver called something out the window at him. A car passed him, not slowing at all. If a guy is dumb enough to stroll down the middle of a highway, he deserves to get run over, thought Joshua.

But it was a hell of a lot safer out here than on the shoulder, or taking a short cut through the desert.

Clouds were rolling toward him from the Gulf of California, where Tucson's summer monsoons usually originated. But it was unusual in the fall to see great bulbous thunderheads that looked like fat black whales. Fall rain was generally from the north, from a high pale gray overcast.

Jagged lightning struck the desert in front of him, and then thunder boomed with a shattering crack like a howitzer. And then he saw two more strikes of lightning and heard the thunderous explosions. The wind came up, and the Indian summer day fled before the threatening storm.

Damn, he thought, the top is down on the car. Well, can't do anything about that. He started jogging again, hoping to beat the rain home. He crossed his left arm over his chest and held it tightly to his body with his right arm and hand, clutching the miner's pick against his mechanical arm. He neared Valencia Road and saw the airport control tower a half mile to his left. It hadn't occurred to him before that he would run right into Tucson's airport, and the pleasant surprise of it made him run even faster. He looked back down the highway and saw the black sedan creeping up the shoulder toward him.

He ran in the middle of Valencia Road toward the access road to the terminal. Traffic was a little heavier here, and several drivers called out to him derisively. He hardly heard them. His chest was aching and his left shoulder was so sore that every jarring step rebounded painfully through him. A massive clap of thunder detonated overhead, followed by two smaller explosions. Several lightning strikes fulminated around the airport. There were two taxis parked in front of the terminal. Rain began to pelt down, and then it turned to hail. He ran up to the lead cab and pulled the rear door open awkwardly, holding on to the pick with the same hand.

He jumped into the back seat and sat up stiffly.

"What the hell ya think yer doin'?" the driver said, looking back at him. He picked up a tire iron from the seat and brandished it toward Joshua.

"Take it easy, pal," Joshua gasped, trying to catch his breath. "I got a flat tire back up the Nogales Highway."

"You tryin t' change it wi' that?" The driver looked at the pick.

"No, no," Joshua gasped. "Just brought it for my son, do some rock collecting." He breathed deeply a few times to catch his breath and steady himself.

The driver put the tire iron back on the seat. "Where to, bud?"

"The BIA, over on Indian Agency Road."

The driver nodded and started the old brown Chevy. He drove out of the airport and turned left on Valencia Road. He studied Joshua in the rearview mirror.

"You that lawyer over t' the BIA?"

"Which lawyer?"

The driver chuckled. "Yeah, I reckon ya are." He had a fat face, round cheeks pushing up his lower eyelids and shrouding watery hazel eyes. He had a three-day growth of salt-and-pepper whiskers and a crew cut of bristly gray hair.

"I seen yer pitcher in the papers a coupla months

back. Ain't got nothing t' do in this hack 'cept'n read, mos' a the time. Read the papers a lot. Yer some kinda ballsy sombitch, I give ya credit for that."

"Thanks, I'm flattered." Joshua's face was empty of emotion.

The driver snorted and then laughed. He looked at Joshua through the rearview mirror. "Yer a real ballbuster." He shook his head appreciatively and clucked his tongue.

Joshua stared out the window at the downpour. The driver pulled off Valencia onto Indian Agency Road, a long mud puddle, and parked in front of the BIA. Joshua handed him two dollars.

"Hey, thanks, bud," the driver said. "You easterners is always big wi' the tips. You knock em dead now, hear."

Joshua got out and splashed through the mud, up the steps, and into the Bureau. Frances Hendly stood up slowly behind the smeary reception window.

"What happened?" she asked.

"Just got caught in the rain. Nothing," Joshua said. He waved at her reassuringly and then realized he still had the miner's pick in his hand. Frances's eyes bulged.

"Oh, sorry," he said. "Had a flat tire."

She stared at him. Joshua walked down the hallway toward his office. Chuy Leyva was sitting behind his desk. On the desk was a checkerboard. Joshua walked in. Chuy stood up and looked a little sheepish.

"This is my brother, Solomon," he said, gesturing toward the young man across the desk.

Solomon stood up and nodded. "Nice to meet you, Mr. Rabb." He was tall and strongly built like Chuy, but not as handsome. His cheeks were lightly scarred by acne, common among the Papagos, and his face was fuller than his brother's, meatier.

Joshua put the pick on the desk and extended his hand to Solomon. They shook hands. "Good to meet you," Joshua said.

"You got caught in the rain, huh?" Chuy asked.

"Yeah. My car had a flat. It's down on the Nogales Highway. Can you give me a lift?"

"Sure, sure. We'll bring Sol. He's great at changing tires in the rain." He chuckled.

Solomon grimaced. " 'Cause he carries a gun, he thinks he's big medicine."

"I need some of that medicine right now," Joshua said.

They ran through the slackening rain and climbed into Chuy's pickup. By the time they reached the car, the rain had stopped.

"You had hubcaps this morning, didn't you?" Chuy said.

Joshua nodded slowly.

"You can't leave a car alone out here," Solomon said. "Those hubcaps are worth ten bucks at a junkyard."

They got out of the pickup and walked up to the Chevy. The driver's seat had been slashed. The stuffing was pulled out in handfuls and scattered in the car. Joshua stood stiffly by the car door looking at the seat. He breathed deeply to suppress his anger and frustration. He walked to the trunk. It had been broken open. He took out the jack, but the jack handle and the tire iron were missing.

▼▲▼

Joshua drove the car to Hal Dubin City, and Hal came out to survey the damage to the upholstery.

"Shouldn't leave a nice set a wheels like this unattended," he said.

"I didn't have much choice. Anyway, what do you care, it's business for you. I need some of your best *cockamoon*."

Dubin laughed and smiled broadly at Joshua. "You're a funny guy. Whattaya do?"

"I'm a lawyer."

Dubin nodded. "I didn't figger you for a violinist." He snorted gleefully. "Aw right, pure *cockamoon* with cotton batting costs you fifty little ones."

"I don't have any little ones. To me they're all giants. And I don't want you trying to take advantage of my good nature and soft heart. Twenty-five."

Dubin surveyed him and pursed his lips in thought. "*Nu*, what can I do? I wanna make you happy. You got a deal. Bring the car around to the upholstery shop in back. I'll get Hidalgo and the *shvartzer* on it right now." He shrugged. "*Gesheft iz a bissel schwach* [Business is a little slow]."

Joshua drove the car to the back and parked. He walked into the store through the rear door. Dubin was at a desk near the rear, filling out a sales slip. Joshua handed him twenty-five dollars. Dubin put the bills in his pants pocket and walked into the workroom to tell Hidalgo what to do. He came back a moment later.

"Come on, take a load off. It'll be forty-five minutes, an hour." Dubin sat down in a plush armchair.

Joshua sat on the couch beside it.

"So what brings you to Tucson?"

"Took a bullet in my lung in the war. Doctors at the VA in Brooklyn said Tucson was the best climate for pulmonary problems. How about you?"

"*Shvartzers* moved into Crown Heights like you wouldn't believe. I had a nice shop. But the neighborhood turned, you know, just wasn't the same place anymore. Then my wife reads in *Life* magazine about Tucson and wide open spaces and says, 'Let's go,' and that's it. I sold the place to my wife's cousin Berl, he should only rot in hell, the *gonnif*, and here I am." He shrugged and looked around his store. "It ain't Goldberg's, but it's a living."

"Goldberg's is pretty expensive. I looked at his furniture."   "Yeah, he's a fucking crook. Tried to put me out of business when I opened last year. Went to Pima County zoning, told them I wasn't zoned here for a department store. Cost me plenty. Had to hire a lawyer, Harold Adamson, you know him?"

Joshua shook his head.

"Real wheeler-dealer, from one of the old families here. Cost me a *grand*. Had to grease ten assholes, but I kept the store." He grimaced. "I owe Goldberg for that. You know he ain't even Jewish no more?"

Joshua shook his head.

"Cat'lic, I swear to God. He converted a couple years ago. Wasn't good business being a *yidl* out here in the sticks. So now he's a Cat'lic." He shook his head in disgust. "So what kind of law you into? Maybe I'll use you next time, huh?"

"Well, mostly I'm doing criminal cases right now. I'm working part-time for the BIA at San Xavier, and I'm kind of out of the mainstream."

Dubin stared at him soberly and nodded slowly. "Why don't you come into Tucson and open an office? You'll never get any real business all the way out there."

"I don't have the money right now to open an office. It'll take me a while."

"I own a little place down on Speedway, right across from the University. An old house, needs a little fixing up. You could put an office in the front, the living room and the little den off it, and you'd still have the kitchen and three bedrooms upstairs. You got a family?"

"Two kids. My wife died in a car accident."

Dubin sighed lugubriously. "I got a daughter, Barbara, she's twenty-three, can't find a fuckin man that's good enough for her. This one's too skinny, this one's too short, this one's only an insurance salesman and that ain't good enough for her. Kids, I'm telling you." He looked solemnly at Joshua. Joshua felt as though he were being appraised through a loupe by a jeweler. "Maybe you'll come to dinner? We'll talk about this little piece of property I got. Maybe even Barbara will be home for a change." He frowned. "Always these goddamn dude ranches. She loves to ride horses. Dresses up like Dale Evans, boots and everything. She goes to El Dorado for a week, to the Flying Y, nothing's too good for her. Money is like piss to her." He shook his head as though disgusted, but his eyes were eagerly studying Joshua's.

Hidalgo walked into the showroom and called out, "The car's ready."

Joshua stood up. Hal Dubin stood up reluctantly.

"I'm going to call you," he said. "Maybe my wife'll throw a brisket in the oven for Shabbos, huh?"

Joshua nodded.

"Good, good. You think about it. Right across from the University. Great location." He shook Joshua's hand avidly.

CHAPTER
FIFTEEN

Hanna stood in front of the bathroom mirror, brushing her rich brown hair until it glistened. It fell softly to the top of her shoulders. She pouted her lips and applied the new lipstick she had bought at McClellan's last week and admired the color in the mirror.

Thanksgiving sure was different in Tucson than it had been in Brooklyn. Grandma would roast a big turkey and make cranberry sauce out of fresh berries and take down the blueberries she'd canned up in the Catskills in August and bake a delicious pie. After the sumptuous meal, they would go to Coney Island. There was usually snow on the boardwalk when they walked to Coney Island, a little over a mile away, to go on the Ferris wheel and the loop-de-loop and all the other rides.

But not here in Tucson. Grandma and Grandpa were back in Brooklyn, and here there was no snow. In fact, there were just a bunch of mud puddles from yesterday's storm. And instead of turkey, she was probably going to get pork and beans or something horrible like that. Of course, the weather was beautiful right now. You had to give Tucson credit for that. Fifty-five degrees with a cool breeze and a

cloudless azure sky the color of the lisianthus that
Magdalena had planted beside the front porch. But
no Coney Island here. No carnival, no cotton candy,
no ice cream cones, no organ grinders with cute
little monkeys.

"I think you're too old for that stuff anyway," she
whispered to her image in the mirror. She dabbed
a touch more rouge on her cheeks and admired the
results. She walked into the living room and sat
down on the overstuffed chair and smoothed her
pleated black wool skirt, trying not to wrinkle it.
She was wearing silk stockings, black patent-leather
flats, a long-sleeved hot pink silk blouse, and a pale
pink shawl over her shoulders. The clothes had been
her mother's.

Joshua was reading the newspaper on the couch,
and he looked at her and flinched.

"What's wrong, Daddy? Do I look awful?"

He smiled softly at her. "No, honey. You look just
like your mother. Beautiful and delicate."

She smiled broadly at him.

"You going to a prom or something?" Adam asked.
He was on the floor next to the big radio.

"No. I'm going to Mark Goldberg's for
Thanksgiving."

"We're going to the Reservation," Adam said.
"Chief Macario is having a big goat roast like last
summer." He wrinkled his cheeks a little and forced
a smile.

"You'll live," Hanna said.

Adam rolled his eyes.

They heard the sound of a car pulling into the
front yard and splashing through a long mud puddle. A moment later came a knock on the door.

"Have a nice time, honey," her father said.

"Thanks, Daddy." She stood up and straightened her skirt. She walked to the door and opened it.

"Wow, you're gorgeous," Mark Goldberg said, his hazel eyes wide and gleaming. She pulled the door closed behind her.

▼▲

At three o'clock, Joshua and Magdalena drove to Black Mountain, where the big barbecue pits that the Papagos used for their celebrations were. Early in the morning, Magdalena and her grandmother Ernestina had slaughtered a kid, skinned and gutted it, made long slits in the flesh, filled the slits with garlic cloves, and spitted it over one of the pits. It was roasted deep brown now and smelled fabulous.

The Antone family was gathered around a large fire, and next to them was Francisco Romero's family. Francisco had been chief of the tribe for over a year, since Macario Antone's retirement. Joshua and Magdalena sat next to Macario. Adam rode Golden Boy through the mud in the bottom of the irrigation ditch across from his house and loped easily through the barren half-mile-long field behind San Xavier Mission, across Mission Road, and over to Black Mountain. Adam rode up behind his father and just stood there, not getting off the horse. Macario admired the new bridle and saddle vociferously and Adam beamed proudly.

"Any more cholera deaths?" Francisco asked Joshua. He had stiff white hair spilling around his shoulders, which contrasted sharply with his riveting black eyes and deep brown leathery skin. He was wrinkled and wiry and almost twenty years younger than Macario, though Macario's hair still had flecks of black in it and he looked hardly a day older than Francisco.

"No one dead in the last week," Joshua answered. "The word got out to everybody to boil their water, and the Indian Health Service has been treating all our wells off the Santa Cruz. It looks like we've got it under control."

"How long till they finish the sewer plant?" Francisco asked.

Joshua shrugged. "Four months if it comes in on schedule. But there may be a delay."

"Yah, I read about it," Macario said. "Papers say this Avra Valley Concrete guy is pulling a fast one on the Office of Land Management. Talk is he's supplying duck shit with gray dye in it and calling it concrete." He laughed and Francisco joined in.

Joshua grimaced. Sharp ribbing was common among the Papagos, and he knew that there was nothing malicious in the laughter of these men. They had all been through a brutal summer together, and they trusted each other and treated each other like family.

"Well, we'll be finding out pretty soon," Joshua said. "The judge ordered it tested."

"Yah, I saw that in the paper, too," Macario said. "He ordered samples brought up from Mexico." He rolled his eyes, and Francisco burst out laughing.

"You kidding?" Francisco said.

Macario shook his head widely from side to side.

Francisco slapped his thigh and chortled. "The judge gonna send the 7th Army to guard the guys who's gonna get the samples?"

"Shit! The 7th Army couldn't even stop Pancho Villa from raiding a few haciendas," Macario said. "It took General Pershing and the *whole* goddamn Army to stop him. It's going to take General MacArthur's Rainbow Division to get a chunk of concrete out of Nogales!"

The men hooted and slapped their thighs. Joshua smiled, too. Luckily it wasn't his obligation to get the samples for the test. He'd had enough of Nogales.

Chuy walked up and sat down next to Magdalena. "What's so funny?" he whispered to her.

"The concrete testing down in Nogales," she whispered.

He nodded. "The judge thinks he snaps his fingers and says, 'Make it happen,' and suddenly it happens. He doesn't know Mexico."

Magdalena chuckled.

"But I bet we could do it," Chuy said.

She looked at him quizzically. "Do what?"

"You and I could go dressed like *peones* and nobody would even notice us."

"I'm not risking my life for a bucket of cement."

"Where's your sense of adventure?" he chided her good-naturedly.

"Well under control. I get my adventure in safer ways."

"We can do that, too." He winked and grinned.

She felt herself blushing and looked away. "Only my husband will do that."

He shrugged. "Okay, we'll get married. The Indian way. I'll put my saddle by the entrance to your *olas kih*." He had a teasing smile on his face.

She looked at him and smiled. "And twenty minutes later when you're happy and content you'll take your saddle and ride off into the sunset."

"That's the Indian way."

"I'm an 'acculturation girl,' remember. I like it the white man's way. Whoever I let into my bed puts a ring on my finger in front of a priest and stays with me forever."

"You mean even when you're old and gray and your chins are hanging down to your belly button?"

"You think you're going to stay twenty-six and black-haired and beautiful like Mr. America?"

He laughed.

"You're going to lose your teeth and get a big stomach and your hair will look like Chief Francisco's," she said, looking soberly at him, "but I will still love you."

His flippant grin faded, and he looked at her seriously. He reached out and took her hand, and she slid close to him.

Joshua watched them whispering together and was happy for both of them. The look on Magdalena's face reminded him of the Black Madonna he had seen at a Brazilian art exhibit in New York. It was a carved ebony statue with the most beautifully serene face he had ever seen. Magdalena could have been the model.

Ernestina crooked her finger at her granddaughter, and Magdalena walked over to the roast kid with her. She held a large ceramic platter while Ernestina sliced off hunks of meat and piled the platter high. Then Magdalena walked around the campfire and everyone took some of the meat in their hands. Ernestina walked behind her with pitchers of saguaro wine. A little girl picked out

sweet corn from a steaming kettle set into the barbecue coals and passed the corn out to everyone
who wanted it.

Adam walked Golden Boy over to a patch of grass-
like plants with tiny magenta flowers and dropped
the reins. He got off the horse, and it began grazing contentedly.

Macario Antone called out, "No, no! Don't let
him graze there. That's locoweed. It'll give him stag-
gers and maybe kill him."

Adam picked up the reins and walked the horse
over to a patch of bear grass. He dropped the reins
again. Golden Boy nickered and shook his head and
began nibbling on the bear grass. Adam sat down
beside Joshua and took a hunk of goat meat off the
platter when Magdalena passed by.

"Tastes good, huh?" his father said.

Adam carefully bit off a little piece and chewed
slowly. His face brightened. "I thought it was going
to taste like an old shoe. But this is okay."

Joshua laughed. "It's better than okay. It's
delicious."

Adam curled up the corners of his nose and ate
another little bite. "I like chicken better." He took
a corn cob from the young Indian girl and put the
rest of the goat meat on the ground. One of the half
dozen dogs trotting around immediately ran over,
snapped up the piece of meat, and trotted off.

"There are starving children all over the world
who would have loved to have eaten that," Joshua
said.

"Sorry, Dad. I wish I could have given it to one
of them."

Joshua looked at his son and laughed.

"Can I go ride Golden Boy now, Dad?"

"Okay, but be back home by dark. It's getting dark a lot earlier now."

"Thanks, Dad." Adam walked over to his horse. He led him to a boulder and stood him beside it. He climbed the boulder and jumped onto the horse's back. He rode slowly toward the Santa Cruz River.

"Stay away from Mrs. Antone's cows," Joshua called after him.

▼▲

Hal Dubin called Joshua at the BIA on Friday morning to invite him to dinner Saturday night. Joshua realized that he was a new piece of meat being inspected by the daughter—what was her name? Barbara? Whatever. But more important than that was the office/home that Dubin had hooked him with. A real salesman, Dubin, and a first-rate "hook and reel." Hook the sucker with some cheap piece of merchandise, reel him in until he ends up buying something four times more expensive that he doesn't want or need. But Joshua did want to explore the office suggestion. After all, this little paradise on Indian Agency Road would come to an end sometime. The sooner the better!

So Joshua was hooked, and he took down the directions to get to Dubin's house. He found it easily. It was a sprawling red brick ranch-style house in the foothills of the Catalina Mountains, a couple of miles north on Campbell Avenue, overlooking all of Tucson. The house was beautiful, huge, furnished lavishly in pieces that could not be found at Hal Dubin City.

Hal was drinking straight whiskey like a stable hand. His words were already beginning to slur before dinner. His wife Rebecca was tall and shapely and wore bleached blond hair beautifully coiffed in a permanent. She had the face of a woman who had survived long years with a hard man.

Barbara was a wonderful surprise. She was tall and slender, had light brown hair in a ponytail, and very large breasts. She wore a closely tailored taupe silk blouse, and her breasts pushed out the front of it. She sat across the table from Joshua at dinner and glanced demurely at him from time to time. She was spectacularly pretty, with a strong face, dimpled chin, lambent brown eyes. She untied the ribbon holding her hair and combed it with her fingers. It fell thick and shiny to her shoulders. Lifting her arms up like that pushed her breasts even harder into the tight blouse.

Hal was a little too drunk to talk business, so the dinner conversation lapsed into short flurries about the weather, horses, Crown Heights, Tucson. After dinner, Barbara suggested that Joshua and she sit out in the backyard by the swimming pool. It was a breezeless, cool evening. They sat under the huge, spreading limbs of a mesquite tree. The moon was full and bright, and Joshua's eyes adjusted quickly to the dark.

"Did Daddy tell you all that stuff about me being wild and shiftless?"

Joshua laughed. "Wild, yes, I think he said something like that. But shiftless? No."

"He tells everybody that," she said, her voice sour.

"Where he comes from, girls are supposed to be married at eighteen and having their first son at nineteen."

"I know. I come from the same place."

"Is that what you think, too?"

"No. I think that a girl is supposed to live her life in whatever way she wishes, and an overbearing father pushing her to get married shouldn't make her feel guilty if she wants something else."

She looked at him, and a smile grew on her face. "That's a nice thing to say."

"I believe it."

"I believe you do," she said softly.

Patio lights on six foot tall poles around the yard suddenly went on. Hal Dubin walked onto the patio through the sliding glass doors. "Nice night, huh?" he said, his voice slurry. He took a long swallow from the drink in his hand.

Barbara looked regretfully at Joshua and shrugged. "Sorry about Daddy," she whispered. "I hope we can do this again, just the two of us."

Joshua nodded. "I'd like that," he said, rising as Hal walked unsteadily toward them. "I'd like that a lot."

CHAPTER
SIXTEEN

"You wanna go to Bible School with me?" Jimmy Hendly asked. It was almost ten o'clock on Sunday morning.

"Naw," Adam said. "My dad got real mad at me the last time I went with you."

"What for?"

Adam shrugged. "He says I have to go to Temple Emanu-El instead, 'cause we're Jewish."

"Well, that don't make no difference." Jimmy sounded indignant. "Pastor Freemantle says that bringin' along Jews is good 'cause we can try 'n show 'em the light."

"The light?"

"That's what the pastor calls it."

"What's that?"

"Heck, I dunno." Jimmy shrugged. "I ain't got no idea."

"Well, I can't go anyway. I'll see you after."

"Where ya gonna be?"

"With Golden Boy. Probably down by the reservoir."

"Hey, could Geronimo have some a yer hay? We run out, and Dad said we can't get none till tomorrow when the feed store opens."

"Sure. I'll take Golden Boy out. Bring Geronimo to the shed."

"Will yer dad get mad?"

"He isn't even here. He went down to Tumacacori this morning with Chuy Leyva for some reason or other. I think someone died there yesterday."

"Okay, I'll bring Geronimo." Jimmy jogged toward his house.

Adam went into the shed and saddled Golden Boy. The horse was asleep on his feet and awoke abruptly, snorted, and swished his tail as Adam worked the steel bit into his mouth. Adam led him out of the shed and tied him to a steel ring on a post beside it. The manger was empty. Adam took a pitchfork out of the shed and forked some hay into it from the small pile next to the shed. A few minutes later, Jimmy led Geronimo into the shed and tethered him to the manger. The horse began eating noisily.

"Thanks a lot," Jimmy said. "I guess he's real hungry. I'll see ya at the reservoir after Bible School." He made a face and walked away.

Adam felt as free as a bird. He was supposed to go to Sunday School at Temple Emanu-El this morning, but Chuy had come over to the house early to tell Joshua that there were two more Papagos dead in a shack near Tumacacori Mission. The Indian Health Service doctor was meeting them there at nine o'clock to see if the cholera epidemic had broken out again. So there was no one to drive Adam all the way to Temple Emanu-El in downtown Tucson. Adam was elated, freed from his usual Sunday-morning drudgery. He climbed on Golden Boy's back with the help of the wooden step cut into the hitching post. He rode languorously to the reservoir to see if there were any worthwhile bullfrogs hanging around.

A little after noon, Jimmy came home from Sunday School. He made himself a bologna sandwich and went to Adam's horse stall. Geronimo was very sluggish, and Jimmy had to hit him a couple of times on the rump with the hackamore rein to get his attention. He jumped on the horse's back, and they rode toward the reservoir. Jimmy was angry at his horse for being so lethargic. He kicked him in the sides with the heels of his boots, but Geronimo didn't even seem to notice. Suddenly the horse began acting crazy. Jimmy could see Adam sitting on the bank of the reservoir, and he called out for help. Adam ran toward the leaping horse and tried to catch hold of the bridle. Geronimo lurched sidewise, whirled like a rodeo bronc, and knocked Adam to the ground. Then the horse bucked straight up and Jimmy sailed off him onto the ground. Geronimo staggered a few yards away and fell to his knees, then rolled over on his side, and foam began coming out of his mouth.

Adam got up from the ground rubbing his shoulder. He ran toward Jimmy yelling, "You okay, you okay?" There was no answer. Jimmy's head was bent at a weird angle and his tongue was bulging out of his mouth. His eyes were open, but they were eerily flat and sightless. Adam was afraid to touch him. He ran back up the bank of the reservoir and jumped on Golden Boy's back, struggling upright in the saddle. He whipped the horse into a fast canter and reached his house just as his father and Chuy pulled up in

front of it in Chuy's pickup truck with PAPAGO PO-
LICE crudely painted on the doors.

"Dad, Dad!" called Adam, not getting down from
the horse. "Come on! Jimmy got bucked off and
he's hurt bad." Adam spun Golden Boy around and
galloped back toward the reservoir.

Joshua and Chuy jumped back into the pickup
truck. As they neared the reservoir, they saw the
horse lying on its side in the rocky field. A few yards
past him was the boy. The pickup skidded to a stop
on the dirt road. Joshua jumped out and ran up to
Jimmy. He could see immediately that the boy was
dead. His neck was broken, his head twisted at a
wrong angle. Joshua carefully touched Jimmy's ca-
rotid artery, feeling for a pulse. There was none. He
bent his ear to Jimmy's mouth and nose. There was
no breathing.

Adam came up behind his father. "Is he going to
be all right, Dad?"

Joshua stood up and walked to his son. "Stay on
Golden Boy, Adam. Jimmy's dead. You've got to go
get Mr. or Mrs. Hendly. They must be home from
church by now."

Adam began to cry.

Joshua put his hand on his son's knee. "Please,
Adam, go over to the Hendlys'," he said softly. "And
I don't want you coming back here. Put your horse
away and tell Hanna and Magdalena what
happened."

Adam nodded and sniffled miserably. He gasped
to control his breathing. Then he kicked Golden
Boy in the sides and strapped his neck with the
reins, and the horse began a slow gallop back up
the road by the irrigation ditch.

"He's been poisoned," Chuy said. He knelt beside Geronimo's foaming mouth. The horse groaned.

Chuy took his revolver out of his holster, held it to the middle of the horse's forehead, and pulled the trigger. The sharp crack of the .357 echoed off the bank of the reservoir. Joshua got up and stood by Chuy.

"Why do you say poisoned?"

"That foam. I've seen horses die like that. One from eating green mesquite beans. A couple from locoweed."

"But that just means they might have eaten it on their own. Nobody had to give it to them?" Joshua asked.

"Yes, sure," Chuy said, looking oddly at Joshua. "You think this might be intentional?"

Joshua looked grim. "Anything can happen around this place."

"Well, we're going to find out. I'll take his stomach and liver over to Dr. Niditch at the Livestock Board. He'll test them."

"On Sunday?"

"I know where he lives," Chuy said. He walked to the pickup and opened the metal tool case bolted into the front of the bed. He rummaged around and took out a bucket and a coil of hemp rope. He came back to the horse. He took a long bowie knife out of the sheath on his gun belt, stood over the horse at its back, and slashed a two-foot incision in the horse's abdomen. Intestines and other organs spilled out onto the ground. The stink was nauseating. Chuy quickly tied both ends of the stomach and cut it free. He dropped it in the bucket. He groped inside the entrails for the liver, found it, cut off a large lobe, and put it in the bucket. His arms were covered with blood. He put the bucket in the bed of the pickup, walked up the reservoir bank, and washed his arms in the water.

"You go on," Joshua said. "I'll wait here with Jimmy."

Chuy drove away. Joshua sat down in front of Jimmy, and the shock of it suddenly gripped him. He wept for the little boy, for his parents, and finally in shamed gratitude that it was not his own son lying broken in the dirt.

▼▲▼

The ambulance took Jimmy to Tucson Mortuary downtown; Joshua went in it with Edgar.

Edgar was silent and practically stupefied at first. But when the mortician wheeled Jimmy into a cold-storage locker and slammed the door shut, the full finality of it hit Edgar and he began to tremble. Then tears came, and he sat on a bench in the mortuary chapel for two hours and wept on and off. Joshua sat next to him, his arm around Edgar's shoulders, and stared at the pulpit and the wilting flowers around it and the coffin stand in front of it, left over from the last funeral. How did any person find God at the death of an eleven-year-old? How could any person find solace in such a place as this?

Joshua tried to keep his dormant memories from rising angrily like demonic incubuses in his mind's eye, but he couldn't suppress them. He saw the concentration camp that his company had found, just outside the little Czechoslovakian town called Medzibiez. Besides the dozens of hollow-eyed, emaciated survivors, many of whom died in the days following their liberation, there were mounds of decomposing, reeking corpses behind the four wooden barracks. Joshua was Major Rabb then, commanding a rear-guard company in Patton's push across Germany and Czechoslovakia to Vienna. And his company had been sent to occupy the "prison camp" in the forest. But it was not a prison like any Joshua or his men had ever seen. It was a place where human beings, who had committed no crimes except for being alive at the wrong time and in the wrong place, were worked to death or sent to their deaths in gas chambers.

Joshua had walked into the crematorium, not knowing what it was, and the dirt floor in front of the row of ten huge ovens was covered with ashes. The first several ovens were empty. But there was a body in the fourth. It was a little boy, nine or ten. He was well fed and pink-skinned and beautiful, with a mop of curly brown hair. He must have been one of the sex toys from the barracks with the FELD-HÜREN sign over the door. His eyes had been eaten out, probably by the half dozen rats that were now feasting on the remains of his right leg. Joshua trained his .45 pistol on the pack and fired, and the rats scurried into the darkness at the far end of the oven. The bullet rebounded around the steel chamber walls and ricocheted over his shoulder into the wall behind him. But he didn't even notice. He just stared at the eyeless face of the boy. The mouth was open and pursed like the rictus of a baby sparrow in his nest. Joshua couldn't stop weeping.

He wept now and was ashamed for not being stronger, for not being able to give strength to Edgar in this time of his overwhelming grief. Chuy Leyva came into the chapel and sat in the rear pew, several rows behind Edgar and Joshua, not wanting to intrude on them. It was four o'clock when Edgar stood up, shakily at first, and Joshua stood up beside him. They had stopped crying an hour ago, and now their faces were gray and drawn. They walked outside to the pickup truck, and Chuy drove to Edgar's house.

"I'll come with you," Joshua said.

"No," Edgar said. "Frances 'n me need to handle this thing ourselves." His voice was hoarse and weak. "But I'd appreciate if you'd drive us over to the cemetery tomorrow. I won't feel like drivin."

Joshua nodded. "I'll be here at nine o'clock in the morning."

Edgar walked stiffly into his house.

Chuy drove to Joshua's house and parked. "It's like I thought. Locoweed."

Joshua turned to the Papago policeman and forced himself to concentrate. "How'd he get hold of it?"

Chuy shrugged. "It grows wild all over the fields out here. A little bit of it won't hurt them, but then one day they'll eat too much of it and do just what Geronimo did."

Joshua nodded.

"But there's one more thing," Chuy said slowly. "There's a bunch of it in the hay pile beside your shed."

"What?" Disbelieving.

"Come with me. I'll show you."

They walked to the shed. Chuy leaned over the pile of hay and pulled out a handful of strawlike stems with tiny dried magenta flowers. "Have you noticed this before?" Chuy asked.

Joshua shook his head. "No, I just got those two bales at Southwest Feed last Friday. I brought them out here and cut the wires and didn't see anything like that."

"Well, it could just be here by accident, got baled up with the alfalfa when they harvested the field. But the way it's laid in there, it looks like someone might have intentionally put it there on the pile. See, the alfalfa is pressed flat and crosswise when they bale it. But all this locoweed is just thrown in, like it wasn't baled along with the hay."

Joshua stared at Chuy. "In other words, somebody intended this for Golden Boy, and for Adam to be lying in the mortuary."

"Looks that way to me," Chuy said. "But we can't be certain. It might just have been an accident."

Joshua stared at the locoweed. Billy the Cat dismembered in the living room. The flat tire on the highway, and one of Callan's hands—he was sure of it the more he thought of it—slashing up the car seats and stealing the jack handle, because Chester Milliken had been killed with a jack handle. It was Joshua's last warning. And then this. Locoweed in the hay. Callan's men had built the shed. They knew the layout of the property here.

"I need a big favor from you, Chuy." Joshua looked intently at the Indian. "I need you to take Hanna and Adam and Magdalena over to the BIA office in Sells and look after them for a few days. There are several beds there and a bathroom. It's not safe here for them."

Chuy nodded. "When?"

"After the funeral tomorrow. Let's say three o'clock."

"Okay, Mr. Rabb. How about you? Are you going to be safe here?"

"I'll be all right."

"These are mean people."

"Right now I feel mean, too," Joshua muttered.

▼▲▼

The Monday-morning newspaper carried the obituary of James Herman Hendly, eleven years old, killed in a riding accident. So when the Rabbs and Hendlys got out of Joshua's yellow convertible in Evergreen Cemetery's parking lot, many others were there. A dozen kids from Jimmy's class at Sunnyside School, twice that many adult friends of Edgar's and Frances's, mostly from the Pentecostal Church they attended every Sunday. There were also twenty Indians, a group from Sells representing the Tribal Council, Chief Romero and his wife, former Chief Antone and his wife and granddaughter Magdalena, and several of the boys whom Jimmy and Adam played with at the reservoir.

Among the cars in the parking lot was Diana Thurber's red Cadillac convertible with the white top. She stood by the driver's door, dressed in a simple black suit and plain black short heels, her hair in a bun.

Edgar and Frances walked toward the open grave where Pastor Freemantle stood. He held an open Bible before him and read the Psalms in a strong, sonorous voice. He wore his thick gray-blond hair in a meticulously combed high pompadour. He was about sixty years old, with pouchy pink cheeks and light brown eyes, tall, well fed, and dressed in a very expensive-looking black silk suit. He wore a braided black leather bolo tie with a Mexican silver cinch in the shape of a thunderbird, studded with turquoise stones.

The pastor's voice resonated over the grave: "Let not your heart be troubled. Ye believe in God, believe also in me. In my Father's house are many mansions. If it were not so, I would have told you. I go to prepare a place for you. And if I go and prepare a place for you, I will come again and receive you unto myself, that where I am, there ye may be also. And whither I go ye know, and the way ye also know."

Pastor Freemantle closed the Bible and placed it on the small portable podium beside him. He raised his arms in a hugging gesture and smiled at Edgar and Frances as they neared the grave. "Come stand with me," he said, "and be assured that your son is entering the kingdom of heaven. Come and we will exalt in the wisdom of our Savior who has chosen little Jimmy to be at his side at this time."

Frances and Edgar walked up beside the pastor and stood weeping. Their bodies trembled. Edgar wore a threadbare black wool suit, a little too small to be buttoned over his ample paunch. Frances wore a black pillbox hat and long veil that hid her face. Her plain black shirtdress reached to the tops of her brown laced shoes.

Adam stood off to the side with his classmates and the Indian children. They all wore teary-eyed looks of dread. They were in their school clothes, plaid shirts and Levis and cowboy boots. Hanna stood beside her father feeling very sick. She had worn her plainest dark gray shift. She wished that she could wear a black dress more suitable for this horrible place, but she didn't have one. She had long since outgrown the black dress that Grandma had bought her to go to Mommy's funeral, almost two years ago.

Mark Goldberg walked up beside Hanna. Tears came to her eyes and rolled down her cheeks. He put his arm around her shoulders, and he looked away so that she wouldn't see his tears.

Jimmy lay in a four-foot-long knotty pine box beside the grave. The box was painted white and varnished so that it glistened in the sunlight. Edgar and the pastor and Joshua and Chief Macario and Chief Romero and a man Joshua didn't know picked up the ends of the three ropes under the coffin and lifted it. Joshua used only his right hand, but the coffin was very light, and they lowered it easily into the grave. Frances gasped and shuddered and fell to her knees. Two ladies nearby rushed to her and helped her up.

The pallbearers stood back from the grave. Edgar wept softly, and Joshua stood next to him with his arm around his slumped, shivering shoulders. Tears streamed down Joshua's cheeks.

Pastor Freemantle reached his arms upward in a hieratic gesture. His face was soft and peaceful, and he smiled toward the heavens. 'Praise the Lord! Praise the Lord! We have perfect faith in the wisdom and justice of our Lord Jesus. Receive the soul of this innocent lamb, and may he ever stand by Thy side in the eternal peace and joy of life everlasting. Amen and Amen."

The mourners began slowly walking away from the grave. Edgar bent over and threw a handful of dirt on the coffin, as did Joshua and Hanna and Mark and several others. Diana walked up to the grave and threw a handful of dirt into it. She straightened up and caught Joshua's tear-filled eyes. Edgar went over to Frances, put his arm around her, and led her slowly away from the grave.

Diana walked up to Joshua. "I'm terribly sorry," she whispered.

Joshua swallowed and wiped his eyes with the sleeve of his black wool suit. They were alone by the graveside now, staring at each other. "You are so beautiful," Joshua said, his voice gravelly. "You take my breath away. But you are the antithesis of the pastor's words of comfort." He stared balefully at her. "Callan did this. He intended it to be Adam in that grave."

She recoiled from him. "How can you say such terrible, cruel things to me? The only sin I've committed is loving you."

"Your love is as dangerous as a diamondback rattler."

Her mouth opened wide and she looked hard at him as though to fathom how he could be so stupid and vicious. "You can't believe that. You can't believe that Uncle George could be so evil. You don't even know him, and yet you judge him and condemn him. You think that you're a fair and just man, but you're a phony. Uncle George hasn't done anything to you to earn that kind of hatred."

"Cut the Uncle George bullshit!" Joshua muttered savagely. "Everybody around here knows you're a prostitute from Kansas City who started screwing the old man after his wife died. And now you're both trying to screw me!"

Her mouth gaped open. Then she gritted her teeth and swung her right hand at his face to slap him. He caught her hand in his and pushed her away. She stumbled backward and almost fell. He strode away from the grave to his car. She stared after him, angry, humiliated, and hot blood pinkened her cheeks.

▼▲▼

The Hendlys returned to their house and the Rabbs to theirs. Adam lay on the floor next to the radio. He was miserable and listless, and from time to time he began sobbing. Then the tears would stop as abruptly as they had come.

Hanna had left the cemetery with Mark. Joshua didn't worry anymore about her being with him. He couldn't go along on every date as the chaperone. And he trusted her. She was a good girl. And she was a nice girl, too, with the kind of mature tenderness that any man would find alluring.

Magdalena sat in the overstuffed armchair darning a sock. She was lost in her own thoughts.

Adam got up off the floor a little after one o'clock. "I'm going over to the reservoir, okay, Dad?"

Joshua nodded. "Don't take Golden Boy. We've got to have him checked by a vet."

"I know, Dad. I'll be back in a couple of hours."

Joshua hadn't changed his clothes after the funeral. He sat torpidly on the sofa, brooding and silent. He had hardly slept the night before, and he was exhausted.

"Why don't you go to sleep for a while?" Magdalena said.

Joshua looked at her as though he noticed for the first time that she was in the living room with him. "I'm too numb to move," he mumbled.

"Come, I'll help you," she said.

She came over to him, took his right hand, and led him into his bedroom. He sat on the edge of his bed. She helped him off with his suit jacket and tie and white shirt. Then she unstrapped his aluminum arm and laid it beside the bed. She knelt before him and unlaced his shoes, pulling them off and then his socks. He unbuckled his belt and she tugged his pants off.

"I feel like *I'm* the one who died," he whispered. Tears came to Magdalena's eyes. She bent forward and kissed Joshua on the forehead. He lay back and closed his eyes. Magdalena left the room quietly and closed the door soundlessly.

When he awoke, it was almost three o'clock. A little note on the bedstand in Magdalena's careful handwriting said, "Went with Chuy. Be back by three."

He got out of bed and put on his bathrobe. No one was home. He took a hot shower and let the water massage his shoulders for ten minutes. He felt as though life would go on and he would endure. He dressed in Levis and a polo shirt, turned on the radio, and sat back on the sofa. He sat lethargically, staring at the carved wooden harp and brown fabric that covered the front of the big radio. Some big band from the Algonquin Hotel in New York City was playing swing music, and Joshua listened vacantly.

There was a loud knock on the front door.

"Come in," Joshua called out, sitting upright on the sofa.

Edgar Hendly walked in. He was dressed in the same clothes from the funeral, but he had removed the ill-fitting jacket. His face was taut, angry looking, and his eyes were hostile and burning. He waved a sheet of paper in front of Joshua.

"You didn't tell me," he gasped. He swallowed and tried to slow his breathing. "You didn't tell me they murdered my boy." His eyes glowed savagely.

"Take it easy, Edgar." Joshua got up from the sofa and put his arm around him.

Edgar shook his arm off. "How could you do that, you sombitch?" His voice was plaintive, and he began weeping.

"What happened, Edgar?"

Edgar handed him the sheet of paper. It was written in a jerky, sloppy hand: "Mr. Hendly, it was not your child who was to be punished for the wrongdoing of Joshua Rabb. It was his son. You have paid a terrible price for Rabb's actions." It was unsigned.

Joshua looked at Edgar. "Where'd you get this?"

"Someone slipped it under the front door."

"I'm terribly sorry," Joshua said. "I wish they'd killed me instead."

Edgar studied Joshua's eyes. Then he slumped down on the sofa and his body shook with sobs. The tears receded slowly.

"I was going to tell you after the first shock wore off," Joshua said, sitting beside Edgar. "We found locoweed in the hay. We weren't sure it was intentional." He put the letter between them on the sofa. "This makes it sure. I'm terribly sorry." His voice broke off.

Edgar hunched over silently for minutes, and his crying stopped. He sat back in the sofa and his body relaxed.

"I know you didn't mean nothin bad by what you been doin with this concrete thing. I been yer friend for six months now. I know what yer made of." He looked with understanding at Joshua. "But I told ya before, ya cain't try to be more *just* than *God*. Always the moralist, tryin to do what you think God would do."

Joshua swallowed down a feeling of nausea. He felt dirty.

"I told ya and told ya, sometimes with some a these assholes ya gotta just look the other way. Ya gotta let em steal a few bucks. Otherwise they turn into rabid coyotes and rip the throats outta the people ya love. Eventually they'll get to you, after they've destroyed everything you hold dear, and they'll tear yer heart out for a nickel." He breathed deeply and rubbed his eyes. "Next they'll kill Adam and rape yer girl and leave her to bleed to death in the desert and be eaten by vultures." He paused and looked earnestly at Joshua. "You ready for that? Are yer scruples that mighty?"

Joshua gritted his teeth and looked away from Edgar's accusing eyes. He had no answers, only a pervasive and gnawing sense of guilt.

Edgar got up heavily and left the house.

Suddenly Joshua was frightened. He remembered that Adam had left hours ago for the reservoir. He was in danger. Joshua ran out of the house, jumped into his car, and gunned it toward the reservoir. A minute later he saw a dozen boys on the bank, mostly Indian boys, and Adam. Adam looked up and

waved at him. Joshua sat for a few moments, waiting
for his heart to stop beating so fast. He caught his
son's eye again, and Adam came to the driver's side
of the car.

"Time to go, Adam."

Adam nodded and got into the car. "Do we have
to go to Sells?" His voice was whiny. He looked
unhappily at his father.

"Yes. I'm sorry. Just for a week or so, until I get
to the bottom of this. I don't want you getting hurt."

As they neared their house, Mark Goldberg pulled
his car up in front of it. Hanna got out and waved
at Mark, and he backed his car up and drove away.
She walked onto the porch and waited for her father
and Adam. They went into the house.

"Pack enough clothes for a week," Joshua said.

Hanna and Adam went silently to their rooms.
Joshua flopped down on the couch. Magdalena
came through the front door. She went up to Joshua
and looked earnestly at him.

"You feeling better?" she asked softly, disarmingly.

He looked into her eyes, and there was deep caring in them, ingenuous and unsullied. He smiled at
her and nodded. "I feel much better."

"Good," she said. "I brought along a few clothes
and things in the truck. Are Hanna and Adam
ready?"

"They're packing."

"I'd better help." She walked into Adam's room.

Joshua handed the letter to Chuy. He read it intently and grimaced. "Well, now we know for sure."

Joshua nodded.

"Don't worry about your family, Mr. Rabb. I'll
take care of them."

"I know," Joshua said. "Please call me Joshua."

"Yes, sir."

Magdalena came into the living room and set one cardboard valise next to the door. Hanna carried another to the door. Chuy picked up both suitcases and put them in the bed of the truck. Magdalena waited in the cab. Joshua kissed Hanna and Adam. He felt tears coming again and rubbed his eyes hard.

"I'll call as soon as everything's all right," he said.

They nodded and walked to the pickup. He closed the door, not wanting to see them drive off. He felt hollow inside, deserted and despairing. He sat down on the couch, but he couldn't force himself to listen to the music playing softly from the radio.

Water stains on the wall caught his eye. Why had such unsightly stains eluded him before? They were right up there at the joint with the ceiling. There must be a leak in the roof. Have to get that fixed. But right now? Well, isn't there some paint in the shed? White paint left over when Callan's men built it? They had a gallon of white paint and two brushes. They're probably in the shed.

He walked out the kitchen door and went to the shed. Golden Boy was sleeping. On the dirt floor in the corner was the paint. The brushes were on top of the can. One of them was dried stiff as a stone. The other had been cleaned and the bristles were reasonably pliable. He picked up the can of paint and brought it into the house. One of the dinette chairs felt sturdier than the others, and he brought it into the living room and placed it directly under the stained part of the wall and ceiling. Holding the can while painting presented a hindrance, but

Joshua strapped on his mechanical arm and latched the stainless-steel prongs onto the wire handle of the paint can. No problem. He let go of the handle and pried the lid open with one of the prongs. The lid was glued down by old paint, but it opened easily from the force of his steel hand. Well, look at that, he mused pleasantly. Another valuable use for Captain Hook. "I'm going to call you Captain Hook," he said to his hand. Penny used to call me that, he thought, but that was long ago, a lifetime ago. "Do your thing," he said earnestly to his hand. He bent it up to his mouth and kissed the prongs as their christening. "I now christen you Captain Hook."

He clenched the paint bucket handle carefully and climbed on the chair. Only a few drops fell on the unvarnished terra-cotta-tiled floor. He dipped the paintbrush into the paint and wiped off the excess carefully against the rim of the can. He felt like Michelangelo at the Sistine Chapel, standing awkwardly on scaffolding, painting God creating the world. Joshua swept the brush in a long arc across the lower edge of the rusty stains. "That's God's hand reaching out to Adam," he murmured, holding his breath a little to control his brush just so. "That's it, that's it," he said softly. "Now we'll do God's face." He dipped the brush again and stroked it gently against the rim and began daubing at the long stain on the right.

There was a knock on the door, not a vigorous rapping, but kind of a timorous tapping. "Come a rapping come a tapping on my chamber door. Quoth the raven," he whispered to himself, climbing carefully down from the chair. He put the can on the floor and the brush on top of it and opened the door.

Edgar Hendly stood there, looking oddly at Joshua. Sheriff Pat Dunphy stood behind him, appearing even more pink-faced than Joshua had seen him before. He must be hitting the sauce pretty good, Joshua thought. His nose was developing the alcoholic fat bumpiness that W. C. Fields wore as a trademark.

"You paintin?" Edgar asked, looking at Joshua like a psychiatrist looks at his patient who just came in for his session and sat down on the couch wearing nothing but a loincloth and lipstick war paint stripes on his cheeks and forehead.

Joshua swallowed, realizing that he looked a little foolish. "Stains," he said, pointing up to the ceiling.

Edgar nodded. "Pat and me need the note."

"Sure, sure. Come in. It's around here somewhere."

The men came into the living room and stared at the open paint can on the floor and the widening ring of white paint on the tiles around the dripping can.

"Oughta clean that stain up fast, Mr. Rabb," Dunphy said. "Gonna fuck up yer floor permanent."

"Yeah, better find some thinner," Joshua said. He walked out of the kitchen door, leaving Edgar and the sheriff looking at each other with raised eyebrows. He came back empty handed a moment later.

"Can't find any," Joshua said. "Guess I'll go over to Pedrano's Hardware. They must sell it, huh?" He looked inquiringly at the sheriff.

"Yeah, I reckon," Dunphy drawled.

Edgar picked the letter up from the couch and handed it to the sheriff. Dunphy pursed his lips and studied it. He shook his head and breathed deeply. "Like to find these cocksuckers. Yessir, sure would."

"Just look over at the Lazy G Ranch," Joshua said. "One of the hands did it, and George Callan ordered it. I can point out the hand to you."

Dunphy studied him. "You got some proof or just a wild hair up yer ass?"

Joshua's face lost its soft carelessness. He stared hard at the shitkicker cowtown sheriff whose word in this little place was law and whose act was that of God's anointed.

"Has Edgar told you what's been going on with Callan's contract?" Joshua asked.

"Yeah, I done heard about it. Normal shit with a gover'ment contract, ain't it?"

"Maybe. But there've been two murders now. Chester Milliken and Jimmy. That makes it not so normal."

Dunphy shrugged. "I ain't sayin there ain't *somebody* been pullin some bad shit here. What I'm sayin is how I prove it's Callan."

"Go out there and kick him in the balls a couple of times. He'll tell you," Joshua said. "Or are you only a tough guy with defenseless women?"

The blood drained from Dunphy's cheeks, and his pale blue eyes appeared to glow red. "You got a serious fuckin mouth on you, boy. I done tol' ya before to keep yer fuckin mouth shut around me. Ya better take my advice." He clenched both hands into white-knuckled fists.

"Come on, knock off this shit," Edgar growled. "My boy's rottin in a stinkin grave and you two guys 're at each other like alley cats in heat." He glared at Pat Dunphy. "Joshua's right, it's Callan behind all this shit. He killed my boy. Now what're ya gonna do about it?" Edgar's face was fierce.

The challenge silenced Dunphy and straightened his shoulders like a private dressed down by a colonel. His fists uncoiled, and the belligerence left his face. It was one thing to rip the New York Jewboy a new asshole. That was just recreation. But you couldn't do that shit to Edgar. Edgar was Tucson-born and bred, and he worked for Senator Lukis for twenty years before the senator pulled the right strings to get him appointed superintendent of the BIA. Rabb was just a pissant, but Edgar had heavy connects.

"Come on, gott damn it, I'm askin ya. What're ya gonna do?" Edgar said truculently.

"Aw right, take it easy, Edgar," Dunphy said. He held up both hands in a halt gesture. "I'll go out and talk to Callan."

Edgar shot him a look of disgust. "Oh yeah? And what'll ya say to him? 'Hey, Georgie, you kill old Edgar's boy? Fess up now.' "

Dunphy gritted his teeth. "What the hell ya expect me t'do, Edgar? Just sorta mosey on up to him over at the M.O. Club and cuff him and throw him in jail? What the hell am I gonna charge him with, and how am I gonna prove it?" He was back on firm ground again, and his shoulders relaxed.

Edgar scowled and shook his head in frustration. He looked at Joshua for help. Joshua shrugged and looked away morosely.

"Fuckin guy can get away with murder?" Edgar asked rhetorically.

"Listen, Edgar," Dunphy cajoled, "you really ain't got no proof a that. All ya got is a note. Now the fact is that the whole thing coulda been a accident, no more'n that. Just a horse gettin hold a some bad feed. And then somebody wantin to fuck with yer mind writes ya this note. The note just don't prove nothin, even if we had a chance in the world a findin out who wrote it."

"Come on," Edgar said to the sheriff, his voice soiled with disgust. "Let's go over to the FBI. Maybe Collins got a idea or two."

"It ain't his jurisdiction," Dunphy said. "It didn't happen on Federal land."

"Piss on you guys and alla yer jurisdiction bull-shit. My boy's been murdered, and all I wanna see is Callan swingin from a crossbeam with a noose around his neck."

Edgar wheeled abruptly about and walked toward his car. Pat Dunphy cast a sour look at Joshua and followed Edgar.

Joshua closed the door and surveyed the paint can and brush. "Crazy son of a bitch," he muttered. "Get a grip on it, Joshua boy."

He put the lid on the can and punched it down with the heel of his hand. He took the can and brush back to the shed. He drove distractedly to the hardware store and bought a pint of paint thinner. He saturated a rag with it and rubbed vigorously on the terra-cotta tiles, turning the ring of white paint drips into an amorphous gray smudge. He sat back against the wall and stared sullenly at it.

Somehow the bells from Mission San Xavier impinged on his consciousness. They signaled the end of mass every day like a bugler signaled retreat in an Army camp. The sound wafted to him on the mild winter breeze of Tucson. It beckoned him. He went into his bedroom and took the leather-covered *chumash* out of the bedstand drawer. His father had given it to him when he went into the Army in 1942. His father had held up his hand and spread the forefinger and middle finger from the other two fingers and incanted the priestly blessing: *"Y'vere-checha adoshem v'yishm'recha ..."*

"I hope he does bless me and keep me and watch over me, Dad," Joshua had said, touched by his father's sentimentality, but hardly ready to throw his fate into the hands of a God who had never seemed available to answer prayers in the past. Like the week he prayed steadily that Annette Morovich would go to the prom with him. Or the time he prayed that the pimples would go away on his chin before his date with Maria Pulverini. They weren't such tough requests that God should have had trouble with them. But Annette had gone to the prom with Danny Shimkus and the pimples had seemed to be permanent. He had hardly ever opened Dad's Bible, but he always carried it with him. If nothing else, it was a link with home, a reminder that there was a reason for being in terrible places, Normandy, the Ardennes Forest, Medzibiez. And when he had been wounded near the tiny town in Luxembourg with the prescient name of Diekirch, they had shipped him to a military hospital in Antwerp, and the only thing to read other than a book of O. Henry stories was the Bible. So he had practically memorized it. And as a book of stories—if nothing else— it made fascinating reading.

He sat on the edge of the bed and stared at the

cover of the Bible. "Joshua ben-Aryeh-Lev" was imprinted in gold on the bottom right corner. His father's name was Richard, his Hebrew name Aryeh-Lev, "The Lion Hearted." A fitting name for him.

Joshua felt the sense of connection rise in him, as it often did when he held this book. He would begin to feel the presence of family. Mom lighting candles on Friday night, Rachel helping her set the table, the smell of *cholent* from the kitchen, garlicky and familiar, his father sitting in the big chair under the lamp reading a page or two of Talmud, Hanna and Adam sitting dutifully on the floor in front of him, listening to him spin wisdom from the rabbis of the Talmud and tales from the Hassidic rabbis of his youth in Russia.

Joshua stared wistfully at the homey images cascading before his mind's eye, playing on the cover of the Bible like a motion picture lights up a screen. The Bible was working its magic on him. He got up and took off his mechanical arm. He was wearing a short-sleeved polo shirt, and Captain Hook was too shocking when seen in all his glory. He left the house and walked across the yard to the irrigation ditch. It was muddy in the bottom, just a trickle of water in it, and he walked down to a narrow sandbar where he could cross over to the Reservation without ruining his shoes. It was sunset, and the top half of the sun was behind the crenellated crest of Black Mountain. Vermillion light diffused over the mountain, streaked with purple wisps of feathery clouds. A pair of gophers stood nearby on the mound of dirt surrounding their hole and sniffed the evening air. A vulture circled in the sky fifty yards away, waiting for some doomed desert creature to surrender its life. A great black beetle clung to a newly born lime green cholla pad a couple of inches long and an inch wide, and the beetle nibbled on the top of it like a kid taking bites out of the edge of a cookie.

Joshua found a tall flat stone and sat down on it. The last peal of the bell from the Mission tower proclaimed the end of the day. The light began fading quickly to dreary gray.

"Can you hear me, God?" Joshua said in a normal conversational voice. "I'm here to talk to you about some problems I've been having." He paused and looked around, gathering his thoughts the way he would when addressing a jury on closing argument. "My dad used to tell me about Rabbi Yitzchak of Berdichev, how he would shake his hand at the heavens and scold you for neglecting us. Well, I'm not going to be quite so petulant, because I don't know you nearly as well as Rabbi Yitzchak claimed to. I just wouldn't feel real comfortable doing that. But I hope you'll forgive me if I tell you that I think you're doing a shitty job down here. I mean, I haven't asked you for very much in my life, you know, a couple of dates and a pimple or two, and I guess you were too busy to focus on little shit like that. After all, you had a big war to worry about. Of course, you didn't show a hell of a lot of compassion for six and a half million Jews who were being shoved into ovens. But the rabbis say that you work in wondrous ways, and nothing proves it better than that. I mean, that much suffering by innocent people, tolerated by a God of love and justice, is wondrous by any definition. And now I have this personal problem which doesn't quite compare to six and a half million, let alone another hundred million killed by bombs and bullets, and I feel kind of funny asking you like this, but then I'm supposed to feel close to you and have faith that 'your goodness and mercy will follow me all the days of my life'—that's what my dad always used to tell me— so let me ask just this one favor: I want you to make sure my kids don't get hurt. They don't deserve anything like that. So keep them safe. And I promise you this: if you fuck with me on this one, if you let somebody hurt Hanna or Adam, I'm going to hunt you down like a rabid dog until you have nowhere to hide and blow your brains out."

He sat tensely, watching the last ember of the sun slide below Black Mountain and draw all of its light down with it.

"Now I know I'm not supposed to talk this way to you, God, because everybody says that you listen and hear and bring down an awful retribution on those who stray from your path of righteousness or doubt your infinite wisdom. I guess Pastor Freemantle believes that, because he was doing all he could to turn Jimmy's murder into some nugget of bliss in God's plan. But I don't see any plan that looks quite that good, and I don't see any retribution for the scum who murdered him. And I don't see any prospect that you're going to handle this any better than you've handled the other shit that's been going on."

Joshua was speaking into coal darkness now.

"So with all due respect to Pastor Freemantle and Rabbi Yitzchak and all the other folks who think you're doing just fine, allow me to share with you my view that you've fucked up real badly the last few years, and I just don't feel comfortable relying on you to set things right. Edgar says to me all the time that I'm trying to be more *just* than *God*. Well, I don't know what that means, because being more just than God isn't a hell of a lot of justice at all. So I guess I'm going to have to look after my family and my friends all by myself, and not worry about what you think or how you would handle it. You had your chance, and from what I see, you didn't do so well. Now it's up to me."

He stood up and focused his eyes on the few dim glows of porch lights across the irrigation ditch. He walked slowly to his house.

The bottle of Mexican gin—"Ginebra Classica," it said on the label—was almost full. Edgar had brought it over once for some reason or other, Joshua couldn't remember, and they'd only had a couple of drinks. The stuff could remove the rust from a trailer hitch. It gave you a heartburn as soon as you poured it into a glass. Joshua poured a tumblerful and drank it down. He coughed and wheezed a moment. Then he poured another tumblerful. He went into the living room and slumped onto the sofa. Tears streamed from his eyes. "I'm sorry, God," he gasped. "I didn't mean to talk dirty to you."

He drained the glass determinedly, and by the time he reached the dregs, the desired effect had been achieved. He was so blind that he could not see. His mind was so numb that he could not think. He stretched out on the sofa and fell into deep sleep.

CHAPTER
SEVENTEEN

Joshua awoke with a thumping headache so severe that he had to lie down again as soon as he tried to get out of bed. The pulsing in his temples was percussive, like timpani playing a crashing solo in an atonal symphony. It was four in the morning and still pitch dark. He slowly swung his legs over the side of the bed and lifted his head guardedly from the pillow. He kneaded his forehead, trying to rub away the percutaneous pain that was incising through his skull into his brain.

He stumbled into the kitchen, put coffee on the stove, and sat down to wait. Some interminable time later, he drank it black and hot, and its hoped-for therapeutic effect began to work. The caffeine began to dilate the constricted blood vessels in his temples, and the throbbing lessened. He stood for long minutes under the shower, turning his head this way and that to let the water beat on his forehead and temples and reproach the pain. It worked, and by the time he had shaved and brushed his teeth and dressed in a white starched shirt, black tie with diagonal black stripes, and pinstriped black double-breasted suit, he felt as though he might survive the day. He studied himself in the bathroom mirror and saw new wrinkles around his puffy eyes. I look like I just came off a two-week bender, he thought. Judge Velasco's liable to throw me in the drunk tank.

The thought of Franklin Carillo's trial today sobered him even more. And then he thought of J. T. Sellner, what kind of story would be in this morning's newspaper, and a small pounding attacked his temples again. He took his briefcase with the Carillo file in it and went out to his car. It was still dark, but the summit of Martinez Hill on the east was developing form in the early light. He drove to downtown Tucson, to the Jury Box Cafe across from the courthouse. He dropped a nickel on the stack of newspapers on the sidewalk outside the front door and pulled one of the papers out.

He sat in a booth, ordered corned-beef hash and poached eggs, and thumbed through the newspaper for the inevitable Carillo story. There it was on page 3. Some things you can count on in life. JUDGE TO DECIDE EVIDENCE was the headline.

By J. T. Sellner. Judge Bernardo Velasco, newly appointed to replace Judge Fran Rooks, who died in October, will make his first critical decision as a judge today. He has been asked by defense attorney Joshua Rabb to suppress the gun found during a Pima County Sheriff's Department search of Carillo's home. If he grants the "Motion to Suppress," the gun cannot be used as evidence in Carillo's trial. Two ballistic experts have tested the gun, according to Chief Deputy County Attorney W. Randolph Stevens, and they will testify that it was the probable weapon used by Carillo to murder Victoria Grant and her four-week-old baby Alicia, as well as to assault nineteen-year-old U of A coed Arlene O'Donnell.

According to Prosecutor Stevens, Motions to Suppress are normally only permissible in Federal Court. This case is different because it involved a state officer's search of a suspect's house on federal land. The officer was not aware that the house was on the San Xavier Papago Reservation. Judge Velasco is therefore being asked to decide "a case of first impression," as Stevens called it, and there was no higher court precedent which required the judge to rule one way or the other. "He's free to follow his conscience," Mr. Stevens said. "Let us all hope that the conscience of the judge is in accord with that of the people of Tucson."

Mr. Rabb came to Tucson from Brooklyn after his wife died in an influenza epidemic.

Joshua grimaced. The damn reporter still can't get Rachel's death right. *I ought to sue her for libel or something, or for just being an asshole.* The rest of the story was a rehash of the BIA lawyer's clash with Mission Sand and Gravel last summer. Some of it was true. He disgustedly threw the newspaper down on the table.

Randy Stevens came into the cafe and walked over to Joshua. "You mind?" he asked.

"No, of course not," Joshua said.

Stevens sat down and ordered bacon and eggs. "You see J. T.'s story?"

Joshua nodded.

"She's a first-class cunt," Stevens said. "She's known the judges around here all of her life and screwed every one of them. Shit! She probably screwed old Fran Rooks after he was dead." He chuckled, sneering. "Now she screws them in the papers every chance she gets."

"And me, too," Joshua said.

"Yip," Stevens said. "Thank God she lays off of

me. I have kind of thin skin. I'd have to charge her with criminal seditious libel."

"Didn't that go out with Peter Zenger about two hundred years ago?"

"Not around here!" Stevens laughed maliciously.

They ate breakfast without much conversation. They were both preoccupied with the coming trial, though neither of them mentioned it. Stevens left for his office at a few minutes before nine. Joshua stayed in the booth, drinking cup after cup of black coffee and reading the newspaper from front to back. At three minutes before ten, he walked to Judge Velasco's courtroom. It was crowded with spectators conversing in hushed respectful voices. Carillo was sitting at the defense table wearing the distinctive plaid cowboy shirt that Joshua had bought for him. Solomon Leyva, Chuy's brother, sat inconspicuously in the rear of the courtroom wearing an identical shirt.

Erma Carillo was in the first row behind the railing. She had for once eschewed the dramatic cane-banging entrance.

At almost the same moment that Joshua sat down next to Carillo, the bailiff came through the rear door and banged his gavel on the judge's bench. Judge Velasco came into the courtroom and sat in his big leather chair. He leaned forward over the bench and peered at the people in front of him.

"Show the presence of both counsel," Velasco said, "as well as the defendant."

The court reporter began writing on the stenographer's pad on his small desk.

"With respect to the defendant's motion to suppress," the judge placed several sheets on the bench in front of him, "I have reached the following decision." He perched his readers on the end of his nose and read. "I hold that all evidence obtained by search and seizure on a federal reservation or enclave, in violation of the Constitution, is inadmissible in a state court."

Stevens gasped audibly. Joshua opened his eyes wide and stared in shock at the judge.

"Since the Fourth Amendment's right of privacy has been declared enforceable against the states through the due process clause of the Fourteenth, it is enforceable against them by the same sanction of exclusion as is used against the federal government. Were it otherwise, then just as without the *Weeks* rule, the assurance against unreasonable federal searches and seizures would be merely 'a form of words,' valueless and undeserving of mention in a perpetual charter of inestimable human liberties.

"In extending the substantive protections of due process to all constitutionally unreasonable searches on federal land, even when the evidence is to be used in a state court, it is logically and constitutionally necessary that the exclusion doctrine—an essential part of the right to privacy—be also insisted upon as an essential ingredient of the right recognized by the *Weeks* case.

"My holding is not only the logical dictate of prior cases, but it also makes good sense. There is no war between the Constitution and common sense. Presently, a federal prosecutor may make no use of evidence illegally seized, but a state's attorney across the street may, although he supposedly is operating under the enforceable prohibitions of the same Amendment. Thus the state, by admitting evidence unlawfully seized, serves to encourage disobedience to the Federal Constitution which it is bound to uphold.

"There are those who say, as did Justice (then Judge) Cardozo, that under our constitutional exclusionary doctrine the criminal is to go free because the constable has blundered. In some cases this will undoubtedly be the result. But there is another consideration—the imperative of judicial integrity. The criminal goes free, if he must, but it is the law that sets him free. Nothing can destroy a government more quickly than its failure to observe its own laws, or worse, its disregard of the charter of its own existence. My decision, founded on reason and truth, gives to the individual no more than that which the Constitution guarantees him, to the police officer no less than that to which honest law enforcement is entitled, and to the courts, that judicial integrity so necessary in the true administration of justice."

The few individuals in the courtroom who had any idea what the judge's words meant gasped in shock. Randy Stevens breathed deeply and shook his head.

"Are you ready to begin, Mr. Stevens?" the judge asked.

Randy stood up and glanced at the judge. "I'm afraid, your honor, that your decision has caught me off guard. I am not prepared to proceed at this time without the gun as evidence." He thought for a moment. "I would ask your honor for an open continuance so that I can appeal your decision to the Supreme Court of Arizona as a certified question."

The judge shook his head. "I don't think it would

be fair to the defendant to keep him in jail indefinitely while you go up on appeal. Unless, of course, you're willing to admit him to bail that he can make."

"He's too dangerous to let him out, your honor."

"Then proceed with your opening statement, Mr. Stevens."

The prosecutor clenched his jaw and repressed his anger. "If the court please, I would ask for a continuance of two weeks so I can prepare for this trial—without the gun as evidence. I've got to rethink my proof."

Velasco looked at Joshua. "Mr. Rabb?"

Joshua was still stunned by the judge's ruling. He felt pleased and magnanimous. "No objection, your honor."

"Okay," Velasco said. "One week from today at ten. Fish or cut bait." He banged his gavel and walked off the bench.

There was an uneasy stirring in the courtroom.

"What happened this time?" Erma Carillo blurted waspishly behind Joshua.

"Take it easy, Mrs. Carillo," Joshua said, turning around. "The judge ruled in Franklin's favor on the gun."

"You mean it?" she asked, her pinched hateful look loosening and becoming a tentative smile.

"Yes," Joshua said.

Chuy Leyva, wearing a shirt exactly like Solomon's and Franklin Carillos's, came into the courtroom. Solomon walked up to him and said something, and both of them left. Joshua put papers slowly into his briefcase, waiting for the crowd of bewildered, frustrated, angry spectators to disperse.

A few among them pedantically informed the others
what the judge's long legalese speech meant, and
the look on many of their faces was hostile. They
filed out of the courtroom. Joshua waited until they
were gone. He could hear some of them milling
about in the corridor, their raised voices vexed
and combative.

Randy Stevens had also lingered in the courtroom. "Come on," he said to Joshua, "we'll go the
back way. I don't want you getting killed out there."

Joshua smiled wryly. "I would have thought after
the judge got done that you'd be happy with a
lynching party."

"For Velasco, not for you," Stevens said. He
laughed. "Bernie and I have been banging on each
other in this courthouse for a lot of years. Now
he's got me by the balls and he's squeezing." Randy
shrugged. "Part of the game, that's all. You did okay,
wrote a good motion."

"Thanks."

"But I'll kick your ass in trial. I'm not letting that
dirtball killer back on the street. He'll be after *our*
kids next."

Joshua rolled his eyes and said nothing. They left
through the rear door of the courtroom. A dozen
churlish spectators waited in the corridor, angry and
frustrated that they couldn't vent their anger on the
eastern shyster defense lawyer.

▼▲▼

Joshua sat in his office at the BIA, his feet up on
the desk, leaning back as far as the swivel chair
would allow. The residue of last night's bout with

the Mexican gin and today's court session had left him enervated, slightly nauseous. His head was throbbing again. Neither Edgar nor Frances had come to work, and Joshua decided to look in on them. He couldn't comfort them in their grief. No one could. But he could be there for them. That's what friends were for.

He walked down the hallway toward the entrance, using his cane. His left foot had begun to hurt an hour ago. An old man stood in the lobby, his shoulders slumped defeatedly. He was tall and cadaverous, wearing filthy overalls with flakes of cow manure crusted on the cuffs and around the soles of his laced work boots. He turned sad gray eyes toward Joshua and deferentially removed a battered rust-colored felt cowboy hat. His hair was thick and mostly blond.

"You the lawyer?" he asked. The way he pronounced it, it sounded like "liar."

"Yes, I am." Joshua stopped in front of him.

"I been readin 'bout ya."

Joshua nodded.

"I need yer help. Or anyway, my boy needs yer help. That's the same."

"What can I do for you?"

"Can we talk here?"

"We can go in my office," Joshua said. He walked back to his office and sat down in the swivel chair. He gestured toward the oak desk chair.

"Naw, mister." The old man stood fidgeting in front of the desk, nervously fingering the brim of his hat and turning it in front of him. "I got the barnyard all over my pants 'n boots. I'll just stand."

"It's all right, really. Please sit down and relax."

The old man sat down on the edge of the chair, then settled back into it. "My boy Hubie needs yer help, Mr. Rabb. He killed a ostrich over at the zoo, and they're holdin 'im on a charge of burglary and grand theft and poachin and God knows what all."

"Why did he kill an ostrich?"

The old man shifted uncomfortably on the chair. "Hubie is mighty slow, Mr. Rabb. His mama had a real hard labor with 'im and he came out with the cord around his neck, all blue and still. And the doctor said he had some brain damage from bein deprivated of oxygen, or somethin like that. Anyways, Hubie been real slow all his nineteen years. He'll get hold of a little likker and turn mean crazy. Last year he got into a fight at the Manhattan Bar, over t' the bus terminal, and prit near killed a guy. They made 'im go to court on that one, and old Judge Rooks put 'im out on probation, he called it, let 'im come on back home. But he told 'im he'd better not be makin no more ruckus. And now this happened, and they got Hubie in the county jail. I'm real worried, Mr. Rabb."

"But I still don't know why your son killed the ostrich, Mr.—"

"Hoskins. Isaac Hoskins. Well, he just done it. He snuck into the zoo 'bout six or seven in the mornin last Saturday and was throwin paint thinner on it and then throwin matches at it. It caught on fire and burned to death. He didn't even run away. He climbed the fence into the cage and sat with it. They found 'im still in there at eight o'clock." The old man grimaced. "Can ya help 'im?"

Joshua shrugged. "I don't know. I'll have to talk to him."

"I'd be much obliged, Mr. Rabb." The old man stood up and fished in his big overalls pocket. He pulled out a roll of bills tied with a piece of hemp cord and handed it to Joshua.

"Thanks, that's fine," Joshua said. He put the roll of bills in his pocket. "I'll visit your boy later this afternoon, Mr. Hoskins."

Joshua walked with the old man down the corridor and watched him go out to an ancient rusty Model T Ford pickup truck with splintery wood side panels and a crank engine. The old man rotated the crank in the hole below the radiator, once, twice. The motor caught the third time. He drove slowly away. Joshua locked the front door of the Bureau, left through the rear door, and locked it behind him.

He knocked on the front door of the Hendly house, and Edgar opened the door, peeked out, and then opened it wider to let Joshua in.

Edgar was too morose to carry on a conversation, and Frances didn't even come out of the bedroom. Joshua got up to leave after a few minutes. He hugged Edgar at the doorway and kissed him on the cheek. Edgar held Joshua away for a moment and studied his face, then hugged him hard. Tears dripped from his eyes and he turned away embarrassedly.

Joshua limped to his car. It was a chilly day, clear and crisp azure, and the sun was far south toward Mexico. It was having a hard time delivering heat at this oblique angle. Joshua reached in his pocket and pulled out the roll of bills. He untied the string and counted the money. Sixty-eight dollars, probably every cent the old man had, stashed bill by bill in a cigar box in the corner of his closet. Joshua felt guilty, as though he were stealing.

He drove to the Pima County Jail. He sat in the small interview cubicle and waited for them to bring Hubert Hoskins to him.

The boy was small and wiry. Freckles covered his face. Sandy hair jutted out in a cowlick. He was no more than five foot four and a hundred twenty or thirty pounds. His hands were horny tough, a farmer's hands, and he looked like Ma and Pa Kettle's nephew from the adjoining farm. He smiled impishly at Joshua and sat down on the chair across from him.

"How are you, Hubie? Your dad asked me to come see you."

"Am I gettin out soon, Mister?" Hubie's face was eager.

"I don't know about that, Hubie. Right now, I need to ask you a few questions about the ostrich."

"They're mean in here," Hubie said. "Some guys pulled down my pants and tried to do me like a cow, ya know. I punched one of em, but then some big guys held me down." His face became frightened, and he looked entreatingly at Joshua. "I wanna go home."

"I'm going to try to do that, Hubie. But first I have to ask you some questions."

"They make fun a me alla time, call me 'dummy' and 'Little Bo Peep.' And one guy pulled out his thing and rubbed it real big and long and squirted me in the face whilst a couple a them others held me down. I wanna go back home. I don't like this place."

"Why did you kill the ostrich, Hubie?"

"What's 'at?"

"You know, that big bird at the zoo."

"Oh yeah, the one with the long skinny legs. Well, I didn't mean to kill it. I just wanted to play with it. I got a little pitcher book with pitchers a zoo animals all cute 'n cuddly, and I just wanted to play with it like the boy done in the book."

"But you burned it to death, Hubie. Do you know that?"

The boy considered Joshua's words for a moment, cocked his head, pursed his lips, and squinted. "Well, I reckon I got into some a old lady MacAnally's 'shine and done drunk too much. I cain't quite recollect."

"Did you ever go to school, Hubie?"

"Naw, I never been. I always wanted to, ya know, 'cause the other kids all had fun there. I'd see em out on the playground jumpin rope and spinnin on this merry-go-round thing, ya know. But Pa always said I was too important on the farm. Anyways, some old lady come out t' the house a few times and gave me some papers, 'test' she called em, and told me and Pa that I didn't have t' go t' school. I got plenny a pitcher books, though. I look at em alla time."

Joshua nodded and smiled at him. "Okay, Hubie. It was nice talking to you. I'll try to get you out real soon."

Hubie grinned at him and nodded. He shuffled out of the interview room. Joshua walked to the security cage with three sheriff's deputies inside.

"I'd like to see the jail commander," he said.

"What's up, Mr. Rabb?" asked one of the deputies.

"Just get the commander," Joshua said.

The deputy shrugged and picked up the telephone. Joshua walked over to the doorway and stared out at the purpling day. Low lavender clouds like feather pillows were gathering.

"What's up, pal?"

Joshua turned around. A thin middle-aged man in a clean tan uniform with a major's brass oak leaf on each epaulet stood before him squarely, paratroop boots planted as though he were about to do combat.

"You've got a boy in here, Hubert Hoskins. He's being homosexually abused by some other inmates. You should put him in protective isolation."

"Says who?"

"Says me. I'm his lawyer."

"Listen, lawyer man, I run the jail. You just run your fairy ass outta here." The man's eyelids twitched over flat brown eyes.

Joshua clenched his fist. He could feel the heat of the blood rushing to his cheeks. His temples began to pound. He stepped toward the jail commander and suddenly felt a fist slam into his right kidney from behind. He fell to his knees, the pain lancinating, and he fought for consciousness. Someone kicked him in the ribs and he sprawled on his stomach, the wind knocked out of him. He gasped for breath. He felt himself being pulled out of the building and rolled down the cement entry ramp. He ended up in a heap in the dirt at the bottom of the ramp. Finally breath came again to his lungs. He stood up shakily. Someone was watching him from a second-story window, but the glass was mirrored by sunlight, and Joshua couldn't see who it was. He limped painfully to his car. He drove to the courthouse and went into the county attorney's office.

Randy Stevens looked up from his desk and raised his eyebrows at Joshua. "That black suit of yours is going to need a little cleaning."

"Yes. I ran into a dirt pile over at the jail. I was asked by a boy's father to go talk to him over there. Hubert Hoskins. He set fire to an ostrich."

"Yeah, I know about it. He threw some paint thinner on it and lit it with matches. Pretty sick."

"Sick is right. The boy is retarded. He's one hundred percent M'Naghten, doesn't know right from wrong."

Randy shook his head. "No he's not. We're not prosecuting him, the probation office is revoking him."

Joshua shrugged. "That doesn't make him sane."

"No, of course not. It just prevents you from invoking the M'Naghten insanity defense."

"I still don't get it."

"In Arizona's procedure with a probation revocation proceeding, his only defense is that he didn't do it. If he admits to it, he gets the time left on his original sentence. If he denies it and demands an adjudication hearing, it's just a fast trial in front of the judge. No jury. If the judge determines that he did it, he revokes the probation. The sentence is mandatory. There's no insanity defense for a revocation, because the judge doesn't sentence him on this crime, he simply imposes the prison sentence for which he was out on probation. For Hubie that's about four years. He got in a fight last year and put a guy in the hospital. Got five years probation for battery."

Joshua shook his head. "Listen, Randy, this boy is no Franklin Carillo, he's just a sad retarded kid. Incarceration isn't going to do a damn thing for him or us. And right now he's being sexually abused in the jail. I asked the jail commander to put him in isolation, and this is what I got." He pointed to the dirt on his suit.

"Yeah, Major Heffner is a prickly sort of guy," Randy said. "And I haven't got any more say with him than you do."

"More prick than prickly," Joshua said. "Who's his boss?"

"Pat Dunphy. Go talk to him."

Joshua frowned. "That would do a lot of good."

Randy shrugged. "Well, it's either that, or talk to Charlie Weston. He's the probation officer."

Joshua nodded and walked out. His head was aching painfully. His left leg was sore and his missing toes throbbed.

CHARLES WESTON—PIMA COUNTY PROBATION was the sign on the door at the end of the corridor. Joshua knocked on the door and walked into a cramped office with dog-eared files stacked against the walls all the way to the ceiling. Behind the small olive-drab steel desk was a man about Joshua's age, big, burly, with a thick head of red curly hair, disarming dark green eyes, and an engaging smile.

"What can I do for you?" he said.

"I'm Joshua Rabb." He extended his hand toward Weston. "I represent Hubert Hoskins."

"Yeah, I've read about you."

Weston shook his hand, and the smile faded from his eyes. "And what are you going to tell me, Mr. Rabb? That Hubie's crazy as a June bug in

December and shouldn't be in jail? He needs hospitalization?"

"I think it's pretty obvious."

Weston nodded. "I tried him on probation for a year, Mr. Rabb. I got a little bit of compassion myself." He wheeled himself out from behind the desk. Joshua hadn't noticed that he was sitting in a wheelchair. Weston's legs had been amputated at midthigh. "A mortar in France, Mr. Rabb. About six seconds after I hit Omaha Beach."

Joshua held up his steel hand. "Czechoslovakia."

"Well, you had a longer war than I did. Anyway, I've got compassion for the boy. But I have nowhere to put him. He's dangerous to himself and others, and you can't overlook that. But if I put him up in the State Mental Hospital in Phoenix, some really blown-out shit-for-brains is going to kill him. There's no supervision up there. It's just a goddam cesspool for warehousing human garbage. So I have to keep him here."

"But he's being put in the barrel by the queers every night. The kid doesn't deserve that."

Weston shrugged and frowned. "I feel for Hubie, Mr. Rabb, I really do, but I got no control over that. A guy gets himself thrown in the joint, he takes whatever gets dished out over there. It's not a rest home for cardinals and kings, it's a holding tank for killers and rapists and thieves."

"Well, at least drop the revocation. Then Stevens will have to try him for the burglary. I can defend on insanity, and the judge can put him in a mental institution."

"That's what I'm telling you, Mr. Rabb. There is no 'institution.' " He mouthed the word articulately.

"This is Arizona. We have one state hospital. Period. It isn't like we've got a whole mental health network set up to handle problems like this." He shrugged. "That's the way it is."

Joshua extended his hand to Weston. Their handshake was firm.

"Nice meeting you," Joshua said.

"You married?"

"No."

"Me neither. Blast took off my dick." Weston looked matter-of-factly at Joshua. "That doesn't make me real attractive to the ladies. So I hang around Danny's Billiard Parlor, down on Congress. A lot of the guys do, sheriff's deputies, lawyers, bums like us." His eyes lit up his face. "Come on around and play a game of eight ball some time."

"Thanks," Joshua said. "But I haven't learned to hold a cue yet." He held up his steel hand again.

"Well, I haven't learned to stand up or pee, but that don't stop me from shooting the shit with the boys and having a few beers. And there's a couple of girls hang out there hustling, and they don't care if you've got a dick or not. Suck them off and they're so grateful they'll make your asshole sing!"

Joshua laughed. "Take it easy, Charlie."

He passed the door to the county law library, went inside, and sat down on a chair with a padded leather seat. He rubbed his forehead and closed his eyes. Maybe he could get the judge to issue a writ. A writ of what? A writ of *rachmunis*. A small smile crept over his face. That's what they called it in Brooklyn, where practically everybody in the courthouse was Jewish. They called any writ that was really nothing more than a legal favor from a judge a writ of *rachmunis,* mercy. That's what he needed now, a little mercy for Hubie Hoskins. But how? He stopped rubbing his forehead and opened his eyes. The set of Arizona Revised Statutes was on the top shelf along the wall to his left. He went over and pulled out Volume One, "Constitution."

He thumbed the pages to the United States Constitution and turned to the Bill of Rights. The first few amendments didn't apply at all. Then he read the "cruel and unusual punishment" clause of the Eighth amendment. That's it! It's got to be cruel and unusual punishment to subject a nineteen-year-old retarded boy to homosexual assaults in a jail.

He took the book down the hallway to Judge Velasco's chambers. The secretary told him that the judge had already left for the day. Joshua glanced at his wristwatch. He hadn't realized that it was almost four-thirty.

"Could you do me a favor and call over to Judge Buchanan's office and see if he's still in?"

The secretary dialed the phone and asked if Judge Buchanan was in chambers. She hung up and shook her head. "No, Mr. Rabb. He left at three o'clock. His secretary, Mrs. Hawkes, said to tell you the Transcon hearing is back on the calendar for ten o'clock tomorrow. She called your office twice to tell you."

Joshua walked back to the law library and replaced the book on the shelf. Poor Hubie would have to spend another night in the general population. The thought made Joshua wince. He drove wearily home and ate cold chile from a big pot in the icebox. He mixed a glassful of water with a teaspoon of bicarbonate of soda and drank it down with difficulty. His mouth felt dry, and he swallowed down two aspirins along with another glass of water. He switched on the radio and sat down stiffly in the overstuffed chair.

"The Green Hornet" was on. He was stalking some gangland hood who had rolled a drunk. Joshua concentrated on listening to the program to distract himself, to relax. It worked. The headache slowly lessened, and his body gradually lost its tenseness.

CHAPTER EIGHTEEN

By nine o'clock in the morning, Joshua had tediously one-finger-typed a writ of habeas corpus for Hubert Hoskins. It asked Judge Velasco to order that the boy be released from jail and placed in a private mental health treatment facility in Tucson at state expense. It alleged that the incarceration of a retarded boy in the general population of the Pima County Jail, where he was repeatedly subjected to homosexual abuse, was cruel and unusual punishment in violation of the Eighth Amendment to the United States Constitution.

In the Tucson telephone book were listings for two private hospitals, Serenity Acres and McFadden Hospital. Joshua spoke on the telephone to the administrators of both hospitals and decided that McFadden Hospital would be a suitable place for Hubie. The only problem was the $80 per month that it cost.

Joshua drove downtown and parked next to the courthouse. He went into Judge Velasco's chambers, and the judge's secretary told him to knock and go in but be careful. The judge was in a rage this morning.

Bernie Velasco was sitting back in his chair, staring at the ceiling, his feet on his desk, when Joshua walked in. Velasco slowly came forward in his chair and removed his feet from the desk. He gestured for Joshua to have a seat in one of the desk chairs.

"I've got a writ of habeas corpus for a boy at the jail, Judge. I'd like you to consider it."

Velasco reached over the table, and Joshua handed him the three typewritten pages. The judge read slowly, and his face took on a mordant scowl.

"What is this, a joke?" Velasco asked.

Joshua was surprised at his reaction. "No joke, your honor. Just a little humane treatment for a pathetic boy."

Velasco dropped the papers on his desk. "I guess you haven't seen the paper yet?"

Joshua shook his head.

The judge picked it up and began reading:

Judge Velasco ruled that the murder weapon, found by the Sheriff's Department upon a search of Carillo's home, could not be used in evidence by the state. Professor Walter Adelgarth at the University of Arizona's College of Law called the ruling "unprecedented, an exercise in judicial mischief by a new judge who is ignoring the United States Supreme Court's repeated admonitions that the *Weeks* rule permitting the suppression of illegally seized evidence applies only to the Federal government in Federal cases." Professor Adelgarth was astounded that Judge Velasco would make such a sweeping ruling that endangered the capacity of the state to convict a very dangerous criminal. "It is the kind of judicial activism that scoffs at the legislature and makes hash out of our historic belief in states' rights unimpeded by the heavy hand of federal interference," said the professor.

Velasco stopped reading and stared bitterly at Joshua. "Pretty good press, huh?"

Joshua shook his head. "No, pretty terrible. I'm sorry."

"Now you want me to put Hubert Hoskins in a private rest home at county expense." Velasco's face was drawn, his eyes hooded and narrowed. "He's the boy who set fire to the ostrich over at the zoo, isn't he?"

Joshua nodded.

"Well, I guess you didn't pay any attention to the outcry around here when that happened. You were probably too busy with your own hassles. But I sure remember. There wasn't anybody too anxious to treat the boy with kid gloves."

"The mob isn't right just because it's loud and unruly."

Velasco snorted and shook his head. "Bullshit platitudes like that are great for law school debates about right, truth, and justice. But it doesn't quite work that way in real life. I can't just snap my fingers and take someone charged with a felony out of jail and put him in a sanitarium and make the taxpayers foot the bill."

Joshua said nothing. Velasco handed the three typewritten sheets to him. "No writ."

Joshua left the office angry and frustrated. He drove to Scott Street by the U.S. Post Office and parked. It had begun drizzling just moments before, and now a steady rain was falling from a nacreous overcast. He ran into the building and walked up the stairs to the courtroom. He sat down in the end chair at the defendants' table. George Callan was already seated at the table with Harry Chandler. They conversed in angry, hoarse whispers.

Taft Greer, wearing an elegant blue pinstriped

suit and black bowler hat, led his entourage to the plaintiffs' table. Henry Jessup and Dan Swirling looked pleased and eager. A third man was with them.

After a few minutes, the court reporter sat at her desk, the bailiff struck the wooden block with the gavel, and Judge Buchanan took the bench. He looked particularly grave this morning, his blue eyes more exhausted and careworn than usual.

"Show the presence of the parties and counsel. This is the time set for the continued hearing on Plaintiff Transcon Construction Company's order to show cause. Taft, you have some evidence about the quality of the concrete?"

"We do indeed, your honor," said Greer, rising dramatically from his chair and speaking stentorially. "Plaintiff calls Professor Thomas Bower."

The middle-aged man sitting in the first row of spectator seats got up, walked over to the bailiff, and took the oath to tell the truth. He sat down in the witness chair.

"State your occupation, please," Greer said, hooking his thumbs in the armholes of his vest.

"Professor of chemistry, University of Arizona."

"How long have you been so employed?"

"Since I received my doctorate from the Massachusetts Institute of Technology in 1927." He was a bland-looking man with close-cropped graying brown hair and brown eyes. He wore a shapeless charcoal gray suit.

"Did you test certain concrete at my request last week?"

"I did."

"Please tell the court what you found."

"Objection," Chandler said, standing up. "No foundation."

"Right," said the judge. "Give us some foundation, Taft."

"Do you have any experience in testing concrete?"

"Yes, sir. I was the inspector on two bridge projects for the Corps of Engineers during the war, one over the river at El Camino del Cerro, the other one up near Phoenix over Indian Bend Wash."

"How did you acquire the samples you tested from the sewage project in Nogales?"

"In three ways. Mr. Jessup cut out a foot square of just-laid concrete from the culvert, he took a bucket of fresh concrete from one of the trucks, and he hammered out a bucketful of dried concrete from a section of the culvert that had been poured about four weeks ago."

"Objection," Chandler said. "Hearsay. Move to strike as nonresponsive. He can't testify to acts of others unless he observed them."

"Sustained," said the judge.

"I avow to the court that Mr. Jessup would testify that he performed those acts," Greer said.

Buchanan frowned. "All right, overruled. But let's try to comply with the rules of evidence, Taft."

"Did you test the concrete?" Greer asked.

"Yes, sir."

"Where?"

"In my lab at the university."

"Please tell us the results."

"The results were uniform. The freshly poured concrete had eighteen percent tricalcium aluminate. The drying piece had a little over seventeen percent.

The dried sample had almost eighteen percent calcium sulfoaluminate."

George Callan bit his lower lip and stared malignantly at the chemist.

"Is that Type 5 concrete?"

"No, sir. It's not even an acceptable Type 2."

"Is that an appropriate-quality concrete for a sewage system?"

"No. The sulfates in sewage will chemically combine with the tricalcium aluminate to form calcium sulfoaluminate. This will engender other chemical reactions, causing cyclical expansion and contraction in the concrete which will cause cracking in a year or two. Within five years the cracking will eventually undermine the integrity of the culvert system."

"Thank you," Greer said. He sat down.

Harry Chandler spent the next twenty minutes cross-examining the professor about the reliability of the tests used and whether the samples could have been tainted artificially. The cross-examination was fruitless. The professor was excused from the witness stand and left the courtroom.

"Any testimony?" Judge Buchanan asked, looking unhappily at Harry Chandler.

"Not at this time, your honor. We were unprepared for this testimony." Chandler's voice was subdued. "I request a week's continuance so that we can test the concrete ourselves."

The judge sucked in both cheeks and pursed his lips. He sighed and folded his hands in front of him on the bench. "You've had plenty of time for that, Harry. I think it's my duty to vacate the award to Avra Valley Concrete Company of United States

Contract"—he squinted at the file in front of him—
"4732 slash 46. It's also my obligation under the
law to hold a hearing on disgorgement." He looked
at Chandler.

Harry stood up. "Your Honor, the results of the
testing take us very much by surprise. We're just
not prepared to go forward with a disgorgement
hearing at this time. It's premature."

"How much time will you need?"

Harry shrugged. "We've got to get the concrete
tested. And if it really isn't Type 5, then we have to
prepare for the disgorgement hearing. That means
getting accountants down here. We'll have to get
the books and records of the corporation. It'll take
a week, maybe ten days."

Taft Greer shot out of his chair. "Your honor, I
don't—"

Judge Buchanan cast a vicious glance at Greer.
"Sit down, sir! You and your clients are not parties
to a disgorgement hearing. Only the Office of Land
Management and Mr. Callan and his company."

Greer sat down slowly, embarrassed at being
chastised in front of his clients.

Buchanan fixed his former partner with a school-
marmish look. "Listen, Harry, you've known for a
week that this might happen. I can't give you another week. You be ready this afternoon to tell me
why I shouldn't pierce the veil. And you, Mr. Rabb,"
he said, looking at Joshua, "you be ready to tell me
how much money the U.S. government wants back.
I'll see you gentlemen here at one-thirty." He
walked off the bench.

Henry Jessup whooped. He stood up and slapped
Taft Greer on the shoulder.

George Callan sat stonily at the table, his jaw clenched so hard that his lips were blanched white.

Joshua walked through the rear door into the judge's secretary's office.

"Good morning, Mr. Rabb," she said pleasantly.

"Good morning, Mrs. Hawkes." Joshua forced what he hoped was a pleasant smile. He took the folded writ of habeas corpus out of his inner jacket pocket.

"I'd like to see the judge," he said.

"Is it about a writ for Hubert Hoskins?"

Joshua nodded, surprised.

"Judge Buchanan thought you might want to see him about that. He asked me to tell you that Judge Velasco called him this morning before the hearing and talked to him about it. Judge Buchanan won't issue the writ."

Joshua stared at the elderly woman. She shrugged apologetically. He put the papers back in his pocket and left the judge's chambers. He spent the next two hours sitting glumly in Georgette's Diner. The open-faced hot beef sandwich was tasteless, and the Coke was flat. He felt a wave of melancholy wash heavily over him and oppress him. He would have to ask the judge to order that Avra Valley Concrete reimburse the entire five million dollars it had received so far. Nothing else would be appropriate following this morning's testimony indicating clear fraud. But that wasn't all of it. If the corporation didn't have sufficient assets on hand to repay the five million dollars, and the Avra Valley corporation was defunct and therefore almost certainly penniless, then the judge would "pierce the corporate veil" and order George Callan to pay the money out of his personal funds. That could mean Federal marshals auctioning off the Lazy G Ranch and everything on it to raise the money. Not that George didn't deserve it. But Joshua knew him well enough by now to know that George wouldn't take it lying down. Someone would get killed. Maybe more than one.

At one-fifteen, Joshua walked slowly back to the courtroom. Jessup and Swirling were sitting at the plaintiff's table. Taft Greer stood by a window, hands laced behind his back, staring at the street below. Joshua sat down at the defense table.

The bailiff came into the courtroom a few moments later. He glanced at his watch. "Any of you gentlemen seen Mr. Chandler or Mr. Callan?"

"Nope," Greer said.

Joshua shook his head. It was one thirty-five. The bailiff frowned and left the courtroom.

Ten minutes later, Chandler entered the courtroom. His suit appeared even baggier than usual. His tie was loosened, the top button of his shirt was open, and his face was flushed. A minute later the court reporter, bailiff, and judge came into the courtroom. Judge Buchanan sat in his deep chair and stared acidulously at Harry Chandler.

"Show the presence of all counsel and parties except for defendant George Callan," Buchanan said. "Talk to me, Harry."

"George Callan took off in his car without a word after the court session, and I haven't seen him since. I have no idea where he's gone."

"Does he think he'll get a continuance with a cheap trick like that?" Buchanan asked.

Harry Chandler rose from his seat. His normally

soft eyes were hard and muddy and angry. "Now I'll tell you what, Judge, I haven't got a clue what's on George's mind. Except that I think he was deeply and genuinely shocked by the testimony of Dr. Bower this morning, just as I was. I think that George Callan deserves to have a little more time in this matter, and I think the court's rush to judgment is arbitrary and capricious."

Judge Buchanan flinched and peered angrily at his former partner.

"I haven't been able to locate Mr. Callan's accountant, Henry Murchison," Chandler continued in an irate tone. "He is in Albuquerque on business. I haven't been able to locate Andy Sillweg over at the Bank of Douglas. His secretary said that he went to Casa Grande this morning, won't be back till later. In short, I am unprepared to proceed and to represent my client adequately. And I still believe that we are entitled to test the concrete ourselves and present evidence to the court. We must have a continuance for one week."

Buchanan gritted his teeth and stared morosely at Chandler. He turned his face toward Joshua. "It's your call, Mr. Rabb."

Joshua stood up. "The government will not oppose any reasonable continuance so long as the court issues a restraining order to the Bank of Douglas directing the sequestration of all construction funds being held for distribution to Avra Valley Concrete—there should be over thirteen million dollars there—as well as a cease and desist order directing Avra Valley and its subsidiaries to cease any work on the sewage project pending further order of this court."

Chandler rose quickly from his chair. His voice was scathing. "That's absolutely improper, your honor. You can't prejudge this case without allowing ample and appropriate time for a complete and thorough hearing on the merits." His voice and demeanor became solicitous. "Just give us two days, Friday at ten in the morning."

The judge shook his head. "Friday is the day for releasing the funds at the Bank of Douglas, isn't it, Mr. Rabb?"

Joshua nodded.

"Here's what I'm going to do for your client, Harry." Buchanan leaned heavily on the bench, looking down his nose at Chandler through his spectacles. "I'm sequestering the takeout money being held by the bank, but I won't C and D the project itself, and I won't render judgment on the fraud claim. George can show good faith by continuing with the construction. I'll give you a week to get your case prepared. I won't make any ruling on the merits of this matter until you've had ample opportunity to present all the evidence you think is necessary. Be back here next Wednesday at ten o'clock. That's going to be your opportunity. Mrs. Hawkes," he looked down at the court reporter, who was also his secretary, "please prepare a preliminary injunction ordering the Bank of Douglas to freeze the construction takeout loans on U.S. Contract 4732 slash 46. Have the marshal's office serve it on the bank forthwith." He walked off the bench.

Greer and his clients left the courtroom noisily, jubilant. Chandler stood at the table, rubbing his mouth and chin hard. He glanced at Joshua with sad, tired eyes. "Bad business, this," he mumbled.

"Awful bad." He shook his head and walked out of the courtroom.

Joshua waited enough time for Chandler to walk to his office. He didn't feel like arguing with anyone, especially not George Callan's lawyer. He was using his cane today, and he thunked out of the courtroom and down the stairs to the sidewalk. Greer and Jessup and Swirling were standing there, chatting together pleasantly.

"Well, I guess that does it, huh, Mr. Rabb?" called out Henry Jessup.

Joshua stopped and turned to him. "Does what, Mr. Jessup?"

"Why, terminates the contract, Mr. Rabb. Now it comes to me."

"Not yet, Mr. Jessup. We have another hearing next week, and if the judge really does terminate the contract, then I'm going to have to check the Code of Federal Regulations to see how I'm required to proceed. I think I'm going to have to put the project out for rebids."

Jessup's smile became a pugnacious frown. "What's that bullshit about?" His voice was thick and breathy from anger. "You're supposed to award it to the next lowest bidder. That's me." He pointed a stubby forefinger at his own chest.

"I don't think so, Mr. Jessup. Once the project is under way, if the contract award is set aside, I think I'm required to call for public bids."

Jessup turned to Taft Greer. "What's this shit about, Taft? You said I'd get the project."

"Now hold your horses," Greer said. "Just leave it to me. This man don't know what he's talking about." He pointed at Joshua.

Jessup turned back to Joshua, his rage unassuaged. "I've taken about all I'm going to from you, you fuckin lowlife kike. If I don't get that job, you're a fuckin corpse. You hear what I'm saying?" He was screaming.

Dan Swirling took Jessup's arm. "Take it easy, Henry. The whole world is hearing what you're saying."

Jessup whipped his arm free and stared savagely at Joshua. He lowered his voice to a thick muttering. "Hiding your kids in Sells with them Indians isn't going to keep them safe, you cocksucker bastard. You're all fresh meat if I don't get that contract."

Joshua stepped toward him. Swirling wrapped his arms around Jessup from behind and pulled him away. Jessup didn't resist this time. He let himself be pulled ten feet away from the steel blue eyes and parted lips of Joshua Rabb's enraged face. Then he squirmed out of Swirling's hold.

"Mind what I tell you, you lowlife bastard." He shook his finger at Joshua.

Joshua walked slowly toward him, his white knuckled fist holding his cane resting over his shoulder like a bullwhip handle. Jessup turned around and jogged toward a big Oldsmobile sedan parked across the street. Swirling and Greer followed at a fast walk, looking back anxiously to make sure they weren't being pursued.

Joshua was so angry that he could hardly catch his breath. He watched the car pull away from the curb and continue down Broadway until it turned left.

Was it Jessup, not Callan? Did Jessup try to kill Adam and get Jimmy Hendly by mistake? Joshua stood trembling with anger. A mild drizzle began to fall from the cinder gray overcast sky. He didn't feel it, not until he heard a crack of thunder and looked up. Fat droplets fell now and wet his face and hair. His suit jacket became heavy and hung uncomfortably on his aching left shoulder. He lifted his stainless-steel-pronged hand and stared at the water pouring off it as if from a rainspout. He brought the tip of the gnarled mesquite branch cane down from his shoulder and put the end of it between the prongs. He manipulated the cables expertly and squeezed the prongs closed. Hard. Harder. They easily crushed the inch-thick hardwood and severed the tip. It fell into the gutter and washed away in the swirling gush of rainwater.

Squishing cane tips isn't exactly getting me anywhere, he thought. Adam and Hanna had better come home. They were no longer hidden safely away.

Joshua drove to the BIA and called the BIA office in Sells. There was no answer. He began to get frightened for them, imagining a rush of horrible possibilities. He tried in vain to push away the fear. He had to keep moving, to do something to divert his attention. He drove down to his house and changed into Levis and a cowboy shirt. He took the .45 revolver and a box of shells out to the car and drove toward Sells. The weather had worsened, but he hadn't been paying attention. He passed the newly constructed culvert at Coyote Creek and noticed the heavy flow of water rushing through it. He looked south toward the Baboquivari Mountains and saw black clouds hovering over them. The hazy look of the air between the clouds and mountains meant that it was raining heavily.

Soon the rain swept across the Ajo Highway in sheets. On the asphalt portion of the highway, driving was smooth. But on those stretches where the asphalt had been worn down and washed away over the years, the roadway was becoming puddled.

It was a little after three, and Joshua decided to wait out the rain. He didn't want to get his car embedded in a foot of mud. There was virtually no traffic along the Ajo Highway, and it might take a day or two before someone came by who could help tow him out of the mire.

The torrential downpour here in the high foothills forty miles from Tucson was the most powerful rainstorm Joshua had ever experienced. Lightning zapped earthward, and seconds later would come the crash of thunder. It was as dark as late dusk. The convertible top began to leak in several places, and a steady series of drips soaked Joshua's trousers. There was nowhere to sit that was much of an improvement. The storm blew fast across the highway and vanished rapidly into the desert, leaving only the hazy look of the rainfall to betray its continued vitality. The darkness dissipated, and the sun began to burn through patchy pale pink and white cotton-candy clouds. The rain stopped.

Joshua got out of the car and walked down the road to where the asphalt ended. He stepped carefully onto the dirt and was surprised at how hard the ground was. The rain had washed over the humped roadway and collected in the gulleys on both sides. The sky had become almost clear, a gemlike turquoise, and the sun sparked the myriad raindrops on the plants by the road. There were no flowers now in the early winter, so his attention was drawn to the various brilliant greens and yellows of the leaves and bracts and sepals of the flowering plants and the pads and tubercles of the cacti.

He walked back to his car and drove without incident to Sells. The ramshackle hovels could not be brightened or romanticized by the sun or washed pristine by the rain. They were simply drab and depressing.

It was after four when he finally pulled up outside the BIA office. Chuy Leyva's pickup was parked in front. Adam ran out to greet him and hugged him happily. Hanna came out more demurely, as befitted a fifteen-year-old lady, and she beamed happily when her father told her that they were going home.

Magdalena rode back with Chuy. Hanna and Adam went with Joshua. He put the top down and the mild air washed them. Joshua stopped at a small farm on the Nogales Highway, a half mile from Valencia Road.

"I'll just be a minute," he said.

It was after six. He knocked on the front door. It opened a crack and then all the way.

"I'm sorry to have to tell you that I can't get Hubie released, Mr. Hoskins. They're going to revoke his probation next week, and he's going to be sentenced to Arizona State Prison for the remainder of the sentence on the aggravated battery charge, about four years."

Isaac Hoskins sniffed and looked imploringly at Joshua. "Ain't nothin ya can do?"

Joshua shook his head grimly.

"What's 'at, Ike?" asked an old woman limping up

to the door. She was tall and pole thin, wearing her wispy white hair in a straggly loose bun. Her eyes were an odd amber color. She was wearing a faded brown Mother Hubbard that hung shapelessly down to the tops of her bare, filth-blackened feet. The floor of the shack was dirt. She held up a smudgy lorgnette pinned by a cord to her chest pocket and squinted at Joshua.

"Just Hubie's liar, Aggie," Isaac Hoskins said. "He says he cain't do nothin t' help our boy."

Aggie stared at Joshua through the lorgnette and then dropped it. She was chewing tobacco, and a black crust ringed her mouth. A little spittle dripped down her chin. She turned away and receded into the shack.

Joshua pulled the wad of bills out of his pocket. It was still tied with the string. "Here. I can't take your money, Mr. Hoskins, since I can't do anything to help Hubie."

"No, no, Mr. Rabb." He pushed away the extended hand. "Ya still gotta be with 'im at the hearing. I got a paper today says the hearing is next Friday. Hubie needs you, Mr. Rabb."

"But I'm telling you that I can't help him. I tried. The hearing's just a formality. Hubie's going to be sent to prison."

"Then let it happen with a real liar by his side, Mr. Rabb. I don't want him to think that his ma 'n me abandoned 'im."

Joshua nodded. "Okay, Mr. Hoskins. I'll represent him." He smiled gravely at the old man and walked back to the car.

"That's where Hubie lives," Adam said.

"How do you know Hubie?" his father asked.

"Me and Jimmy came here and Jimmy told me about him."

"When was that?"

"On Halloween night, when we were trick or treating, and that guy in the car tried to scare us." Adam's face instantly looked pained and he stopped speaking. He had forgotten that he wasn't supposed to say anything about that. He saw the alarm in his father's eyes and knew that he was about to be forbidden to leave home except to go to school.

His father stared at him. They still hadn't left the Hoskins place.

"Why didn't you tell me?"

"I just forgot, Dad. It wasn't anything. Jimmy and me weren't scared or nothing."

"Exactly what happened?"

"A car followed us in the dark. And then its lights went on right in front of us and a man jumped out in a witch's mask and spooked the horses, and both me and Jimmy got bucked off. Then the car just drove away."

"Well, you can stay close to the house for the time being," Joshua said. "Understand?"

He had the look on his face that you didn't argue with. "Yeah," Adam said quietly.

Joshua started the car and backed out the long driveway to the Nogales Highway. The situation was getting clearer now. Much clearer. Halloween had been the first day that Jessup and Swirling had come to see him. It was at his office that Jessup had threatened him, tried to force him to vacate the contract award to George Callan. Joshua remembered how angry he had become, being goaded by Jessup. And that night somebody scared the boys.

Then there was Billy the Cat. And Chester Milliken. It would appear to everybody that the only one with a motive to murder Milliken was Callan. And Jimmy's death that should have been Adam's happened right after the court hearing, when Judge Buchanan ordered the concrete tested. Again, only Callan would be suspected. That was right around the same time that the Mexican followed me down the Nogales Highway and I had a flat tire. I thought the guy was one of George Callan's hands, but he could have been working for Jessup. Damn! It's time to go out to the Lazy G and see if I can find the guy. If not, I'll go over to Transcon and look for him. Maybe I've been dead wrong about George Callan. And Diana? God, it would be great if she's really his niece and not just some Kansas City whore! Come on, God. Just this one time. It's the only favor I'll ever ask. He thought about the times they had spent together and began to feel wistful.

He parked in front of the little adobe house beside Chuy's pickup. Chuy was in the chicken coop dropping feed for the fluttering chickens. Magdalena was in the kitchen, heating the pot of green chile on the stove.

Adam turned on the radio and lay down on the floor in front of it. Rochester said something to Mr. Benny. Adam laughed, but Joshua didn't even hear it. He was trying to piece together what had happened, with Jessup as the villain this time instead of Callan. Jessup made a better fit, a much better fit.

CHAPTER
NINETEEN

Joshua drove to the Callan ranch the next morning. Diana opened the door and stared unsmilingly at him. "What do you want?"

"To talk to you," Joshua said.

"I've heard enough from you." Her eyes were hurt. Her voice was acrid.

"Look, I'm sorry. I've been thinking about it for days. I was very upset. I just jumped to some conclusions that don't seem right anymore." He shrugged. "I'm sorry. I want to talk to you about it."

She lingered a moment, holding onto the door, making the decision whether to slam it in his face. Then she turned and walked into the house, leaving the door open.

Joshua followed her into the kitchen and sat down at the dinette table.

"George here?"

"No, he went to Nogales yesterday." She stood at the sink washing lima beans in a tightly woven string bag. "When he got back from court, he was angrier than I've ever seen him. He said he was going down to Nogales to get some samples of the concrete and bring it to the University for testing."

"I don't think the tests will turn out any differently."

She turned a severe look at him. "Well, I do. Whatever you may think, my uncle is an honest man. If he says he's pouring Type 5 concrete, then that's exactly what he's doing."

Joshua said nothing.

"Uncle George called Governor Calderon yesterday at noon, when he came home. He asked Alfonso to check if Jessup or anyone else had been down there getting concrete to test. Alfonso called him back an hour later and told him nobody had taken any samples. Two of Alfonso's men checked the whole length of the culvert, and there were no chunks taken out of it anywhere or patched places. The samples that Jessup brought to the University were phony."

Joshua shook his head and sighed. "I don't know who to believe anymore."

"Well, it's damn sure time for you to take sides! You just can't keep sitting on the fence chewing grass straws and watching those bastards ruin my uncle's life!" She began to cry.

"I want to see your birth certificate," Joshua said.

She looked at him disgustedly. "Drop dead."

"I really want to see your birth certificate."

"You want to make sure I'm a human being and not a dog or a muskrat?"

"You know what I want."

"What'll it prove? Maybe my mother was married to George's brother and he died and my stepfather's name is on the birth certificate. Or maybe my mother is George's sister and was married previously, so her name wasn't Callan."

He stared at her and said nothing. She fidgeted at the sink with the bag of beans and dropped them in the sink.

"I love how you believe in me." She wept quietly.

Joshua went to her and wrapped his arm around her. He had left Captain Hook at home. She shook free of him and strode out of the kitchen. He stood glumly staring out the window.

She came back five minutes later and took the bag of beans out of the sink and laid it on the sideboard. She put a tall stock pot under the faucet and began filling it. Joshua turned around, walked back to the dinette, and sat down at it. There was a folded half sheet of paper on the table in front of him. He opened it and smoothed it flat. It was a little stiff and crinkly with age. "Certificate of Live Birth," was its heading. Handwritted entries on the printed form indicated that Diana Thurber was born to Harold T. Thurber and Margaret Thurber (maiden name Callan) on February 6, 1922. The signature of the Administrator of Kansas City Memorial Hospital was embossed with a seal that said, "Registrar of Births—Wyandotte County," and there was another signature under it. A gold seal was pasted below that, embossed on the top with the words AD ASTRA PER ASPERA, and under that with a spray of stars, two covered wagons, a horse plow in a wheat field, a steamboat on a river, a church house, and the sun rising over mountains.

Joshua stared at the birth certificate and began to smile. Diana was cutting the bag open and pouring the beans into the stock pot on the oven burner.

"You could have shown this to me before," he said quietly.

"You could have had a hell of a lot more faith in me. I didn't think I had to prove to you that I was a real person."

"I'm sorry. I've been a real ass."

She turned toward him, her face softer. "You can say that again."

" 'If thou meet thine enemy's ass going astray, thou shalt surely bring it back to him.' Genesis 23."

She allowed a hesitant smile. "Always the lawyerly retort."

"I'm trying to impress you."

"I've been impressed since I first saw you at the M.O. Club."

He walked slowly to her and raised his hand to her cheek. His hand was trembling. She touched it and pressed it to her cheek. Tears came to Joshua's eyes. He swallowed and tried to keep them away, but he could feel them rolling down his cheeks.

"What's this about?" she whispered.

"I'm happy." He sniffed and looked at her and felt so full of emotion that words weren't appropriate. He drew her to him and they kissed. He tasted the salt of their tears.

"I want to see the two hands who led your Lippizaner back to the barn the day I was out here and you were riding *dressage*."

"You still suspicious?" She looked up at him.

"Not of you. But I just have to know."

"What did they do?"

"I think one of them gave me a flat tire and followed me. He slashed my seat covers."

She frowned. "That doesn't sound like Chico or Miguel. They'll be out in the barn, changing the straw.

They do it every Thursday morning. Wait, I'll go with you."

They walked to the barn behind the horse ring. Two men were pitchforking matted, soggy straw out of a horse stall. Diana exchanged a few pleasantries with them, and then she and Joshua walked to his car.

"Miguel looks like him," Joshua said. "But it's not him." He felt very relieved. But the loss of his previous certainty began to make him nervous. He would have to go over to Transcon's plant and look around. A dangerous enterprise at the moment. It was eight in the morning. They walked hand in hand back into the house. Diana was wearing a loose cotton shirtdress. She had no makeup or lipstick on. She led him down the hallway to her bedroom and locked the door. She unbuttoned the dress and let it fall to the floor around her. She was naked and gorgeous, like Botticelli's Venus, and he couldn't take his eyes from her. She basked in his look. She stepped to him and unbuttoned his plaid shirt and Levis. He touched her delicately, the curve of her breast, her puckered nipple, the soft curls of hair covering her vulva. She drew in her breath with a little gasp and shuddered slightly.

▼▲▼

He got dressed and sat down on the edge of the bed. She rolled toward him and pressed her face against his knee.

"Will you come to dinner when Uncle George gets back? I want you two to be friends again."

"Yes. But George may not be quite so eager. I'm involved in a hearing with him that could affect a lot of things."

"I know, he told me. But it's all going to turn out just fine. I feel it." She smiled at him earnestly. "He called me last night from the Fray Marcos Hotel. Said he'd be back this morning. He had the samples to take over to the University."

"I want to marry you," Joshua said. He didn't know why. The words just came, spontaneously, inexorably.

Her mouth opened in surprise. Then she smiled softly and tears came to her eyes. She nodded and sniffled.

He kissed her lightly and lingered, aroused again by the delicate perfume that she touched to her neck and breasts. She dressed and they walked reluctantly to his car. He drove away. She looked after him until the yellow convertible crested the small rise in the road.

CHAPTER TWENTY

Hanna walked into Joshua's office in the Bureau. "Dad, somebody pushed a wood crate off a truck into our front yard."

It was Friday afternoon. Joshua glanced at his wristwatch. It was a little before five. Hanna must have just come home from school.

"Who?" Joshua asked.

She shrugged. "Just a big stake truck and a Mexican guy. I didn't recognize him."

"What's in the box?"

"I don't know. But it smells real bad."

"Maybe a shipment of perfume from McClellan's."

She laughed.

Joshua walked with his daughter to their house. In the front yard was a large wooden crate.

"Go get the crowbar out of the shed, and let's see what's in it," Joshua said. An offensive smell kept him back a few feet from the crate.

Hanna brought him the crowbar, and he approached the three-foot-high box, trying to breathe shallowly. He pried off one of the top planks and then a second one. A man wearing an expensive linen western suit covered with blood was folded into the box. His face and head weren't visible.

"Go sit on the porch," Joshua said to Hanna.

"What's wrong?" She looked at him in alarm.

"There's a dead person in here," he said.

She gasped.

He took the crowbar and pried two cross slats from the side. When he removed the third slat, he saw George Callan's lusterless pale blue eyes staring visionlessly at him. There was a small bullet hole in his cheek, just below his eye. Blood had poured down and caked black on his lower face and chin and neck, turning his white cotton shirt and white leather bolo tie black.

Joshua swallowed hard. He walked to Hanna, who was sitting stiffly on the porch steps, and put both of his hands on her shoulders. "It's George Callan. Go back to the Bureau and tell Mr. Hendly and Chuy and make sure they call Roy Collins, the FBI man."

Hanna gulped and ran toward the BIA. Joshua slumped down on the porch steps. He stared at the box, sickened, confused. At least one thing was now certain: George Callan wasn't behind all of the trouble. It was Jessup. Joshua sat brooding on the porch steps, holding his breath a little each time the breeze shifted and blew a jolt of the cloying odor of death toward him.

Chuy and Edgar came jogging toward the box. Edgar stopped a dozen feet short, sniffed the air like a blue tick hound, and walked toward the house instead. He sat down beside Joshua.

"I been thinkin there are better things to do than work for the gover'ment," Edgar said. "Fuckin dangerous lately. My boy'd still be alive . . ." His cheeks reddened, his eyes became wet, and he sniffed.

"Don't blame yourself for any of this," Joshua said. He felt a deep sense of guilt over Jimmy. And Jimmy's death hadn't had anything to do with Edgar. It had been Joshua's fault. "What's happening around here has nothing to do with us. It's an old feud as bad as the Hatfields and McCoys, except these people are killing each other over money."

Edgar nodded. "It's as old as the Good Book: 'Ye serpents, ye generation of vipers, how can ye escape the damnation of hell?' "

"Well, Edgar, I'm proud of you. You finally quoted something from the Bible that's really in it."

Edgar snorted. "I've had reason to be readin it a whole lot lately." His voice trailed off.

Again Joshua felt the gnawing pain of guilt over Jimmy's death. As much as he could rationalize it, the truth was unavoidable: Jimmy had died instead of Adam.

Chuy stood a few yards from the crate, staring at George Callan. Roy Collins drove up in an aging gray Ford sedan with the great seal of the United States painted on the doors. The eagle had chipped off the seal, and all that was left of the motto was GOD WE T.

Collins got out and walked over to the crate. He applied a daub of Vicks under his nose from a small jar that he put back in his seersucker jacket pocket.

"Who opened the box?" he called out.

"I did," Joshua responded.

"Touch him?"

"No."

Collins nodded. He poked and felt the body in various places. Then he picked up the crowbar and pulled off the remaining planks on the side.

Hanna and Adam walked down Indian Agency Road toward their house. They stopped in the road fifty feet away. Hanna had her arm around Adam's shoulders.

The sound of a siren in the far distance became louder. It grew like a slow drumroll to a crescendo as the coroner's ambulance turned off Valencia onto Indian Agency Road. Hanna and Adam edged to the side of the road to let it pass.

Sheriff's Deputy Paul Wheaton got out, pulled a thick cigar out of his breast pocket, lit it up, puffed a few long puffs, and walked up to Collins. They spoke together quietly, Collins pointed at the body several times, and then Wheaton walked to the rear of the ambulance and pulled out a gurney. He wheeled it next to the box and braced it there with his left leg. Collins pulled on Callan's suit jacket tail and the body of the old man flopped onto the gurney, bounced against Wheaton's shin, and settled dead still. Rigor mortis kept it rigid, bent almost double at the waist. Collins and Wheaton wheeled the gurney to the ambulance and lifted it inside. They came back toward the porch.

"Howdy, Mr. Rabb," Wheaton said. "Can I put you in my report as the official identification?"

Joshua nodded.

"Did he have any next of kin?"

"Yes. A niece." Joshua swallowed. "I guess I'd better go out to the ranch and tell her."

"Well, if you could stop down at the coroner's office and sign the certificate?"

"Yes, sure, I'll come right now. It's on the way to the ranch." Joshua drew himself up from the porch slowly and heavily. He walked up to Chuy. "Will you stay in the house with the kids tonight? I may not be back."

"Sure, Mr. Rabb."

Joshua walked over to Hanna and Adam. "You two all right?"

Both of them nodded. Hanna looked frightened. Adam chewed his lower lip.

"You told me we'd move, Daddy," Hanna said, her voice quavering.

"We will, honey. Chuy's going to stay in the house tonight. He'll take care of you. I've got to go out to Callan's ranch and I may be back real late. Tomorrow we'll look for somewhere to live. Okay?"

She nodded.

"Can I take Golden Boy?" Adam sniffed.

"You bet. We won't go anywhere without him. Now you two mind Magdalena and Chuy, hear?"

"We will, Dad," Hanna said.

▼▲▼

When Joshua got to the coroner's office downtown, Dr. Stanley Wolfe was filling out the death certificate.

"You could set up a little office down the street," the coroner said wryly. "Save you a lot of travel time."

"I do seem to spend an inordinate amount of time with you, Stan."

The doctor made a sour face. "You got a real bumper crop of corpses out in your neck of the woods, especially with the cholera."

Joshua nodded grimly. He signed his name in the "witness" block and happened to notice that the block next to it, "Time of Death," was filled in with "1000 hours to midnight." The "Cause of Death" box read "5 gunshot wounds, .38 or larger."

"Stan, you've put down last night between ten and midnight as the time of death."

The doctor nodded.

"But he was in a hotel in Nogales, Sonora."

Dr. Wolfe shrugged. "I'm pretty sure about the time of death. I don't guess at things like that."

"I know, I know. I wasn't questioning you. I was questioning me. I don't know how he could've been killed at the hotel at midnight, five .38 caliber or higher gunshot wounds, without the whole town hearing it."

Dr. Wolfe splayed the fingers of both hands. "Beats me," he said.

"Okay, thanks. I'll be making arrangements for a funeral in the next day or two."

"I'm sending him over to the refrigerator at Tucson Mortuary. He's already going fast. Once it starts, keeping him cold isn't going to stop it. You'd better have your funeral soon."

Joshua nodded. He drove to the Lazy G Ranch. It took over a half hour, and by the time he got there he had thought it all out.

As he parked beside the white picket fence, Diana came out the door and walked toward him.

"What's wrong?" Her eyes were troubled.

"What do you mean?"

"You came driving down that dirt road fifty miles an hour. There must be something wrong."

Joshua grimaced. "Yeah. Come here." He walked up to her and hugged her. "Your uncle's dead," he said softly, holding her close.

Her body suddenly tensed and her breathing stopped. Then her breath came out in a groan and she collapsed against his chest. He lifted her with great difficulty, cradling her legs in his mechanical arm, and carried her into the house. She was disoriented, not unconscious, and he sat her on the couch in the living room. Her body was slack. He poured a large drink of tequila into a glass at the bar along the end of the room and brought it to her. She swallowed a mouthful, coughed, absently wiped the perspiration from her forehead, and sat up slowly. She took another large swallow. She sat for a moment, letting it work down to her toes.

"How did it happen?" she whispered.

Joshua sat down beside her and took her free hand in both of his. "Somebody shot him."

Her eyes and mouth flew open in shock, and then they closed slowly.

"That bastard Jessup," she growled hoarsely. "But I didn't think he'd do anything this terrible."

"I don't think he did."

She focused slowly on him. "But who else would have any reason to?"

"Alfonso Calderon."

She stared at Joshua for a moment, waiting for him to tell her that he was just joking. He didn't.

"I don't get it," she said.

"George was killed last night around midnight. You told me this morning that he called you from the Fray Marcos in the evening. He was going to stay overnight."

She nodded.

"So he was killed in Nogales, shot five times with a high-caliber handgun. Most likely at the hotel.

With that many shots, somebody had to hear the noise. Nothing, especially five gunshots, goes unnoticed in Nogales. And if Jessup or Swirling or one of their men had done it, they'd never get across the border. Only one man could have done it: Alfonso Calderon."

"But they were like brothers."

"Brothers fight. Brothers kill each other. George must have realized that Alfonso was turning out crap concrete. After all, what did Alfonso care? He already got the first three or four million dollars off the front end. The rest of it was to be George's. So what did Alfonso care if the project got shut down? It was all George's money being lost."

Diana was listening intently.

"George must have confronted Alfonso and gotten killed. Maybe Agostino Diaz, the chief of the *Federales,* actually pulled the trigger, or the pimp Juan Iturbe, or a hundred other scumbags that Alfonso controls, but only Alfonso had the power to authorize it down there. He's the law. If anyone else had killed Alfonso Calderon's blood brother, he'd be executed in the town square in front of everybody."

Joshua nodded at her in his certainty. "It's got to be Calderon."

"Then he killed the chemist, too, to keep him from testing?"

Joshua nodded.

"And tried to kill Adam, to keep you from making any trouble over the contract?"

Again Joshua nodded. "It all makes sense. And nothing else makes better sense."

"Poor Uncle George," Diana said. She began to cry softly. "Poor Uncle George."

Joshua hugged her. She shuddered and wept harder, and then her shoulders stopped shaking and the tears slowly stopped.

It was almost six-thirty. Constanza came into the living room. "Mr. Callan be here dinner, *Señorita?*"

Diana got up and put her arm around the maid. She walked with her into the kitchen, speaking softly to her in Spanish. Joshua could hear the maid's loud weeping. Slowly it stopped. Diana came in a few moments later. She had a pitcher of margaritas and two glasses on a tray.

"I gave her the weekend off. She's worked for Uncle George for thirty years, and she's really upset."

They each drank a margarita and felt a little better. Just being together was therapy. After two more margaritas, Diana led Joshua into the bedroom. They fell asleep in each other's arms, and he awoke at two in the morning to her soft sobbing. He comforted her, and they made love.

"I have to go," he whispered.

"I don't want you to go, ever," she said.

"I can't stay here. I've got two kids at home." He sat up on the edge of the bed and strapped on his mechanical arm.

"Bring them here to live."

He stopped moving. "What?"

"All of you come live here," she said resolutely.

"How would that look?"

"Who cares? I need you. I love you. You said you want to marry me."

He stood up, walked around the bed, and turned on the lamp. She squinted in the light for a moment and then looked earnestly at him.

"I do want to marry you," Joshua said. "But obviously now isn't the right time."

"I know. We'll have to wait a few weeks after the funeral. People would talk. But there's no reason that you shouldn't move out here. Besides the master bedroom, there are three other bedrooms and separate guest quarters with its own bathroom and kitchen. You take the guest quarters. Hanna and Adam can have two of the bedrooms. I'll move into Uncle George's room. That way none of the servants or the hands will talk, and we can be together all the time. I love you very much."

She pushed down the covers and reached toward him with both hands. Her breasts and slender waist rose to him. He sat down on the edge of the bed and they kissed. They made love again, long and caring and solicitous to each other, like two people truly in love.

"We'll be over by noon," he whispered.

"I love you so," she whispered.

He got dressed, switched off the light, waited for his eyes to accustom themselves to the darkness, and kissed her nipple.

"Ummmm," she said. "Come here." She stretched out both of her arms.

He stood up quickly to elude her embrace and laughed. "Not again right now. I'll have to have a pecker transplant."

▼▲▼

They drove out to the Lazy G Ranch with the convertible top down and the cool wind whipping their hair. Then Chico and Adam took the pickup truck and the horse trailer back to pick up Golden Boy. They released him in the huge pasture behind the house and he nickered and swished his tail, loped about twenty yards, looked around at his old friends, and began grazing contentedly on the hock-high ryegrass.

Hanna hadn't been to the ranch before. Joshua walked with her around the stables and the corral and the huge pasture. She lingered at the trailing roses in the long red brick box by the front door.

"You're going to marry her, aren't you, Daddy?" She looked at him soberly.

"Yes, honey. Probably in a month or so."

She nodded. "She's very pretty, Daddy." Her voice broke a little, and tears misted her eyes.

Joshua hugged her. "I'll never love any woman more than I love you. I promise."

She wept softly, and he hugged her close.

"I wish Mommy didn't die," she whispered.

"Me, too," he said hoarsely.

They stood together for a few minutes, and then she dried her eyes with a red hankie from the back pocket of her Levis.

"Do I get to be maid of honor?"

He laughed. "We'll have to talk to Diana. It's her wedding too, you know."

Hanna grinned. "A blue tulle skirt with a long-sleeved satin top and *peau de soie* heels, like I saw in Goldberg's window?"

He laughed again, genuinely pleased. "Let's talk to Diana."

▼▲▼

Diana was rivetingly beautiful in the black velvet dress. Tears streamed silently from her eyes. She had given Hanna a plain black wool suit from her own closet to wear. They sat together, holding each other's hand, in the back seat of the black Packard limousine, driven by Miguel.

Joshua hadn't prodded Adam to come to the funeral. For a boy of eleven, he had been to more funerals than most people attend in a lifetime.

Hanna's hair was a shade darker brown than Diana's, but they both shone red in the bright afternoon sun by the mausoleum at Evergreen Cemetery. It was a small marble building topped by a bronze statue of the archangel Michael. Inside there was room for three or four people to stand in the corridor between the vaults on either side. George's mother and father were here, on the north side, and George lay beside them. On the other side were his wife, her parents, and her father's brother. There are enough empty crypts in here for me and Diana and the kids, Joshua thought glumly.

The service was held outside the mausoleum. A great chunk of Tucson's gentry was there, paying their last respects to one of the last old-time pioneers of southern Arizona.

Arthur O'Leary stood with his son Mike. Arthur was dressed in a black western suit. He held a black cowboy hat over his heart. His eyelids were red-rimmed, his eyes watery, and his breath a little boozy. Mike was dressed in a dark gray wool suit, expensive, tailored to show off his powerful shoulders and trim waist. His blond hair glowed literally golden in the sun. When he came through the receiving line, he bussed Diana's cheek, as did some others, but his lips came very close to hers. Too close, Joshua thought, feeling like pushing him away from her. Then Mike shook hands strongly with Joshua and moved on, taking his father by the arm and walking him slowly toward their Cadillac in the parking lot.

Harry Chandler went through the receiving line, smiled bravely at Diana, and held on to Joshua's hand after the handshake. He pulled Joshua aside, far enough away from the others to converse in confidence.

"It's all over," Harry said low.

"What do you mean?"

"The hearing with Transcon this Wednesday, and the potential disgorgement hearing."

Joshua nodded. "Great."

"I talked to Buck yesterday. Since he never made a ruling on the merits of whether George was knowingly involved in a fraud, and since he can't hold a disgorgement hearing with a dead man, the matter is moot. He's vacating the award of the contract to Avra Valley Concrete Company, and that's the end of it. George's personal estate won't be involved."

"What happens to the five million dollars?"

Harry shrugged. "Uncle Sam eats it."

Joshua nodded. "Then all I do is put the contract out for bids and start over?"

"You do whatever the Code of Federal Regulations and the OLM manual says. And by the way," Harry added in a confidential tone, "I'm the one who drafted George's will. Diana Thurber gets everything."

Joshua nodded and walked back to the receiving line.

▼▲▼

"You are one slick motherfucker, I give you that." Henry Jessup leered at him.

It was Monday afternoon. Jessup and Taft Greer sat in the straight oak chairs in Joshua's office at the BIA. Dan Swirling leaned against the doorjamb, his hands stuffed in his pants pockets.

"Yes, sir. I take my hat off to you," Jessup said. "You are the only motherfucker in this whole goddamn deal who comes out smelling like a rose. You get the farmer's daughter, the finest ranch in southern Arizona, five million bucks, and a shiny new silk tie."

Joshua involuntarily glanced down at his tie. It was one of George Callan's, out of George's bedroom closet that Diana had emptied last night, putting all the stuff in boxes. Except for a few ties that Joshua had admired. He looked hard at Henry Jessup and said nothing.

"I want that contract."

"You have a better chance than anyone else. I'm publishing the specs in the newspaper tomorrow. You already know precisely what's called for and how the others will probably bid."

"I don't think it's necessary for you to publish," Greer drawled, his voice deep and resonant in the small office. "Transcon ought to be entitled to the contract by default."

Joshua thumbed through a three-ring binder on his desk, found the correct page, turned the binder around, and pushed it toward Greer. "This is the Office of Land Management Policy Manual. It says I've got to republish. If you have a better idea, you've got to run it by the Director of the OLM in Washington."

Greer read the page slowly. "Or the Regional Director in Los Angeles?"

Joshua shrugged. "Him, too. If Melvin Scruggs gives me a directive, I follow it."

Greer nodded. "Okay. I'll have to get on my broom and go have a chat with Mel." He winked at Henry Jessup.

"Some smart motherfucker," Jessup said, walking out of the office.

Edgar came into Joshua's office a few minutes later. "What're them snakes smilin about so cheery?"

"I guess I charmed them."

Edgar snorted. "Yip. Do a little oboe serenade fer them crooks and hope they don't plant their fangs in yer eyeball." He breathed deeply and clenched his jaw. "Let's go get a drink. I need a drink."

Joshua looked at him in surprise. "Edgar! It's only eleven o'clock in the morning. And you're a Baptist or a Holy Roller or something. You're not supposed to be guzzlin booze." Joshua laughed.

Edgar looked back at him seriously, not letting himself be cajoled by the humor. "We'll take Chuy with us. I need a drink." He walked out of Joshua's office.

Chuy drove the Indian Police pickup with Joshua and Edgar next to him. Edgar was brooding darkly, and there was no conversation among them. Chuy parked in front of a small stucco building off the Nogales Highway. It had no sign on it. The stale smell of beer and piss and vomit exuded out the open door and intensified when they walked inside.

It was dark enough that the chipped Formica bar looked like well-worn wood from twenty feet away. A few Mexicans and Indians sat on stools, hunched over the bar. Two Indians played checkers at a small corner table. Several of the men had cigarettes in their mouths, and the smoke hung in the dank air like a cirrus cloud.

They sat down at a rickety round wooden table in the empty corner. *"Una botella de ron,"* Chuy called out, signaling with his hand to the bartender.

The fat man reached under the counter and pulled out a bottle of Bacardi light. He brought it to the table, carrying three glasses with his fingers clamped into the tops.

Joshua polished the rim of his glass with the tip of his tie. He held it up and inspected it.

"Don't worry," Chuy said. "Alcohol kills the germs."

Joshua rolled his eyes. Edgar poured himself a glassful and drank half of it. He belched and wiped his lips on his suit jacket sleeve. He drank the rest of it.

"Soon you'll be drinking with both hands," Joshua said.

Edgar sighed deeply and drank another half glass. He coughed and cleared his throat and spat a gob of phlegm on the dirt floor. "I want him dead," he muttered.

Joshua poured rum into his glass and swished it around. He studied the clear liquid. "Who's that?"

"Alfonso Calderon."

Joshua stared at Edgar, then looked over at Chuy and raised his eyebrows quizzically. Chuy stared back at him and shrugged slightly.

"You told me yer theory 'bout Calderon yester-day," Edgar said in a low voice. "Yer a hunnerd percent right. He murdered my Jimmy. I been thinkin hard on it."

Joshua and Chuy sat silently.

"I want him dead. I want to kill him myself. It's the only way I can do justice for Jimmy."

"How about extradition?" Joshua asked.

"Huh!" Edgar snorted. "You think them Meskins are gonna extradite the governor of Sonora? Shit! The only way is I gotta kill him my own self." He drank the rest of his second glass.

"Maybe you ought to lay off that stuff," Joshua said gently. "It'll give you a hell of a headache."

"I've already got a hell of a headache." Edgar sniffed and tears rolled down his cheeks. He poured another glassful of the rum and took a long swallow. He looked at Joshua. "You talk 'bout justice alla time, 'bout doin right and follerin yer conscience. I tell ya this is right. I gotta kill Calderon. An eye fer an eye." He nodded. "An eye fer an eye."

Joshua drank some rum. Chuy drank some rum. Joshua pushed back on the wooden chair and rocked slowly on its rear legs.

"How are we supposed to accomplish this?" Joshua said quietly. "The guy's surrounded by a private army." He stared hard at Edgar. "Provided, of course, that I think you make any sense at all."

Edgar stared back, emboldened by the rum, lisping slightly now. "My boy died instead of Adam. If he'd a killed Adam, you'd a been down there and back already with a bloody straight razor in yer pocket. I know you. Don't tell me it ain't so."

Joshua set the chair on all fours and sat rigidly.

He took a long drink from his glass. "I won't tell you it's not so," he said. "What I'm asking is how you think we can do it without getting killed ourselves?"

Edgar jutted his chin toward Chuy. "Tell him."

Chuy hunched over the table, speaking very low. The other two men brought their heads close to his.

"We can go down there through Poso Verde. It's a Papago village on the Mexican side of the border about fifteen, twenty miles from Newfield on the big Reservation. There's no border station there, just a barbed-wire fence. We'll cut it, go to Poso Verde. I have a cousin there. We'll drive down to Hermosillo on the back roads in his truck, Sonora plates. In Hermosillo we'll look for the governor. He's either there or in Guaymas. We'll be a formal delegation from the BIA/OLM, wanting to discuss the sewage project and the concrete problems with him. He'll meet with us. There'll be a couple of bodyguards around, but probably not even in the room with us. They won't be suspecting anything. Edgar'll kill him. We'll leave in our truck, staying off Highway 15 and coming back through Poso Verde. When they discover the murder, they won't be looking for a Mexican truck on the back roads, they'll be covering the border crossings, Nogales, Sasabe, Lochiel, Naco, Douglas. There won't be anybody at Poso Verde." Chuy stopped speaking and looked at the other two men. "Once we're back here we're okay."

"How come you're willing to get involved in this?" Joshua asked quietly, jutting his chin toward Chuy.

The Indian shrugged. "What are friends for? I don't think it can be done any other way than I planned it, and Edgar needs my help. And what he wants to do needs doing."

Joshua breathed deeply and nodded slowly. He thought for a moment and frowned. "How about us getting extradited to Mexico?" Joshua said. "Have you thought about that?"

Edgar dismissed the question with a wave of his hand. "Them Meskin officials ain't much bothered by political assassinations. It opens up new job opportunities for em. They'll be spendin all their time tryin to pick a successor. Anyways, there ain't been a extradition to Mexico that I can remember in fifty years."

Joshua took a long drink of rum. "You two guys been thinking about this for a while, huh?"

Both of them nodded.

"When?" Joshua asked.

"What's wrong with tomorrow?" Edgar said.

"I've got the Carillo trial."

"Then Thursday."

Joshua settled back in his chair. "Henry Jessup called me a smart motherfucker. He wouldn't think I was so smart if he saw me now."

"Yer the one always talkin 'bout doin right," Edgar said, "and how ya gotta take risks. What's righter than this?"

"What's riskier?"

"I dunno. I ain't thinkin about that. I'm thinkin about Jimmy and Adam." Edgar looked grimly at Joshua. "Whattaya say?"

Joshua stood up. "I've got to think about it. Let's get out of here."

Edgar dropped two dollar bills on the table and

drank the rest of the rum out of the bottle. They walked out of the bar.

▼▲▼

The courtroom was crowded. Chuy and his brother sat in the last row as inconspicuously as they could. They wore matching plaid cowboy shirts, identical to the one that Franklin Carillo was wearing. The defendant sat next to Joshua staring morosely ahead.

The jury was selected in an hour. Twelve men sat in the box, waiting for the trial to begin. Judge Velasco opened the file on the bench. "Show the continued trial of Franklin Carillo and the presence of both counsel and the defendant. The jury has been sworn. Proceed, Mr. Stevens."

Before Randy could call his first witness, Joshua stood up. "We invoke the rule, your honor."

"Very well," said the judge. "Randy, you have any witnesses in the courtroom?"

Stevens looked around. "Arlene O'Donnell and Dr. Wolfe."

"Bring them forward."

The girl and the coroner walked up to the judge's bench. The clerk of the court stood before them holding a Bible. "Raise your right hands, please. Do you swear to tell the truth, the whole truth, and nothing but the truth, so help you God?"

"I do," murmured the girl.

"Yes," said Dr. Wolfe.

The clerk sat down. Judge Velasco said, "You have been placed under the rule. This means that you may not remain in the courtroom until after you have testified. Until you testify, you must remain outside in the hallway, and you must not discuss your testimony with any persons except Mr. Stevens or Mr. Rabb. Is that clear?"

They both nodded.

"All right, please wait in the hallway."

They walked out of the courtroom.

"Deputy Simms," Judge Velasco said.

"Yes, sir." The bailiff stood up at his small table.

"Stand at the courtroom door. Question anyone who wishes to enter. Direct all witnesses to be seated in the hallway and not to discuss the case."

"Yes, your honor." Simms walked to the rear of the courtroom and stationed himself in front of the door.

The judge settled back in his chair and nodded at Stevens.

"State calls Arlene O'Donnell," Randy said.

A moment later she stood in the witness box and looked around anxiously.

"You can be seated, Miss O'Donnell," the judge said. "You've already been sworn."

She testified precisely as she had at the preliminary hearing. Carillo had picked her up hitchhiking near Ajo and Mission Roads. She wanted to go to the University, but he drove onto the bank of the Santa Cruz River. He raped her. He forced her to suck on him. He shot a big gun off by her ear. Then he drove her to the University and dropped her off. Randy Stevens sat down.

Joshua Rabb stood up slowly, with as much drama as he could muster. He wore a black wool suit and vest and black on black striped silk tie. The gold pocket watch, his grandfather's watch from Russia, was in his vest pocket, and the gold watch chain was hooked into the middle button of his vest. A twenty-two-karat gold coin from England and a fourteen-karat gold medallion in the form of some obscure Czarist Russian crest dangled from the end of the chain. He had scrubbed the stainless-steel prongs of his hand with a Brillo pad and Boraxo this morning. They sparkled under the bright courtroom lights.

Joshua cross-examined Arlene O'Donnell casually for several minutes, rehashing some innocuous elements of her testimony, putting her at ease. He strolled slowly back and forth in front of her by the jury box railing. His left foot had hurt like hell this morning, for some reason, so he was using a shiny new black-painted wooden cane.

Suddenly he wheeled toward her and jabbed at her with his steel hand. "You gave him your name and telephone number," he thundered.

She nodded, her mouth open in fright.

"The jury can't hear you, Miss O'Donnell," he chastised her.

"Yes." She began to cry.

"You told us that this vicious animal had just raped you and forced you to put your mouth on his penis."

She nodded.

"The jury can't hear you, Miss O'Donnell," he stormed.

"Yes," she murmured.

"*He* didn't ask you for your name and telephone number, did he, Miss O'Donnell? You *volunteered* it."

She sobbed louder.

"The gentlemen of the jury are waiting for your answer, Miss O'Donnell," Joshua said quietly. He sat down heavily, making a show of it, not waiting for her to answer him. She wept loudly at the witness stand.

You are a fucking prince, Joshua thought, staring straight ahead and keeping his face bland. You should win the Nobel Prize for fucking princes of the defense bar who can carve up innocent little girls with practiced poise and polish so that degenerate scumbags can go free. "You are a prince of the justice system, Mr. Joshua Rabb, attorney at law. We present you the Nobel fucking Prize, for you are among the biggest and bestest pieces of shit in the western world. We are proud to give you this symbol of your momentous achievement." And some old fart wearing a salt-and-pepper beard and a monocle on a gold chain hangs a ribbon around his neck with a gold medal that reads, *"For courageous service to justice by destroying the honest testimony of a thousand witnesses. Anno Domini 1946."*

He listened listlessly to the gruesome testimony of the coroner, letting the jurors see that it was unimportant to him, and when it was his turn to examine Dr. Wolfe, he had but one very carefully worded question: "Do you have any admissible evidence of any nature whatsoever that links Franklin Carillo to these tragic murders?"

"No, sir," Dr. Wolfe said. His eyes flickered and his cheeks became red, and Joshua could see him straining to keep from blurting out to the jury that the police had seized a .44 magnum Ruger, *Carillo's* Ruger, from his own bedroom closet, which was the murder weapon, but which had been ruled inadmissible by the judge.

"Thank you, doctor."

Dr. Wolfe walked out of the courtroom. Stevens called Wanda Tucker as his next witness. Before the bailiff could open the courtroom door to summon her, Joshua stood up and addressed the judge.

"Your honor, I have a motion to make outside the hearing of the jury."

"Well, approach the bench and tell me what's on your mind, Mr. Rabb."

Joshua and Randy walked to the side of the bench away from the jury. The judge hunched over it.

Joshua whispered, "I want to have two other Indians, approximately the same size and shape as Carillo, wearing the same shirts, sit at the defense table with Carillo when this woman is asked to identify the man she saw that night."

Randy was angry. He kept his voice low with difficulty. "This is circus crap, Judge! She's already identified him once before at the preliminary hearing."

"She identified the only man in jail clothes in the courtroom," Joshua whispered. "That hardly lends great credence to her testimony, your honor. This man is on trial for his life. Justice requires that the identification be free of taint or unduly suggestive conditions."

Velasco sighed deeply and settled back into his chair. He tapped his readers idly on the bench. "Those two Indians in the back with the matching shirts?"

"Yes, your honor," Joshua said.

Velasco pursed his lips and studied them. "Very well, seat them next to Franklin Carillo."

Randy winced and fixed the judge with an angry scowl.

"That's my ruling, Mr. Stevens," Judge Velasco said, his voice cold. "Proceed."

Joshua waved his arm toward Chuy and Solomon. They walked to the defense table and sat down beside Franklin Carillo. Several of the jurors stirred, looking uncomfortably at each other.

The elderly white-haired woman took the witness stand and testified that she had seen an Indian man around the laundry room at midnight, right about the time that Victoria and her four-week-old baby Alicia were kidnapped.

"Do you see that same man in the courtroom today, Mrs. Tucker?" Stevens asked.

She squinted toward the defense table. She opened her cloth purse and took out a pair of thick rimless spectacles. She squinted through them at the Indians.

"Well, there's three of them bucks there. How'm I supposed t' tell em apart?"

"Would you be able to see them more easily if you were closer to them?" Stevens asked.

"Well, yes, that might help some."

"Your honor?" Stevens looked at the judge.

Velasco nodded.

"All right, Mrs. Tucker," Randy said. "Please come down from the witness stand here in front of the defense table."

She walked up next to him and scrutinized each of the Indians.

"Just cain't rightly say," she mumbled, "I done

identified him onct. At that other court thing a
month or two back."

"Move to strike, your honor," Joshua said.

"Yes," Velasco said, sitting forward and looking
soberly at the jurors. "You are not to consider the
remark that Mrs. Tucker has just made. Anything
that may have happened outside of this courtroom
is not evidence that you may consider. Her statement is stricken." He turned to Stevens. "Curb Mrs.
Tucker's appetite for loose talk, sir."

"I apologize to the court. Mrs. Tucker, just answer yes or no: Do you see here the man you saw
that night?"

She shook her head slowly. "I think it's this one,"
she said, pointing at Franklin, "but I cain't say it's
not this one." She pointed at Chuy and shrugged.

"All right, Mrs. Tucker. You may resume your seat
at the witness stand," Stevens said.

"I have no questions, your honor," Joshua said,
standing up. "She needn't take the stand again if
Mr. Stevens is finished." You bet he's finished, he
thought. He sat down, and his left foot wasn't hurt-
ing any longer. Thank God almighty, I'm cured at
last! The Nobel fucking Prize for princes of justice
has cured my foot. I bet if I pull my shiny shoe
off right now I'll have four new toes. Hallelujah!
Hallelujah! Praise the Lord!

The state rested its case. Joshua rested the defense. The Fifth Amendment to the United States
Constitution prevented the prosecution from calling
Franklin Carillo as a witness. And Joshua did not
call the alibi witness, Mrs. Bojorquez. There was a
limit to what even a Nobel fucking Prize prince of
justice could do on behalf of a guilty client. He

looked back at Erma Carillo and smiled. She stared at him with naked hatred.

Stevens delivered a slam-bang closing argument, summoning up all of the fury of the community at the shocking nature of the crimes that Franklin Carillo had committed. "Animals like this cannot be freed simply because the state doesn't have a photograph of him pulling the trigger."

Joshua stood up and limped toward the jury box, supporting himself with the cane. Just like Lionel Barrymore would do it, he thought. Or better yet, Clarence Darrow, standing before the jurors in Tennessee, defending a sad little schoolteacher who had told his students that they were just a bunch of monkeys. He'd fixed those jurors with a stare, hooked his thumbs in his suspenders, and mesmerized them. Come to think of it, they had promptly convicted the hapless teacher.

"Gentlemen of the jury," Joshua said, his voice deep and reverent, "it is my opportunity at this time to ask you to fulfill one of the great privileges of free men in a free land. You and only you will decide the fate of this poor Indian boy accused of heinous crimes." He paused. He looked sadly at Franklin Carillo. He looked earnestly into the troubled faces of the jurors.

Not only the Nobel Prize. We're talking Academy fucking Award! Cheers from the movie stars sitting around the tables. He takes the Oscar tenderly in hands, looks tearfully out at the clapping celebrities, and thanks them humbly for the honor of which he is so undeserving.

"I always wear black on days like this," Joshua said, "when a poor man is seated before his peers and relies on their collective conscience as his only protection from his own death. Days like these are terrible days, burdensome days, days we would all like to skip." Joshua's voice was tender and resonant. "Frank would like to skip it, too. He'd much rather be somewhere else." Joshua's voice got lighter, a friend confiding in other friends. "I'm reminded of something that W. C. Fields said. He said he always hated Philadelphia. It's a terribly boring city. He spent a week there one night." Joshua chuckled. The faces of the jurors loosened up just a little. Two of them cracked smiles, three, four. "But he said that the most fitting thing he could think of to put on his tombstone would be, 'On the whole, I'd rather be in Philadelphia.'" Joshua laughed, fully their friend now, shootin the shit over the back fence with the neighbors. All of the jurors smiled. Their shoulders relaxed. They looked back at him with respectful eyes, willing to be his friends.

"I'm sure that Frank would much rather be in Philadelphia than sitting here under the shadow of his own tombstone."

Several of the jurors glanced sympathetically at Carillo. There was no evidence that he had had anything to do with the tragic murders of the mother and her baby. And as to the college girl, well, a girl doesn't give her phone number to a rapist.

I got them, Joshua thought. They're hooked. Now I reel them in.

▼▲▼

Joshua and Diana sat on the sofa, drinking margaritas. They looked lazily through the sliding-glass living room door. The setting sun cast fuchsia and lavender shadows on the pasture and the grazing horses. It was the perfect setting for a painting by Gainsborough of the English countryside or a farm in southern France by Corot. But the paradise was here, now, and Joshua was adrift on its beauty and serenity.

Adam was at the stables behind the corral, currying Golden Boy. Hanna sat in the armchair beside the couch.

"You've got to be kidding," she said, her eyes wide with distress. "They acquitted him?"

Joshua nodded.

"Of *everything*?"

He nodded again and sipped his drink.

"How could you be a part of that, Dad? It's a criminal act."

"No it isn't, honey." Joshua shook his head and spoke softly to his daughter. "It's the highest achievement of our American civilization, that the vast and overwhelming power of the state cannot crush the life out of even one tiny little powerless human being without presenting real evidence that proves, beyond a reasonable doubt to a moral certainty, that he deserves to be crushed. Today the state couldn't do that. The jurors did the only thing they could honorably do."

"God, Dad, what bullshit. Franklin Carillo raped and murdered an innocent woman and raped and murdered her *four-week-old baby*. And he *admitted* it to you."

"Honey, I keep telling you it isn't ladylike to use words like that."

"Which word, Daddy? Was it bullshit, or rape, or murder, or admitted?"

He sipped his drink. "I know that it's awfully hard to understand. It's even hard for me to keep it in perspective sometimes. But it's the best justice system that has evolved from many centuries of experimenting by the greatest minds of all the civilizations of western man."

"You mean like Hitler. Like how the Germans evolved over many centuries to go from human beings to man-eating animals?"

"That was a system gone awry," Joshua said.

"Maybe our justice system has gone awry."

He fixed her with a sarcastic look. "Do you have a better idea?"

She shrugged. "I think you should just shoot him."

He raised his eyebrows. "That's your idea of justice?"

"Well, why not? He confessed horrible crimes to you that carry the death penalty. Why shouldn't you be the agent of justice and execute him? Would it be any different than the Nazis you killed in the war?"

He looked at her soberly, and he had no retort.

She was annoyed by his obstinacy. "Would that be more wrong than what happened today?" she said. "Letting a murderer like that go free can't prove the high quality of our legal system. Only punishing a dangerous criminal can do that." She looked crossly at her father.

"Okay, you two," Diana soothed, defusing the confrontation. "Let's talk about the weather or something."

▼▲▼

Hanna and Adam went crabbily to bed at ten o'clock. Now that they lived so far out of Tucson, they had to get up a half hour earlier on school mornings so that Joshua could drop them off on the way to the BIA. Hanna had shot petulant glances at her father all evening, bringing up time and again the injustice of letting Franklin Carillo go free. Finally, in frustration, Joshua reminded her that it was not he, but a jury of twelve other men, who had acquitted Carillo.

"And I guess you had nothing to do with that, huh, Dad?" she said innocently.

"I just did my job."

"Then why were you all dressed up like you never usually dress, all in black with your big gold watch and chain? You looked like you were trying to make them think you were Abraham Lincoln, Old Honest Abe, 'Take my word on it, gentlemen of the jury, butter wouldn't melt in my mouth.' "

"Bedtime," Joshua announced.

"Yeah, that's the only way you'll win this argument, huh, Dad?"

He frowned at her, and she and Adam traipsed sulkily to their bedrooms.

Joshua exhaled with feigned exhaustion and let his shoulders sag. "Whew, she's a pistol."

Diana nodded and smiled. "She's special, Joshua, very special. Both of them are. You're a lucky man."

He smiled back at her and nodded. The radio was on, and Joshua focused on the music. It was from the Algonquin Hotel in New York City, some big band playing some swing music he didn't recognize.

A few minutes later, Diana moved over on the couch and rested her head on his shoulder.

"I bet you're exhausted," she said.

He nodded. She reached across him and switched off the lamp. She ran her hand down his polo shirt to his gym shorts. He had no underwear on, and she put her hand under the lax elastic band and held him. "Not too tired, though, huh?" she said gutturally.

"Never," he whispered. "Oh, I forgot to tell you, I'm going to Los Angeles for a couple of days. Edgar and I have to go to the Regional OLM and check on the sewage project contract. Transcon's all over me to award it to them, and I got a call this afternoon from Mel Scruggs. He wants to talk about it."

"When will you be back?" Her lips were on him, her tongue flicking the soft underside.

He groaned and sucked in his breath. "Thursday night or Friday morning," he gasped. "We're taking the train. Oooooh."

He jerked and held his breath to stifle his groans. His body slowly relaxed.

"I just wanted to make sure you remember me when you're gone," she whispered.

"I love you."

"I love you, too."

They kissed, and then they walked hand in hand to his bedroom in the guest quarters.

CHAPTER
TWENTY-ONE

"Are you out of your mind?" Joshua said, his eyes flashing at Edgar.

It was just getting light, a little after seven Thursday morning. He was standing with Edgar in front of the BIA as Chuy drove up in the blue pickup. Magdalena was beside him on the seat.

"It's the only way," Edgar said. "A couple of Mexican peons driving in the truck are a lot better than Chuy alone or the three of us. You and me are gonna ride on a mattress in the bed a the truck, under a tarp."

"But it's too dangerous for Magdalena. I won't let her come."

"It's not yer call. It's hers. She's full growed and plenny smart enough to decide fer herself. And it's the best chance we got of gettin back alive."

Magdalena walked up to Joshua. "I want to do this. I'll drive in Hermosillo and in Guaymas, if we have to go there. We can get away much faster and better than if you have to park the truck somewhere."

"This is too damn dangerous, Magdalena. I can't let you do this."

"I *want* to do it. I *need* to do it. Calderon can't

get away with what he's done. And you have been
my friend when I've needed you. Now it's my turn."
Her eyes flickered with the memory of Joshua driving her to the *Clinica de las Mujeres* in Nogales.

Joshua was disarmed by the intensity in her eyes.
He nodded his head reluctantly. "Okay. Have you
said anything about this to Hanna or Adam or anyone else?"

She shook her head resolutely.

"Let's go," he said. He walked to the rear of the
truck bed and climbed into it. Edgar followed him.
They were both dressed in business suits and shirts
and ties, to pull off their "official visit" to the Governor of Sonora. The mattress and tarp were clean,
and they settled under the tarp. It was a forty-degree
morning, and the warmth under the canvas felt
good.

They changed trucks in Poso Verde with Chuy's
cousin, a sheep rancher. The truck he lent them
was larger and more powerful. It was a three-and-
a-half-ton Ford stake truck, and it had hauled everything at one time or another. They had to hose out
the bed and let the wood planks dry a little before
putting the mattress down. In this deserted back-
country of Sonora, they rode most of the six hours
to Hermosillo sitting up and uncovered. Twenty
miles outside of the Sonoran capital, Joshua and
Edgar pulled the tarp over themselves. Magdalena
took the wheel from Chuy.

It was a cool, humid day. A thick overcast hung
close to the earth. It began to drizzle. Magdalena
pulled into the parking lot next to the State Building. It was after three o'clock, siesta time, and there
were few cars there. Chuy removed the rear stake

panel and set it against the floor of the bed as a ladder to the ground. Edgar and Joshua climbed down. It began to rain harder. The three men ran into the government building. Chuy had changed into his newest police uniform shirt, and he spoke to the young receptionist in fluent Spanish. She sat behind a drop-front maplewood desk and batted her eyelashes at him. Joshua and Edgar stood a short distance away.

She made a call on the telephone. Chuy came over to Joshua. "He's here, in the living quarters. She's calling his secretary."

They stood there a moment. Down the stairs came the young man whom Joshua had seen at the same drop-front desk when he had come here last month. The young man walked toward Joshua and smiled. "The governor will see you gentlemen, of course. You're Mr. Rabb?"

Joshua nodded.

"Yes, yes, I remember. Some weeks ago, wasn't it? Please follow me." He walked up the stairs.

Joshua and Edgar and Chuy walked behind him. They followed him down the left corridor on the second landing. It had a maroon deep-pile carpet. The walls were Louis XIV carved wood, painted baby blue. Several antique chairs lined the corridor, but no one was sitting in them. The young man opened one of the baroquely carved double doors at the end of the corridor and stood aside for the three men to enter. He closed the door behind them.

It was an enormous sitting room, all in the same Louis XIV decor. The floor was covered with what appeared to Joshua to be genuine Persian carpets. There were several sofas and low tables and a dozen

chairs, upholstered in silk chinoiserie. The tables
had gilded curved legs. The wooden walls were high,
painted pale rose, and the top frieze was gilded. It
was the most opulent room that Joshua had ever
seen.

Governor Calderon came toward Joshua, all
smiles, holding out his hand. Another man stood
next to a table filled with liquor bottles, behind a
long sofa. He wore servant's clothes from Napole-
onic times, a gold vest, black velvet knee britches,
white stockings, and patent-leather pumps with silk
bows. Chuy went directly toward him.

"How delightful to see you, Joshua. Terrible about
George's death. When I heard about it, I was shattered." The governor was dressed in a brocaded
black smoking jacket and tuxedo trousers with a
stripe down the side.

Joshua swiftly gripped the governor's outstretched
arm at the wrist, between the prongs of his steel
hand. Calderon instantly stopped; his eyes bulged
open, and his tongue stuck out of his mouth. Joshua
lifted his arm higher, and the governor stood breathlessly on tiptoes trying to relieve the pain.

In the same instant, Chuy pulled a hunting knife
out of the sheath under his shirt at the small of his
back and pressed the tip of the blade into the side
of the servant's neck. A trickle of blood dripped onto
his gold vest. Chuy reached around the man's back,
took an automatic pistol out of the man's shoulder
holster under the vest, and pushed it into the waist-
band of his Levis.

Edgar stepped in front of the governor. He pulled
a straight razor out of his pocket and flicked it open.

Joshua pushed Calderon back slowly to a sofa and

released his steel prongs. Calderon flopped back onto the sofa and sat bug-eyed, rubbing his wrist, looking fearfully from Joshua to Edgar.

"I didn't kill George Callan, I swear it. It wasn't me. He was like my brother."

"Fuck George Callan," Edgar snarled. "This is for my boy Jimmy." Edgar stepped close in front of him and raised the straight razor.

"No, no, no, no, no! I didn't do it," Calderon blurted out. He raised both arms and crossed them over his face and neck as a shield. "It was Arthur O'Leary and his son Michael."

Joshua and Edgar looked at each other. Edgar held the straight razor close toward Calderon.

"What kind of bullshit is this?" Joshua said.

"No, no, no, I swear on the Holy Virgin, I had nothing to do with it." He kept his arms over his face.

"You were George's partner in the concrete deal."

"No, no, no, no, no! I had nothing to do with it."

"It was your plant in Guaymas that turned out the concrete," Joshua persisted, his voice rough.

Calderon slowly lowered his arms slightly and peered up at the two men in front of him. "You must listen to me," he pleaded. "I have never owned a concrete plant in Guaymas or anywhere else. My family has raised cattle for over three hundred years. Whoever told you this was lying."

"George Callan told me," Joshua growled. "He told me he transferred all of his equipment from Avra Valley to your plant."

Calderon shook his head vigorously. "It's just not so," he whined. "I swear it. Young Michael O'Leary had the idea to supply concrete from a plant here in Sonora. His father Arthur and George went along with it. George used his Avra Valley plant as a front. They put all of the equipment in Imuris, a village in the Pinito Mountains about fifty miles south of Nogales. The Magdalena River runs through there, there's plenty of sand, and there's a huge abandoned shed where the *Ferrocarril Sudpacifico* used to repair railway cars. That's where they put the plant." He lowered his arms to his lap.

Joshua stared at Edgar. Edgar nodded. "Yeah, that's the little town were ever'body lives in abandoned boxcars on the spur track up on the hill by the highway."

"That's right, that's right," Calderon said eagerly.

"Then why did Callan get killed?" Joshua asked, looking viciously at the governor.

"He thought they were really putting out Type 5 cement. They'd already gotten five million dollars, George got a million of it, the O'Learys got three—" He stopped short and gulped.

"And you got a million?" Joshua said.

"This is Mexico," Calderon whined. "I'm the Governor of Sonora. This is how we do it."

"So George was about to be the fall guy in Jessup's lawsuit, and he wanted the money back from the O'Learys so he wouldn't lose everything when the judge terminated his contract and ordered him to return the five million dollars?"

Calderon nodded.

Joshua straightened up and stood back.

"But you still ain't said nothin about my boy," Edgar snarled, raising his straight razor threateningly.

Calderon immediately raised his arms again as a shield. "I never even heard about it until afterward," he wailed. "I didn't have anything to do with such a thing. My people wouldn't go into the United States. They have no protection there."

Edgar straightened up slowly. He gritted his teeth and looked grimly at Joshua.

"How d' we know if he's tellin the truth?"

Joshua shook his head. He breathed deeply. "I don't know anything anymore."

"You'll go to Imuris. You'll see the plant," the governor pleaded. "You'll see, you'll see." He lowered his arms cautiously, studying the men in front of him.

"Yeah, we'll be dead before we leave this building," Edgar said hoarsely.

Joshua nodded.

"No, no, no! I'll come with you. We'll go to Imuris. Then you leave me at the border in Nogales."

Edgar looked at Joshua. Joshua shrugged. "Might work," he said. "Is he your bodyguard?" Joshua glanced at the liveried servant standing stiffly next to Chuy, the knife blade pressed to his throat.

The governor nodded.

"We'll take him, too," Joshua said. "Is there a back way out of here?"

"Yes. Through there, it's my sleeping quarters. There's a stairway down the back of the building."

"What's back there?"

"A small street."

Joshua quickly gripped the governor's wrist again in his steel prongs. Calderon gasped. Joshua pulled and Calderon scrambled up from the sofa, trying to keep his arm steady.

"If you make just one funny move or sound, I'll

rip your hand off," Joshua said evenly and looked the governor in the eye.

Calderon nodded, his eyes twitching in terror.

It was pouring outside. Edgar jogged to the parking lot on the other side of the building and came back in the truck a few minutes later. Magdalena looked frightened. Joshua released Calderon's wrist and pushed him up into the bed of the truck, following him. Edgar and the bodyguard climbed in after them. They lay down on the mattress under the tarp. Chuy replaced the truck gate and got into the cab with Magdalena.

They drove uneventfully up Highway 15. At times the downpour was so heavy that Magdalena could hardly see the road. She slowed to a crawl, straining to see ahead of her. At one o'clock in the morning, she finally pulled off the highway onto the muddy track leading into Imuris. It was raining even harder here in the mountains. She drove jerkily toward the huge shed by the engorged Magdalena River and parked.

The men climbed down from the bed of the truck, stiff, soaked, exhausted. Edgar took a flashlight out of the glove compartment. They walked into the shed. It was filled with piles of sand, pea gravel, larger aggregate, four huge kilns for making cement, great mounds of limestone and shale and steel plate, and a conveyor belt reaching out the back of the building toward the river. Several concrete mixer trucks were parked on the far side by the lift-up doors.

"What d' we do?" Edgar said glumly.

"I can't drive anymore," Magdalena said. "I need some sleep."

"We'd better stay here tonight," Joshua said.

"Chuy and I will take turns sleeping and watching these guys."

There was no further discussion. Everyone was too exhausted. Edgar brought the tarp in from the truck. He and Magdalena lay down on it. The governor and his bodyguard lay down on the bare ground. Joshua and Chuy sat down against the shed wall.

"Me first," Chuy said. "You sleep. I'll wake you up at four."

Joshua nodded. He slid down, folded his good arm under his head, and fell quickly asleep.

▼▲▼

They reached the Nogales border station at eight o'clock in the morning. The Mexican inspector stood at attention, his eyes bulging, as Governor Calderon barked at him to let them pass. Magdalena drove the truck up to the American Customs Inspection booth. The inspector came out as the men climbed out of the truck. Chuy ejected the clip on the ground and handed the automatic pistol to the bodyguard. The governor and his bodyguard walked quickly back into Mexico. The inspector watched the transaction with a queer look on his face. He walked up to Joshua.

"That guy that looked like a doused rat is the Governor of Sonora." He looked closely at Joshua.

" 'Zat right?" Joshua said.

The inspector looked from Joshua to Edgar to Magdalena to Chuy. He read the patch on Chuy's sleeve.

"What the fuck's going on?" he asked Chuy.

Chuy shrugged.

The inspector once again slowly appraised them all. Then he shrugged and shook his head and walked into his booth.

An hour and fifteen minutes later they arrived at the BIA and parked.

"Let's go to Benson and talk to Arthur and Mike," Edgar said.

Joshua nodded.

"I'll take the truck back to Poso Verde and get the pickup," Magdalena said.

The men got into Joshua's convertible. It was an hour drive to Benson. Edgar pointed to a dirt road turnoff. "That's Art's place," he said.

Joshua drove down the dirt road. Dust billowed behind the car. It hadn't rained here, and the morning was bright and sunny and warm. They neared the large ranch house, nestled in front of a low rocky hill. The place appeared to be deserted. Joshua drove past the house to a stable. A workman was forking hay into a wheelbarrow. Joshua stopped the car and turned off the engine. The workman turned around, startled, and watched the three men walk toward him. His eyes narrowed as he recognized Joshua.

He was the Mexican in the black car, the one who had offered to help fix the flat tire. Joshua was ten feet from him, walking steadily toward him. The Mexican aimed the pitchfork at him and hurled it like a spear. Joshua leapt aside, but one prong of it caught his suit coat sleeve and tore it open. The Mexican pulled a switchblade out of his back pocket, the blade flashed open, and the man jumped toward Joshua.

Joshua smashed straight forward with his mechanical arm. The knife slashed through Joshua's jacket and glanced off his aluminum arm. The prongs of the steel hand caught the man's throat and crushed his Adam's apple. He collapsed to the ground, clutching his throat, trying to breathe.

The three men stood there watching him writhe.

"I reckon that's the guy who done it, huh?" Edgar looked at Joshua.

Joshua nodded. "He wanted to help me fix a flat out on the Nogales Highway. Just like he helped Chet Milliken. I'd bet he put the locoweed in the hay and delivered George Callan in the crate."

Edgar nodded grimly.

"I guess I could give him a tracheotomy," Joshua said. "I learned some first aid in the army."

"Shit," Edgar muttered. He hawked up a wad of phlegm and spat it in the dying man's purpling face.

The three men walked to the ranch house. The front door was locked. Chuy kicked it until the jamb splintered and the door burst open. They searched every room. There was no one in the house. They walked back to the yellow Chevy convertible. The Mexican had stopped moving. His eyes bulged almost out of the sockets, and his tongue was black and hugely swollen and stuck three inches out of his mouth.

"Reckon we'll look fer Art 'n Mike some other time, huh?" Edgar said. "I'm a little tired."

Joshua nodded. He and Chuy lowered the convertible top. They drove back to the BIA.

▼▲▼

Joshua was exhausted. He parked by the red Cadillac at eleven o'clock in the morning. Several other cars and trucks were parked there. A half dozen hands were cleaning out the huge corral. He never ceased to marvel at the rich activity on this marvelous ranch. Diana's ranch. His ranch.

He unlocked the front door and went inside. No one was around. The kids were at school. Diana must be in Tucson shopping. He went into the kitchen for something to eat.

There was a loud groan, like a smothered scream. He turned and listened. He heard it again. It was coming from one of the bedrooms. He ran toward them. Diana's bedroom door was shut. He opened the door and ran inside the darkened room. A naked man was on top of her, raping her. The man jerked his head around. It was Michael O'Leary.

Joshua grabbed a fistful of his long yellow hair and pulled him off of Diana. He threw O'Leary on the floor and kicked him in the chest. O'Leary rolled away and leapt up, as agile as a cougar. He came toward Joshua. Joshua kicked him in the groin as hard as he could. O'Leary doubled over. Joshua smashed a right uppercut directly up into the man's nose and O'Leary sprawled on his back unconscious, his nose broken and bleeding profusely.

"Oh, thank God, thank God you came," Diana sobbed. She huddled on the bed, holding her arms around her legs.

Joshua walked over to her to comfort her. Then he froze. Suddenly he knew. He simply knew. He stood by the bed watching her. He began to feel nauseous, and a dreadful realization thudded in his brain.

She slowly stopped sobbing and peeked at him. She read his look and began to whimper. "You don't think that I—" gasp. "You don't believe—" sob. "I love you, Joshua." Earnest sad brown eyes.

"What an asshole," Joshua murmured. "How can anybody be as big an asshole as me?" He stared at her. "You suckered me the whole time, right from the beginning."

She got on her knees and reached for him. "Joshua, I did it for you. I love you. Uncle George got scared. He thought they were going to force him to pay back the whole five million dollars. He couldn't get it back from Alfonso or Art O'Leary. He was going to sell the ranch. *Our ranch,* Joshua. Our ranch. I couldn't let that happen."

"So you got Mike to have the Mexican kill him."

She settled back on her haunches and looked at him seductively. "For you and me, Joshua," she whispered. "For us." She held out her arms for him.

"God, you are gorgeous," he muttered.

Mike O'Leary groaned and began to move on the floor. Joshua walked over to him and kicked him hard in the jaw. O'Leary rolled over on his side and his arms splayed out. Blood bubbled from his mouth.

Joshua walked into the living room and called the FBI office. He went into his room, took a quick hot shower, dressed in Levis and a cowboy shirt and loafers, and waited for Roy Collins.

▼▲▼

"I'll book him for criminal fraud on a federal contract and murder," Collins said. "But first, I guess I better take him by the emergency room over at St. Mary's Hospital. There aren't any medical facilities up at the Mount Lemmon Detention Center."

He helped the handcuffed man into the back seat of the gray Ford.

"Yes, I think there are. They use the nurse over at the Ranger Station." Joshua thought a moment. "Then again, there might not be a nurse up there right now."

"You all right?" Collins said.

"Right as rain." Joshua frowned and walked into the house.

Diana was wearing a bathrobe, sitting on the sofa in the living room. She had a half full tumbler in her hand and a bottle of tequila on the table beside her. "What's going to happen to me?" she wailed.

Joshua went into his room and packed his clothes in a valise. He put it by the front door. He took two more valises into Hanna's and Adam's rooms and packed their belongings.

"You can't leave me like this," Diana howled from the living room.

Joshua loaded the valises into the back seat of the car. Alfredo, the ranch hand who had delivered the horses to Adam and Jimmy, walked up to Joshua.

"What's goin on, Mr. Rabb?"

Other hands were standing still and watching.

"I'm moving back to the BIA, Alfredo. Can you bring Golden Boy over there to the shed you built?"

"Sure, Mr. Rabb. Right now you want him?"

Joshua nodded. He got in the car and drove away.

Later that day, he picked Hanna up at Tucson High as she came out of her last class at four o'clock. They drove to Sunnyside and picked up Adam fifteen minutes later. By the time they got home, Golden Boy was stolidly munching hay in his shed.

CHAPTER
TWENTY-TWO

The winter sun in Tucson has the wonderful capacity to bring great warmth to the earth. The sun shines like this in Brooklyn sometimes in the winter, Joshua thought, but you can still freeze your balls off. That's the difference between Tucson and Brooklyn. Well, there are plenty of other differences, too. He sat on the porch steps on Friday morning and stared toward the mission. The domes glowed in the sunlight. Several quail swooped up from beneath a creosote bush and flapped across the irrigation ditch. They landed in the front yard and began pecking at seeds visible only to them. It had been cold last night, twenty-five degrees, and the last of the honeysuckle stalks beside the porch steps lay prostrate on the thawing ground.

It was almost eight-thirty, and the Mission bell began ringing, summoning the worshippers to mass. Several black-clad Papago women and a few old men walked to the church. Joshua walked to his car and drove downtown to the courthouse.

Hubie Hoskins was already there, sitting handcuffed at the defense table in Judge Velasco's courtroom. From behind he looked like Adam, except

Adam's hair was darker. Joshua felt hollow and weak.

Hubie had a fresh scab by the side of his mouth and a black eye on the same side. His father stood behind the railing, talking to him about the crops, and how hard it was plowing the field without his help.

Joshua sat down beside the boy. "How are you, Hubie?"

His freckled cheeks wrinkled up in a pained look. "Am I gettin out today, mister?"

Joshua shook his head. "I don't think so. I think you're going to have to spend some time in Florence at the prison. But it's better up there. You'll have a lot of freedom. You can do farm work during the day and they have basketball courts and baseball fields." It was true, but it sounded a great deal better than it really was.

"Will there be those kind of guys up there, mister, you know, like down here?"

Joshua swallowed. "Yes, there will. But maybe you'll be able to make friends with some good guys, and you can all protect each other." Bullshit, Joshua thought, pure bullshit. You're going to be like a rag doll with a pack of dogs. He began to feel sick. Tears pressed against his eyelids and he tried to blink them away.

Charlie Weston wheeled into the courtroom. He said a cheery hello to Joshua. Joshua nodded to him. The bailiff and the court reporter came in, followed by Judge Velasco. He sat down at the bench and opened the file on it.

"This is the adjudication hearing on the revocation petition in the matter of Hubert Billy Hoskins. Mr. Rabb, you're representing Mr. Hoskins?"

"Yes, your honor."

"What is your response to the petition?"

"Not responsible by reason of mental incompetency, your honor."

Velasco sighed and grimaced. "I'd like to help Mr. Hoskins out, counselor, but that's an improper plea under Arizona law in a revocation proceeding. Did he set fire to the ostrich or not?"

"He performed that physical act without any requisite mental state of criminality, your honor."

Velasco nodded. "What do you think I should do, Mr. Rabb? Should I ignore the problem and let him go? And next time he throws matches around and burns down somebody's house—maybe with somebody in it—it will be my fault. Will I have performed my obligation to this community, Mr. Rabb?"

"The boy needs treatment, your honor. I would ask the court to put him into an institution that is equipped to handle these problems."

"And who will pay, Mr. Rabb? I don't have the authority to order the state or Pima County to pay these charges out of public funds. I simply lack that power, Mr. Rabb."

Joshua said nothing. He stared glumly ahead of him. Isaac Hoskins was crying behind him.

"I can't put him in the Arizona State Hospital, Mr. Rabb. There's insufficient supervision there. He would be in danger. So there's only one choice I have, and it's a terribly unpleasant one for me. But it is the law, and I am bound to follow it, Mr. Rabb, as are you. I am revoking probation and ordering that Hubert Billy Hoskins be remanded to the custody of the warden of Arizona State Prison for three years eleven months and six days, the remainder of his prior sentence." He banged his gavel and walked off the bench.

Two sheriff's deputies who had been sitting quietly in the jury box led Hubie out of the courtroom. Isaac Hoskins trudged slowly out the door.

"Haven't seen you over at Danny's Billiard Parlor," Charlie Weston called back, wheeling his chair toward the door.

Tears were spilling down Joshua's face, and he had no voice. He didn't answer. He rubbed his eyes hard with his fist, and then he just sat there, staring torpidly into space.

Bernie Velasco came walking into the courtroom. He had taken off his black robe and had on a tan suit. He sat down on the chair next to Joshua. "Shit deal, huh?"

Joshua nodded.

"You want to hear the punch line?"

Joshua looked at him.

"Buck Buchanan just called me. Mike O'Leary made his bail this morning. Two million dollars cash posted in overflowing cardboard boxes. Brought in by his father Art."

Joshua breathed deeply. "Frank Carillo gets acquitted. Mike O'Leary walks free, like an Oriental potentate. He'll probably never do another day in jail. And Hubie Hoskins gets four years in the joint." He looked searchingly at the judge. "Is this really happening?"

Velasco shook his head grimly. "Is there a place where they do this better?"

"Maybe ancient Athens," Joshua said. "Maybe the real fathers of democracy did it right."

"You mean those guys who forced Socrates to drink hemlock?"

Joshua shrugged his sagging shoulders. "I guess nobody gets it right all the time. Maybe they just had a better average than we do."

They got up and walked slowly out of the courtroom.

The following is an excerpt from *Nothing but the Truth*, Richard Parrish's forthcoming sequel to *Versions of the Truth*, to be published by Dutton in January, 1995.

Joshua Rabb slouched in the slightly lopsided swivel chair behind his desk. It was ten o'clock in the morning, and a lawyer from Brooklyn named Moses Petrovich had called just an hour ago, asking for an appointment for himself and a friend, a businessman who needed some advice. The two men sat now in the straight wooden chairs in front of Joshua's desk. Moses was quite large, the other short and thin.

"I don't quite understand," Joshua said, looking from the big man to the small one.

"It's not so hard to understand. How's a New York City lawyer named Moses Petrovich going to fare in Tucson, Mr. Rabb?" the big man asked.

Joshua shrugged. "They won't elect you mayor, but you won't go to jail for it. Joshua Rabb isn't much of an improvement."

All three men laughed easily. "Well, Mr. Rabb, your modesty is laudable," said the big man. "But we're from the city, and we like to deal with *landsmen*, and you're the only Jewish lawyer in Tucson. We did some checking, and we're sure you can do a fine job."

"I appreciate the vote of confidence, Mr. Petrovich—"

"Moish, please, just call me Moish."

"Okay," Joshua smiled pleasantly. He was right. A guy called Moish didn't have a chance in Tucson. "So what can I do for you."

"Mr. Lansky has been my friend and client for years, and he finds himself in a bit of a problem with the federal government."

Meyer Lansky nodded his head and spread his arms, splaying his fingers, showing at once his innocence and helplessness.

"A friend of his, Benny Siegel, just built a hotel in Las Vegas," Petrovich said, studying Joshua's face for a sign of recognition. "The Flamingo Hotel."

Joshua nodded. "I've read about Mr. Siegel and the Flamingo Hotel. Supposed to be the nicest one in Las Vegas. The big contractor in Phoenix built it. What's his name, Ward, Warren?"

"Webb," offered Meyer Lansky. "Del Webb." Lansky was small, short and slender, and meticulously dressed in a dull gray sharkskin suit, starched white shirt, gray wool tie, and simple black wing-tipped shoes. By contrast, Petrovich was wearing a flowered Hawaiian-type beach shirt and bright yellow pants and white suede sandals over white silk socks. Both men were in their forties.

"Right," Petrovich said. "Del Webb built it and Mr. Siegel and his partners got their financing from the Valley National Bank in Phoenix."

"Are you one of the partners?" Joshua asked. He was concentrating hard, trying quickly to put together the threads of information about the infamous Bugsy Siegel. You couldn't read the newspapers without occasionally seeing stories about the Flamingo. It was famous, reported to have cost between three and six million dollars to build, at least three times more than any other casino in Las Vegas, and also reported to be almost bankrupt.

"Me? No. But the FBI thinks that Mr. Lansky is."

"Why is the FBI interested?"

"Mr. Lansky has interests in some clubs across the line from New York City and Miami and some other places that entertain gamblers. The papers like to call them 'carpet joints'?"

Mention of "carpet joints" suddenly jogged Joshua's memory of the newspaper and magazine articles he had read about Lansky. "But gambling is legal in Las Vegas, I thought."

"Right again. But anytime Mr. Lansky's name turns up, the FBI develops an interest. In this case, they think he helped provide certain restricted materials during construction."

"Like what?"

"Well, a few tons more structural steel than was authorized in the quota that Mr. Siegel was given, some decorative marble they say came from Italy. A few other things."

"I'm still not following. If Mr. Lansky isn't a partner

and didn't supply these materials, how can we have any exposure?"

"Well," Petrovich said, "if he isn't and if he didn't, he won't." He smiled affably.

Joshua nodded. "Okay, so maybe he is and maybe he did, so what exactly is the problem?" He looked directly at Meyer Lansky.

"The problem is I need *tzuris* [trouble] with the FBI like I need another *tuchus*," Lansky said. "Benny's in way over his head and I got serious men looking for assurances from me about the safety of their investment. *Goyim*, not *landsmen* like us. They have no *hertzen*." He patted his heart. "If the FBI gets into this, it's just one more knife in my guts."

Joshua nodded. Now he had made the full connection between Siegel and Lansky. He remembered reading several articles in the *New York Times* ten, twelve years ago. Lansky and Siegel had been partners with New York's most famous mobster, Charlie "Lucky" Luciano until Luciano was sent to prison in 1936 or 1937.

Joshua sat back in his chair, wary and suspicious. "Well, what can I do? Have you been charged? Is an investigation going on?"

Moses Petrovich took a sheet of paper out of his briefcase and slid it across the desk. Joshua picked it up. "But this is a subpoena duces tecum to a grand jury in Nevada," he said, "for Benjamin Siegel's construction records, not for Meyer Lansky."

"It's only a matter of time if they get Benny's records that they come after Mr. Lansky."

Joshua looked at the lawyer soberly. "I'm still not getting it, Moish."

Petrovich pulled a white letter-size envelope out of his briefcase. He dramatically counted out ten hundred-dollar bills and laid them on the desk. "They have brothers and sisters inside," he said, holding up the envelope. "Are you getting it better now?"

Joshua reached across the desk and picked up the money. He folded it in half and put it in his shirt pocket. "No, not really. But if you think this will help, I don't want to disappoint you." He looked amiably from one man to the other.

Lansky laughed. "I like this fuckin' guy. Moish. I like this guy."

All three men laughed. Joshua took the money out of his pocket and placed it on the desk in front of Lansky. "What do I have to do to earn Mr. Lansky's thousand?"

"No, no, no! It's not Mr. Lansky's. You got it from me. It's important you remember that." There was no humor in Petrovich's voice.

"Call me Meyer. I like you," Lansky said. "He's smart," he said, turning to Moses Petrovich, "he's a smart boy." "Smart" sounded like "smot."

Joshua smiled a friendly smile. The thousand dollars was a huge amount of money. He had defended first-degree murder cases for much less.

"The problem is that Meyer also got a subpoena," Petrovich said. He took another sheet of paper out of his briefcase and handed it to Joshua. It was a subpoena duces tecum from the federal grand jury in Phoenix for the records of Meyer Lansky.

"Del Webb also got a subpoena for Phoenix," Petrovich said.

Joshua nodded. "Okay, I'm getting the picture." He looked at the date on the subpoena. "This is next Thursday, June 12. You'll have to bring me the records to review."

"There ain't no records," Lansky said. "My name ain't on no records for the contruction of the Flamingo Hotel. That I can guarantee."

Joshua settled back in his chair. "Then why do you need me, Meyer, what is the thousand for? And why aren't you up in Phoenix hiring a lawyer?"

"I'm the kind a guy goes somewhere, suddenly everybody knows. The FBI comes sniffin'. The IRS knocks on my door. I always hire a lawyer when I go someplace so I can call when I need. I'm living here now in Tucson. My wife and me was divorced in February. She's back in New York with two of my kids, Paul and Sandra. The oldest one, Irving, I got here with me. Doctors told me this was the best place I could come for Irving, he's got some health problems. *Kenna Hurra*"—he knocked with his knuckles on the seat of the wooden chair—"he'll be all right. I bought a house over by the university, got a old friend lives near there. He has a son same age as Irving."

"So what do you want me to do about the subpoena?"

"You come with me to Phoenix next week, I'll testify, we'll come back. That's all. This ain't my first time."

Joshua looked at him soberly. "Listen, Meyer, I know you think I'm a boob from the middle of nowhere, but I lived in Brooklyn until a year ago, and I've read about you and Lucky Luciano and Bugsy Siegel, and even out here we have newspapers and magazines. It's hardly a thousand dollars worth of work taking a train ride with Meyer Lansky to Phoenix and back. I've got to know what this is really about."

"I got a big piece of the Flamingo," Lansky said. "It in't on paper. But it's big money. Some of my associates also got big interests. I'm talking serious business here. This ain't good what's going on with the grand jury. My friends don't like that Benny got himself in trouble over bullshit." He twisted his mouth sourly. "Marble, fuckin' Italian marble, shit like that." He shook his head. "It ain't good we get publicity and investigations. I got to keep the fields away from me and my associates."

Joshua nodded. "Okay. I understand. But you have to understand that I'm just a lawyer. There are rules, I follow them."

"I ask you to do something else? No. I hire you because you got a good reputation, you're an honest guy. I need a honest guy." Lansky pushed the stack of hundred-dollar bills across the desktop to Joshua. "Just call it a retainer, so if I need you at midnight sometime you won't resent havin' to get outta bed."

Joshua laughed. "I don't have a phone. To get me out of bed, you'll have to drive all the way out here."

"No phone?" Lansky said, disbelieving. "This is 1947 already, not the Middle Ages. Fix it up, Moish. Get my Tucson lawyer a phone. My lawyer gotta be a *machier* [big shot]." Turning back to Joshua, "This I throw in extra."

"Thank you, Meyer. I'm sure my daughter will be thrilled. She can talk to her friends every night for two hours."

The three men laughed. "Give him my number, Moish," Lansky said.

Petrovich wrote on the back of one of his business cards and handed it to Joshua, who walked to the door of his small office, opened it and shook hands with both men as they left. Joshua went back to the desk, put the folded bills in his shirt pocket, and smiled broadly.